Also by
John Edgar Wideman

Introduction
by Walton Muyumba

1

John Edgar Wideman has been my most important teacher, though
I didn't attend any of the universities where he taught. Already
well into my undergraduate studies when I first read the stories in Wideman's *Damballah*, it still stands as the moment my education really began.
As the child of Congolese immigrants and simultaneously an inheritor
of the Western Hemispheric Black experience, especially in the United
States, I was entangled in multiple lines of descent and responsibility. Like
so many other young Black Americans coming of age in the late 1980s
and early 1990s, I was trying to create an identity on my own terms. But
I also felt a need to extend the political advancements previous generations accomplished in the liberation movements throughout the African
diaspora.

None of this was easy to narrate to myself or others. Because my literary
education began very traditionally—Chaucer, Shakespeare, Keats, Austen,
Dickens, and Woolf—I didn't have models for creating stories about my liminality. Luckily, other parts of my formal (and informal, often subterranean)
training included listening to, reading, and watching canonical artists of the
African diaspora: Achebe and A Tribe Called Quest; Gwendolyn Brooks and

James Baldwin; Morrison and Makeba; Bird and Dizzy; Richard Wright and Frantz Fanon; Spike Lee and Public Enemy; Miles and Coltrane; Kincaid and Walcott; Ellington and Monk; Wole Soyinka and August Wilson. They offered me an abundance of beauty, feeling, and intelligence. But it wasn't until I read *Damballah*—electric with Wideman's modernist experimentation and his orchestra of voices—that I began, as Ralph Ellison puts it in *Invisible Man*, "creating the uncreated features" of my own face.[1]

During a period of rudderless wandering, intellectual adjustment, and growing psychological awareness, Wideman's first story collection guided me as no other artwork could at the time. Even three decades on, the collection's title story, "Damballah," continues to shape my understanding of how the strongest Afro-diasporic traditions are maintained and renewed. In that piece, Wideman flips the American slave story on its head: rather than describing his characters bound by their subjugation, Wideman draws our attention to Orion, a fish-gathering griot, whose daily ritual summons Damballah Wedo. The primordial father in the Vodou pantheon, Damballah signals both the ancient past and assures the future.

Parsing "Damballah" for the first time, I noticed, just as the young, unnamed slave boy–protagonist does, that Orion embodies his freedom defiantly. Proudly African, Orion designates the crossroads with the Kongo sign, calls for Damballah's guidance, and creates an African/American tradition. When the boy catches the spirit and learns to make the sign and speak the word, he's also learning that prayerful, linguistic action powers self-invention. When the plantation's master and overseer find out that Orion has maintained his West African religious practices, the penalty is deadly: they sever Orion's head from his body. At the story's end, the boy retrieves Orion's head, carrying it to the ceremonial site. Listening to Orion's stories once again, he blesses the head and sets it adrift to the waiting fish. In that act, the boy takes up the ritual as if born to it, as if born from Orion's head—the narrative tradition passing cyclically, mouth to mouth, like life-giving resuscitation.

Damballah, *Hiding Place*, and *Sent for You Yesterday* form *The Homewood Trilogy*. The overarching story those works describe begins with Sybela Owens, a slave who ran to freedom with Charlie Bell, the slave master's son. They established Homewood, one of Pittsburgh's historically and predominantly African American neighborhoods, during the 1850s. These two characters sit atop the "Begat Chart" in *Damballah*; Wideman molded these characters from family lore about his own ancestors. Though Wideman uses some Homewood street names in his first novel, *A Glance Away*, the district goes unnamed as such. *Damballah* offers readers the first entrée to Homewood specifically.

The stories from *Damballah* in this volume lead readers into the lives of the French and Lawson families. The character John "Doot" Lawson is a writer-translator, if you will; he's collected anecdotes from his family and transposed them into literary fiction. Lawson lives with his own family far away from Pittsburgh, hoping that distance might create opportunities for establishing his writing life free from family disarray and trauma. However, over the course of the trilogy, Lawson discovers that writing about the lives of his maternal grandparents and extended family members, turning their experiences into fiction, allows him the possibility of discovery through characterization and reveals that the roots of his own aesthetic lie in the fertile modes of oral storytelling his family members have crafted. In *Damballah*, Lawson's stories help him locate and traverse various routes leading him back to Homewood.

Readers who imagine Lawson as a surrogate for Wideman or Wideman's stories as autofictions are on the mark. Late in these pages, for example, when readers take up "Maps and Ledgers" (a story that sits at the core of *American Histories*), we'll overhear a brother and sister working back through their family history in a phone conversation. The narrator, the older brother, mentions to his sister that in a previous call they had gotten "deep into the begats, both trying to recall Daddy's grandmother's name and neither could and Owens popped into my mind and I said Owens to you and you said Sybil Owens—wasn't she the slave from down south who came up here to found Homewood and you were right of course and I laughed because I was the one who wrote down the Sybela Owens story and you knew the story from my books or from family conversations."[2]

Notice, however, that the mark is often moving in Wideman's stories. He desires both close connections between his life and his works, and the ambiguities that literary writing can create, holes that allow readers to enter fictional worlds, spaces inside the stories where readers reimagine themselves. Wideman suggests as much in the microstory "You Are My Sunshine" (which appears in *Briefs*). Replying to his French translator's query about an inconsistency between the begat chart frontispiece in *Hiding Place* and the narrative for a character named Shirley, Wideman writes:

> *Shirley's not either, she's both, I want to respond—not only my sister, not only a character—the world of the novel depends on fact and fiction and I'm just a mediator with no answers or changing answers, always more questions than answers, as curious as you are, Jean-Pierre, a translator like you, who at best attempts to mediate irreconcilable differences.*[3]

From story to story in this volume, book to book in his oeuvre, readers ought not search for linear trajectories. Instead, they should notice that Wideman's stories overlap and encompass each other concentrically.[4]

Wideman invites readers to sit alongside him, amid these stories, in liminality, in Great Time, mediating and translating in multiple directions simultaneously. Borrowed from John Mbiti's *African Religions and Philosophy* (1969), Wideman describes "Great Time" as a kind of nonlinear, "ancestral" time. Imagine it as a body of water that one paddles or swims or wades into. "There is no beginning, no end," to ancestral time, Wideman writes.[5] I think that Wideman offers another description of this concept in "Williamsburg Bridge," in which the narrator recalls hearing Sonny Rollins "practicing changes on the Williamsburg Bridge."[6]

Contemplating a suicidal leap into the East River, the narrator realizes that the bridge spans an array of possibilities from the churning river flowing below to Rollins's death-defying improvisatory flights. The saxophonist's improvisational play expressed "color deeper than midnight blue ... Color of disappointment, of ancient injuries and bruises and staying alive and dying and being born again all at once."[7] One does not pass through Great Time unidirectionally. Instead, the artist, the listener, the reader, the imaginer, learns to float in time.

Learning to enter and float in Great Time may be the very lesson the boy interprets from studying Orion so closely. One imagines that the boy learns to enter Great Time through ritual, playing within and with ritual forms, obscuring his practice from scrutiny, while mediating between old and new worlds, and meditating upon narrative meaning. Possibly, I'm speaking about myself: when I entered *Damballah* that first time, I became the watching-listening boy to Wideman's Orion. He taught me to listen to the head and to improvise on it. Reading Wideman's fiction has meant entering into creative exchange with his stories. His work has pushed me to innovate new ways of gathering and embodying my histories and traditions—globally Black, Congolese, American—into ritual practices of cleansing, healing, reconnection, and self-invention.

These selected stories also illustrate that even if selfhood could ever be achieved firmly and finally, such a realization could not assuage or deny human pain. And so, these pages present a writer concerned with physical and existential liberation, emotional and psychological health, expressions of love and satiation of sexual desire, literary aesthetics, and linguistic freedom, and the machinations of the head, the heart, and memory. Wideman is, as great fiction writers often are, a serious, intense noticer of the minuscule, intimate details of human experience. And his characters and voices reflect that careful attention: they represent humans struggling with family legacies, endemic racism and injustice, and looping cycles of community violence and economic limitation. They also laugh, sing, dance, tell stories, philosophize, mourn their dead, celebrate their living, and create beauty. Wideman doesn't write to essentialize Blackness; his stories represent Black experience as the very seat of the practices of possibility and freedom. And in order to maintain those practices, Damballah's guidance is needed in perpetuity.

2

Wideman was born on June 14 1941, in Washington, DC, to Edgar Wideman and Bette French. Soon after the author's birth, the young family moved from DC to western Pennsylvania. He did his primary and secondary education in Pittsburgh, excelling as both a student and an athlete while matriculating at Pittsburgh's Peabody High School. He earned a Benjamin Franklin Scholarship to attend the University of Pennsylvania in Philadelphia. There, he became a member of the Phi Beta Kappa Society and earned varsity letters in track and basketball. Following his senior year basketball season, Wideman was named an All–Ivy League forward. That same year, upon his graduation from Penn, Wideman was awarded a Rhodes Scholarship to attend

New College at Oxford University. In 1966, Wideman completed a thesis in eighteenth-century British literature and earned a PhB from Oxford. He then accepted a Kent Fellowship to attend the Iowa Writers' Workshop at the University of Iowa. He completed his first novel, *A Glance Away*, while in Iowa City and published it in 1967. Since then, Wideman has published nine other novels, five works of creative nonfiction/memoir, and six short-story collections.

Over the course of his esteemed career, Wideman has been awarded numerous accolades, including a MacArthur Foundation Fellowship (1993), the Rea Award for Short Story (1998), Lifetime Achievement Awards from the Anisfield-Wolf Book Awards/Cleveland Foundation (2011) and the Lannan Foundation (2018), the Prix Femina Étranger (2017), the PEN/Malamud Award for Excellence in the Short Story (2019) and the PEN/Faulkner Award for Fiction (twice in 1984 and 1991, the first writer to be so honored). *Father-along* was a nonfiction finalist for the National Book Award (1994). *Brothers and Keepers* and *Writing to Save A Life* were National Book Critics Circle awards finalists in Autobiography (1985) and Nonfiction (2017), respectively. Before his retirement from teaching in 2014, Wideman taught creative writing and literature for five decades at the University of Pennsylvania, the University of Wyoming, the University of Massachusetts at Amherst, and Brown University.

Nearly thirty years have passed since the publication of *The Stories of John Edgar Wideman* (1992), a 432-page compendium of thirty-five stories. That volume contains all the stories from his first three collections: *Damballah*, *Fever*, and *All Stories Are True*. When that book appeared, Wideman was twenty-five years into an already prodigious career: he had ten other titles to his name and he was only fifty-one years old. In 2021, as Wideman approaches his eightieth birthday, the time seems right for a full career retrospective. You might say that it's no longer halftime; Wideman's in the fourth quarter of the game. But Wideman doesn't want to look backward. His momentum only carries him forward to the next project. He continues producing new work as though the game clock doesn't matter.

There are always hard choices to make when preparing a volume of selected works. What stays in play, what gets benched. From readers who've followed Wideman's career closely there are bound to be complaints because their favorite stories aren't here. From readers new to Wideman's stories, there might be complaints because our editorial choices seem to dictate what constitutes the author's strongest efforts without offering up the full catalog for comparison. Having had some minor input in these proceedings, I think this collection decisively illustrates Wideman's angular, innovative storytelling, his linguistic dexterity, his formal range, and his singular position in American literature. And, as an exhibition of Wideman's prowess, this book has been arranged to whet readers' appetites for both the original, individual collections and whatever comes out next from this masterful artist.

Though it's actually a dedication and prefatory note of gratitude, "To Robby" has the flavor and force of a microfiction. In it, Wideman offers his stories to his brother, and to us readers, as the initiation of an epistolary exchange: ". . . these stories are letters. Long overdue letters from me to you. I wish they could snatch you away from where you are."[8] Since the late 1970s, Wideman has been making fiction from the real-life plight of his youngest brother, Robert Wideman. After Robby was arrested and locked up for his participation in an armed robbery and murder, Wideman began an effort to tailor a prose style that might effectuate the tonalities of his brother's voice (in fiction and nonfiction). While many readers regard Wideman's memoir *Brothers and Keepers* as a masterpiece of creative nonfiction, they have not read his stories about carceral time— "Tommy," "Solitary," "All Stories Are True," "What We Cannot Speak About We Must Pass Over in Silence," and "Maps and Ledgers"—for what they are: raw, rare gems, cut and buffed to refract a full spectrum of experiential truths.

"All Stories Are True" is really two linked stories, one about silence and narrative aesthetics, and the other about listening and narrative reception. We might even imagine that these stories are linked letters meant to respond to each other. The story's narrator (who is both Wideman and not Wideman) describes a stay at his mother's place in Homewood as he prepares to visit his youngest brother in prison. Waking early for his drive to the prison, the narrator stands, coffee in hand, in the front doorway of his mother's house, observing her as she silently takes in the quiet morning street from her front porch. Thinking through his return to Pittsburgh, the narrator finds himself imagining the layers of his mother's narrative memory while simultaneously anticipating the visit with his brother.

Mapping and murmuring the names of Homewood streets in mantra, the narrator recognizes something like his literary inheritance in her silence. The realization allows him to enter his mother's aesthetic, use it as a navigation tool, and find his way into his brother's cell. Knowing "the names of streets can open like the gates of a great city, everyone who's ever inhabited the city, walked its streets, suddenly, like a shimmer, like the first notes of a Monk solo, breathing, moving, a world quickens as the gates swing apart."[9] (Later in these pages you'll find "Weight," another story about mothers and storytelling; it's gorgeous and reads like a kind of sibling to "All Stories Are True.")

Pay special attention to Wideman's sentence-level artistry at the beginning of "What We Cannot Speak About We Must Pass Over in Silence." Notice his penchant for building the momentum of thought-experience through contingency: commas, conjunctions, and clauses. Wideman has rhymed and aligned the story's two opening sentences metrically, announcing a specific pace. However, in the third and fourth lines, the author breaks that structure as though he realized the necessity of a freer physics of sound, one capacious enough to mash up or collage the sensory and the psychological as a unified state of being. The fifth, sixth, and seventh sentences— like a concertina's bellows—flux space and time to create the layeredness of simultaneity. The narrator's description tumbles into an "unending instant" of anxious first steps, heat, sorrow, critical noticing, self-awareness, and anticipated returns.

This story is another example of Wideman mediating between imagination and personal life. The fiction both veils and reveals Wideman. For example, when the narrator here compares his emotional spaces to his sun-deprived, cell-like apartment—"In a certain compartment of my heart where compassion's supposed to lodge, but there's never enough space in cramped urban dwellings so I store niggling self-pity there too, I try to find room also for all the millions of poor souls who have less than I have, who would howl for joy if they could occupy as their own one corner of my dreary little flat"—it's possible Wideman is speaking of himself.[10]

Also notable is the fact that Jake, Wideman's second-born son, is serving a life sentence in an Arizona prison for killing a fellow camper during a summer camp group trip to the Southwest in 1986. Because the son has demurred collaboration with his father and has requested that the father not speak of him in interviews, in those Wideman stories with characters whose circumstances resemble Jake's, the author has employed those characters as catalysts for the narrators' exploration of their own psychological states. And often, those narrators are writers.

There is a long line of death, trauma, violence, and silence about those terrors in Wideman's family history. The author has acknowledged and grappled with this barbed truth in his tremendous works of creative nonfiction. In his stories, Wideman doesn't have space or time to wrangle with causes, so he drills down to the effects, elaborating the emotional consequences for characters confronting their demons or repeating subtle violences through silence or passing on traumas generationally as though they are genetic material or inherited debt.

In "Maps and Ledgers," for example, the narrator remembers a phone call from his panicked mother announcing that his father had been arrested for killing a man. But the father doesn't "serve time for murder" because the defense attorney "plea-bargained self-defense and victim-colored like my father anyway so they chose to let my father go."[11] But this circumstance initiates a cycle of fathers, sons, and brothers in the narrator's family who are incarcerated for violent, sometimes murderous crimes. The narrator suggests this kind of transference carries some "precedents from Greek mythology," born, as it seems, of curse or tragic fatedness. The narrator recognizes his mother's call as an omen. And like Oedipus upon learning his fate, the narrator tells himself "get away . . . and none of this happens."[12]

"Maps and Ledgers" is a reckoning with "Across the Wide Missouri," a painful and beautifully wrought early story about paternal silence and emotional withholding. There, John Lawson realizes that he's acquired his own father's habit of self-centered distance; he also notices that the gods, if you will, have gifted his young son with impressionable emotional sensibility: "Things don't touch him. They imprint. You can see it sometimes. And it hurts. He already knows he will suffer for whatever he knows. Maybe that's why he forgets so much."[13] There is a hint here, in tone, that Lawson registers his son's sensitivity and forgetfulness as a set of keys that might open an exit from paternal inheritances. It's difficult, however, to not read the narrator's final crushing sentences as the author's eerie, muffled premonition about Jake Wideman's future.

Wideman too is susceptible to suffering for whatever he knows about African American experience, the American carceral system, and the ironies of human life. His stories suggest that though we, the imprisoned and the so-called free, shall all run out of life time eventually, addressing that truth allows us to access other truths about imagination, dreaming, kinship, love, liberation, and hope. These selected stories are equipment for deciphering the complex entanglements of living. I hear the faintest echo among these narratives, like a ghost note in the collection's rhythm, a whispered valediction tiding in from the sea of Wideman's other works: "Hold on, Your Brother."[14] If these stories are letters, then this sign-off is apt here because it's also a benediction, an exhortation, and an encouragement. Perhaps I hear this resonance because it's the perfect closing bracket after Wideman's opening inscription. He's dedicated *You Made Me Love You* to "All those coming up after: stay in the struggle." Individually and collectively, these stories show us how to float inside Great Time, willing from its vastness the very truths that give our lives meaning and fuel us for battles ahead.

3

To me, no one in American letters sounds like Wideman. His unique, forceful musicality stems, in part, from his close study of blues idiom literature and lyricism. His career-long interrogation of African diasporic experience, his returning continually to Homewood, to visiting rooms of carceral institutions in Arizona and western Pennsylvania, his attempting repeatedly to mine his family history, to enter and understand the revolutions of his characters' psychologies, to evoke the specific intonations of invented voices, is his fingering the jagged grain of myth, memory, and material experience. As with Ralph Ellison's definition of the blues, Wideman's stories arise from "an impulse to keep the painful details and episodes of a brutal experience alive in [his] aching consciousness" in order to "transcend it, not by the consolation of philosophy but by squeezing from it a near-tragic, near-comic lyricism."[15]

Taking cues from Albert Murray's *Stomping the Blues* (1976), Wideman has developed a personal aesthetic from blues idiom practices—the enduring, workable forms and styles in dance, literature, and the oral, visual, and musical arts. In his essays about Murray's blues theory, Wideman explains that the "dues which must be paid in order to play the blues involve the same self-restraint, discipline, and grounding in idiomatic tradition to which any artist must submit."[16] Those practices have lasted over time because artists creating in the tradition continue improvising new ways of documenting Black life and states of human feeling. Their experiments and innovations—often born from performance modes localized by block, neighborhood, city, or region—critique, revise, extend, and renew the tradition. As Murray argues consistently across his works, improvisation is imperative to Black American life and to the perpetuation of the idiom. Wideman's art is rooted in Homewood's idiom thus; it rises from the blues aesthetic tradition and speaks universally.

It's worth noting that Wideman has learned as much about producing blues idiom fiction from his publishing generation—Toni Morrison, Toni Cade Bambara, Gayl Jones, Ishmael Reed, James Alan McPherson, Leon Forrest—as he has from Ellison or Murray. And I've learned as much about improvisation from reading Wideman as I have from listening to Billy Strayhorn and Mary Lou Williams, Art Blakey and Paul Chambers, Earl Hines and Ahmad Jamal, Billy Eckstine and Dakota Staton, all high-order blues idiom musicians hailing from Pittsburgh. Wideman's experiments with story form bring to mind the sensation of listening to improvisatory musical play. Take, as examples, his way of forging phrases into the run-on sentences of his characters in thought, his juxtaposing differently shaped fragments against or overlapping one another, or his propensity for pasting various swatches of story within the contextual boundaries of a larger primary narrative.

Perhaps no other story captures Wideman's improvisatory play like "The Silence of Thelonious Monk." Reading about Arthur Rimbaud's hellish love affair with Paul Verlaine, the narrator begins mixing the poets' quarrelsome love story with the story of his own souring affair. Imagining the poets' infamous standoff at Gare du Midi, the narrator constructs a motion picture of the action while recalling lines from the third section of Verlaine's

"Il pleure dans mon coeur...": *"Il pleure dans mon coeur/ Comme il pleut sur la ville."* Just as Verlaine's verse tides into narrator's mind, it's overtaken by the music cutting across the alleyway and into his room: "Monk's music just below my threshold of awareness, scoring the movie I was imagining, a soundtrack inseparable from what the actors were feeling, from what I felt watching them pantomime their melodrama."

Monk enters the narrative musically, then he quickly becomes a character in the fiction. His presence inspires the narrative's structure, shifting as it does from the narrator's riffing on distant lovers and potentially deadly breakups, to his direct interactions with the pianist's silences, to his reminiscing in tempo:

> *Listening to Monk, I closed the book... Then you arrived. Silently at first. You playing so faintly in the background it would have taken the surprise of someone whispering your name in my ear to alert me to your presence. But your name, once heard, I'd have to confess you'd been there all along.*[17]

In the mix of train whistles, pop guns, French symbolist poetics, and be-bop innovations, I hear, just below Monk's roundabout midnight vamping, Wideman scratching a sample of Leroy Carr's "How Long, How Long Blues": "Went to the station, didn't see no train. / Down in my heart, I have an aching pain." I also hear the narrator fingering a jagged, crepuscular blues lick about love and silence, about silences in love or on the piano keyboard remaining unrequited but still full of possibility.

From the eloquence of Monk's "sometimes comic, sometimes manic and threatening" silences to the "wordless choruses" that gospel singers sometimes hum or moan in order to express the ineffable, the unspeakable, Black musicians can shuttle across space and time through these moments of fecund quietude. While Wideman cannot replicate the immediacy of musical silences, he can create intimacy through his play in African American literary language that is "rich with time and silence."[18]

But these improvisational possibilities aren't merely musicological. They're also physical, athletic. The promise of what might be or could be played with, on, or in the body, funds Wideman's elegantly framed narrative, "Doc's Story." The large frame is a narrative about playground basketball, male communal story exchange, and the hope for overcoming personal insecurities and socially determined racial constructs. Within that outline is a tale about Doc, a professor and playground legend, who continues to hoop in spite of having lost his eyesight. Believing in Doc's prowess, his ability to feel his way through the game blindly, to shoot and score guided by his other senses, suggests to the narrator that other human realities might be surmounted through faith, feeling, and inventive storytelling.

Had he been able to carry Doc's story from the playground court's male community back to his white lover, exchanging it for her narrative, the narrator wonders, could he have saved the love affair? Could he have convinced her to stay with him? Could their story exchange have spurred him to improvise manhood braided from hope, love, and flight? Could they overcome being "opposites attracting"?[19]

In the space between their opposing positions is where all the uncertain, sometimes scary, possibly silent, often pleasurable play of self-becoming and love happen. And as it pertains to forms of manhood in Wideman's stories, this is the space where the many complex, contradictory aspects of masculinity get revised and remixed as "new rules, new priorities, that disrupt the known" forms of heterosexual Black manhood in favor of something more open, indeterminate, and emotionally available.[20] First published in *Esquire* in 1986, "Doc's Story" might be the first example of what the author describes in his excellent basketball book, *Hoop Roots*, as his labor to fashion prose with "the immediate excitement of process, of invention, of play" at the core of playground basketball.[21]

Drawing the body, movement, and improvisation together in language and narrative might also be called collage. Throughout his career, Wideman has pointed toward filmmakers, painters, and sculptors in order to highlight visually what he's producing formally in writing. Among the artists who regularly appear in Wideman's writing, Romare Bearden is especially important. Bearden's oeuvre and art theories underwrite Wideman's literary practice.[22] Here, for instance, the story "Collage" is Wideman's attempt to get "Bearden to save the life of Jean-Michel Basquiat." Set at some point in the mid-1980s, Wideman imagines the two painters in conversation while they "spray-paint graffiti in a vast graveyard of subway cars."[23] Though Bearden and Basquiat maintained studios one mile apart from each other in lower Manhattan, there's no record of their ever meeting.

As they exchange ideas about art—Bearden the mentor, Basquiat the up-and-coming understudy—the younger painter notices that Bearden's artworks remind him of his dead mother's old habit of telling stories that "flatten perspective. Cram in everything, everyone, from everywhere she's been." Basquiat realizes that Bearden and his mother both create democratically, "each detail counts equally, every part matters as much as any grand design. . . . Meaning depends on point of view." But Wideman's invented Basquiat, stops himself from belaboring the point because all he needs to say is "*Dance.* Mom talking story or Bearden at the turntable mixing cutouts with paint with fabrics with photos with empty spaces invite people to dance."[24] And later, as though answering Basquiat's thought, Bearden adds that "collage envisions new pasts as well as new futures."[25]

Undoubtedly, Wideman's unveiling himself through metafiction: the painters both produced artworks that could serve as models for the author's approach to form in fiction. In their discussion of theory, the painters are describing how the story "Collage" has been made and how to read it. And Wideman is shifting from collage to palimpsest by recycling and layering ideas from his other works onto this story.[26] Wideman's reuse is like Monk or Rollins repeating musical licks on different tunes during different recording sessions or like Basquiat's "SAMO" appearing in spray paint on disparate buildings on Manhattan's Lower East Side and in oil on many different canvases repeatedly. And it's improvisational in that Wideman is using the material that's available to describe new insights or signal new directions. In his essay "The Architectonics of Fiction," Wideman argues that "a story should somehow contain clues that align it with tradition and critique tradition, establish the new space it requires, demands, appropriates, hint at how it may bring forth other things like itself, where these others have, will, and are coming from."[27]

Wideman's theory of fiction is good to have in mind when taking in his microstories. In the fullness of its 102 microfictions, *Briefs* reiterates many Widemanian themes and subjects, and yet it is alive with newness. It's an echoing novel of ideas that's been exploded and then rearranged as a Bearden-esque collage. The twenty-nine briefs present here maintain that effect. For instance, "Now You See It," a one-sentence word cascade about blank space on the page, best represents the author's idea about visuality and imagination. The blank space houses "everything the writer does not know, cannot know."[28]

Charged rhythmically, word by word, "Witness" demands to be read out loud. Told from the first-person perspective of a wheelchair-bound observer, the story is about watching a young man's murder, the policing of the crime scene, and, subsequently, the young man's family mourning his death at the scene. We enter in medias res, apropos of nothing: "Sitting here one night six floors up on my little balcony when I heard shots and saw them boys running." Wideman positions readers as witnesses too, guiding us to imagine the dead boy's parents and baby sister arriving "at the spot the boy died," where they "commence to swaying, bowing, hugging, waving their arms about," and "look like they grief dancing, like the sidewalk too cold or too hot they had to jump around not to burn up."[29]

Maybe this goes without saying, but Wideman's fragments, improvisations, and collages are political forms. The author's formal designs project his imagined futures. Wideman's forecasts suggest that love and liberation be the governors of our personal and political lives. He takes enormous risks by imploring readers to relinquish their passive reading habits in favor of potentially liberating engagement with his challenging, experimental forms. To find their way in and through these stories meaningfully, readers must play improvisationally alongside and against the author.

Wideman has admitted that his willingness to exhaust adequacy may create dissatisfaction among readers, that urging them to witness, charging them to interrogate their habits of imagination, may actually encourage them—as he writes in "Surfiction"—to "fall away as if each word is a well-aimed bullet."[30] His works force us to confront that "what we are accustomed to acknowledging as awareness is actually a culturally learned, contingent condensation of many potential awarenesses."[31]

In this ream of stories, "Fever" is Wideman's chief and most complex exploration of the short narrative form as a conduit for readers to release themselves to the full spectrum of awarenesses. "Fever" demonstrates how an improvised literary form might actualize simultaneity and multiplicity.

The story describes Philadelphia's devastating yellow fever plague of 1793. Wideman eschews streamlined, plotted fiction in favor of a structure that narrates the past and projects the future at once. Collaging several fragments and multiple points of view, the author follows Richard Allen, the founder of the Bethel African Methodist Episcopal Church, and his work with the prominent Philadelphia doctor Benjamin Rush; he explores the etymological basis of "dengue" in both the Swahili and Spanish languages; he enters the consciousness of an unnamed African questioning his gods and his mortality while bound in the hold of a slave ship; he illustrates the transhistorical American fear of Black bodies as contagion carriers; and he documents how quickly those fears become feverish blisters of hatred spreading in conflagrate flares across a city (or across the centuries of the nation's history) in the merciless stranglehold of a strange and decimating virus. In effect, Wideman has collaged an access point into Great Time.

Though this story began as his search for the source of the city's historical, viral infection of racecraft, "Fever" also speaks truthfully and emphatically about contemporary America: a nation caught in the clutches of a pandemic and political malfeasance while remaining locked in civil conflict with the engineers of white supremacy. In other words, "Fever" is a daring feat of imagination. And in his design and realization of this literary collage, Wideman has produced a short fiction masterpiece.

Wideman's stories provoke readers to bear witness to their own individual lives. He seems to detail this conviction in the sentence-length, short-short fiction "Shadow": "He notices a shadow dragged rippling behind him over the grass, one more silent, black presence for which he's responsible."[32] After we've learned to attend to ourselves responsibly—following a learning process that includes interrogating the language intensely, adapting it to "the infinite geography of [our] inner imaginative worlds, the outer social play, [and] the constant intercourse of both," and improvising narrative forms that stimulate the full range of our receptors—the author hopes we may be able to bear witness to and take responsibility for our collective emotional, social, and political failures.[33] This, of course, demands a deeper, more radical action: bearing witness to and taking responsibility for one another.

Perhaps that's what the story "JB & FD" illustrates about John Brown and Frederick Douglass. Wideman's characters imagine themselves "stepping into" other bodies in order to envision the world from new angles of perception. Not only do these two radical actors of American history see themselves anew through others' eyes, that creative action generates great empathetic understanding in each of them. Even more, as the story's narrator realizes, radical imagining frees us to forget who we are, who we are supposed to be, "and it is perfection." The narrator listens for the voices of his main characters "sealed within the silence" of a stand of trees in Brittany, France, and "for a small instant [he's] inside them, and it lasts forever."[34]

You Made Me Love You—playful, prayerful, intricate, inviting—challenges readers to reimagine themselves radically and improvisationally. Opening yourself to Wideman's structures, sounds, and sentences will liberate you from yourself, thus expanding and renewing your sense of self, time, and experience. This is Damballah's instruction, this is Great Time's bequest, and this is the meaning of the blues. Pleasure will arise from dancing with this master on his own terms and to his own tunes. Delight will come from recognizing in Wideman's voices and silences your own intonations and noticing in his layered mélange the reflected contours of your own face.

Damballah
(1981)

To Robby

S tories are letters. Letters sent to anybody or everybody. But the best kind are meant to be read by a specific somebody. When you read that kind you know you are eavesdropping. You know a real person somewhere will read the same words you are reading and the story is that person's business and you are a ghost listening in.

Remember. I think it was Geral I first heard call a watermelon a letter from home. After all these years I understand a little better what she meant. She was saying the melon is a letter addressed to us. A story for us from down home. Down Home being everywhere we've never been, the rural South, the old days, slavery, Africa. That juicy, striped message with red meat and seeds, which always looked like roaches to me, was blackness as cross and celebration, a history we could taste and chew. And it was meant for us. Addressed to us. We were meant to slit it open and take care of business.

Consider all these stories as letters from home. I never liked watermelon as a kid. I think I remember you did. You weren't afraid of becoming instant nigger, of sitting barefoot and goggle-eyed and Day-Glo black and drippy-lipped on massa's fence if you took one bit of the forbidden fruit. I was too scared to enjoy watermelon. Too self-conscious. I let people rob me of a simple pleasure. Watermelon's still tainted for me. But I know better now. I can play with the idea even if I can't get down and have a natural ball eating a real one.

Anyway... these stories are letters. Long overdue letters from me to you. I wish they could tear down the walls. I wish they could snatch you away from where you are.

Damballah:
Good Serpent of the Sky

"Damballah Wedo is the ancient, the venerable father; so ancient, so venerable, as of a world before the troubles began; and his children would keep him so: image of the benevolent, paternal innocence, the great father of whom one asks nothing save his blessing.... There is almost no precise communication with him, as if his wisdom were of such major cosmic scope and of such grand innocence that it could not perceive the minor anxieties of his human progeny, nor be transmuted to the petty precisions of human speech.

"Yet it is this very detachment which comforts, and which is evidence, once more, of some original and primal vigor that has somehow remained inaccessible to whatever history, whatever immediacy might diminish it. Damballah's very presence, like the simple, even absent-minded caress of a father's hand, brings peace.... Damballah is himself unchanged by life, and so is at once the ancient past and the assurance of the future....

"Associated with Damballah, as members of the Sky Pantheon, are Badessy, the wind, Sobo and Agarou Tonerre, the thunder.... They seem to belong to another period of history. Yet, precisely because these divinities are, to a certain extent, vestigial, they give, like Damballah's detachment, a sense of historical extension, of the ancient origin of the race. To invoke them today is to stretch one's hand back to that time and to gather up all history into a solid, contemporary ground beneath one's feet."

One song invoking Damballah requests that he "Gather up the Family."

Quotation and citation from Maya Deren's *Divine Horsemen: The Living Gods of Haiti*

A Begat Chart

1860s Sybela and Charlie arrive in Pittsburgh; bring two children with them; eighteen more born in next twenty-five years.

1880s Maggie Owens, oldest daughter of Sybela and Charlie, marries Buck Hollinger; bears nine children among whom are four girls—Aida, Gertrude, Gaybrella, Bess.

1900s Hollinger girls marry—Aida to Bill Campbell; Gaybrella to Joe Hardin (three children: Fauntleroy, Ferdinand, Hazel); Bess to Riley Simpkins (one son: Eugene)—except Gert, who bears her children out of wedlock. Aida and Bill Campbell raise Gert's daughter, Freeda.

1920s Freeda Hollinger marries John French; bears four children who survive; Lizabeth, Geraldine, Carl, and Martha.

1940s Lizabeth French marries Edgar Lawson; bears five children among whom are John, Shirley, and Thomas.

1960s Lizabeth's children begin to marry, propagate—not always in that order. John marries Judy and produces two sons (Jake and Dan); Shirley marries Rashad and bears three daughters (Keesha, Tammy, and Kaleesha); Tommy marries Sarah and produces one son (Clyde); etc. . . .

FAMILY TREE

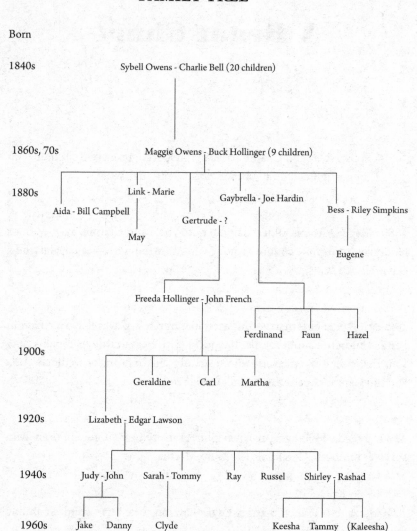

Born

1840s   Sybell Owens - Charlie Bell (20 children)

1860s, 70s   Maggie Owens - Buck Hollinger (9 children)

1880s

Link - Marie

Aida - Bill Campbell   Gaybrella - Joe Hardin

Gertrude - ?   Bess - Riley Simpkins

May

Eugene

Freeda Hollinger - John French

Ferdinand   Faun   Hazel

1900s

Geraldine   Carl   Martha

1920s   Lizabeth - Edgar Lawson

1940s   Judy - John   Sarah - Tommy   Ray   Russel   Shirley - Rashad

1960s   Jake   Danny   Clyde   Keesha   Tammy   (Kaleesha)

Damballah

O rion let the dead, gray cloth slide down his legs and stepped into the river. He picked his way over slippery stones till he stood calf deep. Dropping to one knee he splashed his groin, then scooped river to his chest, both hands scrubbing with quick, kneading spirals. When he stood again, he stared at the distant gray clouds. A hint of rain in the chill morning air, a faint, clean presence rising from the far side of the hills. The promise of rain coming to him as all things seemed to come these past few months, not through eyes or ears or nose but entering his black skin as if each pore had learned to feel and speak.

He watched the clear water race and ripple and pucker. Where the sun cut through the pine trees and slanted into the water he could see the bottom, see black stones, speckled stones, shining stones whose light came from within. Above a stump at the far edge of the river, clouds of insects hovered. The water was darker there, slower, appeared to stand in deep pools where tangles of root, bush, and weed hung over the bank. Orion thought of the eldest priest chalking a design on the floor of the sacred *obi*. Drawing the watery door no living hands could push open, the crossroads where the spirits passed between worlds. His skin was becoming like that in-between place the priest scratched in the dust. When he walked the cane rows and dirt paths of the plantation he could feel the air of this strange land wearing out his skin, rubbing it thinner and thinner until one day his skin would not be thick enough to separate what was inside from everything outside. Some days his skin whispered he was dying. But he was not afraid. The voices and faces of his fathers bursting through would not drown him. They would sweep him away, carry him home again.

In his village across the sea were men who hunted and fished with their voices. Men who could talk the fish up from their shadowy dwellings and into the woven baskets slung over the fishermen's shoulders. Orion knew the fish in this cold river had forgotten him, that they were darting in and out of his legs. If the whites had not stolen him, he would have learned the fishing magic. The proper words, the proper tones to please the fish. But here in this blood-soaked land everything was different. Though he felt their slick bodies and saw the sudden dimples in the water where they were feeding, he understood that he would never speak the language of these fish. No more than he would ever speak again the words of the white people who had decided to kill him.

The boy was there again hiding behind the trees. He could be the one. This boy born so far from home. This boy who knew nothing but what the whites told him. This boy could learn the story and tell it again. Time was short but he could be the one.

"That Ryan, he a crazy nigger. One them wild African niggers act like he fresh off the boat. Kind you stay away from less you lookin for trouble." Aunt Lissy had stopped popping string beans and frowned into the boy's face. The pause in the steady drumming of beans into the iron pot, the way she scrunched up her face to look mean like one of the Master's pit bulls told him she had finished speaking on the subject and wished to hear no more about it from him. When the long green pods began to shuttle through her fingers again, it sounded like she was cracking her knuckles, and he expected something black to drop into the huge pot.

"Fixin to rain good. Heard them frogs last night just a singing at the clouds. Frog and all his brothers calling down the thunder. Don't rain soon them fields dry up and blow away." The boy thought of the men trudging each morning to the fields. Some were brown, some yellow, some had red in their skins and some white as the Master. Ryan black, but Aunt Lissy blacker. Fat, shiny blue-black like a crow's wing.

"Sure nuff crazy." Old woman always talking. Talking and telling silly stories. The boy wanted to hear something besides an old woman's mouth. He had heard about frogs and bears and rabbits too many times. He was almost grown now, almost ready to leave in the mornings with the men. What would they talk about? Would Orion's voice be like the hollers the boy heard early in the mornings when the men still sleepy and the sky still dark and you couldn't really see nobody but knew they were there when them cries and hollers came rising through the mist.

Pine needles crackled with each step he took, and the boy knew old Ryan knew somebody spying on him. Old nigger guess who it was, too. But if Ryan knew, Ryan didn't care. Just waded out in that water like he the only man in the world. Like maybe wasn't no world. Just him and that quiet place in the middle of the river. Must be fishing out there, some funny old African kind of fishing. Nobody never saw him touch victuals Master set out and he had to be eating something, even if he was half crazy, so the nigger must be fishing for his breakfast. Standing there like a stick in the water till the fish forgot him and he could snatch one from the water with his beaky fingers.

A skinny-legged, black waterbird in the purring river. The boy stopped chewing his stick of cane, let the sweet juice blend with his spit, a warm syrup then whose taste he prolonged by not swallowing, but letting it coat his tongue and the insides of his mouth, waiting patiently like the figure in the water waited, as the sweet taste seeped away. All the cane juice had trickled down his throat before he saw Orion move. After the stillness, the illusion that the man was a tree rooted in the rocks at the riverbed, when motion came, it was too swift to follow. Not so much a matter of seeing Orion move as it was feeling the man's eyes inside him, hooking him before he could crouch lower in the weeds. Orion's eyes on him and through him boring a hole in his chest and thrusting into that space one word, *Damballah*. Then the hooded eyes were gone.

On a spoon you see the shape of a face is an egg. Or two eggs because you can change the shape from long oval to moons pinched together at the middle seam or any shape egg if you tilt and push the spoon closer or farther away. Nothing to think about. You go with Mistress to the chest in the root cellar. She guides you with a candle and you make a pouch of soft cloth and carefully lay in each spoon and careful it don't jangle as up and out of the darkness following her rustling dresses and petticoats up the earthen steps each one topped by a plank which squirms as you mount it. You are following the taper she holds and the strange smell she trails and leaves in rooms. Then shut up in a room all day with nothing to think about. With rags and pieces of silver. Slowly you rub away the tarnished spots; it is like finding something which surprises you though you knew all the time it was there. Spoons lying on the strip of indigo: perfect, gleaming fish you have coaxed from the black water.

Damballah was the word. Said it to Aunt Lissy and she went upside his head, harder than she had ever slapped him. Felt like crumpling right there in the dust of the yard it hurt so bad but he bit his lip and didn't cry out, held his ground and said the word again and again silently to himself, pretending nothing but a bug on his burning cheek and twitched and sent it flying. Damballah. Be strong as he needed to be. Nothing touch him if he don't want. Before long they'd cut him from the herd of pickaninnies. No more chasing flies from the table, no more silver spoons to get shiny, no fat, old woman telling him what to do. He'd go to the fields each morning with the men. Holler like they did before the sun rose to burn off the mist. Work like they did from can to caint. From first crack of light to dusk when the puddles of shadow deepened and spread so you couldn't see your hands or feet or the sharp tools hacking at the cane.

He was already taller than the others, a stork among the chicks scurrying behind Aunt Lissy. Soon he'd rise with the conch horn and do a man's share so he had let the fire rage on half his face and thought of the nothing always there to think of. In the spoon, his face long and thin as a finger. He looked for the print of Lissy's black hand on his cheek, but the image would not stay still. Dancing like his face reflected in the river. Damballah. "Don't you ever, you hear me, ever let me hear that heathen talk no more. You hear me, boy? You talk Merican, boy." Lissy's voice like chicken cackle. And his head a barn packed with animal noise and animal smell. His own head but he had to sneak round in it. Too many others crowded in there with him. His head so crowded and noisy lots of time don't hear his own voice with all them braying and cackling.

Orion squatted the way the boy had seen the other old men collapse on their haunches and go still as a stump. Their bony knees poking up and their backsides resting on their ankles. Looked like they could sit that way all day, legs folded under them like wings. Orion drew a cross in the dust. Damballah. When Orion passed his hands over the cross the air seemed to shimmer like

YOU MADE ME LOVE YOU 13

it does above a flame or like it does when the sun so hot you can see waves of heat rising off the fields. Orion talked to the emptiness he shaped with his long black fingers. His eyes were closed. Orion wasn't speaking but sounds came from inside him the boy had never heard before, strange words, clicks, whistles and grunts. A singsong moan that rose and fell and floated like the old man's busy hands above the cross. Damballah like a drum beat in the chant. Damballah a place the boy could enter, a familiar sound he began to anticipate, a sound outside of him which slowly forced its way inside, a sound measuring his heartbeat then one with the pumping surge of his blood.

The boy heard part of what Lissy saying to Primus in the cooking shed: "Ryan he yell that heathen word right in the middle of Jim talking bout Sweet Jesus the Son of God. Jump up like he snake bit and scream that word so everybody hushed, even the white folks what came to hear Jim preach. Simple Ryan standing there at the back of the chapel like a knot poked out on somebody's forehead. Lookin like a nigger caught wid his hand in the chicken coop. Screeching like some crazy hoot owl while Preacher Jim praying the word of the Lord. They gon kill that simple nigger one day."

Dear Sir:

The nigger Orion which I purchased of you in good faith sight unseen on your promise that he was of sound constitution "a full grown and able-bodied house servant who can read, write, do sums and cipher" to recite the exact words of your letter dated April 17, 1852, has proved to be a burden, a deficit to the economy of my plantation rather than the asset I fully believed I was receiving when I agreed to pay the price you asked. Of the vaunted intelligence so rare in his kind, I have seen nothing. Not an English word has passed through his mouth since he arrived. Of his docility and tractability I have seen only the willingness with which he bares his leatherish back to receive the stripes constant misconduct earn him. He is a creature whose brutish habits would shame me were he quartered in my kennels. I find it odd that I should write at such length about any nigger, but seldom have I been so struck by the disparity between promise and performance. As I have accrued nothing but expense and inconvenience as a result of his presence, I think it only just that you return the full amount I paid for this flawed *piece of the Indies*.

You know me as an honest and fair man and my regard for those same qualities in you prompts me to write this letter. I am not a harsh master, I concern myself with the spiritual as well as the temporal needs of my slaves. My nigger Jim is renowned in this county as a preacher. Many say I am foolish, that the words of scripture are wasted on these savage blacks. I fear you have sent me a living argument to support the critics of my Christianizing project. Among other absences of truly human qualities I have observed in this Orion is the utter lack of a soul.

She said it time for Orion to die. Broke half the overseer's bones knocking him off his horse this morning and everybody thought Ryan done run away sure but Mistress come upon the crazy nigger at suppertime on the big house porch naked as the day he born and he just sat there staring into her eyes till Mistress screamed and run away. Aunt Lissy said Ryan ain't studying no women, ain't gone near to woman since he been here and she say his ain't the first black butt Mistress done seen all them nearly grown boys walkin round summer in the onliest shirt Master give em barely come down to they knees and niggers man nor woman don't get drawers the first. Mistress and Master both seen plenty. Wasn't what she saw scared her less she see the ghost leaving out Ryan's body.

The ghost wouldn't steam out the top of Orion's head. The boy remembered the sweaty men come in from the fields at dusk when the nights start to cool early, remembered them with the drinking gourds in they hands scooping up water from the wooden barrel he filled, how they throw they heads back and the water trickles from the sides of they mouth and down they chin and they let it roll on down they chests, and the smoky steam curling off they shoulders. Orion's spirit would not rise up like that but wiggle out his skin and swim off up the river.

The boy knew many kinds of ghosts and learned the ways you get round their tricks. Some spirits almost good company and he filled the nothing with jingles and whistles and took roundabout paths and sang to them when he walked up on a crossroads and yoo-hooed at doors. No way you fool the haunts if a spell conjured strong on you, no way to miss a beating if it your day to get beat, but the ghosts had everything in they hands, even the white folks in they hands. You know they there, you know they floating up in the air watching and counting and remembering them strokes Ole Master laying cross your back.

They dragged Orion across the yard. He didn't buck or kick, but it seemed as if the four men carrying him were struggling with a giant stone rather than a black bag of bones. His ashy nigger weight swung between the two pairs of white men like a lazy hammock but the faces of the men all red and twisted. They huffed and puffed and sweated through they clothes carrying Ryan's bones to the barn. The dry spell had layered the yard with a coat of dust. Little squalls of yellow spurted from under the men's boots. Trudging steps heavy as if each man carried seven Orions on his shoulders. Four grown men struggling with one string of black flesh. The boy had never seen so many white folks dealing with one nigger. Aunt Lissy had said it time to die and the boy wondered what Ryan's ghost would think dropping onto the dust surrounded by the scowling faces of the Master and his overseers.

One scream that night. Like a bull when they cut off his maleness. Couldn't tell who it was. A bull screaming once that night and torches burning in the barn and Master and the men coming out and no Ryan.

Mistress crying behind a locked door and Master messing with Patty down the quarters.

In the morning light the barn swelling and rising and teetering in the yellow dust, moving the way you could catch the ghost of something in a spoon and play with it, bending it, twisting it. That goldish ash on everybody's bare shins. Nobody talking. No cries nor hollers from the fields. The boy watched till his eyes hurt, waiting for a moment when he could slip unseen into the shivering barn. On his hands and knees hiding under a wagon, then edging sideways through the loose boards and wedge of space where the weathered door hung crooked on its hinge.

The interior of the barn lay in shadows. Once beyond the sliver of light coming in at the cracked door the boy stood still till his eyes adjusted to the darkness. First he could pick out the stacks of hay, the rough partitions dividing the animals. The smells, the choking heat there like always, but rising above these familiar sensations the buzz of flies, unnaturally loud, as if the barn breathing and each breath shook the wooden walls. Then the boy's eyes followed the sound to an open space at the center of the far wall. A black shape there. Orion there, floating in his own blood. The boy ran at the blanket of flies. When he stomped, some of the flies buzzed up from the carcass. Others too drunk on the shimmering blood ignored him except to join the ones hovering above the body in a sudden droning peal of annoyance. He could keep the flies stirring but they always returned from the recesses of the high ceiling, the dark corners of the building, to gather in a cloud above the body. The boy looked for something to throw. Heard his breath, heavy and threatening like the sound of the flies. He sank to the dirt floor, sitting cross-legged where he had stood. He moved only once, ten slow paces away from Orion and back again, near enough to be sure, to see again how the head had been cleaved from the rest of the body, to see how the ax and tongs, branding iron and other tools were scattered around the corpse, to see how one man's hat and another's shirt, a letter that must have come from someone's pocket lay about in a helter-skelter way as if the men had suddenly bolted before they had finished with Orion.

Forgive him, Father. I tried to the end of my patience to restore his lost soul. I made a mighty effort to bring him to the Ark of Salvation but he had walked in darkness too long. He mocked Your Grace. He denied Your Word. Have mercy on him and forgive his heathen ways as you forgive the soulless beasts of the fields and birds of the air.

She say Master still down slave row. She say everybody fraid to go down and get him. Everybody fraid to open the barn door. Overseer half dead and the Mistress still crying in her locked room and that barn starting to stink already with crazy Ryan and nobody gon get him.

And the boy knew his legs were moving and he knew they would carry him where they needed to go and he knew the legs belonged to him but he could not feel them, he had been sitting too long thinking on nothing for too long and he felt the sweat running on his body but his mind off somewhere cool and quiet and hard and he knew the space between his body and mind could not be crossed by anything, knew you mize well try to stick the head back on Ryan as try to cross that space. So he took what he needed out of the barn, unfolding, getting his gangly crane's legs together under him and shouldered open the creaking double doors and walked through the flame in the center where he had to go.

Damballah said it be a long way a ghost be going and Jordan chilly and wide and a new ghost take his time getting his wings together. Long way to go so you can sit and listen till the ghost ready to go on home. The boy wiped his wet hands on his knees and drew the cross and said the word and settled down and listened to Orion tell the stories again. Orion talked and he listened and couldn't stop listening till he saw Orion's eyes rise up through the back of the severed skull and lips rise up through the skull and the wings of the ghost measure out the rhythm of one last word.

Late afternoon and the river slept dark at its edges like it did in the mornings. The boy threw the head as far as he could and he knew the fish would hear it and swim to it and welcome it. He knew they had been waiting. He knew the ripples would touch him when he entered.

Daddy Garbage

"Be not dismayed
What ere betides . . ."

Daddy Garbage was a dog. Lemuel Strayhorn whose iceball cart is always right around the corner on Hamilton just down from Homewood Avenue is the one who named the dog and since he named him, claimed him, and Daddy Garbage must have agreed because he sat on the sidewalk beside Lemuel Strayhorn or slept in the shade under the two-wheeled cart or when it got too cold for iceballs, followed Strayhorn through the alleys on whatever errands and hustles the man found during the winter to keep food on the stove and smoke in the chimney of the little shack behind Dunfermline. The dog was long dead but Lemuel Strayhorn still peddled the paper cups of crushed ice topped with sweet syrup, and he laughed and said, "Course I remember that crazy animal. Sure I do. And named him Daddy Garbage all right, but can't say now why I did. Must have had a reason though. Must been a good reason at the time. And you a French, ain't you? One of John French's girls. See him plain as day in your face, gal. Which one is you? Lemme see now. There was Lizabeth, the oldest, and Geraldine and one more . . ."

She answers: "Geraldine, Mr. Strayhorn."

"Sure you are. That's right. And you done brought all these beautiful babies for some ices."

"You still make the best."

"Course I do. Been on this corner before you was born. Knew your daddy when he first come to Homewood."

"This is his grandson, Lizabeth's oldest, John. And those two boys are his children. The girls belong to Lizabeth's daughter, Shirley."

"You got fine sons there, and them pretty little girls, too. Can hear John

French now, braggin bout his children. He should be here today. You all want ices? You want big or small?"

"Small for the kids and I want a little one, please, and he'll take a big one, I know."

"You babies step up and tell me what kind you want. Cherry, lemon, grape, orange, and tutti-frutti. Got them all."

"You remember Mr. Strayhorn. Don't you, John?"

"Uh huh. I think I remember Daddy Garbage, too."

"You might of seen a dog around, son, but wasn't no Daddy Garbage. Naw, you way too young."

"Mr. Strayhorn had Daddy Garbage when I was a little girl. A big, rangy brown dog. Looked like a wolf. Scare you half to death if you didn't know he was tame and never bothered anybody."

"Didn't bother nobody long as they didn't bother him. But that was one fighting dog once he got started. Dogs got so they wouldn't even bark when Daddy Garbage went by. Tore up some behinds in his day, yes, he did."

"Wish you could remember how he got that name."

"Wish I could tell you, too. But it's a long time ago. Some things I members plain as day, but you mize well be talking to a lightpost you ask me bout others. Shucks, Miss French. Been on this corner making iceballs, seem like four hundred years if it's a day."

"You don't get any older. And I bet you still remember what you want to remember. You look fine to me, Mr. Strayhorn. Look like you might be here another four hundred at least."

"Maybe I will. Yes mam, just might. You children eat them ices up now and don't get none on them nice clothes and God bless you all."

"I'm going to ask you about that name again."

"Just might remember next time. You ask me again."

"I surely will . . ."

Snow fell all night and in the morning Homewood seemed smaller. Whiteness softened the edges of things, smoothed out the spaces between near and far. Trees drooped, the ground rose up a little higher, the snow glare in your eyes discouraged a long view, made you attentive to what was close at hand, what was familiar, yet altered and harmonized by the blanket of whiteness. The world seemed smaller till you got out in it and understood that the glaze which made the snow so lustrous had been frozen there by the wind, and sudden gusts would sprinkle your face with freezing particles from the drifts as you leaned forward to get a little closer to the place you wanted to go, the place which from your window as you surveyed the new morning and the untouched snow seemed closer than it usually was.

The only way to make it up the alley behind Dunfermline was to stomp right into the drifted snow as if the worn shoes on your feet and the pants legs pegged and tucked into the tops of your socks really kept out the snow. Strayhorn looked behind him at the holes he had punched in the snow. Didn't seem like he had been zigzagging that much. Looked like the tracks of somebody been pulling on a jug of Dago Red already this morning. The dog's trail wandered even more than his, a nervous tributary crossing and recrossing its source. Dog didn't seem to mind the snow or the cold, sometimes even seemed fool enough to like it, rolling on his side and kicking up his paws or bounding to a full head of steam then leaping and belly flopping splay-legged in a shower of white spray. Still a lot of pup in the big animal. Some dogs never lost those ways. With this one, this garbage-can-raiding champion he called Daddy Garbage, Strayhorn knew it was less holding on to puppy ways than it was stone craziness, craziness age nor nothing else ever going to change.

Strayhorn lifts his foot and smacks off the snow. Balances a second on one leg but can't figure anything better to do with his clean foot so plunges it again into the snow. Waste of time brushing them off. Going to be a cold, nasty day and nothing for it. Feet get numb and gone soon anyway. Gone till he can toast them in front of a fire. He steps through the crust again and the crunch of his foot breaks a stillness older than the man, the alley, the city growing on steep hills.

Somebody had set a lid of peeling wood atop a tin can. Daddy Garbage was up on his hind legs, pushing with his paws and nose against the snow-capped cover. The perfect symmetry of the crown of snow was the first to go, gouged by the dog's long, worrying snout. Next went the can. Then the lean-backed mongrel sprawled over the metal drum, mounting it and getting away from it simultaneously so he looked like a clumsy seal trying to balance on a ball. Nothing new to Strayhorn. The usual ungodly crash was muffled by the snow but the dog's nails scraped as loudly as they always did against garbage cans. The spill looked clean and bright against the snow, catching Strayhorn's eye for a moment, but a glance was all he would spare because he knew the trifling people living in those shacks behind Dunfermline didn't throw nothing away unless it really was good for nothing but garbage. Slim pickins sure enough, and he grunted over his shoulder at the dog to quit fooling and catch up.

When he looked back again, back at his solitary track, at the snow swirls whipped up by the wind, at the thick rug of snow between the row houses, at the whiteness clinging to window ledges and doorsills and ragtag pieces of fence, back at the overturned barrel and the mess spread over the snow, he saw the dog had ignored him and stood stiff-legged, whining at a box disgorged from the can.

He cursed the dog and whistled him away from whatever foolishness he was prying into. Nigger garbage ain't worth shit, Strayhorn muttered, half to the dog, half to the bleakness and the squalor of the shanties disguised this bright morning by snowfall. What's he whining about and why am I going back to see. Mize well ask a fool why he's a fool as do half the things I do.

To go back down the alley meant walking into the wind. Wind cutting steady in his face and the cross-drafts snapping between the row houses. He would snatch that dog's eyeballs loose. He would teach it to come when he called whether or not some dead rat or dead cat stuffed up in a box got his nose open.

"Daddy Garbage, I'm gonna have a piece of your skull." But the dog was too quick and Strayhorn's swipe disturbed nothing but the frigid air where the scruff of the dog's neck had been. Strayhorn tried to kick away the box. If he hadn't been smacking at the dog and the snow hadn't tricked his legs, he would have sent it flying, but his foot only rolled the box over.

At first Strayhorn thought it was a doll. A little dark brown doll knocked from the box. A worn out baby doll like he'd find sometimes in people's garbage too broken up to play with anymore. A little, battered, brown-skinned doll. But when he looked closer and stepped away, and then shuffled nearer again, whining, stiff-legged like the dog, he knew it was something dead.

"Aw shit, aw shit, Daddy Garbage." When he knelt, he could hear the dog panting beside him, see the hot, rank steam, and smell the wet fur. The body lay facedown in the snow, only its head and shoulders free of the newspapers stuffed in the box. Some of the wadded paper had blown free and the wind sent it scudding across the frozen crust of snow.

The child was dead and the man couldn't touch it and he couldn't leave it alone. Daddy Garbage had sidled closer. This time the swift, vicious blow caught him across the skull. The dog retreated, kicking up a flurry of snow, snarling, clicking his teeth once before he began whimpering from a distance. Under his army greatcoat Strayhorn wore the gray wool hunting vest John French had given him after John French won all that money and bought himself a new leather one with brass snaps. Strayhorn draped his overcoat across the upright can the dog had ignored, unpinned the buttonless vest from his chest and spread it on the snow. A chill was inside him. Nothing in the weather could touch him now. Strayhorn inched forward on his knees till his shadow fell across the box. He was telling his hands what they ought to do, but they were sassing. He cursed his raggedy gloves, the numb fingers inside them that would not do his bidding.

The box was too big, too square shouldered to wrap in the sweater vest. Strayhorn wanted to touch only newspaper as he extricated the frozen body, so when he finally got it placed in the center of the sweater and folded over the tattered gray edges, the package he made contained half newspaper which rustled like dry leaves when he pressed it against his chest. Once he had it in his arms he couldn't put it down, so he struggled with his coat like a one-armed man, pulling and shrugging, till it shrouded him again. Not on really, but attached, so it dragged and flopped with a life of its own, animation that excited Daddy Garbage and gave him something to play with as he minced after Strayhorn and Strayhorn retraced his own footsteps, clutching the dead child to the warmth of his chest, moaning and blinking and tearing as the wind lashed his face.

An hour later Strayhorn was on Cassina Way hollering for John French. Lizabeth shooed him away with all the imperiousness of a little girl who had heard her mama say, "Send that fool away from here. Tell him your daddy's out working." When the girl was gone and the door slammed behind her, Strayhorn thought of the little wooden birds who pop out of a clock, chirp their message, and disappear. He knew Freeda French didn't like him. Not anything personal, not anything she could change or he could change, just the part of him which was part of what drew John French down to the corner with the other men to talk and gamble and drink wine. He understood why she would never do more than nod at him or say *Good day, Mr. Strayhorn* if he forced the issue by tipping his hat or taking up so much sidewalk when she passed him that she couldn't pretend he wasn't there. *Mr. Strayhorn*, and he been knowing her, Freeda Hollinger before she was Freeda French, for as long as she was big enough to walk the streets of Homewood. But he understood and hadn't ever minded till just this morning standing in the ankle-deep snow drifted up against the three back steps of John French's house next to the vacant lot on Cassina Way, till just this moment when for the first time in his life he thought this woman might have something to give him, to tell him. Since she was a mother she would know what to do with the dead baby. He could unburden himself and she could touch him with one of her slim, white woman's hands, and even if she still called him *Mr. Strayhorn*, it would be all right. A little woman like that. Little hands like that doing what his hands couldn't do. His scavenging, hard hands that had been everywhere, touched everything. He wished Freeda French had come to the door. Wished he was not still standing tongue-tied and ignorant as the dog raising his hind leg and yellowing the snow under somebody's window across the way.

"Man supposed to pick me up first thing this morning. Want me to paper his whole downstairs. Seven, eight rooms and hallways and bathrooms. Big old house up on Thomas Boulevard cross from the park. Packed my tools and dragged my behind through all this snow and don't you know that white bastard ain't never showed. Strayhorn, I'm evil this morning."

Strayhorn had found John French in the Bucket of Blood drinking a glass of red wine. Eleven o'clock already and Strayhorn hadn't wanted to be away so long. Leaving the baby alone in that empty icebox of a shack was almost as bad as stuffing it in a garbage can. Didn't matter whose it was, or how dead it was, it was something besides a dead thing now that he had found it and rescued it and laid it wrapped in the sweater on the stack of mattresses where he slept. The baby sleeping there now. Waiting for the right thing to be done. It was owed something and Strayhorn knew he had to see to it that the debt was paid. Except he couldn't do it alone. Couldn't return through the snow and shove open that door, and do what had to be done by himself.

"Be making me some good money soon's I catch up with that peckerwood. And I'm gon spend me some of it today. Won't be no better day for spending it. Cold and nasty as it be outside, don't reckon I be straying too far from this stool till bedtime. McKinley, give this whatchamacallit a taste. And don't you be rolling your bubble eyes at me. Tolt you I got me a big-money job soon's I catch that white man."

"Seems like you do more chasing than catching."

"Seems like you do more talking than pouring, nigger. Get your pop-eyed self on over here and fill us some glasses."

"Been looking for you all morning, man."

"Guess you found me. But you ain't found no money if that's what you looking for."

"Naw. It ain't that, man. It's something else."

"Somebody after you again? You been messing with somebody's woman? If you been stealin again or Oliver Edwards is after you again . . ."

"Naw, naw . . . nothing like that."

"Then it must be the Hell Hound hisself on your tail cause you look like death warmed over."

"French, I found a dead baby this morning."

"What you say?"

"Shhh. Don't be shouting. This ain't none McKinley's nor nobody else's business. Listen to what I'm telling you and don't make no fuss. Found a baby. All wrapped up in newspaper and froze stiff as a board. Somebody put it in a box and threw the box in the trash back of Dunfermline."

"Ain't nobody could do that. Ain't nobody done nothing like that."

"It's the godawful truth. Me and Daddy Garbage on our way this morning up the alley. The dog, he found it. Turned over a can and the box fell out. I almost kicked it, John French. Almost kicked the pitiful thing."

"And it was dead when you found it?"

"Dead as this glass."

"What you do?"

"Didn't know what to do so I took it on back to my place."

"Froze dead."

"Laid in the garbage like wasn't nothing but spoilt meat."

"Goddamn . . ."

"Give me a hand, French."

"Goddamn. Goddamn, man. You seen it, sure nuff. I know you did. See it all over your face. God bless America . . . McKinley . . . Bring us a bottle. You got my tools to hold so just get a bottle on over here and don't say a mumbling word."

Lizabeth is singing to the snowman she has constructed on the vacant lot next door to her home. The wind is still and the big flakes are falling again straight down and she interrupts her slow song to catch snow on her tongue. Other kids had been out earlier, spoiling the perfect whiteness of the lot. They had left a mound of snow she used to start her snowman. The mound might have been a snowman before. A tall one, taller than any she could build because there had been yelling and squealing since early in the morning which meant a whole bunch of kids out on the vacant lot and meant they had probably worked together making a giant snowman till somebody got crazy or evil and smacked the snowman and then the others would join in and snow flying everywhere and the snowman plowed down as they scuffled on top of him and threw lumps of him at each other. Till he was gone and then they'd start again. She could see bare furrows where they must have been rolling big snowballs for heads and bodies. Her mother had said: "Wait till some of those roughnecks go on about their business. Probably nothing but boys out there anyway." So she had rid up the table and scrubbed her daddy's eggy plate and sat in his soft chair dreaming of the kind of clean, perfect snow she knew she wouldn't see by the time she was allowed out; dreaming of a ride on her daddy's shoulders to Bruston Hill and he would carry her and the sled to a quiet place not too high up on the slope and she would wait till he was at the bottom again and clapping his hands and shouting up at her: "Go, go little gal."

"If you go to the police they find some reason put you in jail. Hospital got no room for the sick let alone the dead. Undertaker, he's gon want money from somebody before he touch it. The church. Them church peoples got troubles enough of they own to cry about. And they be asking as many questions as the police. It can't stay here and we can't take it back."

"That's what I know, John French. That's what I told you."

Between them the flame of the kerosene lamp shivers as if the cold has penetrated deep into its blue heart. Strayhorn's windowless shack is always dark except where light seeps through cracks between the boards, cracks which now moan or squeeze the wind into shrill whistles. The two men sit on wooden crates whose slats have been reinforced by stone blocks placed under them. Another crate, short side down, supports the kerosene lamp. John French peers over Strayhorn's shoulder into the dark corner where Strayhorn has his bed of stacked mattresses.

"We got to bury it, man. We got to go out in this goddamn weather and bury it. Not in nobody's backyard neither. Got to go on up to the burying ground where the rest of the dead niggers is." As soon as he finished speaking John French realized he didn't know if the corpse was black or white. Being in Homewood, back of Dunfermline wouldn't be anything but a black baby, he had assumed. Yet who in Homewood would have thrown it there? Not even those down home, country Negroes behind Dunfermline in that alley that didn't even have a name would do something like that. Nobody he knew. Nobody he had ever heard of. Except maybe crackers who could do anything to niggers, man, woman, or child don't make no difference.

Daddy Garbage, snoring, farting ever so often, lay next to the dead fireplace. Beyond him in deep shadow was the child. John French thought about going to look at it. Thought about standing up and crossing the dirt floor and laying open the sweater Strayhorn said he wrapped it in. His sweater. His goddamn hunting sweater come to this. He thought about taking the lamp into the dark corner and undoing newspapers and placing the light over the body. But more wine than he could remember and half a bottle of gin hadn't made him ready for that. What did it matter? Black or white. Boy or girl. A mongrel made by niggers tipping in white folks' beds or white folks paying visits to black. Everybody knew it was happening every night. Homewood people every color in the rainbow and they talking about white people and black people like there's a brick wall tween them and nobody don't know how to get over.

"You looked at it, Strayhorn?"

"Just a little bitty thing. Wasn't no need to look hard to know it was dead."

"Can't figure how somebody could do it. Times is hard and all that, but how somebody gon be so cold?"

"Times is surely hard. I'm out there every day scuffling and I can tell you how hard they is."

"Don't care how hard they get. Some things people just ain't supposed to do. If that hound of yours take up and die all the sudden, I know you'd find a way to put him in the ground."

"You're right about that. Simple and ungrateful as he is, I won't be throwing him in nobody's trash."

"Well, you see what I mean then. Something is happening to people. I mean times was bad down home, too. Didn't get cold like this, but the cracker could just about break your neck with his foot always on it. I mean I remember my daddy come home with half a pail of guts one Christmas Eve after he work all day killing hogs for the white man. Half a pail of guts is all he had and six of us pickaninnies and my mama and grandmama to feed. Crackers was mean as spit, but they didn't drive people to do what they do here in this city. Down home you knew people. And you knew your enemies. Getting so you can't trust a soul you see out here in the streets. White, black, don't make no difference. Homewood changing . . . people changing."

"I ain't got nothing. Never will. But I lives good in the summertime and always finds a way to get through winter. Gets me a woman when I needs one."

"You crazy all right, but you ain't evil crazy like people getting. You got your cart and that dog and this place to sleep. And you ain't going to hurt nobody to get more. That's what I mean. People do anything to get more than they got."

"Niggers been fighting and fussing since they been on earth."

"Everybody gon fight. I done fought half the niggers in Homewood, myself. Fighting is different. Long as two men stand up and beat on each other ain't nobody else's business. Fighting ain't gon hurt nobody. Even if it kill a nigger every now and then."

"John French, you don't make no sense."

"If I make no sense out no sense, I be making sense."

"Here you go talking crazy. Gin talk."

"Ain't no gin talking. It's me talking and I'm talking true."

"What we gon do?"

"You got a shovel round here?"

"Got a broken-handled piece of one."

"Well get it, and let's go on and do what we have to do."

"It ain't dark enough yet."

"Dark as the Pit in here."

"Ain't dark outside yet. Got to wait till dark."

John French reaches down to the bottle beside his leg. The small movement is enough to warn him how difficult it will be to rise from the box. Nearly as cold inside as out and the chill is under his clothes, has packed his bones in ice and the stiffness always in the small of his back from bending then reaching high to hang wallpaper is a little hard ball he will have to stretch out inch by painful inch when he stands. His fist closes on the neck of the bottle. Raises it to his lips and drinks deeply and passes it to Strayhorn. Gin is hot in John French's mouth. He holds it there, numbing his lips and gums, inhaling the fumes. For a moment he feels as if his head is a balloon and someone is pumping it full of gas and there is a moment when the balloon is either going to bust or float off his shoulders.

"Gone, nigger. Didn't leave a good swallow." Strayhorn is talking with his mouth half covered by coatsleeve.

"Be two, three hours before it's good and dark. Sure ain't sitting here that long. Ain't you got no wood for that fire?"

"Saving it."

"Let's go then."

"I got to stay. Somebody got to be here."

"Somebody got to get another taste."

"Ain't leaving no more."

"Stay then. I be back. Goddamn. You sure did find it, didn't you?"

When John French wrestles open the door, the gray light enters like a hand and grasps everything within the shack, shaking it, choking it before the door slams and severs the gray hand at the wrist.

It is the hottest time of a July day. Daddy Garbage is curled beneath the big wheeled cart, snug, regal in the only spot of shade on the street at one o'clock in the afternoon. Every once in a while his ropy tail slaps at the pavement. Too old for most of his puppy tricks but still a puppy when he sleeps, Strayhorn thinks, watching the tail rise up and flop down as if it measures some irregular but persistent pulse running beneath the streets of Homewood.

"Mr. Strayhorn." The young woman speaking to him has John French's long, pale face. She is big and rawboned like him and has his straight, good hair. Or the straight, good hair John French used to have. Hers almost to her shoulders but his long gone, a narrow fringe above his ears like somebody had roughed in a line for a saw cut.

"Have you seen my daddy, Mr. Strayhorn?"

"Come by here yesterday, Miss French."

"Today, have you seen him today?"

"Hmmm . . ."

"Mr. Strayhorn, he has to come home. He's needed at home right away."

"Well now . . . let me see . . ."

"Is he gambling? Are they gambling up there beside the tracks? You know if they're up there."

"Seems like I might have seen him with a few of the fellows . . ."

"Dammit, Mr. Strayhorn. Lizabeth's having her baby. Do you understand? It's time, and we need him home."

"Don't fret, little gal. Bet he's up there. You go on home. Me and Daddy Garbage get him. You go on home."

"Nigger gal, nigger gal. Daddy's sure nuff fine sweet little nigger gal." Lizabeth hears the singing coming closer and closer. Yes, it's him. Who else but him? She is crying. Pain and happiness. They brought the baby in for her to see. A beautiful, beautiful little boy. Now Lizabeth is alone again. Weak and pained. She feels she's in the wrong place. She was so big and now she can barely find herself in the immense whiteness of the bed. Only the pain assures her she has not disappeared altogether. The perfect white pain.

She is sweating and wishing for a comb even though she knows she should not try to sit up and untangle the mess of her hair. Her long, straight hair. Like her mama's. Her daddy's. The hair raveled on the pillow beside her face. She is sweating and crying and they've taken away her baby. She listens for footsteps, for sounds from the other beds in the ward. So many swollen bellies, so many white sheets and names she forgets and is too shy to ask again, and where have they taken her son? Why is no one around to tell her what she needs to know? She listens to the silence and listens and then there is his singing. *Nigger gal. Sweet, sweet little nigger gal.* Her daddy's drunk singing floating toward her and a nurse's voice saying *no*, saying *you can't go in there* but her daddy never missing a note and she can see the nurse in her perfect white and her daddy never even looking at her just weaving past the uniform and strutting past the other beds and getting closer and singing, singing an ignorant, darky song that embarrasses her so and singing that nasty word which makes her want to hide under the sheets. But it's him and he'll be beside her and he'll reach down out of the song and touch her wet forehead and his hand will be cool and she'll smell the sweet wine on his breath and she is singing silently to herself what she has always called him, always will, *Daddy John, Daddy John*, in time to the nigger song he chants loud enough for the world to hear.

"Got to say something. You the one likes to talk. You the one good with words." John French and Lemuel Strayhorn have been working for hours. Behind them, below them, the streets of Homewood are deserted, empty and still as if black people in the South hadn't yet heard of mills and mines and freedom, hadn't heard the rumors and the tall tales, hadn't wrapped packages and stuffed cardboard suitcases with everything they could move and boarded trains. North. Empty and still as if every living thing had fled from the blizzard, the snow which will never stop, which will bury Dunfermline, Tioga, Hamilton, Kelly, Cassina, Allequippa, all the Homewood streets disappearing silently, swiftly as the footprints of the two men climbing Bruston Hill. John French first, leaning on the busted shovel like it's a cane, stabbing the metal blade into the snow so it clangs against the pavement like a drum to pace their march. Strayhorn next, tottering unsteadily because he holds the bundle of rags and paper with both hands against his middle, thinking, when the wind gives him peace enough, of what he will say if someone stops him and asks him what he is carrying. Finally the dog, Daddy Garbage, trotting in a line straighter than usual, a line he doesn't waver from even though a cat, unseen, hisses once as the procession mounts higher toward the burying ground.

In spite of wind and snow and bitter cold, the men are flushed and hot inside their clothes. If you were more than a few feet away, you couldn't see them digging. Too much blowing snow, the night too black. But a block away you'd have heard them fighting the frozen earth, cursing and huffing and groaning as they take turns with the short-handled shovel. They had decided before they began that the hole had to be deep, six feet deep at least. If you had been close enough and watched them the whole time, you would have seen how it finally got deep enough so that one man disappeared with the tool while the other sat exhausted in the snow at the edge of the pit waiting his turn. You'd have seen the dark green bottle emptied and shoved neck-first like a miniature headstone in the snow. You would have seen how one pecked at the stone-hard ground while the other weaved around the growing mound of snow and dirt, blowing on his fingers and stomping his feet, making tracks as random as those of Daddy Garbage in the untouched snow of the cemetery . . .

"Don't have no stone to mark this place. And don't know your name, child. Don't know who brought you on this earth. But none that matters now. You your own self now. Buried my twins in this very place. This crying place. Can't think of nothing to say now except they was born and they died so fast too. But we loved them. No time to name one before she was gone. The other named Margaret, after her aunt, my little sister who died young, too.

"Like the preacher say, May your soul rest in peace. Sleep in peace, child."

Strayhorn stands mute with the bundle in his arms. John French blinks the heavy snowflakes from his lashes. He hears Strayhorn grunt *amen* then Strayhorn sways like a figure seen underwater. The outline of his shape wiggles, dissolves, the hard lines of him swell and divide.

"How we gonna put it down there? Can't just pitch it down on that hard ground."

John French pulls the big red plaid snot rag from his coat pocket. He had forgotten about it all this time. He wipes his eyes and blows his nose. Stares up into the sky. The snowflakes all seem to be slanting from one spot high over his head. If he could get his thumb up there or jam in the handkerchief, he could stop it. The sky would clear, they would be able to see the stars.

He kneels at the edge of the hole and pushes clean snow into the blackness. Pushes till the bottom of the pit is lined with soft, glowing fur.

"Best we can do. Drop her easy now. Lean over far as you can and drop her easy . . ."

Lizabeth:
The Caterpillar Story

Did you know I tried to save him once myself. When somebody was dumping ashes on the lot beside the house on Cassina Way. Remember how mad Daddy got. He sat downstairs in the dark with his shotgun and swore he was going to shoot whoever it was dumping ashes on his lot. I tried to save Daddy from that.

It's funny sitting here listening at you talk about your father that way because I never thought about nobody else needing to save him but me. Then I hear you talking and think about John French and know there ain't no way he could have lived long as he did unless a whole lotta people working real hard at saving that crazy man. He needed at least as many trying to save him as were trying to kill him.

Knew all my life about what you did, Mama. Knew you punched through a window with your bare hand to save him. You showed me the scar and showed me the window. In the house we used to live in over on Cassina Way. So I always knew you had saved him. Maybe that's why I thought I could save him too.

I remember telling you the story.

And showing me the scar.

Got the scar, that's for sure. And you got the story.

Thought I was saving Daddy, too, but if you hadn't put your fist through that window I wouldn't have had a Daddy to try and save.

Had you in my lap and we were sitting at the window in the house on Cassina Way. You must have been five or six at the time. Old enough to be telling stories to. Course when I had one of you children on my lap, there was some times I talked just to hear myself talking. Some things couldn't wait even though you all didn't understand word the first. But you was five or six and I was telling you about the time your daddy ate a caterpillar.

The one I ate first.

The very one you nibbled a little corner off.

Then he ate the rest.

The whole hairy-legged, fuzzy, orange and yellow striped, nasty rest.

Because he thought I might die.

As if my babygirl dead wouldn't be enough. Huh uh. He swallowed all the rest of that nasty bug so if you died, he'd die too and then there I'd be with both you gone.

So he was into the saving business, too.

Had a funny way of showing it but I guess you could say he was. Guess he was, all right. Had to be when I look round and see all you children grown up and me getting old as sin.

Nineteen years older than me is all.

That's enough.

I remember you telling me the caterpillar story and then I remember that man trying to shoot Daddy and then I remember Albert Wilkes's pistol you pulled out from under the icebox.

That's a whole lot of remembering. You was a little thing, a lap baby when that mess in Cassina happened.

Five or six.

Yes, you were. That's what you was. Had to be because we'd been on Cassina two, three years. Like a kennel back there on Cassina Way in those days. Every one of them shacks full of niggers. And they let their children run the street half-naked and those burr heads ain't never seen a comb. Let them children out in the morning and called em in at night like they was goats or something. You was five or six but I kept you on my lap plenty. Didn't want you growing up too fast. Never did want it. With all you children I tried to keep that growing up business going slow as I could. What you need to hurry for? Where you going? Wasn't in no hurry to get you out my lap and set you down in those streets.

I remember. I'm sure I remember. The man, a skinny man, came running down the alley after Daddy. He had a big pistol just like Albert Wilkes. And you smashed your fist through the glass to warn Daddy. If I shut my eyes I can hear glass falling and hear the shots.

Never knew John French could run so fast. Thought for a moment one of them bullets knocked him down but he outran em all. Had to or I'd be telling a different story.

It's mixed up with other things in my mind but I do remember. You told me the story and showed me the scar later but I was there and I remember too.

You was there, all right. The two of us sitting at the front window staring at nothing. Staring at the quiet cause it was never quiet in Cassina Way except early in the morning and then again that time of day people in they houses fixing to eat supper. Time of day when the men come home and the children come in off the streets and it's quiet for the first time since dawn. You can hear nothing for the first time and hear yourself think for the first time all day so there we was in that front window and I was half sleep and daydreaming and just about forgot I had you on my lap. Even though you were getting to be a big thing. A five- or six-year-old thing but I wasn't in no hurry to set you down so there we was. You was there all right but I wasn't paying you no mind. I was just studying them houses across the way and staring at my ownself in the glass and wondering where John French was and wondering how long it would stay quiet before your sister Geraldine woke up and started to fuss and wondering who that woman was with a baby in her lap staring back at me.

And you told the caterpillar story.

Yes, I probably did. If that's what you remember, I probably did. I liked to tell it when things was quiet. Ain't much of a story if there's lots of noise around. Ain't the kind you tell to no bunch of folks been drinking and telling lies all night. Sitting at the window with you at the quiet end of the afternoon was the right time for that story and I probably told it to wake myself up.

John French is cradling Lizabeth in one arm pressed against his chest. She is muttering or cooing or getting ready to throw up.

"What did she eat? What you saying she ate? You supposed to be watching this child, woman."

"Don't raise your voice at me. Bad enough without you frightening her."

"Give it here, woman."

His wife opens her fist and drops the fuzzy curled remnant of caterpillar in his hand. It lies there striped orange and yellow, dead or alive, and he stares like it is a sudden eruption of the skin of the palm of his hand, stares like he will stare at the sloppy pyramids of ash desecrating his garden-to-be. He spreads the fingers of the hand of the arm supporting the baby's back; still one minute, Lizabeth will pitch and buck the next. He measures the spiraled length of caterpillar in his free hand, sniffs it, strokes its fur with his middle finger, seems to be listening or speaking to it as he passes it close to his face. His jaws work the plug of tobacco; he spits and the juice sizzles against the pavement.

"You sure this the most of it? You sure she only ate a little piece?"

Freeda French is still shaking her head yes, not because she knows the answer but because anything else would be unthinkable. How could she let this man's daughter chew up more than a little piece of caterpillar. Freeda is crying inside. Tears glaze her eyes, shiny and thick as the sugar frosting on her aunt Aida's cakes and there is too much to hold back, the weight of the tears will crack the glaze and big drops will steal down her cheeks. While she is still nodding yes, nodding gingerly so the tears won't leak, but knowing they are coming anyway, he spits again and pops the gaudy ringlet of bug into his mouth.

"I got the most of it then. And if I don't die, she ain't gonna die neither, so stop that sniffling." He chews two or three times and his eyes are expressionless vacant as he runs his tongue around his teeth getting it all out and down. . . .

Someone had been dumping ashes on the vacant lot at the end of Cassina Way. The empty lot had been part of the neighborhood for as long as anybody could remember and no one had ever claimed it until John French moved his family into the rear end of the narrow row house adjoining the lot and then his claim went no farther than a patch beside the end wall of the row houses, a patch he intended to plant with tomatoes, peppers, and beans but never got around to except to say he'd be damned if he couldn't make something grow there even though the ground was more rock and roots than it was soil because back home in Culpepper, Virginia, where the soil so good you could almost eat it in handfuls scooped raw from the earth, down there he learned about growing and he was going to make a garden on that lot when he got around to it and fix it to look nearly as good as the one he had loved to listen to when he was a boy sitting on his back porch with his feet up on a chair and nobody he had to bother with from his toes to the Blue Ridge Mountains floating on the horizon.

Ashes would appear in gray, sloppy heaps one or two mornings a week. The shape of the mounds told John French they had been spilled from a wheelbarrow, that somebody was sneaking a wheelbarrow down the dark, cobbled length of Cassina Way while other people slept, smothering his dream of a garden under loads of scraggly ash. One afternoon when Lizabeth came home crying with ash in her hair, hair her mother had just oiled and braided that morning, John French decided to put a stop to the ash dumping. He said so to his wife, Freeda, while Lizabeth wept, raising his voice as Lizabeth bawled louder. Finally goddamned somebody's soul and somebody's ancestors and threatened to lay somebody's sorry soul to rest, till Freeda hollering to be heard over Lizabeth's crying and John French's cussing told him such language wasn't fit for a child's ears, wasn't fit for no place or nobody but the Bucket of Blood and his beer drinking, wine drinking, nasty-talking cronies always hanging round there.

So for weeks Lizabeth did not sleep. She lay in her bed on the edge of sleep in the tiny room with her snoring sister, afraid like a child is afraid to poke a foot in bath water of an uncertain temperature, but she was frozen in that hesitation not for an instant but for weeks as she learned everything she could from the night sounds of Cassina Way, and then lay awake learning there was nothing else to learn, that having the nightmare happen would be the only way of learning, that after predictable grunts and alley clamors, the cobblestones went to sleep for the night and she still hadn't picked up a clue about what she needed to know, how she would recognize the sound of a wheelbarrow and find some unfrightened, traitorous breath in herself with which to cry out and warn the man who pushed the barrow of ashes that her father, John French, with his double-barreled shotgun taller than she was, sat in ambush in the downstairs front room.

Even before she heard him promise to shoot whoever was dumping ashes she had listened for her daddy to come home at night. He'd rummage a few minutes in the kitchen then she'd listen for the scrape of a match and count his heavy steps as he climbed to the landing; at *twelve* he would be just a few feet away and the candlelight would lurch on the wall and her father would step first to the girls' room, and though her eyes were squeezed as tightly shut as walnuts, she could feel him peering in as the heat of the candle leaned closer, feel him counting his daughters the way she counted the stairs, checking on his girls before he ventured the long stride across the deep well of the landing to the other side of the steps, the left turning to the room where her mother would be sleeping. Once in a while partying all by himself downstairs, he would sing. Rocking back and forth on a rickety kitchen chair, his foot tapping a bass line on the linoleum floor, he'd sing, *Froggy went a courtin and he did ride, uh huh, uh huh.* Or the songs she knew came from the Bucket of Blood. His husky voice cracking at the tenor notes and half laughing, half swallowing the words in those songs not fit for any place but the Bucket of Blood.

Most times he was happy but even if she heard the icebox door slammed hard enough to pop the lock, heard his chair topple over and crash to the floor, heard the steps groan like he was trying to put his heel through the boards, like he was trying to crush the humpback of some steel-shelled roach with each stride, hearing even this she knew his feet would get quieter as she neared the end of her count, that no matter how long it took between steps when she could hear him snoring or shuffling back and forth along the length of a step like he had forgotten *up* and decided to try *sideways*, finally he would reach the landing and the staggering light from the candle her mother always set out for him on its dish beside the front door would lean in once then die with the bump of her parents' door closing across the landing.

Lizabeth could breathe easier then, after she had counted him safely to his bed, after the rasp of door across the landing and the final bump which locked him safely away. But for weeks she'd lain awake long after the house was silent, waiting for the unknown sound of the wheelbarrow against the cobblestones, the sound she must learn, the sound she must save him from.

"It got to be that bowlegged Walter Johnson cause who else be cleaning people's fireplaces round here. But I'll give him the benefit of the doubt. Every man deserves the benefit of the doubt so I ain't going to accuse Walter Johnson to his face. What I'm gon do is fill the next nigger's butt with buckshot I catch coming down Cassina Way dumping ash."

She knew her father would shoot. She had heard about Albert Wilkes so she knew that shooting meant men dead and men running away and never coming back. She could not let it happen. She imagined the terrible sound of the gun a hundred times each night. If she slept at all, she did not remember or could not admit a lapse because then the hours awake would mean nothing. Her vigilance must be total. If she would save her father from himself, from the rumbling cart and the gray, ashy-faced intruder who would die and carry her father away with him in the night, she must be constant, must listen and learn the darkness better than it knew itself.

"Daddy." She is sitting on his knee. Her eyes scale her father's chest, one by one she climbs the black buttons of his flannel shirt until she counts them all and reaches the grayish neck of his long johns. Their one cracked pearl button showing below his stubbled chin.

"Daddy. I want to stay in your hat."

"What you talking about, little sugar?"

"I want to live in your hat. Your big brown hat. I want to live in there always."

"Sure you can. Yes indeed. Make you a table and some chairs and catch a little squirrel, too, let him live in there with you. Now that sounds like a fine idea, don't it? Stay under there till you get too big for your daddy's hat. Till you get to be a fine big gal."

Lizabeth lowers her eyes from his long jaw, from the spot he plumped out with his tongue. He shifted the Five Brothers tobacco from one cheek to the other, getting it good and juicy, and the last she saw of his face before her eyes fell to the brass pot beside his chair was how his jaws worked the tobacco, grinding the wad so it came out bloody and sizzling when he spit.

She was already big enough for chores and hours beside her mother in the kitchen where there was always something to be done. But hours too on the three steps her Daddy had built from the crooked door to the cobbled edge of Cassina Way. Best in the summer when she could sit and get stupid as a fly in the hot sun after it rose high enough to crest the row houses across the alley. If you got up before everybody else summer mornings were quiet in Cassina, nothing moving until the quiet was broken by the cry of the scissors-and-knife man, a jingling ring of keys at his waist, and strapped across his back the flintstone wheel which he would set down on its three legs and crank so the sparks flew up if you had a dull blade for him to sharpen, or by the iceman, who would always come first, behind the tired clomp of his horse's hooves striking Cassina's stones. The iceman's wagon was covered with gray canvas that got darker like a bandage on a wound as the ice bled through. *Ice. Ice. Any ice today, lady?* The iceman sang the words darkly so Lizabeth never understood exactly what he cried till she asked her mother.

"He's saying *Any ice today, lady*, least that's what he thinks he's saying. Least that's what I think he's saying," her mother said as she listened stock-still by the sink to make sure. For years the iceman was Fred Willis and Fred Willis still owned the horse which slept some people said in the same room with him, but now a scowling somebody whose name Lizabeth didn't know, who wore a long rubber apron the color of soaked canvas was the one talking the old gray horse down the alley, moaning, *Ice, ice, any ice today, lady*, or whatever it was she heard first thing behind the hollow clomp of the hooves.

Stupid as a fly. She had heard her daddy say that and it fit just how she felt, sun-dazed, forgetting even the itchy places on her neck, the cries of the vendors which after a while like everything blended with the silence.

Stupid as a fly during her nightlong vigils when she couldn't learn what she needed to know but she did begin to understand how she could separate into two pieces and one would listen for the wheelbarrow and the other part would watch her listening. One part had a daddy and loved him more than anything but the other part could see him dead or dying or run away forever and see Lizabeth alone and heartbroken or see Lizabeth lying awake all night foolish enough to think she might save her daddy. The watching part older and wiser and more evil than she knew Lizabeth could ever be. A worrisome part which strangely at times produced in her the most profound peace because she was that part and nothing else when she sat sun-drugged, stupid as a fly on the steps over Cassina Way.

Bracelets of gray soapsuds circled her mother's wrists as she lifted a china cup from the sink, rinsed it with a spurt of cold water, and set it gleaming on the drainboard to dry. The same froth clinging to her mother's arms floated above the rim of the sink, screening the dishes that filled the bowl. Each time the slim hands disappeared into the water there was an ominous clatter and rattle, but her mother's fingers had eyes, sorted out the delicate pieces first, retrieved exactly what they wanted from the load of dishes. If Lizabeth plunged her own hands into the soapy water, everything would begin to totter and slide, broken glass and chipped plates would gnaw her clumsy fingers. Some larger pieces were handed to her to dry and put away which she did automatically, never taking her eyes from her mother's swift, efficient movements at the sink.

"Lizabeth, you go catch the iceman. Tell him five pounds."

Lizabeth shouted, *Five pound, we want five pound.* She knew better, her mother had told her a hundred times: pounds and miles, *s* when you talking bout more than one, but her daddy said *two pound a salt pork and a thousand mile tween here and home* so when the wagon was abreast of the last row houses and the echo of the hooves and the echo of the blues line the iceman made of his call faded down the narrow funnel of Cassina Way she shouted loud as she could, *Five pound, five pound, Mister.*

The horse snorted. She thought it would be happy to stop but it sounded mad. The driver's eyes went from the little girl on the steps to the empty place in the window where there should be a sign if anybody in the house wanted ice. When his eyes stared at her again, they said you better not be fooling with me, girl, and with a grunt much like the horse's snort he swung himself down off the wagon seat, jerked up an edge of the canvas from the ice, and snapped away a five-pound chunk in rusty pincers. The block of ice quivered as the iron hooks pierced its sides. Lizabeth could see splintered crystal planes, the cloudy heart of the ice when the man passed her on the steps. Under the high-bibbed rubber apron, the man's skin was black and glistening. He hollered once, *Iceman,* and pushed through the door.

If she had a horse, she would keep it in the vacant lot next door. It would never look nappy and sick like this one. The iceman's horse had bare patches in his coat, sore, raw-looking spots like the heads of kids who had ringworm. Their mothers would tie a stocking cap over the shaved heads of the boys so they could come to school and you weren't supposed to touch them because you could get it that way but Lizabeth didn't even like to be in the same room. Thinking about the shadowy nastiness veiled under the stockings was enough to make her start scratching even though her mother washed and oiled and braided her thick hair five times a week.

She waited till the wagon had creaked past the vacant lot before she went back inside. If her pinto pony were there in the lot, nibbling at the green grass her daddy would plant, it would whinny at the sad ice wagon horse. She wondered how old the gray horse might be, why it always slunk by with its head bowed and its great backside swaying slowly as the dark heads of the saints in Homewood AME Zion when they hummed the verses of a hymn.

"That man dripping water in here like he don't have good sense. Some people just never had nothing and never will." Her mother was on her hands and knees mopping the faded linoleum with a rag.

"Here, girl, take this till I get the pan." She extended her arm backward without turning her head. "Pan overflowed again and him slopping water, too." She was on her knees and the cotton housedress climbed up the backs of her bare thighs. Her mama's backside poked up in the air and its roundness, its splitness made her think of the horse's huge buttocks, then of her own narrow hips. Her mama drew the brimful drain pan from under the icebox, sliding it aside without spilling a drop. "Here," her arm extended again behind her, her fingers making the shape of the balled rag. She had to say *Here girl* again before Lizabeth raised her eyes from the black scarifications in the linoleum and pushed the rag she had wrung into her mother's fingers.

"I don't know why I'm down here punishing these bones of mine and you just standing there looking. Next time . . ."

Her mother stopped abruptly. She had been leaning on one elbow, the other arm stretched under the icebox to sop up the inevitable drips missed by the drain pan. Now she bowed her head even lower, one cheek almost touching the floor so she could see under the icebox. When her hand jerked from the darkness it was full of something blue-black and metal.

"Oh, God. Oh, my God."

She held it the way she held a trap that had snared a rat, and for a moment Lizabeth believed that must be what it was, some new rat-killing steel trap. Her mama set the wooden kind in dark corners all over the house but when one caught something her mother hated to touch it, she would try to sweep the trap and the squeezed rat body out the door together, leave it for John French to open the spring and shake the dead rodent into the garbage can so the trap could be used again. Her mama held a trap delicately if she had to touch it at all, in two fingers, as far from her body as she could reach, looking away from it till she dropped it in a place from which it could be broomed easily out the door. This time the object was heavier than a trap and her mama's eyes were not half-closed and her mouth was not twisted like somebody swallowing cod liver oil. She was staring, wide-eyed, frightened.

"Watch out . . . stand back."

On the drainboard the gun gleamed with a dull, blue-black light which came from inside, a dead glistening Lizabeth knew would be cold and quick to the touch, like the bloody, glass-eyed fish the gun lay next to.

"You've seen nothing. Do you understand, child? You've seen nothing and don't you ever breathe a word of this to a soul. Do you understand me?"

Lizabeth nodded. But she was remembering the man in the alley. Must remember. But that afternoon in the kitchen it was like seeing it all for the first time. Like she had paid her dime to the man at the Bellmawr show and sat huddled in the darkness, squirming, waiting for pictures to start flashing across the screen. It had to begin with the caterpillar story.

"I got the most of it then. And if I don't die, she ain't gonna die neither, so stop that sniffling."

Lizabeth has heard the story so many times she can tell it almost as well as her mother. Not with words yet, not out loud yet, but she can set the people—her father, her mother, herself as a baby—on the stage and see them moving and understand when they are saying the right words, and she would know if somebody told it wrong. She is nearly six years old and sitting on her mother's lap as she hears the caterpillar story this time. Sitting so they both can look out the downstairs window into Cassina Way.

Both look at the gray covering everything, a late afternoon gray gathered through a fall day that has not once been graced by the sun. Palpable as soot the gray is in the seams between the cobblestones, seals the doors and windows of the row houses across the alley. Lights will yellow the windows soon but at this in-between hour nothing lives behind the gray boards of the shanties across the way. Lizabeth has learned the number *Seventy-Four-Fifteen* Cassina Way and knows to tell it to a policeman if she is lost. But if she is Lizabeth French, she cannot be lost because she will be here, in this house certain beyond a number, absolutely itself among the look-alikes crowding Cassina Way. She will not be lost because there is a lot next door where her daddy will grow vegetables, and her mother will put them in jars and they will eat all winter the sunshine and growing stored in those jars and there are three wooden steps her daddy made for sitting and doing nothing till she gets stupid as a fly in that same sun, and sleeping rooms upstairs, her sister snoring and the candle poked in before her daddy closes the door across the deep well.

The end house coming just before the empty corner lot is Lizabeth and Lizabeth nothing more nor less than the thinnest cobweb stretched in a dusty corner where the sounds, smells, and sights of the house come together.

Lizabeth watches her mother's eyes lose their green. She sits as still as she can. She is not the worm now like her mama always calls her because she's so squirmy, she is nothing now because if she sits still enough her mother forgets her and Lizabeth, who is nothing at all, who is not a worm and not getting too big to be sitting on people's laps all day, can watch the shadows deepen and her mama's green eyes turn gray like the houses across Cassina Way.

"There was a time Cassina Way nothing but dirt. Crab apple trees and pear trees grew where you see all them shacks. Then the war came and they had a parade on Homewood Avenue and you should have seen them boys strut. They been cross the ocean and they knew they looked good in their uniforms and they sure was gon let everybody know it. People lined up on both sides the street to see those colored troops marching home from the war. The 505 Engineers. Everybody proud of them and them strutting to beat the band. Mize well been dancing down Homewood Avenue. In a manner of speaking they were dancing and you couldn't keep your feet still when they go high-stepping past. That big drum get up inside your chest and when Elmer Hollinger hits it your skin feels about to bust. All of Homewood out that day. People I ain't never seen before. All the ones they built these shacks for back here on Cassina Way. Ones ain't never been nowhere but the country and put they children out in the morning, don't call them in till feeding time. Let them run wild. Let them make dirt and talk nasty and hair ain't never seen a comb.

"That's why I'ma hold on to you, girl. That's why your mama got to be mean sometimes and keep you in sometime you want to be running round outdoors."

Lizabeth loves the quiet time of day when she can just sit, when she has her mama all to herself and her mama talks to her and at her and talks to herself but loud enough so Lizabeth can hear it all. Lizabeth needs her mother's voice to make things real. (Years later when she will have grandchildren of her own and her mother and father both long dead Lizabeth will still be trying to understand why sometimes it takes someone's voice to make things real. She will be sitting in a room and the room full of her children and grandchildren and everybody eating and talking and laughing but she will be staring down a dark tunnel and that dark, empty tunnel is her life, a life in which nothing has happened, and she'll feel like screaming at the darkness and emptiness and wringing her hands because nothing will seem real, and she will be alone in a roomful of strangers. She will need to tell someone how it had happened. But anybody who'd care would be long dead. Anybody who'd know what she was talking about would be long gone but she needs to tell someone so she will begin telling herself. Patting her foot on the floor to keep time. Then she will be speaking out loud. The others will listen and pay attention. She'll see down the tunnel and it won't be a tunnel at all, but a door opening on something clear and bright. Something simple which makes so much sense it will flash sudden and bright as the sky in a summer storm. Telling the story right will make it real.)

"Look at that man. You know where he been at. You know what he's been doing. Look at him with his big hat self. You know he been down on his knees at Rosemary's shooting crap with them trifling niggers. Don't you pay me no mind, child. He's your daddy and a good man so don't pay me no mind if I say I wish I could sneak out there and get behind him and boot his butt all the way home. Should have been home an hour ago. Should have been here so he could keep an eye on you while I start fixing dinner. Look at him just sauntering down Cassina Way like he owns it and got all the time in the world. Your sister be up in a minute and yelling soon as her eyes open and him just taking his own sweet time.

"He won, too. Got a little change in his pocket. Tell by the way he walks. Walking like he got a load in his pants, like other people's nickels and dimes weigh him down. If he lost he'd be smiling and busting in here talking fast and playing with youall and keep me up half the night with his foolishness. Never saw a man get happy when he gambles away his family's dinner. Never saw a man get sour-faced and down in the mouth when he wins."

Lizabeth doesn't need to look anymore. Her daddy will get closer and closer and then he'll come through the door. Their life together will begin again. He is coming home from Rosemary's, down Cassina Way. He is there if you look and there if you don't look. He is like the reflection, the image of mother and daughter floating in the grayness of Cassina Way. There if she looks, there if she doesn't.

She stares at the pane of glass and realizes how far away she has been, how long she has been daydreaming, but he is only a few steps closer, taking his own good time, the weight of somebody else's money in his pockets, the crown of his hat taller than the shadowed roofs of Cassina Way.

Her mama's arms are a second skin, a warm snuggling fur that keeps out the grayness, the slight, late afternoon chill of an October day. She hums to herself, a song about the caterpillar story her mama has just told. Her baby sister is sleeping so Lizabeth has her mother to herself. Whenever they are alone, together, is the best time of the day, even if it comes now when the day is nearly over, sitting at the window in her mama's lap and her mama, after one telling of the caterpillar story, quiet and gray as Cassina Way. Because Lizabeth has a baby sister Geraldine she must love even though the baby makes the house smaller and shrinks the taken-for-granted time Lizabeth was used to spending with her mama. Lizabeth not quite six that early evening, late afternoon she is recalling, that she has not remembered or relived for five years till it flashes back like a movie on a screen that afternoon her mother pulls the revolver from under the icebox.

Her mother screams and smashes her fist through the windowpane. A gunshot pops in the alley. Her daddy dashes past the jagged space where the windowpane had been, glass falling around his head as he bounds past faster than she has ever seen him move, past the empty, collapsing frame toward the vacant lot. A gun clatters against the cobbles and a man runs off down the corridor of Cassina Way.

My God. Oh, my God.

Her mama's fist looks like someone has tied bright red strings across her knuckles. The chair tumbles backward as her mother snatches her away from the jagged hole. Baby Geraldine is yelping upstairs like a wounded animal. Lizabeth had been daydreaming, and the window had been there between her daydream and her daddy, there had been separation, a safe space between, but the glass was shattered now and the outside air in her face and her mama's hand bleeding and her mama's arms squeezing her too tightly, crushing her as if her small body could stop the trembling of the big one wrapped around it.

"Lizabeth . . . Lizabeth."

When her mama had screamed her warning, the man's eyes leaped from her daddy's back to the window. Lizabeth saw the gun but didn't believe the gun until her mama screamed again and flung her fist through the glass. That made it real and made her hear her own screams and made her daddy a man about to be shot dead in the alley.

If a fist hadn't smashed through the window perhaps she would not have remembered the screaming, the broken glass, the shots when she watched her mama drag a pistol from under the icebox and set it on the bloody drainboard.

But Lizabeth did remember and see and she knew that Albert Wilkes had shot a policeman and run away and knew Albert Wilkes had come to the house in the dead of night and given her father his pistol to hide, and knew that Albert Wilkes would never come back, that if he did return to Homewood he would be a dead man.

"You're a fool, John French, and no better than the rest of those wine-drinking rowdies down at the Bucket of Blood and God knows you must not have a brain in your head to have a gun in a house with children and who in the name of sense would do such a thing whether it's loaded or not and take it out of here, man, I don't care where you take it, but take it out of here." Her mother shouting as loud as she ever shouts like the time he teased her with the bloody rat hanging off the end of the trap, her daddy waving it at her mama and her mama talking tough first, then shouting and in tears and finally her daddy knew he had gone too far and carried it out the house . . .

Lizabeth remembered when the gun was dragged from under the icebox so there was nothing to do but lie awake all night and save her daddy from himself, save him from the trespassing cart and smoking ashes and the blast of a shotgun and dead men and men running away forever. She'd save him like her mama had saved him. At least till he got that garden planted and things started growing and he put up a little fence and then nobody fool enough to dump ashes on something belonged to John French.

You ought to paint some yellow stripes and orange stripes on that scar, Mama.

Don't be making fun of my scar. This scar saved your father's life.

I know it did. I'm just jealous, that's all. Because I'll never know if I saved him. I'd sure like to know. Anyway an orange-and-yellow caterpillar running across the back of your hand would be pretty, Mama. Like a tattoo. I'd wear it like a badge, if I knew.

Don't know what you're talking about now. You're just talking now. But I do know if you hadn't been sitting in my lap, I'da put my whole body through that window and bled to death on those cobblestones in Cassina Way, so just by being there you saved me and that's enough saving for one day and enough talk, too, cause I can see John French coming down that alley from Rosemary's now and I'm getting sad now and I'm too old to be sitting here crying when ain't nothing wrong with me.

Across the
Wide Missouri

The images are confused now. By time, by necessity. One is Clark Gable brushing his teeth with scotch, smiling in the mirror because he knows he's doing something cute, grinning because he knows fifty million fans are watching him and also a beautiful lady in whose bathroom and bedroom the plot has him awakening is watching over his shoulder. He is loud and brisk and perfectly at ease cleaning his teeth before such an audience. Like he's been doing that number all his life. And when he turns to face the woman, to greet her, the squeaky clean teeth are part of the smile she devours. This image, the grinning, self-assured man at the sink, the slightly shocked, absolutely charmed woman whose few stray hairs betray the passion of her night with him, a night which was both endless and brief as the time between one camera shot fading and another bursting on the screen, may have been in *Gone With the Wind*, but then again just as likely not. I've forgotten. The image is confused, not clear in itself, nor clearly related to other images, other Rhett Butlers and Scarlett O'Haras and movies flashing on and off with brief flurries of theme song.

It is spring here in the mountains. The spring which never really arrives at this altitude. Just threatens. Just squats for a day or a few hours then disappears and makes you suicidal. The teasing, ultimately withheld spring that is a special season here and should have its own name. Like Shit. Or Disaster. Or something of that order. The weather however has nothing to do with the images. Not the wind or the weather or anything I can understand forces this handsome man grinning at a mirror into my consciousness. Nor do geography or climate account for the inevitable succession— the river, the coins, the song, the sadness, the recollection—of other images toppling him and toppling me because it happens no matter where I am, no matter what the season. In the recollection there is a kind of unmasking. The white man at the mirror is my father. Then I know why I am so sad, why the song makes me cry, why the coins sit where they do, where the river leads.

I am meeting my father. I have written the story before. He is a waiter in the dining room on the twelfth floor of Kaufman's Department Store. Not the cafeteria. Be sure you don't get lost in there. He's in the nicer place where you get served at a table. The dining room. A red carpet. Ask for him up there if you get lost. Or ask for Oscar. Mr. Parker. You know Oscar. He's the headwaiter up there. Oscar who later fell on hard times or rather hard times fell on him so hard he can't work anywhere anymore. *Wasn't sickness or nothing else. Just that whiskey. That's whiskey you see in that corner can't even lift his head up off the table.* Ask for your daddy, Mr. Lawson, or ask for Mr. Parker when you get to the twelfth floor. I have written it before because I hear my mother now, like a person in a book or a story instructing me. I wrote it that way but it didn't happen that way because she went with me to Kaufman's. As far as the twelfth floor anyway but she had to pay an overdue gas bill at the gas company office and ride the trolley back to Homewood and she had to see Dr. Barnhart and wanted to be home when I got there. The whole idea of meeting my father for lunch and a movie was hers and part of her idea was just the two of us, Daddy and me, alone. So my mother pointed to the large red-carpeted room and I remember wanting to kiss her, to wait with her at the elevators after she pushed the button and the green arrow pointed down. If I had written it that way the first time I would be kissing her again and smelling her perfume and hearing the bells and steel pulleys of the elevators and staring again apprehensively through the back of my head at the cavernous room full of white people and the black men in white coats moving silently as ghosts but none of them my father.

The entranceway to the restaurant must have been wide. The way over-priced restaurants are with the cash register off to one side and aisles made by the sides of high-backed booths. Wide but cordoned by a rope, a gold-braided, perhaps tasseled rope, stretched between brass, waist-high poles whose round, fluted bases could slide easily anywhere along the red carpet. A large white woman in a silky floral-patterned dress is standing like she always does beside the pole, and the gold rope swallows its own tail when she loops both ends into a hook at the top of one of the poles.

I must have said then to myself, *I am meeting my father.* Said that to myself and to the woman's eyes which seemed both not to see me and to stare so deeply inside me I cringed in shame. In my shyness and nervousness and downright fear I must have talked a lot to myself. Outside the judge's chambers in the marble halls of the courthouse, years later waiting to plead for my brother, I felt the same intimidation, the same need to remind myself that I had a right to be where I was. That the messages coded into the walls and doors and ceilings and floors, into the substances of which they were made, could be confronted, that I could talk and breathe in the storm of words flung at me by the invisible architects who had disciplined the space in which I found myself.

Daddy. Daddy. I am outside his door in the morning. His snores fill the tiny room. More a storage closet than room, separated from the rest of the house so the furnace doesn't heat it. The bed is small but it touches three walls. His "door" is actually a curtain hanging from a string. We live on the second floor so I am out in the hall, on a landing above the icy stairwell calling to him. *Your father worked late last night. Youall better be quiet this morning so he can get some sleep,* but I am there, on the cold linoleum listening to him snore, smelling his sleep, the man smell I wonder now if I've inherited so it trails me, and stamps my things mine when my kids are messing around where they shouldn't be. I am talking to myself when he stirs in that darkness behind the curtain. He groans and the mattress groans under him and the green metal cot squeaks as he shifts to another place in his dreaming.

I say to myself, *Where is he?* I stare at all the black faces. They won't stay still. Bobbing and bowing into the white faces or gliding toward the far swinging doors, the closely cropped heads poised and impenetrable above mandarin collars. Toomer called the white faces petals of dusk and I think now of the waiters insinuating themselves like birds into clusters of petals, dipping silently, silently depositing pollen or whatever makes flowers grow and white people be nice to black people. And tips bloom. I am seeing it in slow motion now, the courtship, the petals, the starched white coats elegant as sails plying the red sea. In my story it is noise and a blur of images. Dark faces never still long enough to be my father.

"Hey, Eddie, look who's here."

There is a white cloth on the table that nearly hangs to the floor. My knees are lost beneath it, it's heavy as a blanket, but Oscar has another white cloth draped over his arm and unfurls it so it pops like a flag or a shoeshine rag and spreads it on top of the other so the table is covered twice. When Oscar sat me down, two cups and saucers were on the table. He went to get my father and told me he'd be right back and fix me up and wasn't I getting big and looked just like my daddy. He had scraped a few crumbs from the edge of the table into his hand and grinned across the miles of white cloth at me and the cups and saucers. While he was gone I had nudged the saucer to see if it was as heavy as it looked. Under the edge closest to me were three dimes. Two shiny ones and one yellow as a bad tooth. I pushed some more and found other coins, two fat quarters neither new nor worn. So there I was at that huge table and all that money in front of me but too scared to touch it so I slid the ten-pound cup and saucer back over the coins and tried to figure out what to do. Knew I better not touch the tablecloth. Knew I couldn't help spotting it or smudging it if my hand actually touched the whiteness. So I tried to shove the money with the base of the saucer, work it over to the end of the table so it'd drop in my hand, but I couldn't see what I was doing and the cup rattled and I could just see that little bit of coffee in the bottom come jumping up out the cup and me worried that whoever had forgotten the quarters and dimes would remember and surely come back for them then what would I say would I lie and they'd know a little nigger at a big snow-white table like this had to be lying, what else I'm gonna do but lie and everybody in the place know the thief had to be me and I was thinking and worrying and wondering what my father would do if all those people came after me and by that time I just went on and snatched that money and catch me if you can.

"Look who's here, Eddie." And under my breath I said shut up Mr. Oscar Parker, keep quiet man you must want everybody in here listening to those coins rattling in my pocket. Rattling loud as a rattlesnake and about to bite my leg through my new pants. Go on about your business, man. Look who ain't here. Ain't nobody here so why don't you go on away.

Then my father picked up the saucers and balled up the old top cloth in one hand, his long fingers gobbling it and tucking it under his arm. Oscar popped the new one like a shoeshine rag and spread it down over the table. Laid it down quiet and soft as new snow.

"Busboy'll git you a place setting. Eddie, you want one?"

"No. I'll just sit with him."

"Sure looks like his daddy."

"Guess he ought to."

"Guess he better."

I don't remember what I ate. I don't recall anything my father said to me. When I wrote this before there was dialogue. A lot of conversation broken by stage directions and the intrusions of restaurant business and restaurant noise. Father and son an island in the midst of a red-carpeted chaos of white people and black waiters and the city lurking in the wings to swallow them both when they take the elevator to the ground floor and pass through Kaufman's green glass revolving doors. But it didn't happen that way. We did talk. As much as we ever did. Both of us awkward and constrained as we still are when we try to talk. I forget all the words. Words were unimportant because what counted was his presence, talking or silent didn't matter. Point was he was with me and would stay with me the whole afternoon. One thing he must have asked me about was the movies. I believe I knew what was playing at every theater downtown and knew the address of every one and could have reeled off for him the names of the stars and what the ads said about each one. The images are not clear but I still can see the way the movie page was laid out. I had it all memorized but when he asked me I didn't recite what I knew, didn't even state a preference because I didn't care. Going with him was what mattered. Going together, wherever, was enough. So I waited for him at the table. Wondering what I had eaten, running my tongue around in my mouth to see if I could get a clue. Because the food had been served and I had wolfed it down but he was all I tasted. His presence my feast.

He came back without the white coat. He brought a newspaper with him and read to himself a minute then read me bits and pieces of what I knew was there. Him reading changed it all. He knew things I had never even guessed at when I read the movie page the night before. Why one show was jive, why another would be a waste of money, how long it would take to walk to some, how others were too far away. I wanted to tell him it didn't matter, that one was just as good as another, but I didn't open my mouth till I heard in his voice the one he wanted to see.

He is six foot tall. His skin is deep brown with Indian red in it. My mother has a strip of pictures taken in a five-and-dime, taken probably by the machine that was still in Murphy's 5 & 10 when Murphy's was still on Homewood Avenue when I was little. Or maybe in one of the booths at Kennywood

Amusement Park which are still there. They are teenagers in the picture, grinning at the automatic camera they've fed a quarter. Mom looks pale, washed out, all the color stolen from her face by the popping flashbulbs. His face in the black-and-white snapshots is darker than it really is. Black as Sambo if you want to get him mad you can say that. Black as Little Black Sambo. Four black-as-coal spots on the strip. But if you look closely you see how handsome he was then. Smiling his way through four successive poses. Each time a little closer to my mother's face, tilting her way and probably busy with his hands off camera because by picture three that solemn grandmother look is breaking up and by the final shot she too is grinning. You see his big, heavy-lidded, long-lashed, theatrical eyes. You see the teeth flashing in his wide mouth and the consciousness, lacking all self-consciousness and vanity, of how good he looks. Black, or rather purple now that the photos have faded, but if you get past the lie of the color he is clearly one of those *brown-eyed, handsome men* people like Chuck Berry sing about and other people lynch.

"Here's a good one. Meant to look at the paper before now, but we been real busy. Wanted to be sure there was a good one but it's all right, got a Western at the Stanley and it's just down a couple blocks past Gimbels. Clark Gable's in it. *Across the Wide Missouri.*"

The song goes something like this: *A white man loved an Indian Maiden* and la de da / la de da. And: *A-way, you've gone away . . . Across the wide Mis-sour-i.* Or at least those words are in it, I think. I think I don't know the words on purpose. For the same reason I don't have it on a record. Maybe fifteen or twenty times in the thirty years since I saw the movie I've heard the song or pieces of the song again. Each time I want to cry. Or do cry silently to myself. A flood of tears the iron color of the wide Missouri I remember from the movie. *A-way, we're gone a-way . . . Across the wide Missouri.* It's enough to have it in pieces. It's enough to have heard it once and then never again all the way through but just in fragments. Like a spring which never comes. But you see a few flowers burst open. And a black cloud move down a grassy slope. A robin. Long, fine legs in a pair of shorts. The sun hot on your face if you lie down out of the wind. The fits and starts and rhythms and phrases from the spring-not-coming which is the source of all springs that do come.

The last time I heard the song my son called it "Shenandoah." Maybe that's what it should be called. Again I don't know. It's something a very strong instinct has told me to leave alone. To take what comes but don't try to make anything more out of it than is there. In the fragments. The bits and pieces. The coincidences like hearing my son hum the song and asking him about it and finding out his class learned it in school and will sing it on Song Night when the second grade of Slade School performs for their parents. He knew the words of a few verses and I asked him to sing them. He seemed pleased that I asked and chirped away in a slightly cracked, slightly breathless, sweet second-grade boy's voice.

Now I realize I missed the concert. Had a choice between Song Night and entertaining a visiting poet who had won a Pulitzer Prize. I chose— without even remembering *Across the Wide Missouri*—the night of too many drinks at dinner and too much wine and too much fretting within skins of words and too much, too much until the bar closed and identities had been defrocked and we were all clichés, as cliché as the syrupy "Shenandoah," stumbling through the swinging doors out into Laramie's cold and wind.

I will ask my son to sing it again. I hope he remembers the words. Perhaps I'll cheat and learn a verse myself so I can say the lyrics rather than mumble along with the tune when it comes into my head. Perhaps I'll find a way to talk to my father. About things like his presence. Like taking me to the movies once, alone, just the two of us in a downtown theater and seeing him for the whole ninety minutes doing good and being brave and handsome and thundering like a god across the screen. Or brushing his teeth loudly in the morning at the sink. Because I understand a little better now why it happened so seldom. (Once?) It couldn't have been only once in all those years. The once is symbolic. It's an image. It's a blurring of reality the way certain shots in a film blur or distort in order to focus. I understand better now the river, the coins, the song, the sadness, the recollection. I have sons now. I've been with them often to the movies. Because the nature of my work is different from my father's. I am freer. I have more time and money. He must have been doing some things right or I wouldn't have made it. Couldn't have. He laughed when I told him years later about "finding" money on the table. I had been a waiter by then. In Atlantic City during summer vacations from school at the Morton Hotel on the Boardwalk. I knew about tips. About some people's manners and propriety. Why some people treat their money like feces and have a compulsion to conceal it, hide it in all sorts of strange places. Like under the edge of saucers. Like they're ashamed or like they get off playing hide-and-seek. Or maybe just have picked up a habit from their fathers.

Anyway he laughed when I told him and said Oscar probably damned a couple of poor little old white ladies to hell for not leaving him a tip. Laughed and said, *They're probably burning in hell behind you "finding" that money.*

I understand a little more now. Not much. I have sons of my own and my father has grandsons and is still a handsome man. But I don't see him often. And sometimes the grandson who has his name as a middle name, the one who can say "Shenandoah" if he wants to call it that, doesn't even remember who his grandfather is. *Oh yeah,* he'll say. *Edgar in Pittsburgh,* he'll say. *Your father. Yeah. I remember now.*

But he forgets lots of things. He's the kind of kid who forgets lots of things but who remembers everything. He has the gift of feeling. Things don't touch him, they imprint. You can see it sometimes. And it hurts. He already knows he will suffer for whatever he knows. Maybe that's why he forgets so much.

Tommy

He checks out the Velvet Slipper. Can't see shit for a minute in the darkness. Just the jukebox and beer smell and the stink from the men's room door always hanging open. Carl ain't there yet. Must be his methadone day. Carl with his bad feet like he's in slow motion wants to lay them dogs down easy as he can on the hot sidewalk. Little sissy walking on eggs steps pussy-footing up Frankstown to the clinic. Uncle Carl ain't treating to no beer to start the day so he backs out into the brightness of the Avenue, to the early afternoon street quiet after the blast of nigger music and nigger talk.

Ain't nothing to it. Nothing. If he goes left under the trestle and up the stone steps or ducks up the bare path worn through the weeds on the hillside he can walk along the tracks to the park. Early for the park. The sun everywhere now giving the grass a yellow sheen. If he goes right it's down the avenue to where the supermarkets and the 5 & 10 used to be. Man, they sure did fuck with this place. What he thinks each time he stares at what was once the heart of Homewood. Nothing. A parking lot and empty parking stalls with busted meters. Only a fool leave his car next to one of the bent meter poles. Places to park so you can shop in stores that ain't there no more. Remembers his little Saturday morning wagon hustle when him and all the other kids would lay outside the A&P to haul groceries. Still some white ladies in those days come down from Thomas Boulevard to shop and if you're lucky get one of them and get tipped a quarter. Some of them fat black bitches be in church every Sunday have you pulling ten tons of rice and beans all the way to West Hell and be smiling and yakking all the way and saying what a nice boy you are and I knowed your mama when she was little and please sonny just set them inside on the table and still be smiling at you with some warm glass of water and a dime after you done hauled their shit halfway round the world.

Hot in the street but nobody didn't like you just coming in and sitting in their air-conditioning unless you gonna buy a drink and set it in front of you. The poolroom hot. And too early to be messing with those fools on the corner. Always somebody trying to hustle. Man, when you gonna give me my money, man, I been waiting too long for my money, man, lemme hold this quarter till tonight, man. I'm getting over tonight, man. And the buses climbing the hill and turning the corner by the state store and fools parked in the middle of the street and niggers getting hot honking to get by and niggers paying them no mind like they got important business and just gonna sit there blocking traffic as long as they please and the buses growling and farting those fumes when they struggle around the corner.

Look to the right and to the left but ain't nothing to it, nothing saying move one way or the other. Homewood Avenue a darker gray stripe between the gray sidewalks. Tar patches in the asphalt. Looks like somebody's bad head with the ringworm. Along the curb ground glass sparkles below the broken neck of a Tokay bottle. Just the long neck and shoulders of the bottle intact and a piece of label hanging. Somebody should make a deep ditch out of Homewood Avenue and just go on and push the row houses and boarded storefronts into the hole. Bury it all, like in a movie he had seen a dam burst and the floodwaters ripping through the dry bed of a river till the roaring water overflowed the banks and swept away trees and houses, uprooting everything in its path like a cleansing wind.

He sees Homewood Avenue dipping and twisting at Hamilton. Where Homewood crests at Frankstown the heat is a shimmering curtain above the trolley tracks. No trolleys anymore. But the slippery tracks still embedded in the asphalt streets. Somebody forgot to tear out the tracks and pull down the cables. So when it rains or snows some fool always gets caught and the slick tracks flip a car into a telephone pole or upside a hydrant and the cars just lay there with crumpled fenders and windshields shattered, laying there for no reason just like the tracks and wires are there for no reason now that buses run where the 88 and the 82 Lincoln trolleys used to go.

He remembers running down Lemington Hill because trolleys come only once an hour after midnight and he had heard the clatter of the 82 starting its long glide down Lincoln Avenue. The Dells still working out on "Why Do You Have to Go" and the tip of his dick wet and his balls aching and his finger sticky but he had forgotten all that and forgot the half hour in Sylvia's hallway because he was flying, all long strides and pumping arms and his fists opening and closing on the night air as he grappled for balance in a headlong rush down the steep hill. He had heard the trolley coming and wished he was a bird soaring through the black night, a bird with shiny chrome fenders and fishtails and a Continental kit. He tried to watch his feet, avoid the cracks and gulleys in the sidewalk. He heard the trolley's bell and crash of its steel wheels against the tracks. He had been all in Sylvia's drawers and she was wet as a dishrag and moaning her hot breath into his ear and the record player inside the door hiccuping for the thousandth time caught in the groove of gray noise at the end of the disc.

He remembers that night and curses again the empty trolley screaming past him as he had pulled up short half a block from the corner. Honky driver half sleep in his yellow bubble. As the trolley careened away red sparks had popped above its gimpy antenna. Chick had his nose open and his dick hard but he should have cooled it and split, been out her drawers and down the hill on time. He had fooled around too long. He had missed the trolley and mize well walk. He had to walk and in the darkness over his head the cables had swayed and sung long after the trolley disappeared.

He had to walk cause that's all there was to it. And still no ride of his own so he's still walking. Nothing to it. Either right or left, either up Homewood or down Homewood, walking his hip walk, making something out of the way he is walking since there is nothing else to do, no place to go so he makes something of the going, lets them see him moving in his own down way, his stylized walk which nobody could walk better even if they had someplace to go.

Thinking of a chump shot on the nine ball which he blew and cost him a quarter for the game and his last dollar on a side bet. Of pulling on his checkered bells that morning and the black tank top. How the creases were dead and cherry pop or something on the front and a million wrinkles behind the knees and where his thighs came together. Junkie, wino-looking pants he would have rather died than wear just a few years before when he was one of the cleanest cats in Westinghouse High School. Sharp and leading the Commodores. Doo Wah Diddy, Wah Diddy Bop. Thirty-five-dollar pants when most the cats in the House couldn't spend that much for a suit. It was a bitch in the world. Stone bitch. Feeling like Mister Tooth Decay crawling all sweaty out of the gray sheets. Mom could wash them every day, they still be gray. Like his underclothes. Like every motherfucking thing they had and would ever have. Doo Wah Diddy. The rake jerked three or four times through his bush. Left there as decoration and weapon. You could fuck up a cat with those steel teeth. You could get the points sharp as needles. And draw it swift as Billy the Kid.

Thinking it be a bitch out here. Niggers write all over everything don't even know how to spell. Drawing power fists that look like a loaf of bread.

Thinking this whole avenue is like somebody's mouth they let some jive dentist fuck with. All these old houses nothing but rotten teeth and these raggedy pits is where some been dug out or knocked out and ain't nothing left but stumps and snaggleteeth just waiting to go. Thinking, that's right. That's just what it is. Why it stinks around here and why ain't nothing but filth and germs and rot. And what that make me? What it make all these niggers? Thinking yes, yes, that's all it is.

Mr. Strayhorn where he always is down from the corner of Hamilton and Homewood sitting on a folding chair beside his iceball cart. A sweating canvas draped over the front of the cart to keep off the sun. Somebody said the old man a hundred years old, somebody said he was a bad dude in his day. A gambler like his own granddaddy John French had been. They say Strayhorn whipped three cats half to death try to cheat him in the alley behind Dunfermline. Took a knife off one and whipped all three with his bare hands. Just sits there all summer selling iceballs. Old and can hardly see. But nobody don't bother him even though he got his pockets full of change every evening.

Shit. One of the young boys will off him one night. Those kids was stone crazy. Kill you for a dime and think nothing of it. Shit. Rep don't mean a thing. They come at you in packs, like wild dogs. Couldn't tell those young boys nothing. He thought he had come up mean. Thought his running buddies be some terrible dudes. Shit. These kids coming up been into more stuff before they twelve than most grown men do they whole lives.

Hard out here. He stares into the dead storefronts. Sometimes they get in one of them. Take it over till they get run out or set it on fire or it gets so filled with shit and nigger piss don't nobody want to use it no more except for winos and junkies come in at night and could be sleeping on a bed of nails wouldn't make no nevermind to those cats. He peeks without stopping between the wooden slats where the glass used to be. Like he is reading the posters, like there might be something he needed to know on these rain-soaked, sun-faded pieces of cardboard talking about stuff that happened a long time ago.

Self-defense demonstration . . . Ahmad Jamal. Rummage Sale. Omega Boat Ride. The Dells. Madame Walker's Beauty Products.

A dead bird crushed dry and paper-thin in the alley between Albion and Tioga. Like somebody had smeared it with tar and mashed it between the pages of a giant book. If you hadn't seen it in the first place, still plump and bird-colored, you'd never recognize it now. Looked now like the lost sole of somebody's shoe. He had watched it happen. Four or five days was all it took. On the third day he thought a cat had dragged it off. But when he passed the corner next afternoon he found the dark shape in the grass at the edge of the cobblestones. The head was gone and the yellow smear of beak but he recognized the rest. By then already looking like the raggedy sole somebody had walked off their shoe.

He was afraid of anything dead. He could look at something dead but no way was he going to touch it. Didn't matter, big or small, he wasn't about to put his hands near nothing dead. His daddy had whipped him when his mother said he sassed her and wouldn't take the dead rat out of the trap. He could whip him again but no way he was gon touch that thing. The dudes come back from Nam talking about puddles of guts and scraping parts of people into plastic bags. They talk about carrying their own bags so they could get stuffed in if they got wasted. Have to court-martial his ass. No way he be carrying no body bag. Felt funny now carrying out the big green bags you put your garbage in. Any kind of plastic sack and he's thinking of machine guns and dudes screaming and grabbing their bellies and rolling around like they do when they're hit on Iwo Jima and Tarawa or *The Dirty Dozen* or *The Magnificent Seven* or *High Plains Drifter*, but the screaming is not in the darkness on a screen it is bright, green afternoon and Willie Thompson and them are on patrol. It is a street like Homewood. Quiet like Homewood this time of day and bombed out like Homewood is. Just pieces of buildings standing here and there and fire scars and places ripped and kicked down and cars stripped and dead at the curb. They are moving along in single file and their uniforms are hip and their walks are hip and they are kind of smiling and rubbing their weapons and cats passing a joint fat as a cigar down the line. You can almost hear music from where Porgy's Record Shop used to be, like the music so fine it's still there clinging to the boards, the broken glass on the floor, the shelves covered with roach shit and rat shit, a ghost of the music rifting sweet and mellow like the smell of home cooking as the patrol slips on past where Porgy's used to be. Then . . .

Rat Tat Tat . . . Rat Tat Tat . . . Ra Ta Ta Ta Ta Ta Ta . . .

Sudden but almost on the beat. Close enough to the beat so it seems the point man can't take it any longer, can't play this soldier game no longer and he gets happy and the smoke is gone clear to his head so he jumps out almost on the beat, wiggling his hips and throwing up his arms so he can get it all, go on and get down. Like he is exploding to the music. To the beat which pushes him out there all alone, doing it, and it is Rat Tat Tat and we all want to fingerpop behind his twitching hips and his arms flung out but he is screaming and down in the dirty street and the street is exploding all round him in little volcanoes of dust. And some of the others in the front of the patrol go down with him. No semblance of rhythm now, just stumbling, or airborne like their feet jerked out from under them. The whole hip procession buckling, shattered as lines of deadly force stitch up and down the avenue.

Hey man, what's to it? Ain't nothing to it man you got it baby hey now where's it at you got it you got it ain't nothing to it something to it I wouldn't be out here in all this sun you looking good you into something go on man you got it all you know you the Man hey now that was a stone fox you know what I'm talking about you don't be creeping past me yeah nice going you got it all save some for me Mister Clean you seen Ruchell and them yeah you know how that shit is the cat walked right on by like he ain't seen nobody but you know how he is get a little something don't know nobody shit like I tried to tell the cat get straight nigger be yourself before you be by yourself you got a hard head man hard as stone but he ain't gon listen to me shit no can't nobody do nothing for the cat less he's ready to do for hisself Ruchell yeah man Ruchell and them come by here little while ago yeah baby you got it yeah lemme hold this little something I know you got it you the Man you got to have it lemme hold a little something till this evening I'll put you straight tonight man you know your man do you right I unnerstand yeah that's all that's to it nothing to it I'ma see you straight man yeah you fall on by the crib yeah we be into something tonight you fall on by.

Back to the left now. Up Hamilton, past the old man who seems to sleep beside his cart until you get close and then his yellow eyes under the straw hat brim follow you. Cut through the alley past the old grade school. Halfway up the hill the game has already started. You have been hearing the basketball patted against the concrete, the hollow thump of the ball glancing off the metal backboards. The ball players half naked out there under that hot sun, working harder than niggers ever did picking cotton. They shine. They glide and leap and fly at each other like their dark bodies are at the ends of invisible strings. This time of day the court is hot as fire. Burn through your shoes. Maybe that's why the niggers play like they do, running and jumping so much cause the ground's too hot to stand on. His brother used to play here all day. Up and down all day in the hot sun with the rest of the crazy ball players. Old dudes and young dudes and when people on the side waiting for winners they'd get to arguing and you could hear them bad-mouthing all the way up the hill and cross the tracks in the park. Wolfing like they ready to kill each other.

His oldest brother, John, came back here to play when he brought his family through in the summer. Here and Mellon and the courts beside the projects in East Liberty. His brother one of the old dudes now. Still crazy about the game. He sees a dude lose his man and fire a jumper from the side. A double pump, a lean, and the ball arched so it kisses the board and drops through the iron. He could have played the game. Tall and loose. Hands bigger than his brother's. Could palm a ball when he was eleven. Looks at his long fingers. His long feet in raggedy-ass sneakers that show the crusty knuckle of his little toe. The sidewalk sloped and split. Little plots of gravel and weeds where whole paving blocks torn away. Past the dry swimming pool. Just a big concrete hole now where people piss and throw bottles like you got two points for shooting them in. Dropping like a rusty spiderweb from tall metal poles, what's left of a backstop, and beyond the flaking mesh of the screen the dusty field and beyond that a jungle of sooty trees below the railroad tracks. They called it the Bums' Forest when they were kids and bombed the winos sleeping down there in the shade of the trees. If they walked alongside the track all the way to the park they'd have to cross the bridge over Homewood Avenue. Hardly room for trains on the bridge so

they always ran and some fool always yelling, *Train's coming,* and everybody
else yelling and then it's your chest all full and your heart pumping to keep
up with the rest. Because the train couldn't kill everybody. It might get the
last one, the slow one but it wouldn't run down all the crazy niggers screaming and hauling ass over Homewood Avenue. From the tracks you could
look down on the winos curled up under a tree or sitting in a circle sipping
from bottles wrapped in brown paper bags. At night they would have fires,
hot as it was some summer nights you'd still see their fires from the bleachers
while you watched the Legion baseball team kick butt.

From high up on the tracks you could bomb the forest. Stones hissed
through the thick leaves. Once in a while a lucky shot shattered a bottle.
Some gray, sorry-assed wino motherfucker waking up and shaking his fist
and cussing at you and some fool shouts, *He's coming, he's coming.* And not
taking the low path for a week because you think he was looking dead in your
eyes, spitting blood and pointing at you, and you will never go alone the
low way along the path because he is behind every bush, gray and bloody-
mouthed. The raggedy gray clothes flapping like a bird and a bird's feathery,
smothering funk covering you as he drags you into the bushes.

He had heard stories about the old days when the men used to hang out
in the woods below the tracks. Gambling and drinking wine and telling lies and
singing those old-time, down-home songs. Hang out there in the summer
and when it got cold they'd loaf in the Bucket of Blood on the corner of
Frankstown and Tioga. His granddaddy was in the stories. Old John French
one of the baddest dudes ever walked these Homewood streets. Old, big-hat
John French. They said his granddaddy could sing up a storm and now his
jitterbug father up in the choir of Homewood AME Zion next to Mrs.
Washington who hits those high notes. He was his father's son, people said.
Singing all the time and running the streets like his daddy did till his daddy
got too old and got saved. Tenor lead of the Commodores. Everybody saying the Commodores was the baddest group. If that cat hadn't fucked us
over with the record we might have made the big time. Achmet backing us
on the conga. Tito on the bongos. Tear up the park. Stone tear it up. Little kids and old folks all gone home and ain't nobody in the park but who
supposed to be and you got your old lady on the side listening or maybe you
singing pretty to pull some new fly bitch catch your eye in the crowd. It all
comes down, comes together mellow and fine sometimes. The drums, the

smoke, the sun going down, and you out there flying and the Commodores steady taking care of business behind your lead.

"You got to go to church. I'm not asking I'm telling. Now you get those shoes shined and I don't want to hear another word out of you, young man." She is ironing his Sunday shirt hot and stiff. She hums along with the gospel songs on the radio. "Don't make me send you to your father." Who is in the bathroom for the half hour he takes doing whatever to get hisself together. Making everybody else late. Singing in there while he shaves. You don't want to be the next one after him. "You got five minutes, boy. Five minutes and your teeth better be clean and your hands and face shining." Gagging in the funky bathroom, not wanting to take a breath. How you supposed to brush your teeth, the cat just shit in there? "You're going to church this week and every week. This is my time and don't you try to spoil it, boy. Don't you get no attitude and try to spoil church for me." He is in the park now, sweating in the heat, a man now, but he can hear his mother's voice plain as day, filling up all the empty space around him just as it did in the house on Finance Street. She'd talk them all to church every Sunday. Use her voice like a club to beat everybody out the house.

His last time in church was a Thursday. They had up the scaffolding to clean the ceiling and Deacon Barclay's truck was parked outside. Barclay's Hauling, Cleaning and General Repairing. Young People's Gospel Chorus had practice on Thursday and he knew Adelaide would be there. That chick looked good even in them baggy choir robes. He had seen her on Sunday because his Mom cried and asked him to go to church. Because she knew he stole the money out her purse but he had lied and said he didn't and she knew he was lying and feeling guilty and knew he'd go to church to make up to her. Adelaide up there with the Young People's Gospel Chorus rocking church. Rocking church and he'd go right on up there, the lead of the Commodores, and sing gospel with them if he could get next to that fine Adelaide. So Thursday he left the poolroom, *Where you tipping off to, man? None of your motherfucking business, motherfucker*, about seven when she had choir practice and look here, Adelaide, I been digging you for a long time. Longer and deeper than you'll ever know. Let me tell you something. I know what you're thinking, but don't say it, don't break my heart by saying you heard I was a jive cat and nothing to me and stay away from him he ain't no good and stuff like that I know I got a rep that way but you grown enough now to know how people talk and how you got to find things out for yourself. Don't be putting me down till you let me have a little chance to speak for myself. I ain't gon lie now. I been out here in the world and into some jive tips. Yeah, I did my time diddy bopping and trying my wheels out here in the street. I was a devil. Got into everything I was big and bad enough to try. Look here. I could write the book. Pimptime and partytime and jive to stay alive, but I been through all that and that ain't what I want. I want something special, something solid. A woman, not no fingerpopping young girl got her nose open and her behind wagging all the time. That's right. That's right, I ain't talking nasty, I'm talking what I know. I'm talking truth tonight and listen here I been digging you all these years and waiting for you because all that Doo Wah Diddy ain't nothing, you hear, nothing to it. You grown now and I need just what you got . . .

Thursday rapping in the vestibule with Adelaide was the last time in Homewood AME Zion Church. Had to be swift and clean. Swoop down like a hawk and get to her mind. Tuesday she still crying and gripping the elastic of her drawers and saying *No*. Next Thursday the only singing she doing is behind some bushes in the park. *Oh, baby. Oh, baby, it's so good.* Tore that pussy up.

Don't make no difference. No big thing. She's giving it to somebody else now. All that good stuff still shaking under her robe every second Sunday when the Young People's Gospel Chorus in the loft beside the pulpit. Old man Barclay like he guarding the church door asking me did I come around to help clean. "Mr. Barclay, I wish I could help but I'm working nights. Matter of fact I'm a little late now. I'm gon be here on my night off, though."

He knew I was lying. Old bald head dude standing there in his coveralls and holding a bucket of Lysol and a scrub brush. Worked all his life and got a piece of truck and a piece of house and still running around yes sirring and no mamming the white folks and cleaning their toilets. And he's doing better than most of these chumps. Knew I was lying but smiled his little smile cause he knows my mama and knows she's a good woman and knows Adelaide's grandmother and knows if I ain't here to clean he better guard the door with his soap and rags till I go on about my business.

Ruchell and them over on a bench. Niggers high already. They ain't hardly out there in the sun barbecuing their brains less they been into something already. Niggers be hugging the shade till evening less they been into something.

"Hey now."

"What's to it, Tom?"

"You cats been into something."

"You ain't just talking."

"Ruchell, man, we got that business to take care of."

"Stone business, Bruh. I'm ready to T.C.B., my man."

"You ain't ready for nothing, nigger."

"Hey man, we're gon get it together. I'm ready, man. Ain't never been so ready. We gon score big, brother man . . ."

They have been walking an hour. The night is cooling. A strong wind has risen and a few pale stars are visible above the yellow pall of the city's lights. Ruchell is talking:

"The reason it's gon work is the white boy is greedy. He's so greedy he can't stand for the nigger to have something. Did you see Indovina's eyes when we told him we had copped a truckload of color TVs. Shit, man. I could hear his mind working. Calculating like. These niggers is dumb. I can rob these niggers. Click. Click. Clickedy. Rob the shit out of these dumb spooks. They been robbing us so long they think that's the way things supposed to be. They so greedy their hands get sweaty they see a nigger with something worth stealing."

"So he said he'd meet us at the car lot?"

"That's the deal. I told him we had two vans full."

"And Ricky said he'd let you use his van?"

"I already got the keys, man. I told you we were straight with Ricky. He ain't even in town till the weekend."

"I drive up then and you hide in the back?"

"Yeah, dude. Just like we done said a hundred times. You go in the office to make the deal and you know how Indovina is. He gon send out his nigger Chubby to check the goods."

"And you jump Chubby?"

"Be on him like white on rice. Freeze that nigger till you get the money from Indovina."

"You sure Indovina ain't gon try and follow us?"

"Shit, man. He be happy to see us split . . ."

"With his money?"

"Indovina do whatever you say. Just wave your piece in his face a couple times. That fat ofay motherfucker ain't got no heart. Chubby his heart and Ruchell stone take care of Chubby."

"I still think Indovina might go to the cops."

"And say what? Say he trying to buy some hot TVs and got ripped off? He ain't hardly saying that. He might just say he got robbed and try to collect insurance. He's slick like that. But if he goes to the cops you can believe he won't be describing us. Naw. The pigs know that greasy dago is a crook. Everybody knows it and won't be no problems. Just score and blow. Leave this motherfucking sorry-ass town. Score and blow."

"When you ain't got nothing you get desperate. You don't care. I mean what you got to be worried about? Your life ain't shit. All you got is a high. Getting high and spending all your time hustling some money so you can get high again. You do anything. Nothing don't matter. You just take, take, take whatever you can get your hands on. Pretty soon nothing don't matter, John. You just got to get that high. And everybody around you the same way. Don't make no difference. You steal a little something. If you get away with it, you try it again. Then something bigger. You get holt to a piece. Other dudes carry a piece. Lots of dudes out there holding something. So you get it and start to carrying it. What's it matter? You ain't nowhere anyway. Ain't got nothing. Nothing to look forward to but a high. A man needs something. A little money in his pocket. I mean you see people around you and on TV and shit. Man, they got everything. Cars and clothes. They can do something for a woman. They got something. And you look at yourself in the mirror you're going nowhere. Not a penny in your pocket. Your own people disgusted with you. Begging around your family like a little kid or something. And jail and stealing money from your own mama. You get desperate. You do what you have to do."

The wind is up again that night. At the stoplight Tommy stares at the big sign on the boulevard. A smiling Duquesne Pilsner Duke with his glass of beer. The time and temperature flash beneath the nobleman's uniformed chest. Ricky had installed a tape deck into the dash. A tangle of wires drooped from its guts, but the sound was good. One speaker for the cab, another for the back where Ruchell was sitting on the rolls of carpet Ricky had stacked there. Al Green singing "Call Me." Ricky could do things. Made his own tapes; customizing the delivery van. Next summer Ricky driving to California. Fixing up the van so he could live in it. The dude was good with his hands. A mechanic in the war. Government paid for the wasted knee. Ricky said, Got me a new knee now. Got a four-wheeled knee that's gonna ride me away from all this mess. The disability money paid for the van and the customizing and the stereo tape deck. Ricky always have that limp but the cat getting hisself together.

Flags were strung across the entrance to the used-car lot. The wind made them pop and dance. Rows and rows of cars looking clean and new under the lights. Tommy parked on the street, in the deep shadow at the far end of Indovina's glowing corner. He sees them through the office window. Indovina and his nigger.

"Hey, Chubby."

"What's happening now?" Chubby's shoulders wide as the door. Indovina's nigger all the way. Had his head laid back so far on his neck it's like he's looking at you through his noseholes instead of his eyes.

"You got the merchandise?" Indovina's fingers drum the desk.

"You got the money?"

"Ain't your money yet. I thought you said two vans full."

"Can't drive but one at a time. My partner's at a phone booth right now. Got the number here. You show me the bread and he'll bring the rest."

"I want to see them all before I give you a penny."

"Look, Mr. Indovina. This ain't no bullshit tip. We got the stuff, all right. Good stuff like I said. Sony portables. All the same . . . still in the boxes."

"Let's go look."

"I want to see some bread first."

"Give Chubby your keys. Chubby, check it out. Count em. Make sure the cartons ain't broke open."

"I want to see some bread."

"Bread. Bread. My cousin DeLuca runs a bakery. I don't deal with *bread*. I got money. See. That's money in my hand. Got plenty money buy your television sets buy your van buy you."

"Just trying to do square business, Mr. Indovina."

"Don't forget to check the cartons. Make sure they're sealed."

Somebody must be down. Ruchell or Chubby down. Tommy had heard two shots. He sees himself in the plate-glass window. In a fishbowl and patches of light gliding past. Except where the floodlights are trained, the darkness outside is impenetrable. He cannot see past his image in the glass, past the rushes of light slicing through his body.

"Turn out the goddamn light."

"You kill me you be sorry . . . kill me you be real sorry . . . if one of them dead out there it's just one nigger kill another nigger . . . you kill me you be sorry . . . you killing a white man . . ."

Tommy's knee skids on the desk and he slams the gun across the man's fat, sweating face with all the force of his lunge. He is scrambling over the desk, scattering paper and junk, looking down on Indovina's white shirt, his hairy arms folded over his head. He is thinking of the shots. Thinking that everything is wrong. The shots, the white man cringing on the floor behind the steel desk. Him atop the desk, his back exposed to anybody coming through the glass door.

Then he is running. Flying into the darkness. He is crouching so low he loses his balance and trips onto all fours. The gun leaps from his hand and skitters toward a wall of tires. He hears the pennants crackling. Hears a motor starting and Ruchell calling his name.

"What you mean you didn't get the money? I done wasted Chubby and you ain't got the money? Aw, shit. Shit. Shit."

He had nearly tripped again over the man's body. Without knowing how he knew, he knew Chubby was dead. Dead as the sole of his shoe. He should stop; he should try to help. But the body was lifeless. He couldn't touch . . .

Ruchell is shuddering and crying. Tears glazing his eyes and he wonders if Ruchell can see where he's going, if Ruchell knows he is driving like a wild man on both sides of the street and weaving in and out the lines of traffic. Horns blare after them. Then it's Al Green up again. He didn't know how, when, or who pushed the button but it was Al Green blasting in the cab. *Help me Help me Help me . . .*

Jesus is waiting . . . He snatches at the tape deck with both hands to turn it down or off or rip the goddamn cassette from the machine.

"Slow down, man. Slow down. You gonna get us stopped." Rolling down his window. The night air sharp in this face. The whir of tape dying then a hum of silence. The traffic sounds and city sounds pressing again into the cab.

"Nothing. Not a goddamn penny. Wasted the dude and we still ain't got nothing."

"They traced the car to Ricky. Ricky said he was out of town. Told them his van stolen when he was out of town. Claimed he didn't even know it gone till they came to his house. Ricky's cool. I know the cat's mad, but he's cool. Indovina trying to hang us. He saying it was a stickup. Saying Chubby tried to run for help and Ruchell shot him down. His story don't make no sense when you get down to it, but ain't nobody gon to listen to us."

"Then you're going to keep running?"

"Ain't no other way. Try to get to the coast. Ruchell knows a guy there can get us IDs. We was going there anyway. With our stake. We was gon get jobs and try to get it together. Make a real try. We just needed a little bread to get us started. I don't know why it had to happen the way it did. Ruchell said Chubby tried to go for bad. Said Chubby had a piece down in his pants and Ruchell told him to cool it told the cat don't be no hero and had his gun on him and everything but Chubby had to be a hard head, had to be John Wayne or some goddamned body. Just called Ruchell a punk and said no punk had the heart to pull the trigger on him. And Ruchell, Ruchell don't play, brother John. Ruchell blew him away when Chubby reached for his piece."

"You don't think you can prove your story?"

"I don't know, man. What Indovina is saying don't make no sense, but I heard the cops ain't found Chubby's gun. If they could just find that gun. But Indovina, he a slick old honky. That gun's at the bottom of the Allegheny River if he found it. They found mine. With my prints all over it. Naw. Can't take the chance. It's Murder One even though I didn't shoot nobody. That's long, hard time if they believe Indovina. I can't take the chance . . ."

"Be careful, Tommy. You're a fugitive. Cops out here think they're Wyatt Earp and Marshal Dillon. They shoot first and maybe ask questions later. They still play wild, wild west out here."

"I hear you. But I'd rather take my chance that way. Rather they carry me back in a box than go back to prison. It's hard out there, brother. Real hard. I'm happy you got out. One of us got out anyway."

"Think about it. Take your time. You can stay here as long as you need to. There's plenty of room."

"We gotta go. See Ruchell's cousin in Denver. Get us a little stake then make our run."

"I'll give you what I can if that's what you have to do. But sleep on it. Let's talk again in the morning."

"It's good to see you, man. And the kids and your old lady. At least we had this one evening. Being on the run can drive you crazy."

"Everybody was happy to see you. I knew you'd come. You've been heavy on my mind since yesterday. I wrote a kind of letter to you then. I knew you'd come. But get some sleep now . . . we'll talk in the morning."

"Listen, man. I'm sorry, man. I'm really sorry I had to come here like this. You sure Judy ain't mad?"

"I'm telling you it's OK. She's as glad to see you as I am . . . And you can stay . . . both of us want you to stay."

"Running can drive you crazy. From the time I wake in the morning till I go to bed at night, all I can think about is getting away. My head ain't been right since it happened."

"When's the last time you talked to anybody at home?"

"It's been a couple weeks. They probably watching people back there. Might even be watching you. That's why I can't stay. Got to keep moving till we get to the coast. I'm sorry, man. I mean nobody was supposed to die. It was easy. We thought we had a perfect plan. Thieves robbing thieves. Just score and blow like Ruchell said. It was our chance and we had to take it. But nobody was supposed to get hurt. I'd be dead now if it was me Chubby pulled on. I couldna just looked in his face and blown him away. But Ruchell don't play. And everybody at home. I know how they must feel. It was all over TV and the papers. Had our names and where we lived and everything. Goddamn mug shots in the *Post-Gazette*. Looking like two gorillas. I know it's hurting people. In a way I wish it had been me. Maybe it would have been better. I don't really care what happens to me now. Just wish there be some way to get the burden off Mama and everybody. Be easier if I was dead."

"Nobody wants you dead . . . That's what Mom's most afraid of. Afraid of you coming home in a box."

"I ain't going back to prison. They have to kill me before I go back in prison. Hey, man. Ain't nothing to my crazy talk. You don't want to hear this jive. I'm tired, man. I ain't never been so tired. . . . I'ma sleep . . . talk in the morning, big brother."

He feels his brother squeeze then relax the grip on his shoulder. He has seen his brother cry once before. Doesn't want to see it again. Too many faces in his brother's face. Starting with their mother and going back and going sideways and all of Homewood there if he looked long enough. Not just faces but streets and stories and rooms and songs.

Tommy listens to the steps. He can hear faintly the squeak of a bed upstairs. Then nothing. Ruchell asleep in another part of the house. Ruchell spent the evening with the kids, playing with their toys. The cat won't ever grow up. Still into the Durango Kid, and Whip Wilson and Audie Murphy wasting Japs and shit. Still Saturday afternoon at the Bellmawr show and he is lining up the plastic cowboys against the plastic Indians and boom-booming them down with the kids on the playroom floor. And dressing up the Lone Ranger doll with the mask and guns and cinching the saddle on Silver. Toys like they didn't make when we were coming up. And Christmas morning and so much stuff piled up they'd be crying with exhaustion and bad nerves before half the stuff unwrapped. Christmas morning and they never really went to sleep. Looking out the black windows all night for reindeer and shit. Cheating. Worried that all the gifts will turn to ashes if they get caught cheating, but needing to know, to see if reindeer really can fly.

Solitary

To reach the other world you changed buses twice. The first bus took you downtown and there you caught another to the Northside. Through the Golden Triangle, across the Sixth Street Bridge, the second bus shuttled you to Reed Street on the Northside where you waited for one of the infrequent expresses running out Allegheny River Boulevard to the prison. With perfect connections the trip might take an hour and three quarters each way but usually a whole day was consumed getting there and getting back with the visit to her son sandwiched between eternities of waiting. Because the prison was in another world. She hadn't understood that at first. She had carried with her into the prison her everyday expectations of people, her sense of right and wrong and fairness. But none of that fit. The prison mocked her beliefs. Her trips to see her son were not so much a matter of covering a certain distance as they were of learning the hostile nature of the space separating her from him, learning how close and how far away he would always be. In the time it took to blink, the time it took for a steel gate to slam shut behind her, he would be gone again, a million miles away again, and the other world, gray and concrete, would spring up around her, locking him away as abruptly as the prison walls.

One Sunday, walking the mile from the prison gate to the unsheltered concrete island which served as a bus stop and shivering there for over an hour in freezing November rain she had realized the hardships connected with the visits to her son were not accidental. The trips were supposed to speak to her plainly. Somebody had arranged it that way. An evil somebody who didn't miss a trick. They said to reach him you must suffer, you must fight the heat and cold, you must sit alone and be beaten by your thoughts, you must forget who you are and be prepared to surrender your dignity just as you surrender your purse to the guard caged outside the waiting room entrance. In the prison world, the world you must die a little to enter, the man you've traveled so far to see is not your son but a number. He is P3694 and you must sit on a hard, wooden bench in a filthy waiting room until that number is called. Then it's through steel doors and iron bars and buzzing machines which peek under your clothes. Up stairs and down stairs and across a cobbled corridor dark and chill even in summer and you are inside then and nothing you have brought from the outside counts. Not your name, your pain, your love. To enter you must be prepared to leave everything behind and be prepared when you begin the journey home to lose everything again.

That is the trip she must take to see him. Not hours and buses but a brutal unraveling of herself. On the way back she must put herself together again, compose herself, pretend the place she has been doesn't exist, that what surrounds her as the bus lumbers along the boulevard is familiar and real, that the shopping center and factories and warehouses crowding the flanks of Allegheny River Boulevard served some useful, sane purpose and weren't just set out to taunt her, to mock her helplessness. Slowly she'd talk herself into believing again. This bus will take me to Reed. Another will cross the bridge into town. I'll catch the 88 and it will shudder over the parkway and drop me five blocks from home. And when I am home again I will be able to sit down in the brown chair and drink a cup of coffee and nod at some foolishness on TV, and nothing I do, none of these little lies which help me home again will hurt him or deny him. Because he is in another world, a world behind stone walls higher than God's mercy.

Sometimes she says that to herself, says the prison is a place her God has forsaken. But if He is not there, if His Grace does not touch her son then she too is dwelling in the shadow of unlove. If she can make the journey to the Valley of the Shadow, surely He could penetrate the stone walls and make His presence known. She needs weeks sometimes to marshal her strength for the trip. She knows what it costs her: the sleepless nights, the rage and helplessness, the utter trembling exhaustion bracketing the journey. How she must fight back tears when she sees his face, hears his voice. How guilt and anger alternate as she avoids people's faces and shrinks into a corner of a bus. She prays the strangers won't see her secrets, won't laugh at her shame, won't shatter in the icy waves of hatred pouring from her frozen heart. She knows her blood pressure will soar sky high and the spasms of dizziness, of nausea will nearly knock her off her feet. She needed weeks to prepare for all of that and weeks of recovering before she gathered strength enough to begin planning another trip, but she rode the buses and walked the miles and waited the eternities. Surely the walls weren't too tall, too thick for Him. He could come as a cloud, as a cleansing wind.

The prison was built close to the river. She wondered if the men could see it from their cells. She had meant to ask Tommy. And if her son could see it, would the river flowing past make him feel better or feel worse. In spring the sloping bank beyond the iron fence of the visitors' parking lot turned green. The green wasn't fair, didn't make sense when she noticed it for the first time as she stopped in the asphalt and gravel margin between the prison's outer wall and the ten-foot-tall iron fence along the river. A border of green edging the brown river which didn't make sense either as she stopped to blow her nose. For a moment as she paused and stared across the water everything was absolutely still. A wad of tissue was balled in her fist, the river glided brownly, silently past but nothing else was real. Everything so still and quiet she believed that she had fallen out of time, that she had slipped into an empty place between worlds, a place unknown, undreamed of till that moment, a tiny crack between two worlds that was somehow in its emptiness and stillness vaster than both.

The green was sectioned by the iron spears of the fence. Between the sharp points of the spears clusters of spikes riveted to the top railing of the fence glittered in the sun. The sky was blue, the river brown, the grass green. The breeze off the water whispered spring and promised summer but God let his sunshine play in the crowns of needle-pointed spikes. Near the top of the wall she could make out a row of windows deeply recessed, darker than the soot-grimed stones. If Tommy was standing at one of the screened windows could he see the river, the green, the gray pit into which she had slipped?

A coal barge hooted. She stuffed her tissue back in her purse. She thought she could hear the men's voices echoing from behind the walls, voices far away in a cave, or deep inside a tunnel, a jumbled, indistinct murmur out of which one voice would eerily rise and seem to mutter inches from her ear. If she could, she would have run from the yard. The voices hated her. They screamed obscenities and made fun of everything about her. She didn't have the strength to run but wouldn't have run if she could because that would only give them more to laugh at, would bring them howling and nipping at her heels as she fled to the bus stop.

From the visitors' entrance to the bus stop was a walk of nearly a mile. A nameless street paralleled one black prison wall, then crossed a flat, barren stretch of nothing before it intersected Allegheny River Boulevard. From the bus stop she looked back at the emptiness surrounding the prison. The dark walls loomed abrupt and stark. Like the green riverbank the walls had no reason to be there, nothing connected them to the dusty plain of concrete. The walls were just there, like the lid of a roasting pan some giant hand had clamped down. It made no sense but it was there and no one could move it, no one was trying to disturb the squat black shape even though her son was dying beneath it.

This is the church and this is the steeple. Open the doors and out come the people. She let her hands form what she was thinking. Her wiggling fingers were ants scrambling for a wedge of daylight.

Her God had razed the proud walls of Jericho with nothing more than screaming horns. She let her hands fall to her sides and closed her eyes, but the walls were still there when she looked again.

On the first of the buses back to Homewood she tried to think of what she'd say to the others. What she would tell them when they asked, How is he? Should she say he's a million miles away? That his name is different in the other world? That he is heavier, thicker in the shoulders, but the baggy prison clothes hang loosely on his body so he seems like a little boy? Should she say his bitterness toward her is mellowing? Or does his anger hurt her less now only because she has listened so many times to his accusations? He says he has relived every single moment of his life. He turns the days over and over, asking questions, reconstructing incidents, deciding what he should have done, analyzing what he did do and what others did to him. In the story of his life which he dreams over and over again, she comes up a villain. Her love, her fears are to blame. She held the reins too tightly or she let him run loose; she drowned him in guilt with her constant questions, her tears at his slightest trespass or she didn't ever really pay enough attention to him. His hurting words would tear her down. She'd stop trying to defend herself, grow numb. His voice would fade from her consciousness and her mind would wander to a quieter, safer place. She'd daydream and free herself from the choking web of his bitterness. She'd want to ask him why he thought she made these wearying journeys. Did he think she came to be whipped? Did he think he had a right to take out his frustrations on her just because she was the only one who'd listen, who'd travel the million miles to where he was caged? But she wouldn't ask those questions. She'd listen till she drifted to that leaden, numb place where nothing could touch her. If someone to scream at was what he needed, she'd be that someone.

She wouldn't tell them anything like that when they asked, How is he? At the bus stop on Reed Street she rehearsed what she would say, what she always said, *Better. He's doing better. It's a hateful place but he's doing better.* Corrugated tin sheeting and transparent plastic panels formed a back and slanting half-roof partially enclosing the platform. Like standing in a seashell when the roar of traffic buffeted her. This morning only an occasional car rumbled by. All over town they were ripping up the old trolley tracks and asphalting their cobblestone beds but at this end of Reed Street anything that moved rattled against the cobbles like it was coming apart. She was alone till a boy crossing from the far side of the street joined her on the platform. His transistor radio was big as a suitcase and his music vibrated the shelter's tin roof. He was skinny like Tommy had been. A string bean, bean pole like her son Tommy and like him this one pranced when he walked and danced to the music while he was standing still.

Tommy was *Salim* now. She had told them his new name but she had no words for what had happened to his eyes, his cheekbones, the deepening shadows in his face. To herself she'd say his eyes burned, that his flesh was on fire, that the bones of his face were not hard and white, but something kindling beneath his skin, that the fire burned with sharp knife edges and his skin hung on the points of flame and the dark hollows of his face were where the fire shone blackly through his brown skin. His eyes screamed at her. It hurt him to be what he was, where he was, but he had no words for it either. Only the constant smoldering of his flesh, the screaming of his eyes.

"He's stronger, much stronger. The Muslim business and the new name scare me but it's something for him to hold on to. They have their own little group. It gives him a chance to be somebody. He has his bad days of course. Especially now that the weather's getting nice. He has his bad days but he's made up his mind that he's going to stay on top of it. He's going to survive."

She'd say that. She'd answer with those words each time one of them asked about him. She'd say the words again and again till she was certain she believed them, till she was certain the words were real.

He'd been in the Behavior Modification Unit six weeks now. Six weeks out of the six months of solitary confinement they'd slapped on him. They called it the B.M.U., the Hole. To her it was a prison within a prison. Something worse happening after she thought she'd faced the worst. Twenty-three hours a day locked in his cell. Forty-five minutes of exercise in the yard if a guard was free to supervise him. If not, tough. Twenty-four hours alone in a ten-by-eight box. One meal at eleven, the other at two. *If you could call them meals, Mom.* Nothing till the next eleven o'clock meal except coffee and a hunk of bread when he was awakened. Two meals in three hours and no food for the next twenty-one. A prison within a prison. A way of telling him and telling her never to relax, never to complain because things could always get worse.

Instead of staying on the last bus till it reached her stop she got off at Frankstown and Homewood. They had both stood when the visiting room guard called his number. Tommy had wrapped his arms around her and hugged her, drawn her as close as he could to the fires alive inside him. Then he had turned from her quickly, striding across the scarred floor toward the steel gate from which he had entered. He hadn't turned back to look at her. The smell of him, the warmth, the strength of his arms circling her so suddenly had taken her breath away. She had wanted to see his face again, had almost cried out at those shoulders which were a man's now, which sloped to his arms and long, dangling hands and tight round butt and gangly legs with his bare ankles hanging down out of the high-water prison pants. She had believed nothing could hurt more than the bottled-up anger he spewed at her but she had been wrong. The hug hurt more. His arms loving her hurt more. And when he turned like a soldier on his heel and marched away from her, eyes front, punishing the floor in stiff, arm-rigid strides she was more alone than she had ever been while he raged.

So she stepped off the bus at Frankstown and Homewood because she didn't want to be alone, didn't want to close her front door behind her and hear the bolts and chains clicking home in the stillness, and didn't want to greet the emptiness which would rush at her face, pelt it like the dusty, littered wind when it raced across the barren plain outside the prison walls.

This was his street, Tommy's stomping ground. One hot summer night they'd burned it. Looted and burned Homewood Avenue so the block between Hamilton and Kelly was a wasteland of vacant lots and blackened stone foundations and ramshackle wooden barricades guarding the craters where stores and shops had once done business. This was the same Homewood Avenue her daddy had walked. Taller than the buildings in his high-crowned, limp-brimmed hat. Big-hat John French strutting like he owned Homewood and on his good nights he probably did, yes, if all the stories she had heard about him were true, he probably did own it. Her father, her sons, the man she married, all of them had walked up and down Homewood Avenue, so she got off before her stop because she didn't want to be alone. They'd walk beside her. She could window-shop in Murphy's 5 & 10, listen to the music pouring from the open door of the Brass Rail and Porgy's Record Shop, look at the technicolored pictures advertising coming attractions at the Bellmawr show. She could hear it and see it all, and walk in the company of her men even though the storefronts were boarded or demolished altogether or transformed to unfamiliar, dirty-looking shops and her men were gone, gone, gone.

On the far corner of Homewood and Kelly the brick-and-stone Homewood AME Zion church stood sturdy and solid as a rock. She almost crossed over to it. Almost climbed the cement steps and pushed through the red door. She knew she'd find silence there and knew at the foot of the purple-carpeted aisle she could drop to her knees in a familiar place and her God would listen. That if she left her pride in the ravaged street and abandoned her hate and put off her questions He would take her to His bosom. He would bathe her in the fount of His Grace and understand and say well done. She almost stepped off the broken curb and ran to His embrace but the stolid church they had purchased when white people started running away from Homewood didn't belong on the avenue this afternoon. She stared at it like she'd stared at the prison and the green riverbank. He had to have a plan. For her life or anybody's life to make sense He had to have a plan. She believed that and believed the plan would reveal His goodness but this long day she could only see gaps and holes, the way things didn't connect or make sense.

Now she knows she is walking to the park. Homewood Avenue with its ghosts and memories was not what had drawn her off the bus early. Homewood Avenue was just a way to get somewhere and clearly now she understood she was walking toward the park.

She turned left at Hamilton, the street where the trolleys used to run.

Then past the library where the name of her great-uncle Elmer Hollinger was stamped on the blackened bronze plaque with the rest of the Homewood veterans of World War I. The family went back that far. And farther when you listened to May and Gert tell about the days when bears and wildcats lived in Homewood and Great-Great-Grandfather Charley Bell was the one first chopped down a tree here. Past the library then across Hamilton and up the hill alongside old Homewood School. The building in which she had started first grade was still standing. Tinny-looking outcroppings and temporary sheds hid most of the old walls but her grade school was still standing. Somewhere she had a picture of her third-grade class posed on the front steps, between the thick columns which supported the porch of old Homewood School. More white faces than black in those days, and long-aproned dresses and stiff collars, and she is a pale spot at the end of one row, couldn't tell she was colored unless you looked real close and maybe not even then. No one was smiling but she remembered those days as happy, as easy, days she quickly forgot so each morning was like starting life all over again, new and fresh. Past the school yard where they're always playing basketball, past the pool the city stopped filling years ago so now it's just a huge garbage can you can smell from blocks away in the summer. At the top of the hill a footbridge to the park crosses the railroad tracks. They say the little house below the bridge on a platform built out from the park side of the tracks was where the trains stopped for George Westinghouse. His private station, and any train his people signaled knew it better stop for him. He was like a king, they said. Owned half of Pittsburgh. The park belonged to him. The two white buildings where the maintenance men keep their tools and tractor were once a stable and a cottage for his servants. It was Westinghouse Park because the great man had donated it to the city. Kids had broken all the windows in the little house. For as long as she could remember it had been an empty shell, blind and gutted, a dead thing beside the tracks.

From the footbridge she could look down on the shape of the park, the gravel paths dividing it into sections, the deep hollow running along Albion Street, the swings and slides in a patch of brown over near the tracks, the stone benches, the whitewashed buildings at the far end. In spite of huge trees blocking her view she saw the park in detail. She had been coming to Westinghouse Park since she was a baby, so she could see it with her eyes closed.

From the bridge the grass seemed a uniform green, a soft unbroken carpet the way it is in her dreams when she comes with her mother and her sisters and brother to sit on the steep sides of the hollow. On summer Sundays they'd wear white and spread blankets on the grass and watch the kids whooping like wild Indians up and down the slope, across the brown floor of the hollow their feet had rubbed bare. She had wondered why her mother dressed them in white then dared them to come home with one spot of dirt on their clothes. She had envied the other children romping and rolling down the sides of the hollow. Sunday is the day of rest, her mother would say, God's peace day, so she'd dress them in white and they'd trudge up Tioga Street toward the park with rolled blankets tucked under their arms. Her mother would read the magazines from the Sunday paper, watch the grown-ups promenade along the paths, and keep track of every breath her children drew. *Mama got eyes like a hawk,* her brother would whisper. *Eyes in the back of her head.* Sooner or later he'd escape just long enough to get grass stains on his knee or backside, just long enough for his sisters to see a white streak flashing in the whirl of dark bodies down in the hollow. Then she'd get mad at her brother, Carl, and join her voice with her mother's summoning him back. *Running with that pack of heathens like he ain't got good sense.* Sometimes her bones ached to tumble and somersault down the green slope, but there were moments, moments afloat with her sisters on the calm, white clouds of their dresses, when she knew nothing could be better than the quiet they shared far away from anyone, each in her own private corner of the bluest sky.

She calls her brother from the open door of the Brass Rail. *Carl, Carl.* Her voice is lost in the swirl of music and talk animating the darkness. The stale odor of beer and pee and disinfectant blocks the entrance. Her brother, Carl, is at the far end of the bar talking to the barmaid. He is hunched forward, elbows on the chrome rail, his long legs rooted in the darkness at the base of his stool. He doesn't hear her when she calls again. The stink rolling in waves from the open door of the men's room works on her stomach, she remembers she's eaten nothing since coffee in the morning. She starts when a voice just inside the door shouts her brother's name.

"Carl. Hey, Carl. Look here, man."

Her brother turns toward the door and frowns and recognizes her and smiles and begins to dismount his stool all at once.

"Hey, Babe. I'm coming." He looks more like their daddy every day. Tall like him, and bald on top like John French, even moving like their father. A big man's gentle, rolling shuffle. A man who walked softly because most things had sense enough to get out of his way. A large man gliding surely but slowly, like John French once did through the streets of Homewood because he wanted to give the benefit of the doubt to those things that couldn't move quite so quickly as others out of his path.

"Could you walk with me a minute? Walk with me up to the park?"

"Sure, Babe. Sure I'll walk with you."

Did he sound like John French? Was his voice getting closer to their father's? She remembers words John French had said. She could hear him laugh or hear his terrible coughing from the living room that year he sat dying in his favorite chair. Those noises were part of her, always would be, but somehow she'd lost the sound of her father's speaking voice. If Carl was getting more like him every day maybe she'd learn her father's voice again.

"I've just been to see Tommy."

"No need to tell me that. All I had to do was look at your eyes and I knew where you'd been."

"It's too much. Sometime I just can't take it. I feel like I'd rather die than make that trip."

"You try and relax now. We'll just walk a little bit now. Tommy knows how to take care of hisself in there and you got to learn how to take care of yourself out here. Did you take your medicine today?"

"Yes. I swallowed those hateful pills with my coffee this morning for all the good they do."

"You know how sick you get when you don't take em. Those pills are keeping you alive."

"What kind of life is it? What's it worth? I was almost to the park. I got as far as the bridge and had to turn around and come back. I wanted to walk over there and sit down and get my nerves together but I stopped halfway across the bridge and couldn't take another step. What's happening to me, Carl? I just stood there trembling and couldn't take another step."

"It's hard. It's hard out here in the world. I know that and you know that, it's hard and cold out here."

"I'm no child. I'm not supposed to break down and go to pieces like I did. I'm a grown woman with grown children. I walked all the way from

Frankstown just to go to the park and get myself together but I couldn't get across that silly bridge. I need to know what's happening to me. I need to know why."

"Let's just walk. It's nice in the park this time of day. We can find us a bench and sit down. You know it'll be better in the park. Mama'll keep her hawk eyes on us once we get to the park."

"I think I'm losing Him."

"Something happen in there today? What'd they do to Tommy?"

"Not Tommy. Not Tommy this time. It's God I'm losing. It's Him in me that's slipping away. It happened in the middle of the bridge. I was looking down and looking over into the park. I was thinking about all those times I'd been to Westinghouse Park before. So much on my mind it wasn't really like thinking. More like being on fire all over your body and rushing around trying to beat down the flames in a hundred places at once and doing nothing but making it worse. Then I couldn't take another step. I saw Mama the way she got after her stroke, the way she was when she stopped talking and walking after Daddy died. You remember the evil look she turned on anybody when they mentioned church or praying. I saw her crippled the way she was in that chair and I couldn't take another step. I knew why she cursed Him and put God out of her life when she started talking again. I knew if I took another step I'd be like her."

She feels Carl's arm go around her shoulders. He is patting her. His big hips get in the way and bump her and she wants to cry out. She could feel the crack begin at the top of her forehead, hear it splitting and zigzagging down the middle of her body. Not his hard hip bone that hurt. She was a sheet of ice splintering at the first touch.

"I'd lose Him if I took another step. I understood Mama for the first time. Knew why she stopped walking and talking."

"Well, I'm here now. And we're gon cross now to the park. You and me gon sit down under those big pretty trees. The oldest trees in Homewood, they say. You musta heard May tell the story about the tree and the bear and Great-Great-Granddaddy Bell killing him with a pocket knife. That woman can lie. You get her riding a bottle of Wild Turkey and she can lie all night. Keep you rolling till your insides hurt."

"Mama was right. She was right, Carl."

"Course she was. Mama was always right."

"But I don't want to be alone like she was at the end."

"Mama wasn't never alone. Me and Gerry were there under the same roof every morning she woke up. And you and Sissy visited all the time. Mama always had somebody to do for her and somebody she could fuss at."

She hears her brother's words but can't make sense of them. She wonders if words ever make sense. She wonders how she learned to use them, trust them. Far down the tracks, just beyond the point where the steel rails disintegrated into a bright, shimmering cloud on the horizon line she sees the dark shape of a train. Just a speck at this distance. A speck and a faint roar rising above the constant murmur of the city. She had never liked standing on the skimpy bridge with a train thundering under her feet. Caught like that on the bridge she wouldn't know whether to run across or leap under the churning wheels.

Her God rode thunder and lightning. He could be in that speck the size of a bullet hurtling down the tracks. If you laid your ear on the track the way Carl had taught her you could hear trains long before you'd ever see them. In a funny way the trains were always there, always coming or going in the trembling rails so it was really a matter of waiting, of testing then waiting for what would always come. The black bullet would slam into her. Would tear her apart. He could strike you dead in the twinkling of an eye. He killed with thunder and lightning.

She stopped again. Made Carl stop with her in the middle of the bridge, at the place she had halted before. She'd wait this time, hold her ground this time. She'd watch it grow larger and larger and not look away, not shut her ears or stop her heart. She'd wait there on the shuddering bridge and see.

Fever
(1989)

Doc's Story

He thinks of her small, white hands, blue-veined, gaunt, awkwardly knuckled. He'd teased her about the smallness of her hands, hers lost in the shadow of his when they pressed them together palm to palm to measure. The heavy drops of color on her nails barely reached the middle joints of his fingers. He'd teased her about her dwarf's hands but he'd also said to her one night when the wind was rattling the windows of the apartment on Cedar and they lay listening and shivering though it was summer on the brass bed she'd found in a junk store on Haverford Avenue, near the Woolworth's five-and-dime they'd picketed for two years, that God made little things closer to perfect than he ever made big things. Small, compact women like her could be perfectly formed, proportioned, and he'd smiled out loud running his hand up and down the just-right fine lines of her body, celebrating how good she felt to him.

She'd left him in May, when the shadows and green of the park had started to deepen. Hanging out, becoming a regular at the basketball court across the street in Regent Park was how he'd coped. No questions asked. Just the circle of stories. If you didn't want to miss anything good you came early and stayed late. He learned to wait, be patient. Long hours waiting were not time lost but time doing nothing because there was nothing better to do. Basking in sunshine on a stone bench, too beat to play any longer, nowhere to go but an empty apartment, he'd watch the afternoon traffic in Regent Park, dog strollers, baby carriages, winos, kids, gays, students with blankets they'd spread out on the grassy banks of the hollow and books they'd pretend to read, the black men from the neighborhood who'd search the park for braless young mothers and white girls on blankets who didn't care or didn't know any better than to sit with their crotches exposed. When he'd sit for hours like that, cooking like that, he'd feel himself empty out, see himself seep away and hover in the air, a fine mist, a little, flattened-out gray cloud of something wavering in the heat, a presence as visible as the steam on the window as he stares for hours at winter.

He's waiting for summer. For the guys to begin gathering on the court again. They'll sit in the shade with their backs against the Cyclone fencing or lean on cars parked at the roller-coaster curb or lounge in the sun on low, stone benches catty-corner from the basketball court. Some older ones still drink wine, but most everybody cools out on reefer, when there's reefer passed along, while they bullshit and wait for winners. He collects the stories they tell. He needs a story now. The right one now to get him through this long winter because she's gone and won't leave him alone.

In summer fine grit hangs in the air. Five minutes on the court and you're coughing. City dirt and park dust blowing off bald patches from which green is long gone, and deadly ash blowing over from New Jersey. You can taste it some days, bitter in your spit. Chunks pepper your skin, burn your eyes. Early fall while it's still warm enough to run outdoors the worst time of all. Leaves pile up against the fence, higher and higher, piles that explode and jitterbug across the court in the middle of a game, then sweep up again, slamming back where they blew from. After a while the leaves are ground into coarse, choking powder. You eat leaf trying to get in a little hoop before the weather turns, before those days when nobody's home from work yet but it's dark already and too cold to run again till spring. Fall's the only time sweet syrupy wine beats reefer. Ripple, Manischewitz, Taylor's Tawny Port coat your throat. He takes a hit when the jug comes round. He licks the sweetness from his lips, listens for his favorite stories one more time before everybody gives it up till next season.

His favorite stories made him giggle and laugh and hug the others, like they hugged him when a story got so good nobody's legs could hold them up. Some stories got under his skin in peculiar ways. Some he liked to hear because they made the one performing them do crazy stuff with his voice and body. He learned to be patient, learned his favorites would be repeated, get a turn just like he got a turn on the joints and wine bottles circulating the edges of the court.

Of all the stories, the one about Doc had bothered him most. Its orbit was unpredictable. Twice in one week, then only once more last summer. He'd only heard Doc's story three times, but that was enough to establish Doc behind and between the words of all the other stories. In a strange way Doc presided over the court. You didn't need to mention him. He was just there. Regent Park stories began with Doc and ended with Doc and everything in between was preparation, proof the circle was unbroken.

They say Doc lived on Regent Square, one of the streets like Cedar, dead-ending at the park. On the hottest afternoons the guys from the court would head for Doc's stoop. Jars of ice water, the good feeling and good talk they'd share in the shade of Doc's little front yard was what drew them. Sometimes they'd spray Doc's hose on one another. Get drenched like when they were kids and the city used to turn on fire hydrants in the summer. Some of Doc's neighbors would give them dirty looks. Didn't like a whole bunch of loud, sweaty, half-naked niggers backed up in their nice street where Doc was the only colored on the block. They say Doc didn't care. He was just out there like everybody else having a good time.

Doc had played at the university. Same one where Doc taught for a while. They say Doc used to laugh when white people asked him if he was in the athletic department. No reason for niggers to be at the university if they weren't playing ball or coaching ball. At least that's what white people thought, and since they thought that way, that's the way it was. Never more than a sprinkle of black faces in the white sea of the university. Doc used to laugh till the joke got old. People freedom-marching and freedom-dying, Doc said, but some dumb stuff never changed.

He first heard Doc's story late one day, after the yellow streetlights had popped on. Pooner was finishing the one about gang warring in North Philly: Yeah. They sure nuff lynched this dude they caught on their turf. Hung him up on the goddamn poles behind the backboard. Little kids found the sucker in the morning with his tongue all black and shit down his legs, and the cops had to come cut him down. Worst part is them little kids finding a dead body swinging up there. Kids don't be needing to find nothing like that. But those North Philly gangs don't play. They don't even let the dead rest in peace. Run in a funeral parlor and fuck up the funeral. Dumping over the casket and tearing up the flowers. Scaring people and turning the joint out. It's some mean shit. But them gangs don't play. They kill you they ain't finished yet. Mess with your people, your house, your sorry-ass dead body to get even. Pooner finished telling it and he looked round at the fellows and people were shaking their heads and then there was a chorus of You got that right, man. It's a bitch out there, man. Them niggers crazy, boy, and Pooner holds out his hand and somebody passes the joint. Pooner pinches it in two fingers and takes a deep drag. Everybody knows he's finished, it's somebody else's turn.

One of the fellows says, I wonder what happened to old Doc. I always be thinking about Doc, wondering where the cat is, what he be doing now . . .

Don't nobody know why Doc's eyes start to going bad. It just happen. Doc never even wore glasses. Eyes good as anybody's far as anybody knew till one day he come round he got goggles on. Like Kareem. And people kinda joking, you know. Doc got him some goggles. Watch out, youall. Doc be skyhooking youall to death today. Funning, you know. Cause Doc like to joke and play. Doc one the fellas like I said, so when he come round in goggles he subject to some teasing and one another thing like that cause nobody thought nothing serious wrong. Doc's eyes just as good as yours or mine, far as anybody knew.

Doc been playing all his life. That's why you could stand him on the foul line and point him at the hoop and more times than not, Doc could sink it. See, he be remembering. His muscles know just what to do. You get his feet aimed right, line him up so he's on target, and Doc would swish one for you. Was a game kinda. Sometimes you get a sucker and Doc win you some money. Swish. Then the cat lost the dough start crying. He ain't blind. Can't no blind man shoot no pill. Is you really blind, brother? You niggers trying to steal my money, trying to play me for a fool. When a dude start crying the blues like that Doc wouldn't like it. He'd walk away. Wouldn't answer.

Leave the man lone. You lost fair and square. Doc made the basket so shut up and pay up, chump.

Doc practiced. Remember how you'd hear him out here at night when people sleeping. It's dark but what dark mean to Doc? Blacker than the rent man's heart but don't make no nevermind to Doc, he be steady shooting fouls. Always be somebody out there to chase the ball and throw it back. But shit, man. When Doc into his rhythm, didn't need nobody chase the ball. Ball be swishing with that good backspin, that good arch bring it back blip, blip, blip, three bounces and it's coming right back to Doc's hands like he

got a string on the pill. Spooky if you didn't know Doc or know about foul
shooting and understand when you got your shit together don't matter if
you blindfolded. You put the motherfucker up and you know it's spozed to
come running back just like a dog with a stick in his mouth.

Doc always be hanging at the court. Blind as wood but you couldn't fool
Doc. Eyes in his ears. Know you by your walk. He could tell if you wearing new sneaks, tell you if your old ones is laced or not. Know you by your
breath. The holes you make in the air when you jump. Doc was hip to who
fucking who and who was getting fucked. Who could play ball and who was
jiving. Doc use to be out here every weekend, steady rapping with the fellows and doing his foul-shot thing between games. Every once in a while
somebody tease him, Hey, Doc. You want to run winners next go? Doc
laugh and say, No, Dupree . . . I'm tired today, Dupree. Besides which you
ain't been on a winning team in a week have you, Du? And everybody laugh.
You know, just funning cause Doc one the fellas.

But one Sunday the shit got stone serious. Sunday I'm telling youall
about, the action was real nice. If you wasn't ready, get back cause the
brothers was cooking. Sixteen points, rise and fly. Next. Who got next? . . .
Come on out here and take your ass-kicking. One them good days when it's
hot and everybody's juices is high and you feel you could play till next week.
One them kind of days and a run's just over. Doc gets up and he goes with
Billy Moon to the foul line. Fellas hanging under the basket for the rebound.
Ain't hardly gon be a rebound Doc get hisself lined up right. But see, when
the ball drop through the net you want to be the one grab it and throw it
back to Billy. You want to be out there part of Doc shooting fouls just like
you want to run when the running's good.

Doc bounce the ball, one, two, three times like he does. Then he raise it.
Sift it in his fingers. You know he's a ballplayer, a shooter already way the ball
spin in them long fingers way he raises it and cocks his wrist. You know Doc
can't see a damn thing through his sunglasses but swear to God you'd think
he was looking at the hoop way he study and measure. Then he shoots and
ain't a sound in whole Johnson. Seems like everybody's heart stops. Everybody's breath behind that ball pushing it and steadying it so it drops through
clean as new money.

But that Sunday something went wrong. Couldna been wind cause
wasn't no wind. I was there. I know. Maybe Doc had playing on his mind.

Couldn't help have playing on his mind cause it was one those days wasn't nothing better to do in the world than play. Whatever it was, soon as the ball left his hands, you could see Doc was missing, missing real bad. Way short and way off to the left. Might hit the backboard if everybody blew on it real hard.

A young boy, one them skinny, jumping-jack young boys got pogo sticks for legs, one them kids go up and don't come back down till they ready, he was standing on the left side the lane and leap up all the sudden catch the pill out the air and jams it through. Blam. A monster dunk and everybody break out in Goddamn. Do it, Sky, and Did you see that nigger get up? People slapping five and all that mess. Then Sky, the young boy they call Sky, grinning like a Chessy cat and strutting out with the ball squeezed in one hand to give it to Doc. In his glory. Grinning and strutting.

Gave you a little help, Doc.

Didn't ask for no help, Sky. Why'd you fuck with my shot, Sky?

Well, up jumped the devil. The joint gets real quiet again real quick. Doc ain't cracked smile the first. He ain't playing.

Sorry, Doc. Didn't mean no harm, Doc.

You must think I'm some kind of chump fucking with my shot that way.

People start to feeling bad. Doc is steady getting on Sky's case. Sky just a young, light-in-the-ass kid. Jump to the moon but he's just a silly kid. Don't mean no harm. He just out there like everybody else trying to do his thing. No harm in Sky but Doc ain't playing and nobody else says shit. It's quiet like when Doc's shooting. Quiet as death and Sky don't know what to do. Can't wipe that lame look off his face and can't back off and can't hand the pill to Doc neither. He just stands there with his arm stretched out and his rusty fingers wrapped round the ball. Can't hold it much longer, can't let it go.

Seems like I coulda strolled over to Doc's stoop for a drinka water and strolled back and those two still be standing there. Doc and Sky. Billy Moon off to one side so it's just Doc and Sky.

Everybody holding they breath. Everybody want it over with and finally Doc says, Forget it, Sky. Just don't play with my shots anymore. And then Doc say, Who has next winners?

If Doc was joking nobody took it for no joke. His voice still hard. Doc ain't kidding around.

Who's next? I want to run.

Now, Doc knows who's next. Leroy got next winners and Doc knows Leroy always saves a spot so he can pick up a big man from the losers. Leroy tell you to your face, I got my five, man, but everybody know Leroy saving a place so he can build him a winner and stay on the court. Leroy's a cold dude that way, been that way since he first started coming round and ain't never gon change and Doc knows that, everybody knows that but even Leroy ain't cold enough to say no to Doc.

I got it, Doc.

You got your five yet?

You know you got a spot with me, Doc. Always did.

Then I'ma run.

Say to myself, Shit . . . Good God Almighty. Great Googa-Mooga. What is happening here? Doc can't see shit. Doc blind as this bench I'm sitting on. What Doc gon do out there?

Well, it ain't my game. If it was, I'd a lied and said I had five. Or maybe not. Don't know what I'da done, to tell the truth. But Leroy didn't have no choice. Doc caught him good. Course Doc knew all that before he asked.

Did Doc play? What kinda question is that? What you think I been talking about all this time, man? Course he played. Why the fuck he be asking for winners less he was gon play? Helluva run as I remember. Overtime and shit. Don't remember who won. Somebody did, sure nuff. Leroy had him a strong unit. You know how he is. And Doc? Doc ain't been out on the court for a while but Doc is Doc, you know. Held his own . . .

If he had tried to tell her about Doc, would it have made a difference? Would the idea of a blind man playing basketball get her attention or would she have listened the way she listened when he told her stories he'd read about slavery days when Africans could fly, change themselves to cats and hummingbirds, when black hoodoo priests and conjure queens were feared by powerful whites even though ordinary black lives weren't worth a penny. To her it was folklore, superstition. Interesting because it revealed the psychology, the pathology of the oppressed. She listened intently, not because she thought she'd hear truth. For her, belief in magic was like belief in God. Nice work if you could get it. Her skepticism, her hardheaded practicality, like the smallness of her hands, appealed to him. Opposites attracting. But more and more as the years went by, he'd wanted her with him, wanted them to be together . . .

They were walking in Regent Park. It was clear to both of them that things weren't going to work out. He'd never seen her so beautiful, perfect.

There should have been stars. Stars at least, and perhaps a sickle moon. Instead the edge of the world was on fire. They were walking in Regent Park and dusk had turned the tree trunks black. Beyond them in the distance, below the fading blue of sky, the colors of sunset were pinched into a narrow, radiant band. Perhaps he had listened too long. Perhaps he had listened too intently for his own voice to fill the emptiness. When he turned back to her, his eyes were glazed, stinging. Grit, chemicals, whatever it was coloring, poisoning the sky, blurred his vision. Before he could blink her into focus, before he could speak, she was gone.

If he'd known Doc's story he would have said: *There's still a chance. There's always a chance. I mean this guy, Doc. Christ. He was stone blind. But he got out on the court and played. Over there. Right over there. On that very court across the hollow from us. It happened. I've talked to people about it many times. If Doc could do that, then anything's possible. We're possible . . .*

If a blind man could play basketball, surely we . . . If he had known Doc's story, would it have saved them? He hears himself saying the words. The ball arches from Doc's fingertips, the miracle of it sinking. Would she have believed any of it?

Surfiction

Among my notes on the first section of Charles Chesnutt's "A Deep Sleeper" there are these remarks:

Not reality but a culturally learned code—that is, out of the infinite number of ways one might apprehend, be conscious, be aware, a certain arbitrary pattern or finite set of indicators is sanctioned and over time becomes identical with reality. The signifier becomes the signified. For Chesnutt's contemporaries reality was I (eye) centered, the relationship between man and nature disjunctive rather than organic, time was chronological, linear, measured by manmade units—minutes, hours, days, months, etc. To capture this reality was then a rather mechanical procedure—a voice at the center of the story would begin to unravel reality: a catalog of sensuous detail, with the visual dominant, to indicate nature, out there in the form of clouds, birdsong, etc. A classical painting rendered according to the laws of perspective, the convention of the window frame through which the passive spectator observes. The voice gains its authority because it is literate, educated, perceptive, because it has aligned itself correctly with the frame, because it drops the cues, or elements of the code, methodically. The voice is reductive, as any code ultimately is; an implicit reinforcement occurs as the text elaborates itself through the voice: the voice gains authority because things are in order, the order gains authority because it is established by a voice we trust. For example the opening lines of Deep Sleeper...

It was four o'clock on Sunday afternoon, in the month of July. The air had been hot and sultry, but a light, cool breeze had sprung up; and occasional cirrus clouds overspread the sun, and for a while subdued his fierceness. We were all out on the piazza—as the coolest place we could find—my wife, my sister-in-law, and I. The only sounds that broke the Sabbath stillness were the hum of an occasional vagrant bumblebee, or the fragmentary song of a mockingbird in a neighboring elm . . .

Rereading, I realize my *remarks* are a pastiche of received opinions from Barthes, certain cultural anthropologists and linguistically oriented critics and Russian formalists, and if I am beginning a story rather than an essay, the whole stew suggests the preoccupations of Borges or perhaps a footnote in Barthelme. Already I have managed to embed several texts within other texts, already a rather unstable mix of genres and disciplines and literary allusion. Perhaps for all of this, already a grim exhaustion of energy and possibility, readers fall away as if each word is a well-aimed bullet.

More Chesnutt. This time from the text of the story, a passage unremarked upon except that in the margin of the Xeroxed copy of the story I am copying this passage from, several penciled comments appear. I'll reproduce the entire discussion.

Latin: secundus-tertius-quar tus-quintus.

"Tom's gran'daddy wuz name' Skundus," he began. "He had a brudder name' Tushus en' ernudder name' Squinchus." The old man paused a moment and gave his leg another hitch.

"drawing out Negroes"—custom in old south, new north, a constant in America. Ignorance of one kind delighting ignorance of another. Mask to mask. The real joke.

My sister-in-law was shaking with laughter. "What remarkable names!" she exclaimed. "Where in the world did they get them?"

Naming: plantation owner usurps privilege of family. Logos. Word made flesh. Power. Slaves named in order of appearance. Language masks joke. Latin opaque to blacks.

Note: last laugh. Blacks (mis) pronounce secundus. Secundus = Skundus. Black speech takes over—opaque to white—subverts original purpose of name. Language (black) makes joke. Skundus has new identity.

"Dem names wuz gun ter 'em by ole Marse Dugal' McAdoo, w'at I use' ter b'long ter, en' dey use' ter b'long ter. Marse Dugal' named all de babies w'at wuz bawn on de plantation. Dese young un's mammy wanted ter call 'em sump'n plain en' simple, like Rastus er Caesar er George Wash'n'ton, but ole Marse say no, he want all de niggers on his place ter hab diffe'nt names, so he kin tell 'em apart. He'd done use' up all de common names, so he had ter take sump'n else. Dem names he gun Skundus en' his brudders is Hebrew names en' wuz tuk out'n de Bible."

I distinguish remarks from footnotes. Footnotes clarify specifics; they answer simple questions. You can always tell from a good footnote the question which it is answering. For instance: *The Short Fiction of Charles W. Chesnutt*, edited by Sylvia Lyons Render (Washington, D.C.: Howard University Press, 1974), 47. Clearly someone wants to know, Where did this come from? How might I find it? Tell me where to look. OK. Whereas remarks, at least my remarks, the ones I take the trouble to write out in my journal,* which is where the first long cogitation appears/appeared [the ambiguity here is not intentional but situational, not imposed for irony's sake but necessary because the first long cogitation—*my remark*—being referred to both *appears* in the sense that every time I open my journal, as I did a few moments ago, as I am doing NOW to check for myself and to exemplify for you the accuracy of my statement—the remark *appears* as it does/did just now. (Now?) But the remark (original), if we switch to a different order of time, treating the text diachronically rather than paradigmatically, the remark *appeared*; which poses another paradox. How language or words are both themselves and *Others*, but not always. Because the negation implied by *appearance*, the so-called "shadow within the rock," is *disappearance*. The reader correctly anticipates such an antiphony or absence suggesting presence (shadow play) between

---

* Journal unpaginated. In progress. Unpublished. Many hands.

the text as realized and the text as shadow of its act. The dark side paradox-
ically is the absence, the nullity, the white space on the white page between
the white words not stated but implied. Forever], are more complicated.

The story, then, having escaped the brackets, can proceed. In this story,
"Mine," in which Chesnutt replies to Chesnutt, remarks, comments, asides,
allusions, footnotes, quotes from Chesnutt have so far played a disproportionate role, and if this sentence is any indication, continue to play a gro-
tesquely unbalanced role, will roll on.

It is four o'clock on Sunday afternoon, in the month of July. The air has
been hot and sultry, but a light, cool breeze has sprung up; and occasional
cirrus clouds (?) overspread the sun, and for a while subdue his fierceness.
We were all out on the piazza (stoop?)—as the coolest place we could
find—my wife, my sister-in-law, and I. The only sounds that break the Sabbath stillness are the hum of an occasional bumblebee, or the fragmentary
song of a mockingbird in a neighboring elm . . .

The reader should know now by certain unmistakable signs (codes) that a
story is beginning. The stillness, the quiet of the afternoon tells us something
is going to happen, that an event more dramatic than birdsong will rupture
the static tableau. We expect, we know a payoff is forthcoming. We know this
because we are put into the passive posture of readers or listeners (consumers)
by the narrative unraveling of a reality which, because it is unfolding in time,
slowly begins to take up our time and thus is obliged to give us something in
return; the story enacts word by word, sentence by sentence in *real* time. Its
moments will pass and our moments will pass simultaneously, hand in glove if
you will. The literary, storytelling convention exacts this kind of relaxation or
compliance or collaboration (conspiracy). Sentences slowly fade in, substitut-
ing fictive sensations for those which normally constitute our awareness. The
shift into the fictional world is made easier because the conventions by which
we identify the real world are conventions shared with and often learned from
our experience with fictive reality. What we are accustomed to acknowledging as awareness is actually a culturally learned, contingent condensation of
many potential awarenesses. In this culture—American, Western, twentieth-
century—an awareness that is eye-centered, disjunctive as opposed to
organic, that responds to clock time, calendar time more than biological
cycles or seasons, that assumes nature is external, acting on us rather than
through us, that tames space by man-made structures and with the *I* as center

defines other people and other things by the nature of their relationship to the *I* rather than by the independent integrity of the order they may represent.

An immanent experience is being prepared for, is being framed. The experience will be real because the narrator produces his narration from the same set of conventions by which we commonly detect reality—dates, buildings, relatives, the noises of nature.

All goes swimmingly until a voice from the watermelon patch intrudes. Recall the dialect reproduced above. Recall Kilroy's phallic nose. Recall Earl and Cornbread, graffiti artists, their spray-paint cans notorious from one end of the metropolis to the other—from Society Hill to the Jungle, nothing safe from them and the artists uncatchable until hubris leads them to attempt the gleaming virgin flanks of a 747 parked on runway N-16 at the Philadelphia International Airport. Recall your own reflection in the funhouse mirror and the moment of doubt when you turn away and it turns away and you lose sight of it and it naturally enough loses sight of you and you wonder where it's going and where you're going and the wrinkly reflecting plate still is laughing behind your back at someone.

The reader here pauses

stream a totally irrelevant conversation:
. . . by accident twenty-seven double-columned pages by accident?

started yeah I can see starting curiosity whatever staring over somebody's shoulder or a letter maybe you think yours till you see not meant for you at all

Picks up in mid-

I mean it started that way

I'm not trying to excuse just understand it was not premeditated your journal is your journal that's not why I mean I didn't forget your privacy or lose respect on purpose.

It was just there and, well we seldom talk and I was desperate we haven't been going too well for a long time

and getting worse getting finished
when shit like this comes down

I wanted to stop but I needed
something from you more than
you've been giving so when I
saw it there I picked it up you
understand not to read but
because it was you you and
holding it was all a part of you

you're breaking my heart

please don't dismiss

dismiss dismiss what I won't dismiss
your prying how you defiled how you
took advantage

don't try to make me a criminal
the guilt I feel it I know right
from wrong and accept whatever
you need to lay on me but I had
to do it I was desperate for something, anything, even if the cost

was rifling my personal life searching
through my guts for ammunition and did
you get any did you learn anything you can
use on me Shit I can't even remember the
whole thing is a jumble I'm blocking it all
out my own journal and I can't remember
a word because it's not mine anymore

I'm sorry I knew I shouldn't as
soon as I opened it I flashed on the
Bergman movie the one where she
reads his diary I flashed on how
underhanded how evil a thing she
was doing but I couldn't stop

A melodrama a god damned Swedish
subtitled melodrama you're going to
turn it around aren't you make it into

The reader can replay the tape at leisure. Can amplify or expand. There is plenty of blank space on the pages. A sin really, given the scarcity of trees, the rapaciousness of paper companies in the forests which remain. The canny reader will not trouble him/herself trying to splice the tape to what came before or after. Although the canny reader would also be suspicious of the straightforward, absolute denial of relevance dismissing the tape.

Here is the main narrative again. In embryo. A professor of literature at a university in Wyoming (the only university in Wyoming) by coincidence is teaching two courses in which are enrolled two students (one in each of the professor's seminars) who are husband and wife. They both have red hair. The male of the couple aspires to write novels and is writing fast and furious a chapter a week his first novel in the professor's creative writing seminar. The other redhead, there are only two redheads in the two classes, is taking the professor's seminar in Afro-American literature, one of whose stars is Charlie W. Chesnutt. It has come to the professor's attention that both husband and wife are inveterate diary keepers, a trait which like their red hair distinguishes them from the professor's other eighteen students. Something old-fashioned, charming about diaries, about this pair of hip graduate students keeping them. A desire to keep up with his contemporaries (almost wrote *peers* but that gets complicated real quick) leads the professor, who is also a novelist, or as he prefers novelist who is also a professor, occasionally to assemble large piles of novels which he reads with bated breath. The novelist/professor/reader bates his breath because he has never grown out of the awful habit of feeling praise bestowed on someone else lessens the praise which may find its way to him (he was eldest of five children in a very poor family—not an excuse—perhaps an extenuation—never enough to go around breeds a fierce competitiveness and being for four years an only child breeds a selfishness and ego-centeredness that is only exacerbated by the shocking arrival of contenders, rivals, lower-than-dogshit pretenders to what is by divine right his). So he reads the bait and nearly swoons when the genuinely good appears. The relevance of this to the story is that occasionally the professor reads systematically and because on this occasion he is soon to appear on a panel at a neighboring university (Colorado) discussing "Surfiction" his stack of novels was culled from the latest, most hip, most avant-garde, new *Tel Quel* chic, anti, non-novel bibliographies he could locate. He has determined at least three qualities of these novels. *One—*

you can stack ten in the space required for two traditional novels. *Two*—they are *au rebours* the present concern for ecology since they sometimes include as few as no words at all on a page and often no more than seven. *Three*—without authors whose last names begin with *B*, surfiction might not exist. *B* for Beckett, Barth, Burroughs, Barthes, Borges, Brautigan, Barthelme . . . (Which list further discloses a startling coincidence or perhaps the making of a scandal—one man working both sides of the Atlantic as a writer and critic explaining and praising his fiction as he creates it: *Barth Barthes Barthelme.*)

The professor's reading of these thin (not necessarily a dig—thin pancakes, watches, women for instance are *à la mode*) novels suggests to him that there may be something to what they think they have their finger on. All he needs then is a local habitation and some names. Hence the redheaded couple. Hence their diaries. Hence the infinite layering of the fiction he will never write (which is the subject of the fiction which he will never write). Boy meets Prof. Prof reads boy's novel. Girl meets Prof. Prof meets girl in boy's novel. Learns her pubic hair is as fiery red as what she wears short and stylish, flouncing just above her shoulders. (Of course it's all fiction. The fiction. The encounters.) What's real is how quickly the layers build, how like a spring snow in Laramie the drifts cover and obscure silently.

Boy keeps diary. Girl meets diary. Girl falls out of love with diary (his), retreats to hers. The suspense builds. Chesnutt is read. A conference with Prof in which she begins analyzing the multilayered short story "A Deep Sleeper" but ends in tears reading from a diary (his? hers?). The professor recognizes her sincere compassion for the downtrodden (of which in one of his fictions he is one). He also recognizes a fiction in her husband's fiction (when he undresses her) and reads her diary. Which she has done previously (read her husband's). Forever.

The plot breaks down. It was supposed to break down. The characters disintegrate. Whoever claimed they were whole in the first place? The stability of the narrative voice is displaced into a thousand distracted madmen screaming in the dim corridors of literary history. Whoever insisted it should be more ambitious? The train doesn't stop here. Mistah Kurtz, he dead. Godot ain't coming. Ecce Homo. Dat's all, folks. Sadness.

And so it goes.

Fever

To Mathew Carey, Esq., who fled Philadelphia in its hour of need and upon his return published a libelous account of the behavior of black nurses and undertakers, thereby injuring all people of my race and especially those without whose unselfish, courageous labours the city could not have survived the late calamity.

Consider Philadelphia from its centrical situation, the extent of its commerce, the number of its artificers, manufacturers and other circumstances, to be to the United States what the heart is to the human body in circulating the blood.

Robert Morris, 1777

He stood staring through a tall window at the last days of November. The trees were barren women starved for love and they'd stripped off all their clothes, but nobody cared. And not one of them gave a fuck about him, sifting among them, weightless and naked, knowing just as well as they did, no hands would come to touch them, warm them, pick leaves off the frozen ground and stick them back in place. Before he'd gone to bed a flutter of insects had stirred in the dark outside his study. Motion worrying the corner of his eye till he turned and focused where light pooled on the deck, a cone in which he could trap slants of snow so they material-ized into wet gray feathers that blotted against the glass, the planks of the deck. If he stood seven hours, dark would come again. At some point his reflection would hang in the glass, a ship from the other side of the world, docked in the ether. Days were shorter now. A whole one spent wondering what goes wrong would fly away, fly in the blink of an eye.

Perhaps, perhaps it may be acceptable to the reader to know how we found the sick affected by the sickness; our opportunities of hearing and seeing them have been very great. They were taken with a chill, a headache, a sick stomach, with pains in their limbs and back, this was the way the sickness in general began, but all were not affected alike, some appeared but slightly affected with some of these symptoms, what confirmed us in the opinion of a person being smitten was the colour of their eyes.

Victims in this low-lying city perished every year, and some years were worse than others, but the worst by far was the long hot dry summer of '93, when the dead and dying wrested control of the city from the living. Most who were able, fled. The rich to their rural retreats, others to relatives and friends in the countryside or neighboring towns. Some simply left, with no fixed destination, the prospect of privation or starvation on the road preferable to cowering in their homes awaiting the fever's fatal scratching at their door. Busy streets deserted, commerce halted, members of families shunning one another, the sick abandoned to suffer and die alone. Fear ruled. From August when the first cases of fever appeared below Water Street, to November when merciful frosts ended the infestation, the city slowly deteriorated, as if it, too, could suffer the terrible progress of the disease: fever, enfeeblement, violent vomiting and diarrhea, helplessness, delirium, settled dejection when patients *concluded they must go* (so the phrase for dying was), and therefore in a kind of fixed determined state of mind went off.

In some it raged more furiously than in others—some have languished for seven and ten days, and appeared to get better the day, or some hours before they died, while others were cut off in one, two, or three days, but their complaints were similar. Some lost their reason and raged with all the fury madness could produce, and died in strong convulsions. Others retained their reason to the last, and seemed rather to fall asleep than die.

Yellow fever: an acute infectious disease of subtropical and tropical New World areas, caused by a filterable virus transmitted by a mosquito of the genus *Aëdes* and characterized by jaundice and dark-colored vomit resulting from hemorrhages. Also called *yellow jack*.

Dengue: an infectious, virulent tropical and subtropical disease transmitted by mosquitoes and characterized by fever, rash, and severe pains in the joints. Also called *breakbone fever, dandy*. [Spanish, of African origin, akin to Swahili *kindinga*.]

Curled in the black hold of the ship he wonders why his life on solid green earth had to end, why the gods had chosen this new habitation for him, floating, chained to other captives, no air, no light, the wooden walls shuddering, battered, as if some madman is determined to destroy even this last pitiful refuge where he skids in foul puddles of waste, bumping other bodies, skinning himself on splintery beams and planks, always moving, shaken and spilled like palm nuts in the diviner's fist, and Esu casts his fate, constant motion, tethered to an iron ring.

In the darkness he can't see her, barely feels her light touch on his fevered skin. Sweat thick as oil but she doesn't mind, straddles him, settles down to do her work. She enters him and draws his blood up into her belly. When she's full, she pauses, dreamy, heavy. He could kill her then; she wouldn't care. But he doesn't. Listens to the whine of her wings lifting till the whimper is lost in the roar and crash of waves, creaking wood, prisoners groaning. If she returns tomorrow and carries away another drop of him, and the next day and the next, a drop each day, enough days, he'll be gone. Shrink to nothing, slip out of this iron noose and disappear.

Aëdes aegypti: a mosquito of the family *Culicidae*, genus *Aëdes*, in which the female is distinguished by a long proboscis for sucking blood. This winged insect is a vector (an organism that carries pathogens from one host to another) of yellow fever and dengue. [New Latin *Aëdes*, from Greek *aedes*, unpleasant: *a-*, not + *edos*, pleasant . . .]

All things arrive in the waters and waters carry all things away. So there is no beginning or end, only the waters' flow, ebb, flood, trickle, tides emptying and returning, salt seas and rivers and rain and mist and blood, the sun drowning in an ocean of night, wet sheen of dawn washing darkness from our eyes. This city is held in the water's palm. A captive as surely as I am captive. Long fingers of river, Schuylkill, Delaware, the rest of the hand invisible; underground streams and channels feed the soggy flesh of marsh, clay pit, sink, gutter, stagnant pool. What's not seen is heard in the suck of footsteps through spring mud of unpaved streets. Noxious vapors that sting your eyes, cause you to gag, spit, and wince are evidence of a presence, the dead hand cupping this city, the poisons that circulate through it, the sweat on its rotting flesh.

No one has asked my opinion. No one will. Yet I have seen this fever before, and though I can prescribe no cure, I could tell stories of other visitations, how it came and stayed and left us, the progress of disaster, its several stages, its horrors and mitigations. My words would not save one life, but those mortally affrighted by the fever, by the prospect of universal doom, might find solace in knowing there are limits to the power of this scourge that has befallen us, that some, yea, most will survive, that this condition is temporary, a season, that the fever must disappear with the first deep frosts and its disappearance is as certain as the fact it will come again.

They say the rat's nest ships from Santo Domingo brought the fever. Frenchmen and their black slaves fleeing black insurrection. Those who've seen Barbados's distemper say our fever is its twin born in the tropical climate of the hellish Indies. I know better. I hear the drum, the forest's heartbeat, pulse of the sea that chains the moon's wandering, the spirit's journey. Its throb is source and promise of all things being connected, a mirror storing everything, forgetting nothing. To explain the fever we need no boatloads of refugees, ragged and wracked with killing fevers, bringing death to our shores. We have bred the affliction within our breasts. Each solitary heart contains all the world's tribes, and its precarious dance echoes the drum's thunder. We are our ancestors and our children, neighbors and strangers to ourselves. Fever descends when the waters that connect us are clogged with filth. When our seas are garbage. The waters cannot come and go when we are shut off one from the other, each in his frock coat, wig, bonnet, apron, shop, shoes, skin, behind locks, doors, sealed faces, our blood grows thick and sluggish. Our bodies void infected fluids. Then we are dry and cracked as a desert country, vital parts wither, all dust and dry bones inside. Fever is a drought consuming us from within. Discolored skin caves in upon itself, we burn, expire.

I regret there is so little comfort in this explanation. It takes into account neither climatists nor contagionists, flies in the face of logic and reason, the good doctors of the College of Physicians who would bleed us, purge us, quarantine, plunge us in icy baths, starve us, feed us elixirs of bark and wine, sprinkle us with gunpowder, drown us in vinegar according to the dictates of their various healing sciences. Who, then, is this foolish old man who receives his wisdom from pagan drums in pagan forests? Are these the delusions of one whose brain the fever has already begun to gnaw? Not quite. True, I have survived other visitations of the fever, but while it prowls this city, I'm in jeopardy again as you are, because I claim no immunity, no magic. The messenger who bears the news of my death will reach me precisely at the stroke determined when it was determined I should tumble from the void and taste air the first time. Nothing is an accident. Fever grows in the secret places of our hearts, planted there when one of us decided to sell one of us to another. The drum must pound ten thousand thousand years to drive that evil away.

Fires burn on street corners. Gunshots explode inside wooden houses. Behind him a carter's breath expelled in low, labored pants warns him to edge closer to housefronts forming one wall of a dark, narrow, twisting lane. Thick wheels furrow the unpaved street. In the fire glow the cart stirs a shimmer of dust, faint as a halo, a breath smear on a mirror. Had the man locked in the traces of the cart cursed him or was it just a wheeze of exertion, a complaint addressed to the unforgiving weight of his burden? Creaking wheels, groaning wood, plodding footsteps, the cough of dust, bulky silhouette blackened as it lurches into brightness at the block's end. All gone in a moment. Sounds, motion, sight extinguished. What remained, as if trapped by a lid clamped over the lane, was the stench of dead bodies. A stench cutting through the ubiquitous pall of vinegar and gunpowder. Two, three, four corpses being hauled to Potter's Field, trailed by the unmistakable wake of decaying flesh. He'd heard they raced their carts to the burial ground. Two or three entering Potter's Field from different directions would acknowledge one another with challenges, raised fists, gather their strength for a last dash to the open trenches where they tip their cargoes. Their brethren would wager, cheer, toast the victor with tots of rum. He could hear the rumble of coffins crashing into a common grave, see the comical chariots bouncing, the men's legs pumping, faces contorted by fires that blazed all night at the burial ground. Shouting and curses would hang in the torpid night air, one more nightmare troubling the city's sleep.

He knew this warren of streets as well as anyone. Night or day he could negotiate the twists and turnings, avoid cul-de-sacs, find the river even if his vision was obscured in tunnel-like alleys. He anticipated when to duck a jutting signpost, knew how to find doorways where he was welcome, wooden steps down to a cobbled terrace overlooking the water where his shod foot must never trespass. Once beyond the grand houses lining one end of Water Street, in this quarter of hovels, beneath these wooden sheds leaning shoulder to shoulder were cellars and caves dug into the earth, poorer men's dwellings under these houses of the poor, an invisible region where his people burrow, pull earth like blanket and quilt round themselves to shut out cold and dampness, sleeping multitudes to a room, stacked and crosshatched and spoon fashion, themselves the only fuel, heat of one body passed to others and passed back from all to one. Can he blame the lucky ones who are strong enough to pull the death carts, who celebrate and leap and roar all night around the bonfires? Why should they return here? Where living and dead, sick and well must lie face to face, shivering or sweltering on the same dank floor.

Below Water Street the alleys proliferate. Named and nameless. He knows where he's going but fever has transformed even the familiar. He'd been waiting in Dr. Rush's entrance hall. An English mirror, oval framed in scalloped brass, drew him. He watched himself glide closer, a shadow, a blur, then the shape of his face materialized from silken depths. A mask he did not recognize. He took the thing he saw and murmured to it. Had he once been in control? Could he tame it again? Like a garden ruined overnight, pillaged, overgrown, trampled by marauding beasts. He stares at the chaos until he can recall familiar contours of earth, seasons of planting, harvesting, green shoots, nodding blossoms, scraping, digging, watering. Once upon a time he'd cultivated this thing, this plot of flesh and blood and bone, but what had it become? Who owned it now? He'd stepped away. His eyes constructed another face and set it there, between him and the wizened old man in the glass. He'd aged twenty years in a glance and the fever possessed the same power to alter suddenly what it touched. This city had grown ancient and fallen into ruin in two months since early August, when the first cases of fever appeared. Something in the bricks, mortar, beams, and stones had gone soft, had lost its permanence. When he entered sickrooms, walls fluttered, floors buckled. He could feel roofs pressing down. Putrid heat expanding. In the bodies of victims. In rooms, buildings, streets, neighborhoods. Membranes that preserved the integrity of substances and shapes, kept each in its proper place, were worn thin. He could poke his finger through yellowed skin. A stone wall. The eggshell of his skull. What should be separated was running together. Threatened to burst. Nothing contained the way it was supposed to be. No clear lines of demarcation. A mongrel city. Traffic where there shouldn't be traffic. An awful void opening around him, preparing itself to hold explosions of bile, vomit, gushing bowels, ooze, sludge, seepage.

Earlier in the summer, on a July afternoon, he'd tried to escape the heat by walking along the Delaware. The water was unnaturally calm, isolated into stagnant pools by outcroppings of wharf and jetty. A shelf of rotting matter paralleled the river edge. As if someone had attempted to sweep what was unclean and dead from the water. Bones, skins, entrails, torn carcasses, unrecognizable tatters and remnants broomed into a neat ridge. No sigh of the breeze he'd sought, yet fumes from the rim of garbage battered him in nauseating waves, a palpable medium intimate as wind. Beyond the tidal line of refuge, a pale margin lapped clean by receding waters. Then the iron river itself, flat, dark, speckled by sores of foam that puckered and swirled, worrying the stillness with a life of their own.

Spilled. Spoiled. Those words repeated themselves endlessly as he made his rounds. Dr. Rush had written out his portion, his day's share from the list of dead and dying. He'd purged, bled, comforted, and buried victims of the fever. In and out of homes that had become tombs, prisons, charnel houses. Dazed children wandering the streets, searching for their parents. How can he explain to a girl, barely more than an infant, that the father and mother she sobs for are gone from this earth? Departed. Expired. They are resting,

child. Asleep forever. In a far, far better place, my sweet, dear suffering one.
In God's bosom. Wrapped in His incorruptible arms. A dead mother with a
dead baby at her breast. Piteous cries of the helpless offering all they own for
a drink of water. How does he console the delirious boy who pummels him,
fastens himself on his leg because he's put the boy's mother in a box and now
must nail shut the lid?

Though light-headed from exhaustion, he's determined to spend a few
hours here, among his own people. But were these lost ones really his people?
The doors of his church were open to them, yet these were the ones who
stayed away, wasting their lives in vicious pastimes of the idle, the unsaved, the
ignorant. His benighted brethren who'd struggled to reach this city of refuge
and then, once inside the gates, had fallen, prisoners again, trapped by chains
of dissolute living as they'd formerly been snared in the bonds of slavery. He'd
come here and preached to them. Thieves, beggars, loose women, debtors,
fugitives, drunkards, gamblers, the weak, crippled, and outcast with nowhere
else to go. They spurned his church so he'd brought church to them, preaching
in gin mills, whoring dens, on street corners. He'd been jeered and hooted, spat
upon, clods of unnameable filth had spattered his coat. But a love for them, as
deep and unfathomable as his sorrow, his pity, brought him back again and
again, exhorting them, setting the gospel before them so they might partake of
its bounty, the infinite goodness, blessed sustenance therein. Jesus had toiled
among the wretched, the outcast, that flotsam and jetsam deposited like a
ledge of filth on the banks of the city. He understood what had brought the
dark faces of his brethren north, to the Quaker promise of this town, this cradle and capital of a New World, knew the misery they were fleeing, the bright
star in the Gourd's handle that guided them, the joy leaping in their hearts
when at last, at last the opportunity to be viewed as men instead of things was
theirs. He'd dreamed such dreams himself, oh yes, and prayed that the light
of hope would never be extinguished. He'd been praying for deliverance, for
peace and understanding when God had granted him a vision, hordes of sable
bondsmen throwing off their chains, marching, singing, a path opening in the
sea, the sea shaking its shaggy shoulders, resplendent with light and power. A
radiance sparkling in this walkway through the water, pearls, diamonds, spears
of light. This was the glistening way home. Waters parting, glory blinking and
winking. Too intense to stare at, a promise shimmering, a rainbow arching
over the end of the path. A hand tapped him. He'd waited for it to blend into

the vision, for its meaning to shine forth in the language neither word nor thought, God was speaking in His visitation. Tapping became a grip. Someone was shoving him. He was being pushed off his knees, hauled to his feet. Someone was snatching him from the honeyed dream of salvation. When his eyes popped open he knew the name of each church elder manhandling him. Pale faces above a wall of black cloth belonged to his fellow communicants. He knew without looking the names of the men whose hands touched him gently, steering, coaxing, and those whose hands dug into his flesh, the impatient, imperious, rough hands that shunned any contact with him except as overseer or master.

Allen, Allen. Do you hear me? You and your people must not kneel at the front of the gallery. On your feet. Come. Come. Now. On your feet.

Behind the last row of pews. There ye may fall down on your knees and give praise.

And so we built our African house of worship. But its walls could not imprison the Lord's word. Go forth. Go forth. And he did so. To this sinful quarter. Tunnels, cellars, and caves. Where no sunlight penetrates. Where wind off the river cuts like a knife. Chill of icy spray channeled here from the ocean's wintry depths. Where each summer the brackish sea that is mouth and maw and bowel deposits its waste in puddles stinking to high heaven.

Water Street becomes what it's named, rises round his ankles, soaks his boots, threatens to drag him down. Patrolling these murky depths he's predator, scavenger, the prey of some dagger-toothed creature whose shadow closes over him like a net.

When the first settlers arrived here they'd scratched caves into the soft earth of the riverbank. Like ants. Rats. Gradually they'd pushed inland, laying out a geometrical grid of streets, perpendicular, true-angled and straight-edged, the mirror of their rectitude. Black Quaker coats and dour visages were remembrances of mud, darkness, the place of their lying in, cocooned like worms, propagating dreams of a holy city. The latest comers must always start here, on this dotted line, in this riot of alleys, lanes, tunnels. Wave after wave of immigrants unloaded here, winnowed here, dying in these shanties, grieving in strange languages. But white faces move on, bury their dead, bear their children, negotiate the invisible reef between this broken place and the foursquare town. Learn enough of their new tongue to say to the blacks they've left behind, *thou shalt not pass.*

I watched him bring the scalding liquid to his lips and thought to myself that's where his color comes from. The black brew he drinks every morning. Coloring him, changing him. A hue I had not considered until that instant as other than absence, something nonwhite and therefore its opposite, what light would be if extinguished, sky or sea drained of the color blue when the sun disappears, the blackness of cinders. As he sips, steam rises. I peer into the cup that's become mine, at the moon in its center, waxing, waning. A light burning in another part of the room caught there, as my face would be if I leaned over the cup's hot mouth. But I have no wish to see my face. His is what I study as I stare into my cup and see not absence, but the presence of wood darkly stained, wet plowed earth, a boulder rising from a lake, blackly glistening as it sheds crowns and beards and necklaces of water. His color neither neglect nor abstention, nor mystery, but a swelling tide in his skin of this bitter morning beverage it is my habit to imbibe.

We were losing, clearly losing the fight. One day in mid-September fifty-seven were buried before noon.

He'd begun with no preamble. Our conversation taken up again directly as if the months since our last meeting were no more than a cobweb his first words lightly brush away. I say conversation but a better word would be *soliloquy* because I was only a listener, a witness learning his story, a story buried so deeply he couldn't recall it, but dreamed pieces, a conversation with himself, a reverie with the power to sink us both into its unreality. So his first words did not begin the story where I remembered him ending it in our last session, but picked up midstream the ceaseless play of voices only he heard, always, summoning him, possessing him, enabling him to speak, to be.

Despair was in my heart. The fiction of our immunity had been exposed for the vicious lie it was, a not-so-subtle device for wresting us from our homes, our loved ones, the afflicted among us, and sending us to aid strangers. First they blamed us, called the sickness Barbados fever, a contagion from those blood-soaked islands, brought to these shores by refugees from the fighting in Santo Domingo. We were not welcome anywhere. A dark skin was seen not only as a badge of shame for its wearer. Now we were evil incarnate, the mask of long agony and violent death. Black servants were discharged. The draymen, carters, barbers, caterers, oyster sellers, street vendors could find no custom. It mattered not that some of us were born here and spoke no language but the English language, second-, even third-generation African Americans who knew no other country, who laughed at the antics of newly landed immigrants, Dutchmen, Welshmen, Scots, Irish, Frenchmen who had turned our marketplaces into Babel, stomping along in their clodhopper shoes, strange costumes, haughty airs, Lowlander gibberish that sounded like men coughing or dogs barking. My fellow countrymen searching everywhere but in their own hearts, the foulness upon which this city is erected, to lay blame on others for the killing fever, pointed their fingers at foreigners and called it Palatine fever, a pestilence imported from those low countries in Europe where, I have been told, war for control of the sea lanes, the human cargoes transported thereupon, has raged for a hundred years.

But I am losing the thread, the ironical knot I wished to untangle for you. How the knife was plunged in our hearts, then cruelly twisted. We were proclaimed carriers of the fever and treated as pariahs, but when it became expedient to command our services to nurse the sick and bury the dead, the previous allegations were no longer mentioned. Urged on by desperate counselors, the mayor granted us a blessed immunity. We were ordered to save the city.

I swear to you, and the bills of mortality, published by the otherwise unreliable Mr. Carey, support my contention, that the fever dealt with us severely. Among the city's poor and destitute the fever's ravages were most deadly and we are always the poorest of the poor. If an ordinance forbidding ringing of bells to mourn the dead had not been passed, that awful tolling would have marked our days, the watches of the night in our African American community, as it did in those environs of the city we were forbidden to inhabit. Every morning before I commenced my labors for the sick and dying, I would hear moaning, screams of pain, fearful cries and supplications, a chorus of lamentations scarring daybreak, my people awakening to a nightmare that was devouring their will to live.

The small strength I was able to muster each morning was sorely tried the moment my eyes and ears opened upon the sufferings of my people, the reality that gave the lie to the fiction of our immunity. When my duties among the whites were concluded, how many nights did I return and struggle till dawn with victims here, my friends, parishioners, wandering sons of Africa whose faces I could not look upon without seeing my own. I was commandeered to rise and go forth to the general task of saving the city, forced to leave this neighborhood where my skills were sorely needed. I nursed those who hated me, deserted the ones I loved, who loved me.

I recite the story many, many times to myself, let many voices speak to me till one begins to sound like the sea or rain or my feet those mornings shuffling through thick dust.

We arrived at Bush Hill early. To spare ourselves a long trek in the oppressive heat of day. Yellow haze hung over the city. Plumes of smoke from blazes in Potter's Field, from fires on street corners curled above the rooftops, lending the dismal aspect of a town sacked and burned. I've listened to the Santo Domingans tell of the burning of Cap François. How the capital city was engulfed by fires set in cane fields by the rebelling slaves. Horizon in flames all night as they huddled offshore in ships, terrified, wondering where next they'd go, if any port would permit them to land, empty-handed slaves, masters whose only wealth now was naked black bodies locked in the hold, wide-eyed witnesses of an empire's downfall, chanting, moaning, uncertain as the sea rocked them, whether or not anything on earth could survive the fearful conflagration consuming the great city of Cap François.

Dawn breaking on a smoldering landscape, writhing columns of smoke, a general cloud of haze the color of a fever victim's eyes. I turn and stare at it a moment, then fall in again with my brother's footsteps trudging through untended fields girding Bush Hill.

From a prisoner-of-war ship in New York Harbor where the British had interned him he'd seen that city shed its graveclothes of fog. Morning after morning it would paint itself damp and gray, a flat sketch on the canvas of sky, a tentative, shivering screen of housefronts, sheds, sprawling warehouses floating above the river. Then shadows and hollows darkened. A jumble of masts, spars, sails began to sway, little boats plied lanes between ships, tiny figures inched along wharves and docks, doors opened, windows slid up or down, lending an illusion of depth and animation to the portrait. This city infinitely beyond his reach, this charade other men staged to mock him, to mark the distance he could not travel, the shore he'd never reach, the city, so to speak, came to life and with its birth each morning dropped the palpable weight of his despair. His loneliness and exile. Moored in pewter water, on an island that never stopped moving but never arrived anywhere. The city a mirage of light and air, chimera of paint, brush and paper, mattered naught except that it was denied him. It shimmered. Tolled. Unsettled the watery place where he was sentenced to dwell. Conveyed to him each morning the same doleful tidings: *The dead are legion, the living a froth on dark, layered depths. But you are neither, and less than both.* Each night he dreamed it burning, razed the city till nothing remained but a dry, black crust, crackling, crunching under his boots as he strides, king of the nothing he surveys.

We passed holes dug into the earth where the sick are interred. Some died in these shallow pits, awash in their own vomited and voided filth, before a bed in the hospital could be made ready for them. Others believed they were being buried alive, and unable to crawl out, howled till reason or strength deserted them. A few, past caring, slept soundly in these ditches, resisted the attendants sent to rouse them and transport them inside, once they realized they were being resurrected to do battle again with the fever. I'd watched the red-bearded French doctor from Santo Domingo with his charts and assistants inspecting this zone, his *salle d'attente*, he called it, greeting and reassuring new arrivals, interrogating them, nodding and bowing, hurrying from pit to pit, peering down at his invisible patients like a gardener tending seeds.

An introduction to the grave, a way into the hospital that prefigured the way most would leave it. That's what this bizarre rite of admission had seemed at first. But through this and other peculiar stratagems, Deveze, with his French practice, had transformed Bush Hill from lazarium to a clinic where victims of the fever, if not too weak upon arrival, stood a chance of surviving.

The cartman employed by Bush Hill had suddenly fallen sick. Faithful Wilcox had never missed a day, ferrying back and forth from town to hospital, hospital to Potter's Field. Bush Hill had its own cemetery now.

Daily rations of dead could be disposed of less conspicuously in a plot on the grounds of the estate, screened from the horror-struck eyes of the city. No one had trusted the hospital. Tales of bloody chaos reigning there had filtered back to the city. Citizens believed it was a place where the doomed were stored until they died. Fever victims would have to be dragged from their beds into Bush Hill's cart. They'd struggle and scream, pitch themselves from the rolling cart, beg for help when the cart passed a rare pedestrian daring or foolish enough to be abroad in the deadly streets.

I wondered for the thousandth time why some were stricken, some not. Dr. Rush and this Deveze dipped their hands into the entrails of corpses, stirred the black, corrupted blood, breathed infected vapors exhaled from mortified remains. I'd observed both men steeped in noxious fluids expelled by their patients, yet neither had fallen prey to the fever. Stolid, dim Wilcox maintained daily concourse with the sick and buried the dead for two months before he was infected. They say a woman, undiscovered until boiling stench drove her neighbors into the street crying for aid, was the cause of Wilcox's downfall. A large woman, bloated into an even more cumbersome package by gases and liquids seething inside her body, had slipped from his grasp as he and another had hoisted her up into the cart. Catching against a rail, her body had slammed down and burst, spraying Wilcox like a fountain. Wilcox did not pride himself on being the tidiest of men, nor did his job demand one who was overfastidious, but the reeking stench from that accident was too much even for him and he departed in a huff to change his polluted garments. He never returned. So there I was at Bush Hill, where Rush had assigned me with my brother, to bury the flow of dead that did not ebb just because the Charon who was their familiar could no longer attend them.

The doctors believe they can find the secret of the fever in the victims' dead bodies. They cut, saw, extract, weigh, measure. The dead are carved into smaller and smaller bits and the butchered parts studied but they do not speak. What I know of the fever I've learned from the words of those I've treated, from stories of the living that are ignored by the good doctors. When lancet and fleam bleed the victims, they offer up stories like prayers.

It was a jaunty day. We served our white guests and after they'd eaten, they served us at the long, linen-draped tables. A sumptuous feast in the oak grove prepared by many and willing hands. All the world's eyes seemed to be watching us. The city's leading men, black and white, were in attendance to celebrate laying the cornerstone of St. Thomas Episcopal African Church. In spite of the heat and clouds of mettlesome insects, spirits were high. A gathering of whites and blacks in good Christian fellowship to commemorate the fruit of shared labor. Perhaps a new day was dawning. The picnic occurred in July. In less than a month the fever burst upon us.

When you open the dead, black or white, you find: the dura mater covering the brain is white and fibrous in appearance. The leptomeninges covering the brain are clear and without opacifications. The brain weighs 1,450 grams and is formed symmetrically. Cut sections of the cerebral hemispheres reveal normal-appearing gray matter throughout. The white matter of the corpus callosum is intact and bears no lesions. The basal ganglia are in their normal locations and grossly appear to be without lesions. The ventricles are symmetrical and filled with crystal-clear cerebrospinal fluid.

The cerebellum is formed symmetrically. The nuclei of the cerebellum are unremarkable. Multiple sections through the pons, medulla oblongata, and upper brain stem reveal normal gross anatomy. The cranial nerves are in their normal locations and unremarkable.

The muscles of the neck are in their normal locations. The cartilages of the larynx and the hyoid bone are intact. The thyroid and parathyroid glands are normal on their external surface. The mucosa of the larynx is shiny, smooth, and without lesions. The vocal cords are unremarkable. A small amount of bloody material is present in the upper trachea.

The heart weighs 380 grams. The epicardial surface is smooth, glistening, and without lesions. The myocardium of the left ventricle and septum are of a uniform meaty-red, firm appearance. The endocardial surfaces are smooth, glistening, and without lesions. The auricular appendages are free from thrombi. The valve leaflets are thin and delicate, and show no evidence of vegetation.

The right lung weighs 400 grams. The left lung 510 grams. The pleural surfaces of the lungs are smooth and glistening.

The esophageal mucosa is glistening, white, and folded. The stomach contains a large amount of black, noxious bile. A veriform appendix is present. The ascending, transverse, and descending colon reveal hemorrhaging, striations, disturbance of normal mucosa patterns throughout. A small amount of bloody, liquid feces is present in the ano-rectal canal.

The liver weighs 1,720 grams. The spleen weighs 150 grams. The right kidney weighs 190 grams. The left kidney weighs 180 grams. The testes show a glistening white tunica albuginea. Sections are unremarkable.

Dr. Rush and his assistants examined as many corpses as possible in spite of the hurry and tumult of never-ending attendance on the sick. Rush hoped to prove his remedy, his analysis of the cause and course of the fever correct. Attacked on all sides by his medical brethren for purging and bleeding patients already in a drastically weakened state, Rush lashed back at his detractors, wrote pamphlets, broadsides, brandished the stinking evidence of his postmortems to demonstrate conclusively how the sick drowned in their own poisoned fluids. The putrefaction, the black excess, he proclaimed, must be drained away, else the victim inevitably succumbs.

Dearest:
I shall not return home again until this business of the fever is terminated. I fear bringing the dread contagion into our home. My life is in the hands of God and as long as He sees fit to spare me I will persist in my labors on behalf of the sick, dying and dead. We are losing the battle. Eighty-eight were buried this past Thursday. I tremble for your safety. Wish the lie of immunity were true. Please let me know by way of a note sent to the residence of Dr. Rush that you and our dear Martha are well. I pray every hour that God will preserve you both. As difficult as it is to rise each morning and go with Thomas to perform our duties, the task would be unbearable if I did not hold in my heart a vision of these horrors ending, a blessed shining day when I return to you and drop this weary head upon your sweet bosom.

Allen, Allen, he called to me. Observe how even after death, the body rejects this bloody matter from nose and bowel and mouth. Verily, the patient who had expired at least an hour before, continued to stain the cloth I'd wrapped round him. We'd searched the rooms of a regal mansion, discovering six members of a family, patriarch, son, son's wife and three children, either dead or in the last frightful stages of the disease. Upon the advice of one of Dr. Rush's most outspoken critics, they had refused mercury purges and bleeding until now, when it was too late for any earthly remedy to preserve them. In the rich furnishings of this opulent mansion, attended by one remaining servant whom fear had not driven away, three generations had withered simultaneously, this proud family's link to past and future cut off absolutely, the great circle broken. In the first bedroom we'd entered we'd found William Spurgeon, merchant, son and father, present manager of the family fortune, so weak he could not speak, except with pained blinks of his terrible golden eyes. Did he welcome us? Was he apologizing to good Dr. Rush for doubting his cure? Did he fear the dark faces of my brother and myself? Quick, too quickly, he was gone. Answering no questions. Revealing nothing of his state of mind. A savaged face frozen above the blanket. Ancient beyond years. Jaundiced eyes not fooled by our busy ministrations, but staring through us, fixed on the eternal stillness soon to come. And I believe I learned in that yellow cast of his eyes, the exact hue of the sky, if sky it should be called, hanging over the next world where we abide.

Allen, Allen. He lasted only moments and then I wrapped him in a sheet from the chest at the foot of his canopied bed. We lifted him into a humbler litter, crudely nailed together, the lumber still green. Allen, look. Stench from the coffin cut through the oppressive odors permeating this doomed household. See. Like an infant the master of the house had soiled his swaddling clothes. Seepage formed a dark river and dripped between roughly jointed boards. We found his wife where she'd fallen, naked, yellow above the waist, black below. As always the smell presaged what we'd discover behind a closed door. This woman had possessed closets of finery, slaves who dressed, fed, bathed and painted her, and yet here she lay, no one to cover her modesty, to lift her from the floor. Dr. Rush guessed from the discoloration she'd been dead two days, a guess confirmed by the loyal black maid, sick herself, who'd elected to stay when all others had deserted her masters. The demands of the living too much for her. She'd simply shut the door on her dead mistress. No breath, no heartbeat, sir. I could not rouse her, sir. I intended to return, sir, but I was too weak to move her, too exhausted by my labors, sir. Tears rolled down her creased black face and I wondered in my heart how this abused and despised old creature in her filthy apron and turban, this frail, worn woman, had survived the general calamity while the strong and pampered toppled round her.

I wanted to demand of her why she did not fly out the door now, finally freed of her burden, her lifelong enslavement to the whims of white people. Yet I asked her nothing. Considered instead myself, a man who'd worked years to purchase his wife's freedom, then his own, a so-called freeman, and here I was following in the train of Rush and his assistants, a functionary, a lackey, insulted daily by those I risked my life to heal.

Why did I not fly? Why was I not dancing in the streets, celebrating God's judgment on this wicked city? Fever made me freer than I'd ever been. Municipal government had collapsed. Anarchy ruled. As long as fever did not strike me I could come and go anywhere I pleased. Fortunes could be amassed in the streets. I could sell myself to the highest bidder, as nurse or undertaker, as surgeon trained by the famous Dr. Rush to apply his life-saving cure. Anyone who would enter houses where fever was abroad could demand outrageous sums for negligible services. To be spared the fever was a chance for anyone, black or white, to be a king.

So why do you follow him like a loyal puppy, you confounded black fool? He wagged his finger. You . . . His finger a gaunt, swollen-jointed, cracked-bone, chewed thing. Like the nose on his face. The nose I'd thought looked more like finger than nose. Fool. Fool. Finger wagging, then the cackle. The barnyard braying. Berserk chickens cackling in his skinny, goiter-knobbed throat. You are a fool, you black son of Ham. You slack-witted, Nubian ape. You progeny of Peeping Toms and orangutans. Who forces you to accompany that madman Rush on his murderous tours? He kills a hundred for every one he helps with his lamebrain, nonsensical, unnatural, Sangrado cures. Why do you tuck your monkey tail between your legs and skip after that butcher? Are you his shadow, a mindless, spineless black puddle of slime with no will of its own?

You are a good man, Allen. You worry about the souls of your people in this soulless wilderness. You love your family and your God. You are a beacon and steadfast. Your fatal flaw is narrowness of vision. You cannot see beyond these shores. The river, that stinking gutter into which the city shovels its shit and extracts its drinking water, that long-suffering string of spittle winds to an ocean. A hundred miles downstream the foamy mouth of the land sucks on the Atlantic's teat, trade winds saunter, and a whole wide world awaits the voyager. I know, Allen. I've been everywhere. Buying and selling everywhere.

If you would dare be Moses to your people and lead them out of this land, you'd find fair fields for your talent. Not lapdogging or doggy-trotting behind or fetch doggy or lie doggy or doggy open your legs or doggy stay still while I beat you. Follow the wound that is a river back to the sea. Be gone, be gone. While there's still time. If there is time, *mon frère*. If the pestilence has not settled in you already, breathed from my foul guts into yours, even as we speak.

Here's a master for you. A real master, Allen. The fever that's supping on my innards. I am more slave than you've ever been. I do its bidding absolutely. Cough up my lungs. Shit hunks of my bowel. When I die, they say my skin will turn as black as yours, Allen.

Return to your family. Do not leave them again. Whatever the Rushes promise, whatever they threaten.

Once, ten thousand years ago, I had a wife and children. I was like you, Allen, proud, innocent, forward-looking, well-spoken, well-mannered, a beacon and steadfast. I began to believe the whispered promise that I could have more. More of what, I didn't ask. Didn't know, but I took my eyes off what I loved in order to obtain this more. Left my wife and children and when I returned they were gone. Forever lost to me. The details are not significant. Suffice to say the circumstances of my leaving were much like yours. Very much like yours, Allen. And I lost everything. Became a wanderer among men. Bad news people see coming from miles away. A pariah. A joke. I'm not black like you, Allen. But I will be soon. Sooner than you'll be white. And if you're ever white, you'll be as dead as I'll be when I'm black.

Why do you desert your loved ones? What impels you to do what you find so painful, so unjust? Are you not a man? And free?

Her sleepy eyes, your lips on her warm cheek, each time may be the last meeting on this earth. The circumstances are similar, my brother. My shadow. My dirty face.

The dead are legion, the living a froth on dark, layered depths.

Master Abraham. There's a gentleman to see you, sir. The golden-haired lad bound to me for seven years was carted across the seas, like you, Allen, in the bowels of a leaky tub. A son to replace my son his fathers had clubbed to death when they razed the ghetto of Antwerp. But I could not tame the inveterate hate, his aversion and contempt for me. From my aerie, at my desk secluded among barrels, bolts, crates, and trunks of the shop's attic, I watched him steal, drink, fornicate. I overheard him denounce me to a delegate sent round to collect a tithe during the emergency. 'Tis well known in the old country that Jews bring the fever. Palatine fever that slays whole cities. They carry it under dirty fingernails, in the wimples of lizardy private parts. Pass it on with the evil eye. That's why we hound them from our towns, exterminate them. Beware of Master Abraham's glare. And the black-coated vulture listened intently. I could see him toting up the account in his small brain. Kill the Jew. Gain a shop and sturdy prentice, too. But I survived till fever laid me low and the cart brought me here to Bush Hill. For years he robbed and betrayed me and all my revenge was to treat him better. Allow him to pilfer, lie, embezzle. Let him grow fat and careless as I knew he would. With a father's boundless kindness I destroyed him. The last sorry laugh coming when I learned he died in agony, fever shriven, following by a day his Water Street French whore my indulgence allowed him to keep.

In Amsterdam I sold diamonds, Allen. In Barcelona they plucked hairs from my beard to fashion charms that brought ill fortune to their enemies. There were nights in dungeons when the mantle of my suffering was all I possessed to wrap round me and keep off mortal cold. I cursed God for choosing me, choosing my people to cuckold and slaughter. Have you heard of the Lamed-Vov, the Thirty-six Just Men set apart to suffer the reality humankind cannot bear? Saviors. But not Gods like your Christ. Not magicians, not sorcerers with bags of tricks, Allen. No divine immunities. Flesh-and-blood saviors. Men like we are, Allen. If man you are beneath your sable hide. Men who cough and scratch their sores and bleed and stink. Whose teeth rot. Whose wives and children are torn from them. Who wander the earth unable to die, but men always, men till God plucks them up and returns them to His side where they must thaw ten centuries to melt the crust of earthly grief and misery they've taken upon themselves. Ice men. Snowmen. I thought for many years I might be one of them. In my vanity. My self-pity. My foolishness. But no. One lifetime of sorrows enough for me. I'm just another customer. One more in the crowd lined up at his stall to purchase his wares.

You do know, don't you, Allen, that God is a bookseller? He publishes one book—the text of suffering—over and over again. He disguises it between new boards, in different shapes and sizes, prints on varying papers, in many fonts, adds prefaces and postscripts to deceive the buyer, but it's always the same book.

You say you do not return to your family because you don't want to infect them. Perhaps your fear is well-founded. But perhaps it also masks a greater fear. Can you imagine yourself, Allen, as other than you are? A free man with no charlatan Rush to blame. The weight of your life in your hands.

You've told me tales of citizens paralyzed by fear, of slaves on shipboard who turn to stone in their chains, their eyes boiled in the sun. Is it not possible that you suffer the converse of this immobility? You, sir, unable to stop an endless round of duty and obligation. Turning pages as if the next one or the next will let you finish the story and return to your life.

Your life, man. Tell me what sacred destiny, what nigger errand keeps you standing here at my filthy pallet? Fly, fly, fly away home. Your house is on fire, your children burning.

I have lived to see the slaves free. My people frolic in the streets. Black and white. The ones who believe they are either or both or neither. I am too old for dancing. Too old for foolishness. But this full moon makes me wish for two good legs. For three. Straddled a broomstick when I was a boy. Giddy-up, giddy-up. Galloping m'lord, m'lady, around the yard I should be sweeping. Dust in my wake. Chickens squawking. My eyes everywhere at once so I would not be caught out by mistress or master in the sin of idleness. Of dreaming. Of following a child's inclination. My broom steed snatched away. Become a rod across my back. Ever cautious. Dreaming with one eye open. The eye I am now, old and gimpy-limbed, watching while my people celebrate the rumor of Old Pharaoh's capitulation.

I've shed this city like a skin, wiggling out of it tenscore and more years, by miles and ells, fretting, twisting. Many days I did not know whether I'd wrenched freer or crawled deeper into the sinuous pit. Somewhere a child stood, someplace green, keeping track, waiting for me. Hoping I'd meet him again, hoping my struggle was not in vain. I search that child's face for clues to my blurred features. Flesh drifted and banked, eroded by wind and water, the landscape of this city fitting me like a skin. Pray for me, child. For my unborn parents I carry in this orphan's potbelly. For this ancient face that slips like water through my fingers.

Night now. Bitter cold night. Fires in the hearths of lucky ones. Many of us still abide in dark cellars, caves dug into the earth below poor men's houses. For we are poorer still, burrow there, pull earth like blanket and quilt round us to shut out cold, sleep multitudes to a room, stacked and crosshatched and spoon-fashion, ourselves the fuel, heat of one body passed to others and passed back from all to one. No wonder then the celebration does not end as a blazing chill sweeps off the Delaware. Those who leap and roar round the bonfires are better off where they are. They have no place else to go.

Given the derivation of the words, you could call the deadly winged visitors an *unpleasantness from Egypt*.

Putrid stink rattles in his nostrils. He must stoop to enter the cellar. No answer as he shouts his name, his mission of mercy. Earthen floor, ceiling, and walls buttressed by occasional beams, slabs of wood. Faint bobbing glow from his lantern. He sees himself looming and shivering on the walls, a shadowy presence with more substance than he feels he possesses at this late hour. After a long day of visits, this hovel his last stop before returning to his brother's house for a few hours of rest. He has learned that exhaustion is a swamp he can wade through and on the far side another region where a thin trembling version of himself toils while he observes, bemused, slipping in and out of sleep, amazed at the likeness, the skill with which that other mounts and sustains him. Mimicry. Puppetry. Whatever controls this other, he allows the impostor to continue, depends upon it to work when he no longer can. After days in the city proper with Rush, he returns to these twisting streets beside the river that are infected veins and arteries he must bleed.

At the rear of the cave, so deep in shadow he stumbles against it before he sees it, is a mound of rags. When he leans over it, speaking down into the darkness, he knows instantly this is the source of the terrible smell, that something once alive is rotting under the rags. He thinks of autumn leaves blown into mountainous, crisp heaps, the north wind cleansing itself and the city of summer. He thinks of anything, any image that will rescue him momentarily from the nauseating stench, postpone what he must do next. He screams no, no to himself as he blinks away his wife's face, the face of his daughter. His neighbors had promised to check on them, he hears news almost daily. There is no rhyme or reason in whom the fever takes, whom it spares, but he's in the city every day, exposed to its victims, breathing fetid air, touching corrupted flesh. Surely if someone in his family must die, it will be him. His clothes are drenched in vinegar, he sniffs the nostrum of gunpowder, bark, and asafetida in a bag pinned to his coat. He's prepared to purge and bleed himself, he's also ready and quite willing to forgo these precautions and cures if he thought surrendering his life might save theirs. He thinks and unthinks a picture of her hair, soft against his cheek, the wet warmth of his daughter's backside in the crook of his arm as he carries her to her mother's side where she'll be changed and fed. No. Like a choking mist, the smell of decaying flesh stifles him, forces him to turn away, once, twice, before he watches himself bend down into the brunt of it and uncover the sleepers.

Two Santo Domingan refugees, slave or free, no one knew for sure, inhabited this cellar. They had moved in less than a week before, the mother huge with child, man and woman both racked by fever. No one knows how long the couple's been unattended. There was shame in the eyes and voices of the few from whom he'd gleaned bits and pieces of the Santo Domingans' history. Since no one really knew them and few nearby spoke their language, no one was willing to risk, et cetera. Except for screams one night, no one had seen or heard signs of life. If he'd been told nothing about them, his nose would have led him here.

He winces when he sees the dead man and woman, husband and wife, not entwined as in some ballad of love eternal, but turned back to back, distance between them, as if the horror were too visible, too great to bear, doubled in the other's eyes. What had they seen before they flung away from each other? If he could, he would rearrange them, spare the undertakers this vision.

Rat feet and rat squeak in the shadows. He'd stomped his feet, shooed them before he entered, hollered as he threw back the covers, but already they were accustomed to his presence, back at work. They'd bite indiscriminately, dead flesh, his flesh. He curses and flails his staff against the rags, strikes the earthen floor to keep the scavengers at bay. Those sounds are what precipitate the high-pitched cries that first frighten him, then shame him, then propel him to a tall packing crate turned on its end, atop which another crate is balanced. Inside the second wicker container, which had imported some item from some distant place into this land, twin brown babies hoot and wail.

We are passing over the Dismal Swamp. On the right is the Appalachian range, some of the oldest mountains on earth. Once there were steep ridges and valleys all through here but erosion off the mountains created landfill several miles deep in places. This accounts for the rich loamy soil of the region. Over the centuries several southern states were formed from this gradual erosion. The cash crops of cotton and tobacco so vital to southern prosperity were ideally suited to the fertile soil.

Yeah, I nurse these old funky motherfuckers, all right. White people, specially old white people, lemme tell you, boy, them peckerwoods stink. Stone-dead fishy wet stink. Talking all the time bout niggers got BO. Well, white folks got the stink and gone, man. Don't be putting my hands on them, neither. Never. Huh uh. If I touch them, be wit gloves. They some nasty people, boy. And they don't be paying me enough to take no chances wit my health. Matter of fact they ain't paying me enough to really be expecting me to work. Yeah. Starvation wages. So I ain't hardly touching them. Or doing much else either. Got to smoke a cigarette to get close to some of them. Piss and shit theyselves like babies. They don't need much taking care anyway. Most of them three-quarters dead already. Ones that ain't is crazy. Nobody don't want them round, that's why they here. Talking to theyselves. Acting like they speaking to a roomful of people and not one soul in the ward paying attention. There's one old black dude, must be a hundred, he be muttering away to hisself nonstop everyday. Pitiful, man. Hope I don't never get that old. Shoot me, bro, if I start to getting old and fucked up in body and mind like them. Don't want no fools like me hanging over me when I can't do nothing no more for my ownself. Shit. They ain't paying me nothing so that's what I do. Nothing. Least I don't punch em or tease em or steal they shit like some the staff. And I don't pretend I'm God like these so-called professionals and doctors flittin round here drawing down that long bread. Naw. I just mind my own business, do my time. Cop a little TV, sneak me a joint when nobody's around. It ain't all that bad, really. Long as I ain't got no ole lady and crumb crushers. Don't know how the married cats make it on the little bit of chump change they pay us. But me, I'm free. It ain't that bad, really.

By the time his brother brought him the news of their deaths . . .

Almost an afterthought. The worst, he believed, had been overcome. Only a handful of deaths the last weeks of November. The city was recovering. Commerce thriving. Philadelphia must be revictualed, refueled, rebuilt, reconnected to the countryside, to markets foreign and domestic, to products, pleasures, and appetites denied during the quarantine months of the fever. A new century would soon be dawning. We must forget the horrors. The mayor proclaims a new day. Says let's put the past behind us. Of the eleven who died in the fire he said extreme measures were necessary as we cleansed ourselves of disruptive influences. The cost could have been much greater, he said I regret the loss of life, especially the half dozen kids, but I commend all city officials, all volunteers who helped return the city to the arc of glory that is its proper destiny.

When they cut him open, the one who decided to stay, to be a beacon and steadfast, they will find: liver (1,720 grams), spleen (150 grams), right kidney (190 grams), left kidney (180 grams), brain (1,450 grams), heart (380 grams), and right next to his heart, the miniature hand of a child, frozen in a grasping gesture, fingers like hard tongues of flame, still reaching for the marvel of the beating heart, fascinated still, though the heart is cold, beats not, the hand as curious about this infinite stillness as it was about thump and heat and quickness.

All Stories Are True
(1992)

All Stories Are True

And for fear of him the guards trembled
and became like dead men.

Matthew 28:4

My mother is standing on her porch. May 10, 1991. Early morning and the street is quiet now, as peaceful as it gets here, as peaceful as it always stays in other neighborhoods, invisible, not a half mile away behind the tree-topped ridge that separates Tokay, Susquehanna, Dunfermline, Seagirt from their neighbors to the west. The litany of streets always sweet on my tongue. I think I murmur their names, a silence unless you are inside my skull, sing them as a kind of background music that doesn't break the quiet of morning. If I'm not reciting them to myself, I hear the names anyway coming from somewhere else, a place that also knows what lies within the sound of these streets said to oneself again and again. Footsteps, voices, a skein of life dragged bead by bead through a soft needle's eye. And knows the names of streets can open like the gates of a great city, everyone who's ever inhabited the city, walked its streets, suddenly, like a shimmer, like the first notes of a Monk solo, breathing, moving, a world quickens as the gates swing apart. And knows my mother is not alone on her porch this May morning. Knows she hears beneath the stillness enveloping her the sound of street names, what is animated when they are recalled. The presence of other souls as palpable as light playing in the edges of her robe. Her mother and father and children. Her brother and sisters. Grands and great-grands. The man I have become and those whom I've lost becoming him. The song of street names a medium in which we all float, suspended, as if each of us is someone's precious, precious child who must never be allowed to slip from the arms cradling, rocking. And knows my mother is listening to time, time voiced in no man-made measurements of days or minutes or years, time playing as it always must, background or foreground or taking up all the space we have, a tape of the street names chanted that releases every Homewood footstep she's ever heard or dreamed.

I'm afraid for her. Experience one of those moments of missing her intensely, her gone, final goodbyes said, though she is here, just ten feet away, through the front door screen, framed by two of the rusty wrought-iron columns supporting the roof. A moment where fear of losing her overwhelms me to such an extent that I am bereft, helpless, unconsoled even by her presence, one price I pay for other moments when she's thousands of miles away and I've needed her and she is there, *there* beside me. After nine months of chemo her hair has grown in again, softer, curlier. Many shades of bushy gray and a crown of lighter hair, nearly white, nearly spun to invisibility by morning. I'm aware as I seldom am of her dimensions, how tall, how wide, how much this woman on the porch with her newborn's hair weighs. I need what is tangible, no matter how small she turns out to be, to offset words like *frail* and *vulnerable* I can't help saying to myself, words popping up though I try not to think them. I hate words with the power to take her away. *Frail. Old.* The effort of denying them makes her disappear anyway. My eyes cross Tokay, counting cobblestones as they go, remarking the incredible steepness of the street slanting out of my field of vision, the broken curbs and littered gutters, settling on the gigantic tree islanded in the delta where Seagirt and Tokay converge and Bricelyn begins. If the downtown wedge of skyscrapers where three rivers meet is the city's Golden Triangle, this could be its Green Triangle. A massive tree centuries old holds out against the odds here across from my mother's house, one of the biggest trees in Pittsburgh, anchored in a green tangle of weeds and bushes, trunk thick as a Buick, black as night after rain soaks its striated hide. Huge spread of its branches canopies the foot of the hill where the streets come together. Certain times of day in summer it shades my mother's front porch. If it ever tore loose from its moorings, it would crush her house like a sledgehammer. As big as it is, its roots must run under her cellar. The sound of it drinking, lapping nourishment deep underground is part of the quiet when her house is empty. How the tree survived a city growing around it is a mystery. For years no more than a twig, a sapling, a switch someone could have snapped off to beat a balky animal, swat a child's behind. I see a dark fist exploding through the asphalt, thrusting to the sky, the fingers opening, multiplying, fanning outward to form a vast umbrella of foliage. The arm behind it petrifies, other thick limbs burst from knots of hardened flesh, each one duplicating the fan of leaves, the delicate network of branches, thinning, twisting as they climb higher and farther from the source. Full-blown in a matter of seconds, ready to stand here across from my mother's house forever, till its time to be undone in the twinkling of an eye, just the way it arrived.

I didn't say any of this to my mother as I pushed through the screen door with my cup of coffee to join her on the porch. Then it was just one quiet thing after the other, a matter of seconds, the sight of her standing still, her back to me, me thinking thoughts that flashed at warp speed but would take forever to unpack, the door creaking, her turning slowly towards the noise, *You up, baby,* a quick welcoming smile before she turns back to whatever it was, wherever she was gazing when I saw her first, small, bathed in the soft, remorseless light of morning, when I heard the sound of Homewood street names playing, transforming a commonplace scene into something else, restoring the invisible omnipresence of time, the enabling medium, what brought you to this moment and will carry you away, how things begin and end, always, you about to step out onto your mother's porch, catching her staring off at something, somewhere, home again, morning again, steamy coffee mug in one hand, sure of what you will do next, your fingers press the doorframe, pushing, absolutely unsure, fearing what will happen next, wondering what's in her eyes, behind them this morning in May, and which ghosts crowd the porch, regretting her privacy you are invading with yours. Who will the two of you together summon if you steal her attention, if you are ready and willing to offer yours, if you can break away from the tune playing over and over in your head and maybe in hers of the street names, sorrow and loss in every syllable when you say them to yourself the way you must to locate yourself here, back home in Pittsburgh this morning, Tioga Susquehanna Seagirt Cassina, praying your mother won't move, won't be gone before you reach her.

You hug each other. Not hard, not soft. Briefly. Long enough to remember everything.

I love my flowers.

A guy was selling them in the gas station. At Braddock and Penn. You know. The two big stations across from one another. A white guy in Mickey Mouse bermudas. He said these hadn't been out in the sun. Too much direct sun's not good for them, he said. These were shoved under a folding table he had set up. Pansies or some other kind, I forget. They just looked pretty to me and I thought you'd like something pretty and growing.

Impatiens. They're beautiful.

And you already have a hook by the door to hang them.

I used to keep a few little plants out here. Then one night just before Easter the flowers grew feet. Woke up one morning and everybody's flowers were gone. I only had a couple nice little plants. Nothing special. But they were gone just like everybody else's up and down both blocks. Flowers grew feet that night and walked away.

You mean somebody ripped off people's flowers.

Should have heard Eva. See the house with the green-and-white aluminum awning. That's Eva's. You know who I mean, don't you. Small brown-skinned woman always dressed nice. Used to ride the bus to town with me to work. Eva had big-time flowers on her porch. Gone that morning like everybody else's and Eva's fit to be tied. She said she was marching down to the corner and beat the black off him with her own two hands if she caught him with one of her flowers. Said she'd know her flowers if she saw them, pot or no pot or new pot she'd know her own flowers and strangle him with her bare hands if she caught him with her flowers.

Somebody selling flowers on the corner.

Right there on Bennett. Day after the night the flowers walked.

No. You got to be kidding.

Huh uh. Some guy down there big as life selling flowers. Had his stand right on Bennett and Bricelyn. No pots. Dog probably sold people's pots somewhere else. He wasn't completely crazy. A flower sale day after everybody's flowers disappeared off their porches.

He's lucky he didn't get shot.

Eva said she was going down there and look for her flowers. Tear him up if she found any. But how could you know for sure. I kinda looked for mine when I passed by that way, but he had everything tied up in plastic bags of dirt so how you supposed to tell. Flowers are flowers. Eva swore she'd know hers, but I didn't notice any commotion down there. Did his business all day. Gone next morning. Walked away like the flowers walked. Never saw the guy before. Don't care if I ever see him again.

A brazen brother.

That's how they do us. Steal anything and everything. Stained-glass windows out the church. I worry about one of them getting into the house.

Sorry-assed junkies.

Dope turns them crazy. Knock you down as soon as look at you. Kids you've watched grow up around here. I don't believe they intend to hurt anybody, but when that sickness is down on them, my, my, my, they'll do anything. I shudder when I think of your brother crazy that way. Him hurting someone or someone hurting him. Those so-called friends of his he'd bring home. Yes ma'am and no ma'am me and all the time I know their dope eyes counting up what they could come back and steal. Tommy knew it, too. God have mercy on me for saying this about my own son, but I believe now that's why he brought some of them around. To steal from me.

Coffee's not hot. Not cold. I try the porch railing with my hand. It feels solid enough. I remember helping Wade from next door mix concrete for the porch. The good feel of doing hard work with my brothers, the three of us, Dave, Ote, and me, Wade's crew sweating into the wet cement, the moment during one cold Iron City break we all felt the presence of the brother missing who should be with us building this porch for our mother. I sit on the rail anchored in our concrete. Ask about Wade.

Poor man had a tough year. Dog died, wife died, he hit that paperboy. Old Wade was way down. Said he wouldn't have made it if it hadn't been for the boy's parents. They didn't blame him. People who witnessed the accident said Wade never had a chance. Going normal speed. The boy rode his bike straight into Wade's car. And thank goodness Wade was on his way to work. So he hadn't been drinking. Wade said if the parents had blamed him for the boy's death, he wouldn't have pulled through.

Dog died. Wife died. That's a rather strange order to put things in, Mother Dear.

You know what I mean. Didn't mean one thing worse than the other or first things first. You know I didn't mean anything like that.

I'm just teasing.

Teasing your fuddle-brained old mother. I know. I know most the time nobody understands what I'm talking about. Half the time don't know my own self. Pay me no mind. I didn't intend any disrespect. Wade loved Nadine dearly and misses her terribly. Loved that raggedy, stump-tailed dog, too. It was just one terrible thing after another falling on the poor man. I don't know how he survived. Thought for a while he was going to drink himself to death. But he'd clean up every morning and drive off to work. Wade's a strong man. A good man, too, in his way.

Sounds like he was Job last year.

I prayed for him. All alone in his house. I know how that feels, rattling around in a house all by yourself.

The porch is holding up fine, isn't it. A little crack by the glider and one where the steps come up but this porch will be here awhile.

Youall did quite a job.

Wade the only one who knew what he was doing. Me and Dave and Ote supplied the muscle.

It was one hot day. I was worried about youall. None of you used to working out in the broiling sun that way.

Little sweat mixed in the cement makes it stronger, last longer. Why you think the Pyramids been standing all these centuries. Good African blood gluing the stones.

What do you think about this idea going around that Egyptians were black.

Better late than never, Mom. I guess. Most of them a mixture of black Africans and brown Asiatics. Look at what part of the world we're talking about. Look at them today. Not exactly a matter of color, though. More about culture. People migrating and invading and mixing since the dawn of time. Everybody's a mongrel. The wonder is it's taken this long for the obvious to be said out loud. Wonder is it's 1991 and the obvious still resisted in some quarters.

I try to change the faces of the people in the Bible. I can't do it. They still look like the faces I saw in Sunday school, in the little picture books we had to study from. No black faces, except for that one dark wise man with Jesus in the manger. When I close my eyes, I still can't put black faces on the Bible people.

Well, we must of had the same books when I was in Sunday school. Maybe that's one of the reasons you had to drag me. Child abuse every Sunday morning.

Bit more child abuse might not have been a bad idea. I felt terrible knowing I was raising a bunch of little heathens.

Anyway, what I started to say is we used those same jive comic books, but the Bible people never were white to me. They never had a color, really. The funny-looking robes and beards and turbans stuck in my mind. But as far as color, well it's Reverend Felder I think of when I think of Bible days and Bible stories. Him up on the pulpit of AME Zion shouting and strutting and banging his big fist. Old Frank Felder black as coal and that's the color of everything he preached. Like his voice tar-brushed the Bible. If the faces in the books weren't black it didn't matter cause black was in charge, telling the story.

I did think of Job more than once when I prayed for Wade. And I guess Job surely did have Wade's face and Wade's face, God bless him, surely isn't white. Poor man bent down under all his burdens. I needed the story of Job to understand how Wade could handle it. Strength to bear up to the worst, no matter what, has to come from somewhere. I needed God and Job. Needed them both to understand how Wade survived what he did.

You know, Mom, people look at you and what you've had to deal with and you're just as much a miracle to them as you say Wade is to you.

God doesn't give you more than you can handle.

Not everybody has that kind of god.

I worry about your brother. Where will he turn now. He's still a Muslim, isn't he. He still goes by his Muslim name.

Told me not long ago he's not as active in the group as he once was. But he does pray. Not as regular as he once did, he says, but he keeps the faith.

I hope he has something. Because this last blow. The pardons board turning him down again without a hearing. He believed they'd almost have to let him go. Didn't see how they could say no.

They say whatever they want to say.

Other times he held something back. In his heart he hoped they'd give him a chance, believed he'd earned a chance, but like you say. He knows they don't have to answer to anybody. Do what they want to do. Every time but this he'd held something back to fight the no.

He's in danger now. Like when he was first locked up and wild and determined to tear the prison apart with his bare hands. Worse now because he's on his own. No crew of young wild ones like him fighting back. All he has is us. And we're out here. All he has really is the chance anybody has. To keep pushing on and try to make something of a life, whatever.

Don't think I can go with you today. I'm too shaky today to face that evil prison. Tell him I'll come next week with Denise and Chance.

Don't want to leave you if you're feeling badly.

I'll be all right here. You go talk to your brother. It's just one of those days. I'll take my pills and sit myself down awhile. I'll get it together, Babe.

Is something specific hurting.

Just one of those not so good days. I'm shaky. I have bad days every now and then. Hug him for me. Tell him I love him. I'll be fine here.

I rise with her. The porch one of those quiet, extrawide, featureless elevators in the hospital where she goes Tuesdays for treatments. Below us the map of streets, veins, arteries. We wait on this floor, at this height. The porch rocks like a Ferris wheel car stopped at the apex of the ride. Perhaps the huge motor's broken. Cable snapped. Gears stripped. We wait and listen for music to drift up from the streets.

My brother's arms are prison arms. The kind you see in the street that clue you where a young brother's been spending his time. Bulging biceps, the rippled look of ropy sinews and cords of muscle snaking around the bones. Skinned. Excess flesh boiled away in this cauldron. Must be noisy as a construction site where the weightlifters hang out in the prison yard. Metal clanking. Grunts and groans. Iron pumped till shoulders and chests swell to the bursting point. Men fashioning arms thick enough to wrestle fate, hold off the pressure of walls and bars always bearing down. Large. Big. Nothing else to do all day. Size one measure of time served. Serious time. Bodies honed to stop-time perfection, beyond vulnerability and pain. I see them in their sun-scoured playground sprawled like dazed children.

Hot today in the visiting area, fiery heat like the day we paddled round in Wade's cement. Row row row your concrete boat. It ain't heavy, it's your brother.

Hey, bro, I'd be the last one to deny I'm fucked up. We both know good and well I've had problems all my life doing what I been supposed to do. Here I sit in this godforsaken hole if anybody needs proof I couldn't handle. Something's wrong wit me, man, but the people who runs this joint, something's real wrong wit them, too.

Pressure in my face muscles from the permanent squint I'm wearing to keep sun out of my eyes. A mask of age. Forehead furrowed, cheeks tensed and hollow, eyes narrow, tiny creases incised at their corners, vision dimmed by the hazy porch of lashes and brow pouting to shade the eyes. Sun cooks my right side. I look past my brother to avoid the direct glare, beyond him to the bricks of the visiting room wall, the glass doors opening to this roofless enclosure where we sit. I listen closely but he's a blur in the center of the space across the round table where my eyes would naturally focus if I wasn't hiding from the sun. I don't need to see him. He will be wearing the same face I am. Pinched and sweaty. Older than it should be. Glazed eyes seeking something other than me to fix on, so what I say is a voice-over, as his is to me, listening while I tour the stones stacked forty feet high that surround us, the glass doors black as water, reflecting scraps of the yard.

Motherfuckers don't say shit for three months. Know I'm on pins and needles every minute of every day since I filed my commutation papers, but don't nobody say one god-blessed single solitary word good or bad for three months. I'm going crazy wit the waiting. And too scared to ask anybody what's happening cause you know how that works. Ask a question and they say *no* just to spite you, just to get you out their face. Limbo, man, for three months. Then last week I'm by the desk in the visiting room waiting for Denise and Chance and the guard at the desk hands me the phone, call for you. Lieutenant's on the line and he says to me Board turned you down. Tells me I can cancel my visit and speak to him now or check by his office later. That's it. Boom. Turned down.

Like getting hit in the chest wit a hammer. Couldn't breathe, man. Couldn't catch my breath for three days. Still can't breathe right. Felt like somebody had taken a hammer and whammed me in the heart.

No warning. No explanation. I'm standing in the visiting room trying to catch my breath and Denise and the baby be in here in a minute. Dying, man, and ready to die. My life was over soon's the lieutenant said Board turned you down.

Weird thing is the night before I had a dream. Woke me up. Couldn't go back to sleep. Dreamed I was in one the offices around here and my papers was on the desk. My papers. What I'd been waiting for all these months and finally there they sat. On top the desk and nobody else around. All I had to do was peep at the last sheet, right. There it'd be in black and white. Yes or no. Couldn't believe it be this easy. So much waiting and praying and begging and cursing boneheads out cause they wouldn't give me a clue. Wouldn't tell me nothing, nothing, and now alls I had to do was turn to the last page and I'd know.

Awful thing was I already knew the answer. Couldn't peep at the bottom sheet cause I already knew. Knew in my heart so I kept standing, staring, too scared to read what I knew I'd find.

Right when the dream ended I did look. Couldn't hold out. Looked and saw *denied* stamped on the last page. Whole dream came back to me soon as I put down that phone in the visiting room. Been *denied* all along. And all along I guess I knowed.

Nothing for three months then I'm waiting for a visit from my old lady and son and I get a phone call. Turned you down. Bam. Take that. Like a hammer in my chest. Tell me that ain't evil, man. Saying no is bad enough. They don't have to treat people like dirt saying it.

My own fault I'm in here. I know I done some bad things. I'm in here, man, doing my time. Uh huh. Hard time. Lots of time for doing wrong. But they treat us like dog shit in here and that's wrong, too. Guys get killed in here. Go crazy. But nobody cares. Long as they keep us locked up they can do us any way they want. Figure we in here, so they don't owe us nothing. But wrong is wrong, ain't it. Just cause we down, is it right to keep on kicking us. Guys get meaner and crazier in here. Every day you see the ones can't take it slipping farther and farther off. Distance in their eyes, bro. Ain't nobody home in them eyes. They shuffle around here like ghosts. Stop speaking to people. Stop keeping theyselves clean. Gone, man. If you been around here any length of time you seen it happen to a lot of guys. You understand how easy it is to tune out and drop off the edge into your own little world. Another planet. You see why guys go off. Why they so cold and mean if they ever hit the street again.

Now our eyes are meeting. The sun's part of the meeting. A sting, a rawness you try to blink away but only make worse as sweat drips and irritates. Only one other table occupied when you sat down at yours. Now no free ones. The visiting room wall forms one end of the outdoor enclosure. Its other three walls rise forty feet at least, smooth blocks of stone topped by razor wire, a walkway, a guard tower in the far corner. At the base of the sheer stone walls fresh plantings, shrubbery dense and spiky bordering the concrete pavement. A few trees, also recently planted, have been spaced along the inside of the walls, each in a square collar of earth the size of a missing section of paving. You register these details for later. You think it will be crucial at some point to remember this yard exactly. You are uncertain why. Then, still listening to what he's saying, you realize how little of your brother's life you can share. This yard, detail by detail, is part of what you do share. You would be compromised if you come away with only a vague recollection. To fight this place, to force it to disappear, you must not miss anything. The map of it in your head makes its horror real, but also is what you must depend upon to plan an escape.

I think I'm finally beginning to understand why they so evil to us. They're scared of the black man. Really scared. More scared than I ever knew. More scared than they know themselves. When I first come in the joint I knew something about the fear. Knew we had something on them. Wild as we was we didn't give them no chance to run game on us. We had learned the hard way coming up running the streets what they thought of us. Crazy killers. Animals. Dope fiends. Niggers you got to lock up or kill before they kill you. That was the deal. So we played the hand dealed us. We was stone outlaws. Fuck wit us you better be prepared to take us down cause if you don't we coming down on you. I was young and hot-blooded and that cowboy-and-Indian gangster shit okay wit me. Bring it on. Let's git down and dirty. Rock and roll. We saw fear in their eyes. We fucked with them to keep it there. But they didn't kill me and, all praises to Allah, I didn't kill a guard. I changed. Wasn't really me in the first place. I was just playing the outlaw role I thought I needed to play to survive the joint. I changed but they stayed scared of me. And they hate me for keeping them scared. My buddy Rick. You remember Ricky from up the hill on Tokay. Took him dying to make me really understand what I'm telling you now. You know he got sick in here. Come in when I did, one of our wild bunch. Take no shit from nobody, none of us. But Rick changed, too. Wised up. Then he got sick, real sick, like I said. They wouldn't treat him. Wouldn't try to find out what was wrong. Why should they. If you scared of some-body, why you gon try and help them, fix them up, make them well so they can jump in your chest again. Huh uh. Ricky just rotted. Chased him away from the clinic. Or handed him a aspirin. You know the story. He shrunk down to nothing. Ninety-three goddamn pounds. Finally they had to stick him in the clinic. Let him rot in the clinic till his mother got to some-body and they transferred Ricky out of here and chained him to a bed in a locked ward in a real hospital and diagnosed stomach cancer. By that time Ricky too far gone to help. Drugged him up so he just nodded away. Didn't know people when they came to see him his mother said. Said he was so weak they unchained him. A cop in the room when she visited, but Ricky just laying there. A pitiful sight, plugged up to machines, not even recognizing his own mama. She was in a chair beside his bed on a Sunday she said it must have been Sunday cause she'd been there a couple hours that afternoon and she works six days a week so it must of been Sunday and Rick been sleeping like he always did the whole time so she was just sitting half sleep herself when Ricky's hand reached over and patted hers where she'd laid it on the blanket. She couldn't believe it she said. Tears started rolling down her cheeks she told me because what his touching her meant she thought was that he was ready to die. Too far gone to get better so she just knew Rick using his last strength to say goodbye.

The cop in the room had a different idea. See, he was still scared of Ricky so Ricky moving that hand meant Ricky was dangerous again. Cop jumped up and started refastening the chains.

None of it makes any goddamn sense. Who they keep. Who they let go. Never give you any reasons. They don't have to give reasons for what they do. They just do it. Denied. They stamp your papers *denied* and that's all the reason they got to give. Denied.

One the dudes they didn't deny, a white boy, he busted out of here not too long ago. Busted out and stayed out till he got tired of running and turned hisself in. Escaped the joint, man, and now they granted him a hearing with the full parole board. What kind of sense do it make.

Maybe you ought to arrange a little vacation for yourself before you apply next time.

Don't think I ain't thought about it. Been keeping my eye on that tree over there. Shimmy up, leap over to the wall. Gone.

Not much of a tree yet.

Yeah, well, it's still pretty scraggly. But I been watching it.

Long time before those branches grow as high as the wall. And you'd still have a pretty good leap.

Guys in here would try. Plenty of them. Scoot up that tree in a minute. Do a super monkey jump.

Branches awful skinny at the top. Even for a monkey.

Right. Right. Skinny enough so you get up there it'll bend to the wall. Ride it like a surfboard.

You got it all figured out, bro.

Told you I've been keeping my eye on that little tree.

This is where you and Denise were when the leaf got out.

At the table closest to the wall. In the shade. Uh huh. We was sitting there but by the time that leaf blew up near the top of the wall both of us on our feet cheering. Other people had got into it, too. Saw what we was watching and that leaf had a whole lot of fans when it sailed over the wall. Would have thought people cheering for the Steelers or somebody's lottery number hit. Wasn't nothing but a leaf me and Denise noticed that had started blowing higher and higher. Each time the wind would grab it, it would circle up higher. Over in that corner like it was riding a draft or a whirlwind or some damn something keeping it up. You know how something dumb catch your attention and you can't let it go. Leaf kept spinning round and round and rising each time it spinned. Like on a yo-yo. After watching it a while you know that leaf has flying out of here on its mind. Every little whip and twist and bounce starts to matter. Before you know it you're blowing with your breath to help it over the wall and you know something inside you will be hurt if that silly leaf can't finish what it started. Whole visiting yard whooping and hollering when it finally blew over the wall.

Denise cried. And damn. It was everything I could do to keep the tears out of my eyes. Everybody in here needed that leaf to go free.

Kind of magic, man, if you was here in the yard and seen it. Know I sound dumb trying to tell you how it was. But that's how it was. Specially for Denise and me cause earlier in the visit she told me she was carrying my baby. We'd already picked names: Jazz Melody for a girl, Chance Mandela if it was a boy. Couldn't help taking the leaf as a sign.

Chance because the odds were stacked against him ever being conceived, let alone born.

Million to one, bro. And Mandela cause Mandela's my man. You know. In the joint like me but still taking care of business.

Chance Mandela. When Mom called and told me he was born the day after Mandela walked out of prison, I couldn't believe it.

Little day-late rascal. But my little guy was close. Real close. Bust out right behind Nelson.

The leaf, the day, the name. Pretty amazing, little brother. Has to be a sign. Gives you something special to fight for. A son, a family. You've come too far to let this denial turn you around.

I think a lot about it. Everything, I mean. When I'm alone at night in my cell. Ain't never really alone no more since they double-bunking everybody, but you know what I mean. When I think about giving up, truth is, nothing but me can pull me back from the edge. I got to do it for me. No matter how much I love Chance and Denise and Mom and youall, nothing, not all the love in the world can fill the hole that opens up when I get down, really down. Only way to save myself is to do it for me. I got to be the reason. I got to be worth saving. Can't live a life for nobody else. Nobody can live one for me. You understand what I'm saying.

I'm trying.

The leaf. I told you how it finally blowed free overtop the wall. Couldn't see it no more. Denise grabbed my hand. She was crying and we was bouncing up and down. People shouting. Some even clapped. But you know something. I'm gonna tell you something I don't tell nobody when I tell about the leaf. The dumb thing blew back in here again.

Backseat

We made love in the belly of the whale. More times than I could count I'd laid her across the funky backseat of Uncle Mac's 1946 Lincoln Continental rusting in the backyard of 712 Copeland Street and opened her fat thighs, jiggly as they wanted to be, but like a compass too, hinged, calibrated so you can keep track of how far they're spreading, a school kind of feeling, a lesson in this thing you're doing to her and you will be tested later, spread her legs and hiked her bottom to one end of the seat so I could crawl in after her and draw the rear door shut behind me. No telling who might look out the kitchen window. What would they think bare frog legs poked out the gaping door of Uncle Mac's pride and joy gathering rust and dust now like Mac himself in the basement playing with his electric trains.

Her name was Tommy. The Lincoln Continental gunmetal red in its prime. Short for Thomasina. A silver-spoked spare wheel attached to the back bumper lengthened the dream car, already long as a limousine, a foot and a half. I'd heard someone say, Ain't she pretty today. Four portholes on each gleaming flank of the hood for extra, nautical elegance. Huh uh. Not in that dirty old thing. Red leather interior. Buck Rogers instrument panel. I'd stolen the blanket over where Italians live from a clothesline after dark, when everybody in my neighborhood knew better than to leave their wash hanging. See how nice it is now. Uncle Mac sported a white yachtsman's cap with a fictitious ship's name in gold stitched on a blue badge above a shiny visor seamed and edged with gold braid. Sail on. Sail on, Mac, with your bad self. She couldn't have been all that ugly. Didn't my mother call her pretty dressed up one Easter in her best. I'm not making this shit up, man. Really don't care what you think, really. Look who's talking, anyway. Many times as I've seen you slinking out the side door of the Bellmawr show with some boogy-bear. Trying to hide and pretend she ain't with you. A fine ride in its day. King of the highway. It was the first year Lincoln put out the Continental, I think. Uncle Mac said when you're old enough to get a license, you can have it. Fix it up. Drive it away. I'm through with it. Just lean on back, girl. Cock your leg up out the way. Hook your heel on the front seatback. Won't give you no baby that way. You be wide open I just be fucking your pussy.

I do. I do. I do do do wop love you.

Don't get bashful with me. No need in you trying to blush. You know you wasn't bashful and shy then. Trying to get me out in Mister Mackinley Overton's nasty old car.

It was like the compasses in plastic trays at school. Most of them busted. Either so tight you can barely prize them open or just flap cause the hinge pin bracket's gone. Start out tight and stiff you push the legs apart till she loosens up, little quivers start in her thighs, her butt muscles pump then she starts doing the Booty-green and it's soft and soppy where your hands up under her and the legs moving on their own now, beating on you in the dark, clamping, dancing.

I hadn't seen her in fifteen years, hadn't touched her in thirty-five, but to-day she decided to remind me and my main man Scott of the good old days.

He used to beg me go out there with him. Didn't always look like I look now, did I. Been big as a house after my kids start coming. Daytime, night-time, didn't make him no nevermind. You know you did. You know. You know. You know you was a dog. Standing here all tongue-tied like you don't remember.

Scott laughs. Well, did you or didn't you, homeboy.

Man. You know after all these years. Be damned if I can remember, man. Pittsburgh all those years ago. Growing up, trying to get slick.

I wink at him. Shield my mouth and lip-synch *Yes. Yes.* So he can read me and she might. And then she says, Good too, wasn't it, and laughs and we all crack up. *Yes. Yes.*

I hear the latest news from Pittsburgh in a phone call from my mother. Grandma holds on. Not eating. Little sip of water or coffee. She seems not to be in pain. Oxygen tube in her nose. She talks, then drifts off. To rest. To sleep. Very weak, very thin. The doctor said, I'm doing nothing to keep her here, nothing that will take her away. Grandma is ninety-eight. Her children were Edgar, Catherine, Eugene. Eugene killed on the island of Guam in the Pacific, a few days after the war with Japan declared over. Sniper or booby trap. Her husbands were Mackinley Overton, the Reverend J. R. Morehead, Otis Fallen, and the first, my grandfather, Harry Wideman, sire of her three children, including Edgar, my father.

I cannot close the great distance between us except by letting myself get too close. Too close means imagining myself beside her bed in the hospital room in Pittsburgh and holding her hand and dealing with the meltdown a touch, flesh to flesh, would begin.

Skin and bones. She's down to skin and bone. Wasting away. We thought she'd live forever. She'd be sick, real sick but she always came back. Flesh has deserted her now. Shrunken down to a whisper under the hospital sheets. She is a large-framed, big-boned woman. Have the bones lost their density, their heft, the power to support her upright, propel her through the world. Flesh is baggage. What good would it do her now. Yet my mother's description makes my grandmother too little, too frail for the journey ahead of her. I don't like to think of her weak and exposed. To survive the passage, she needs padding, meat on her bones. She's not afraid of anything. She carries herself with great independence, dignity. Her style is to be polite, soft-spoken, and sometimes, around white people, invisible, but her manners are superfluous to the iron core of her will. A cover story. A means of getting by, making ends meet. She couldn't be a scared person and remain as tough as she is. Her height, her bearing protect her. I don't like to think of her lying in a bed, reduced in scale. There will be long darkness and cold and shocks of many kinds to meet. I want her robust, those wide hips and broad shoulders bumpered with flesh. She would handle whatever she had to meet, but it worries and hurts me that she's starting out the journey so small.

Pittsburgh is a city of hills piggybacked on other hills. A jumble of streets that climb, jut, slant, crisscross, loop, jook, dead-end as if once there was a plan, an immense symmetrical mound arching toward heaven and houses in neat rows terracing the hump as it thrust upward, but one day the whole thing karate-chopped. Everything split, crumbled, slid. Furrows yawned, gullies opened, houses, trees, streets were stranded on precipitous inclines, the original, stately, turtle-back shape unrecognizable. The whole mess on edge, barely clinging to forty-five-degree hillsides, resigned to the next convulsion that will pitch what's left into the rivers that gird it.

If you're raised in Pittsburgh you grow up aware of edges, ups and downs, the give-and-take-back economic rhythms of the mills, boom-and-bust cycles, the crazy quilt patchwork of borders and turf defined by bridges, trolley car tracks, skin color, language, hills and valleys. People of every imaginable ethnic origin, religion, race, balkanized by the fractured terrain into clans, neighborhoods, and ghettoes isolated as islands in the sea.

My grandmother took me for a ride on the Incline, a funicular railway connecting the lower west end of the city to the heights of Mount Washington. At night in the Incline car, gliding, rattling up the mountainside, Pittsburgh spreading out beneath us, I was mesmerized by the tapestry of lights that winked and twinkled brighter than stars, more real than stars because I could hear them humming and sang back to them, a little Jiminy Cricket my grandmother told me years later, me up on my knees against the seat back, face pressed to the window of the cable car that would have been from another perspective part of the spectacle I was enjoying, an elevator buzzed up to the top floor of Mount Washington, a spark escaping from the profusion of illuminated bridges, highways, chains of auto lights, the wedge of skyscrapers jammed where three rivers—Ohio, Monongahela, Allegheny—converge, turning night to almost day.

My grandmother smiling at the other passengers in the cagelike car, wondering if any of them mind the noise the little boy is making. That's John, my first grandson. I call him Doot. Little Scooddely-Doot chirping like a cricket at the city lights. She wouldn't have spoken aloud to anyone except me and that would be a whisper, close to my ear, twisting in her seat, leaning to peer over my shoulder and see what I was singing at out there. Lookit all the pretty lights pretty lights pretty lights she said I said over and over. Lights lights lights, making up a one-word song and chanting it at the black window. Glowing in the darkness the city before the fall. The city they'd been planning when all the broken hills were still one perfect ark. Lights restored that vision, and I couldn't open my eyes wide enough to take it all in. So I opened my mouth, heart, the works. I remember my grandmother's hand opening, squeezing mine, my weight shifting back off my bare knees that had been pressed into the weave of the seat cushions. Then as I turned again to the window our eyes met. I pointed to the faces suspended out there, ancient versions of hers, mine, hovering in some other place we were passing on our way to the crest of the mountain.

Distance always compounded of distance and closeness, one impossible without the other, you know you are in one city because you are not in another. Distance expresses itself that way. She is in Pittsburgh and you aren't there. Distance announces itself as the necessity of a journey. Of choices. Either go or stay. Plane or car. Time, money trade-offs. Reckonings. Calculations. Everything intervenes. Distance a fence and closeness the green on the other side, always greener, closer because it's on the other side.

Either go today while she's still alive or wait till someone phones to say she's gone. Then go. Go then to gather with the family, one last communal ritual signifying closeness in spite of unbreachable distance. Wait too long and the choice will be snatched out of my hands, or that will seem to be the case, but it's really not, because I know better, know now that I'm deciding as I wait and write.

She's my last surviving grandparent. Two died, Harry Wideman and Freeda French when I was grown, their deaths announced to me long distance over the phone by my mother. John French, Freeda's husband, the first grandparent lost. He was sitting on the toilet, knees rammed against the bathtub rim, a large man in a bathroom too small for him, much too small for a family of six, my grandmother Freeda, my mother, Betty, and her siblings Martha, Geral, and Otis, a tiny bathroom at the top of steep hallway stairs (I'd hear my aunts fly in from work or shopping, hit the front door and make a beeline straight up the steps and slam the bathroom door behind them before the front door stopped shaking), John French was sitting in that bathroom when his heart stopped and he slumped into the space between toilet and tub, unable to fall further, his knees wedged, one arm slung across the sink, no room for him to slide down further into that tight space he cursed every time he slipped off his suspenders and dropped his trousers, but far enough down, big man that he was, none of the women in the house could get him unstuck. Geral ran hollering for Mr. Clark next door. Mrs. Clark drove off for my mother while her husband, Fred, with the women's help propped and dragged my grandfather from the bathroom to the bedroom and laid John French across his son's bed.

I was ten then, going on eleven and it was wintertime. We were hustled into the Clarks' car and driven through icy, snowbanked streets to the house on Finance Street where John and Freeda French had raised their children, where my mother had been forced to raise the five of us when there was no money or no love between her and my father. Going home in a way, my second home on Finance Street in Homewood, but a sudden trip, with no warning, no explanation, a storm-burst of screams and tears and tight-lipped composure, my mother's pale face paler, her eyes red, nothing to say to any of us as we were bundled and bundled ourselves quickly into whatever heavy clothing she grabbed first from the hall closet. No careful layering and buttoning and zippers pulled tight to chin, galoshes fastened toe to shin, scarves wrapped so we were mummified against the cold, the coughs and sneezing and fevers she scared us into believing, because she believed, might steal us away. No. We were dressed helter-skelter in a hurry in anybody's mixmatch stuff. And that was so different, so unlike my mother I knew something terrible had happened. It was that rush into the winter streets, a deep stillness in my mother I knew I should not violate, the questions I couldn't ask, the foolishness and fear hitting me I knew better than to act out in the ride to Finance Street, the firmness and distance of adult voices that said youall sit down here and be quiet, Daddyjohn is upstairs very sick and the hurrying overhead back and forth across the ceiling, the sound of Mr. Clark from next door plodding down the hall stairs, his sigh and low, weary muttering, I'm sorry Miss French sorry sorry, and the front door eased shut behind him and one of my aunts flying back up the steps as soon as Mr. Clark was gone, that's how the death of John French, first of my grandparents to go, was announced.

Tunnels, bridges, tubes, inclines, trolley tracks, giddy banks of steps are the connectors, arteries joining busted pieces of a city. Each has distinctive physical attributes but is also immaterial, a metaphor that contains a message about distance and how we negotiate it, how we build things to embody our deepest desires and fears, arrangements of steel, concrete, stone, timber that fashion us as we use them, speak a language we must learn in order to reach where we're going. Inside the earth, suspended above it, gliding over it as if we've conjured the secret of gravity, control the fickleness of a spinning planet, lift our feet while the earth rotates like a roulette wheel and then set them down again in a different place.

My father's dead brother Eugene, lost in one war, says this about the latest: They're crowing now about winning. You watch. In a while it'll turn to Jim Crowing. Then what will those black boys think who risked their lives and lost their lives to keep a grin on the face of the man who rode Willie Horton bareback to the White House. Twelve, fourteen cops on TV beating that boy with sticks long as their legs. Our young men not even home good from the war yet. What you think they be thinking when they see a black man beat to his knees by a whole posse of cracker cops. Somebody ought to tell them boys, ought to have told me, it happens every time. After every war. Oh yeah. They tell us march off and fight in some jungle or desert. Be heroes and save our behinds. We'll be here rooting for you. But when you come back across the pond, if you make it back, don't forget where you are. You ain't no hero here. You know what you are here. And just in case you don't remember, here's a little reminder. A forget-me-not upside your nappy head. Bop bop a loo bop. Bop bam boom. Rolling around on the pavement beat half to death just in time to welcome our boys home.

I once asked my grandmother Martha to talk to me about her earliest memories. Storytellers on my mother's side of the family had supplied me with bucket-loads of family history, but I knew next to nothing about my father's mother, little about Harry Wideman, his father. Later I would travel to Greenwood, South Carolina, and begin researching my father's father's origins. My father's mother's roots were closer at hand but remained uninvestigated, a few notes at the back of a journal I recorded from one sustained conversation with her about her past, if twenty minutes or so can be considered "sustained." She said her people came from Wrightsville, Pennsylvania, near York. Baers and Lawsons on her father's side, Johnsons and Wrights on her mother's. Though she was called Martha Lawson, Rutledge her real name she said. Her father a white man named Rutledge. She didn't use the word *illegitimate*, but when I asked her if she meant that Rutledge was her natural father but never married to her mother, she nodded and replied, Uh huh, a loud, definite *uh huh* her eyes fixed directly into mine. Not a half clearing your throat Uh huh, but an answer she wished to imprint, to leave no doubt about, an answer foreshortened, abridged, suggesting much she could have said, perhaps should have said, might say on some other occasion, but for now, for her own good reasons Uh huh assumed the weight of all the other untold stories about a girl born out of wedlock in 1892 in a remote, rural southeastern Pennsylvania community, fathered by a white man upon a black woman. A matter-of-fact Uh huh. As matter-of-fact as newspapers at that time reporting on Teddy Roosevelt's charge up San Juan Hill, the massacre of Native Americans at Wounded Knee, Kitchener's expedition in Egypt, the king of Belgium pacifying the Congo, West Africa partitioned, European gunboats in Peking, Indochina annexed by France.

Nothing to regret or be ashamed of. The world was a certain way then and few challenged the rightness of that way. The white man tall in the saddle calling all the shots. His world. His child Martha Irene he could claim, deny, ignore, orphan, kill. The absolute sovereignty he had usurped over all God's children, the irresistibility of his will, superiority of his culture, the insepa-rability of his destiny and dictates from Divine will, these grandiose fictions had penetrated even into the backwaters of Wrightsville, Pa., and abided there so a girl child the instant she emerged from her mother's womb was swaddled in the clothes the emperor had decreed for her, a gown of invis-ibility, of dependency, the status of illegitimacy she must wear all the days of her life, that she would acknowledge nearly a century later, its tattered remnants still clinging Uh huh, uh huh to her grandson. But the thing she acknowledged, and as far as I know never told anyone else, she also denied by not putting the whole sad story into words. *They*, her father, his fathers and sons, all their white cousins scattered across the globe stealing, burn-ing, raping, beating people into submission, *they* and their big sticks had fashioned a world in which she could never be much of anything. She un-derstood that. The power of that world. The harm it would do to her and hers. How they had cheated, abused and disposed of her. But she could also dismiss them and their dirty dog ways. All that was not worth repeating, the whole ugly world they'd created wasn't worth a word, hardly worth a grunt. She was being generous when she uttered Uh huh. That's what the things they'd done amounted to. Not even that. She was granting them the credit of an Uh huh only because her grandson had asked. Needed for some reason to know, to hear her say out loud what they both already knew or *ought* to know as a birthright. Uh huh. She was passing on/sharing with me her gift of language, the power to name, claim, and disclaim. One scornful, curt, clear-eyed, distasteful to her lips part grunt, part incantation in which I heard how *they* for all their fantasies of authority and control and endless scheming and libraries of words, they could never tell the simple truth of her life. Try as they might, they could not usurp her story. In her own good time, in words or deeds or fiery silence, the truth of her witness would be heard. Oh yes. Their side was on the record, it was the record according to their books, laws, customs, schools, and laboratories. Illegitimacy, all their lies and shit, whatever. It was there all right, but it was also nothing. She summed it up and turned it to Uh huh. She'd suffered her life, earned it, and it had little or nothing to do with what *they* said about her over there where they held sway. She had stripped them clean, down to the bone, to their bare asses with no place to run and hide and nothing to cover the shame of their nakedness uh huh.

So you didn't live with your father.

Huh uh.

Did you know him to see him.

Oh yes. Little bitty place like Wrightsville everybody knew everybody else.

You were raised a Lawson.

Yes, sir. Proud of it. And my mother was a Johnson. Baers and Wrights mixed in there, too. Lots of Johnsons and Baers up around York then.

Do you remember anything else. Other family . . .

But the tape stops. The rest of the conversation's lost to me, I'm beginning to fabricate what might have been said. Devise a history I don't know. We can guess it, can't we. Crucial features, at least. How much discipline and silence were required of people growing up black, marginalized, and poor anyplace in America at the apex of the white man's century. But the tape stops because the witness fades from the stand. My grandmother's memories were sparse. She was over ninety when we talked that time. Too late to go back. For her *back* shuttles unpredictably in and out of now. Why chop time again into those little ungenerous cells that confine us most of our lives. Those dark, blind moments when the short view overwhelms, when we're so busy rushing forward we forget about back and up and down and sideways too and the only way out seems up ahead, tomorrow, maybe, in a hurry to be gone.

Been a long time, Doot. Long long time. Your grandmother's an old lady.

Grandma didn't have much she needed to say. Yet I could read things happening in her eyes, in the corners of her mouth where age lines, incised like tribal markings, twitched. Off a screen inside her brow a third unseen eye was reading the story of her life. Pages, chapters consumed faster than a blink. Years, decades displayed on the screen, handfuls of years chewed and swallowed and savored or spit out between breaths. Her long history was being enacted again, her face betrayed the action in minute adjustments. Her chipmunk cheeks, the only place she ever got fat, trembling, flexing, bitten from inside, expressive as the skin of a lake. She was back reliving whatever her memory called up, but living at the speed of light, a fast fast shuffle of scenes people places they say occurs between your next to last and last breath of air on earth.

The show, the spectacle was hers and hers alone to view. No way in. No way out. She wasn't consciously withholding, she simply couldn't do otherwise. Distance between us was not of her making. No more than she had intended to distance herself from Martha Irene Lawson, a skinny yellow girl child playing in a field in Wrightsville, Pa. She was comfortable with distance, its necessity, its tease, the hard passage against all odds and expectations had not left her stranded here, now, an old woman. Instead it freed her to return. To pick and choose. She could verify her life. It continued to happen inside her head, flickering across her invisible eye. And that's all that mattered, perhaps. The force in her yoking her days together. From the beginning to the not quite end yet. Not quite. Yet. The not quite of the end no more distant, illusory, or real than the beginning, as it dances and sways and plays itself out for her again. Energy released someday some instrument may harvest, energy made available for broadcast and replay by technology as commonplace then as what we employ today to hear the dead sing and watch ghosts flutter across a screen.

Long time ago, Doot.

Blankness a moment. My grandmother's eyes unfocused. Or rather focused inward instead of outward. Rolling back the stone. The long-gone days a throng of children exiting into sunlight from a dark cave. Black Orpheus music. La la la la. Lala la la. They are nothing more than a flash of color, a splash of chatter, squabble, singing, laughter. Kid noise and then you begin to make up lives for them. To remember.

We were playing one time in the backyard and my brother, Otis, he said . . .

By the time you open your mouth and turn around the children are gone. You're lying. You're alone. Distance increases driving the vision away, like when you attempt to tell a dream, destroying it with every word. I'm left to construct what I need from her thoughtful silence.

If I hopped a plane to Pittsburgh today, would there be more. More than we've shared already, the infinite history of our lives intersecting. But I need to be beside her bed. In person holding her actual hand. A last touch. On this side. Of what.

I refused to taste let alone eat scrambled eggs till the time my grandmother cooked them for me. Though she was a good cook, even a professional at times—living in and cooking for white families, chef at an Isaly's restaurant on Penn Avenue in East Liberty where my best buddy Scott Payne and I would check in for lunchtime leftovers on our way home from Peabody High School—the first time I ate Grandma's or anybody else's scrambled eggs had less to do with how well she cooked than with where she cooked them the first time she set down a plate of scrambled eggs, bacon, and toast in front of me. Because of where I was, I couldn't say no. Couldn't say much of anything except *yes ma'am* and *yessir*, speaking when spoken to by my grandmother or one of the white faces at the breakfast table in the Ricks' kitchen. My grandmother like a member of the Rick family, they said. Bring your grandson to meet us, they said. So one morning I tagged along in the back of a Lincoln Continental driven by Mr. Overton, the Ricks' chauffeur. Mr. Mackinley Overton, who became Uncle Mac when Grandma left Harry Wideman and moved into Mackinley Overton's place above the Ricks' garage. The scrambled eggs happened right after that move when I was five or six years old. My grandmother chattered all the time about how cute and smart I was and since the Ricks were still holding out hope that one of their children would soon be presenting them with a grandchild they thought maybe a preview would be fun, a vicarious taste through my proud grandmother of what they longed for in their own family. Thus I was invited to breakfast and found myself one early early morning driven through the quietest streets in Pittsburgh. Broad streets, tree-sheltered, immaculate. Houses twice the size of apartment buildings in Homewood, the community where my other grandmother, Freeda French, lived.

The Continental's plush backseat swallowed me. My eyes barely reached window level, windows that magically rose and fell with the touch of a button. I remember leather smell and a reddish glow, a color something like the way our bedroom feels now on sunny mornings when dawn filters through the plum blinds. But then, the color, the softness, the smell, Mr. Overton's board-straight back and big, black chauffeur-capped head, my grandmother's dreamy self-absorption, my worry she was drifting further and further from me, becoming someone else as we passed from the familiar skimpy streets of my neighborhood into a region where houses were too large for anyone to be living inside, then the stillness, the rosy hue immobilized me. I was losing my bearings. Scared to reach out, speak out, reorient myself. I didn't want the ride to end, but I also didn't want to be driven one inch farther from home. For some reason in that leather pit I couldn't help picturing myself as a king on a throne. A tiny, shrunken, frozen king, a Little King like the one in the comics, dwarfed, overwhelmed, so meek and mute no one cares, especially him, that he's king. There I sat, a different color, no bigger than a pea in that immense, upholstered pod, the city tamed and harmless as I'd ever seen it. A warning in the calm, however: You better not stop, better not touch. I prayed we'd turn around. Knew we'd gone too far. Beginning to lose track of who I was, of everything, the dark, wrinkle-necked man in the front seat, the lady gazing out a window humming to herself. Where were we headed. Why. My tongue swelled dry and heavy. I'd lost the power to speak. Only thing making sense the sound of the Lincoln's huge tires buffing those pretty streets clean.

I am a black boy five or six in the kitchen of a white family for whom my grandmother is hired help. Sitting at a table with the white folks while my grandmother in her apron, hair netted into a lump atop her head, serves us a scrambled-egg breakfast. She was beaming as she bustled around, making sure everyone receives enough of what they want on their flower-rimmed plates. Everyone (except me) in their glory. The Ricks because they were treating my grandmother royally by indulging her grandson with a seat at the intimate family table, a little black boy welcomed decades before Sidney Poitier and *Guess Who's Coming to Dinner*. My grandmother because her fabled grandson had achieved one more legendary plateau, sitting big as life at the emperor's table, her rich white employers stamping their seal of approval on the precious Doot she'd advertised to them as cute and smart as a whip, here he was and here she was bathed in reflected glory. Things were changing, maybe they would never be the same again.

All that mellow glory and feeling good just about killed me. I sat through breakfast intent on doing the right thing, determined not to disappoint anybody, not to spill food or get my mouth greasy or talk like a little ignorant picka-ninny. Only the Shadow knows what was running through my five-year-old mind. But the effort glazed my eyes and twisted my tongue. No matter how hard I tried to be something else, I knew I was sitting like a bump on a log, brown and nappy-headed, afraid to say a word other than *yessir, yes ma'am*, eyes down, locked on my plate so nobody could steal them. Was I the only one who knew about the lion crouched in the middle of the table, ready to spring and destroy this nice kitchen, all these fine people, me first, tearing off my head, swiping open my belly with one huge paw. It stinks, it slobbers, its claws drip boogers of red meat. Couldn't anybody else hear the gurgle of its stomach, the low, menacing big-cat purr as its yellow eyes stared at me, waiting for me to commit the mistake that would trigger its charge. A beast as palpable to me as the strips of bacon, triangles of toast, and mound of soft eggs on my plate.

I replied Yes ma'am when eggs were offered because everybody else did. With a salty mouthful of crumbled bacon and buttery crunchy toast, I could barely taste the buttery eggs. A lion to deal with demoted eggs into a minor consideration anyway. What would happen next. Would I explode from the effort of keeping the beast at bay or would it attack, for its own hidden rea-sons, whether I committed a mistake or not. Maybe a tie, a dead heat. Two big bangs sounding like one. Me self-destructing as the lion rips my guts out. Quitting as I'm fired.

So busy lion taming I was actually surprised when I noticed the eggs were gone. Clean plate. One more sign of good breeding, of what a nice little gen-tleman I was. Except everybody else left lots of stuff on their plates. Garbage for my grandmother to scrape into a can, in the kitchen where she periodi-cally disappeared. Because we weren't eating in the Ricks' kitchen after all. It was a breakfast room. Skylights. Green plants. The more I think about the morning at the Ricks' house, the more I remember, the freer I feel to invent what's needed to fill in my memory. A special room for eating breakfast. As unexpected, as bizarre a concept to me as the live lion centerpiece.

I'm sure the Ricks were kind and unfailingly polite, probably bent over backwards to make a child feel at home in an alien atmosphere. I'm sure my grandmother did her best, too. But the experience was dreadful. I summon it up and not many details remain. No specific Rick faces. No Rick names. Just a collective, overwhelming white presence, the smells and noises of the white people responsible. Fear of scrambled eggs overcome, a thousand other fears rushing to fill the vacuum. A funny, deadly lion that somehow accompanied me home, miniaturized but not one iota less threatening or dangerous, bounding up onto a shadowy ledge in the cave of my heart where it feigns sleep but never closes one yellow cat's-eye.

Hey man. See the way that lady coming up the street is walking. Check her out. She old now but you can tell by the way she swish that old booty she done a whole lot a fucking in her day. We were on somebody's stoop. Charlie, who we called Patches or Patchhead because a severe case of tetters had left lighter-colored blotches in his scalp, Charlie, a newcomer who'd only been living on Copeland a couple weeks, was mouthing off about a woman on her way up the block from Ellsworth Avenue where buses and trolleys ran. She sported a dark, white-bordered straw hat, a matching purse squeezed under her bare arm. Summertime. Her bright print dress was fitted at the waist but hung loosely in pleats from her hips, ending halfway between knees and ankles. From the hem of the dress her bony straight legs slanted inward. You'd guess she was bowlegged from the side-to-side pitch of her walk, the steep angling downward from broad hipbones to ankles just inches apart.

Charlie and I didn't get along too well. This was going to make it worse. Because the woman he was sounding on, forcing me to observe in a fashion I never had before (even though once upon a time I had pushed open the bathroom door and she was standing naked in the tub soaping herself and both of us were so surprised I took another half step into the steamy room, seeing and not seeing her, and she scrubbed a few more licks before she said, Oh, it's you, Doot, and I dropped my eyes and backed out, pulling the door to without saying sorry or anything else and now couldn't help fusing and refusing to fuse that close-up of my grandmother's wet anatomy with whatever foul-mouthed point Patches was announcing about the peculiar gait of the woman coming up Copeland), the woman was in fact my grandmother, a fact I wasn't exactly conscious of and Patches didn't know but everybody else on the stoop definitely was aware of so when I finally woke up and smacked Patches hard upside his patchy head, and he leaped for me and we were into a long-overdue rumble, everybody knew Patches was in the wrong and deserved whatever he got. And hoped he got plenty cause it was a shame to put somebody's nice old grandmother in the dirty dozens.

Man, I'da killed Patches he put the mouth on my grandmother that way. But it was not exactly clear if putting somebody's grandmother in the dirty dozens was as bad as putting somebody's mama there. Could be worse. Maybe. But it wasn't clear. We fought, anyway, more scuffle than fight, enough room and other guys between us we mostly hollered back and forth and Patches learned he'd insulted my grandmother and said sorry he didn't mean it man, but he wasn't scared of me and he'd fight me any day, any time but it wasn't over nothing he meant to say cause he hadn't meant no harm, I don't play that shit, man. The air quieter if not entirely clear by the time my grandmother passed the stoop and said, Hi fellas and What a nice bunch of boys and Doot, you come on home in a little minute so you can visit with your grandmother.

I should have kicked his ass good. I never liked him. I think I gave Patches the Patchhead nickname he hated. What I didn't like about him was the permanent sneer on his face. The curl in his lip, the look-right-through-you eyes that said I know you think you can whip me but you better not try. It wasn't even about who was badder, who could whip whose behind, it was about attitude. An ass whipping, no matter who won, wouldn't adjust Patchhead's attitude. I should have tried anyway. He gave me an opening and I should have finished it there and then.

A cold March rain rains down. Some person somewhere may be counting by Marches. Nine Marches left till the end of the century. Then will come the first March in the year 2000. You could count by months or count raindrops striking. How many raindrops will fall before the century ends. A fast count, total mounting higher and higher till rain stops. Then numbers piling up again, flashing faster and faster during the next March downpour, faster even than the numbers registering the national debt accumulating second by second on an electronic billboard in Times Square, but do you reach the new century any quicker counting raindrops or counting months. Is fast sometimes slower. Slower fast. What difference does it make. Approximately 3.2 billion seconds equal a hundred years. If I'd been counting the seconds in my life, I'd be up to about 1.6 billion. My grandmother close to a whole 3.2 billion century's worth. Count down or count up. From either direction you arrive at the same place. No place. The circle closes. An old gospel song asks God: Will the circle be unbroken. Answers itself, closes the circle of faith: *By and by, Lord, by and by. / There's a better home awaiting / In the sky, Lord, in the sky.*

My grandmother Martha Irene was a regular at church. Two of her husbands preached. For nearly twenty years she lived in various parish houses with the Reverend Mr. Morehead who built churches for the greater glory of God in the name of AME Zion. Since the Reverend's death—bless his roan wig, his brace of pastel Cadillacs, the sesquepedalian vocabulary he trotted out in conversations with his college-teacher, writer step-grandson— in the years since she's been in Pittsburgh, finding Otis Fallen at the Vintage Senior Citizens' Center, marrying him then outliving him too, my grandmother has attended Homewood AME Zion. I don't know if she ever severed officially her ties with Reverend Morehead's last church in Ohio, but she's clearly part of the Homewood congregation, a mother of the church, respected, deferred to, a consensus marvel. Though she lies about her age, even if she only carries the ninety-six years she claims in public, she has no right to be as strong, spry, quick-witted as she is. She dresses as if there's still some man, or men, paying special attention to how she looks on her own two good feet, stepping down the aisle of Homewood AME Zion to her accustomed bench in the right center section, two rows from the pulpit. Church members are aware when she's not in her spot. No one in the congregation would dream of occupying it, even when she doesn't. The thought that one Sunday her place will be empty and she might never return may cross someone's mind, but just as quickly is dispelled. She'll make it back. She always does. And if her progress through the front door and down the crimson-carpeted aisle is half of a half step slower, it's also more stately, more dignified. A bad case of flu or a fall or whatever keeps her away, must surely take its toll, she is, after all, constructed of the same flesh and blood as everybody else so we can expect her to slow down a tiny bit. That's part of the marvel. Not so much a matter of Mrs. Martha Fallen getting away with anything. Rather, the grace to bear affliction, to come out the far end of trouble and be recognizable, undefeated, ready for whatever comes next. Uh huh. She'll return next week. In a feathered hat and candy-striped dress, shoes matching purse, fresh and unpredictable. What's Mrs. Fallen wearing today. Did you check out that beautiful silk blouse communion Sunday. Girl, I ain't hit fifty yet and I wish I looked as good in my clothes as Mrs. Fallen. She seems to wear outfits only once. A trick of rotation. Changing accessories, establishing a unique, personal style so you're aware of her, always beautifully dressed, not necessarily the particular suit or dress. She possesses ten or twenty years' worth of choices in her wardrobe because her clothes don't date, classic materials and cuts you don't just pull off a rack. That's also part of the marvel. Not only does she manage to appear in church on her own two feet most every Sunday, but she looks good doing it. A fashion show. Easter parade each Sunday morning.

In spite of preacher husbands and her role as matriarch in Homewood Church, I do not associate my grandmother with religion. Not in her speech, actions nor the depths of her as I perceive them from a cloudy distance, two generations removed. To me she is the worldliest woman in the family. A hardheaded practicality governs her. She seems utterly unsentimental. My father's definitely her son. Aloof, detached, self-sufficient. A habit of masking emotion that's so thoroughgoing, so convincing, you wonder sometimes if emotions really are percolating behind the mask or if the elegant, stylized mask itself has become an emotion, the ultimate, unchanging protective shield of cool indifference. Does what is not expressed count. If so, for what. For whom. Since I'm my father's son, these are not neutral questions. In an unbroken stream I feel the cold rush descend on me, the icy reserve, the cutting off of feeling if feeling threatens to disrupt the illusion of self-control. Is this power to separate myself from my feelings, from my people, a gift, a curse, some unstable mix of both. Should I ask others to trust me, depend on me. Where does the withheld emotion, the denial accumulate. Will it come crushing down one day, the irresistible weight of remorse, or will it be emptiness, a gaunt, turkey-necked bird perched on a fence digesting my insides in its pot belly.

Grandma's different because unlike the other women in the family she's never, in my hearing, spoken passionately of God or spirit, heaven or hell. Never spoken the language of salvation, love, and redemption the others speak. Neither praised transcendent glories above nor testified about here below, the trials and tribulations, toils and snares that try the spirit, break the heart, snatch flesh and breath away. I've never heard her speak of losing a child, or voice the terror that one might be lost. She's never admitted aloud her helplessness, her dependence. My mother, her mother, Freeda French, my aunts, I've seen each one scared. Or hurt or soul weary. Bent down. Dismayed. They would not have survived without their god, his promise of love and divine intervention that doesn't itself resolve trouble but prepares the miracle of faith, the possibility of belief and belief for them becomes a kind of overcoming and resignation that keeps hope alive. I've watched them, heard them when they were knocked down past the point of prayer or singing, yet their religion sustained them, instructed them: *All you got to do is fold your arms and moan a little while.*

The few statements I recall my grandmother making about religion are businesslike, factual, high-church formulaic and cool. She was a preacher's wife responsible for organizational matters, not the mourner's bench. She writes a beautiful hand, letters perfectly formed according to the manual of classic penmanship little black girls copied from diligently at the turn of the century when writing itself, like cleanliness, brought colored people a bit closer to heaven, at least the writing which faithfully mirrored models in the white man's books. Ecstasy of a perfect copy. Starched dresses, ironed hair, skin scrubbed and oiled against ash, shiny shoes, fingernails crisp, snowy ankle-socks, desks in ranks as symmetrical and straight as rows of crosses in Flanders Fields. Church for my grandmother a neat garden, an efficiently arranged chest of drawers. Money in the bank, money kept Swiss-clean, hidden, private, in the vault where it belonged.

They say losing her last child, Eugene, broke her heart. She waited for the mailman every day Eugene was overseas in the war. No one was allowed to touch the mail before she did. Her trips to the mailbox each morning kept him alive, kept his letters, though few and far between and in a childish script nothing, nothing like the good old-fashioned way she'd learned to write, her hand the envy of every church secretary who ever read her quarterly reports, her ritual kept Eugene's letters arriving from distant places and kept away a dreaded telegram from the War Department informing her of her son's death. A vigil unbroken the final two years of World War II. First Edgar gone, then Catherine to the WACS, finally Eugene, last born but the biggest already, finally old enough to enlist if he lied on an extra year. She knew Edgar was a guard in a prisoner-of-war camp, safe, away from the fighting, and Catherine typing at a desk in Washington, D.C., but Eugene was in the Pacific, the bloody, island-hopping road to Tokyo, so it was him mostly she worried about, they say, up some mornings at the crack of dawn and back and forth like a crazy woman, a dozen trips before the time she knew good and well the mailman would arrive.

Perhaps that has something to do with her composure now. The ice in her, the iron, the almost peculiar reserve and quaint sense of decorum. After services, in the fellowship hour when people gather in the church basement for chicken wings and gossip, she'd whisper when she'd ask about my brother, her grandson in prison, as if his whereabouts were a secret, a family shame to be guarded even though everyone in Homewood knew Rob's story, the stories of all the young men cut down, shipped away. But nothing causes her to flinch. I never saw her cry. Or worse, fall into the states my mother and her sisters got in, swaying, quiet, arms folded, dry-eyed when crying would have been a luxury, a release of raging feelings visibly tearing them apart. I'm sorry to hear that, Grandma would say. Or, John French was a fine man. Freeda will miss him. Phrases she'd cobble to wall herself behind, a wall constructed of the bricks she'd counted on the path to the mailbox two years' worth of mornings between 1943 and 1945; sentiments precise as the clipped hedges lining the brick walkway. Perhaps she'd exhausted every ounce of emotional energy and disciplined herself to live on what was left. Shadows and substance. A memory of anxiety, of pain, of giving away everything and receiving nothing in the return mail until weeks after the war was over, weeks after the trek down the brick path from front door to sidewalk was less about hoping for a letter from Eugene or fearing a War Department telegram, than it was a mother's too-good-to-be-true expectation that maybe, just maybe Eugene would be standing there, huge and smiling in his uniform. Weeks of waiting for a surprise she didn't dare speak aloud.

Instead of him home again what the mailman brought her in return for daring to hope, for dying by inches on every trip she took down the brick path, was the notice, finally, weeks, months after the war had ended, that her son Eugene was gone.

There have been times when I didn't know my grandmother's name. I had to stop and try to figure it out. What is she calling herself now. I'd be too embarrassed to ask, if anybody was around at one of those moments to ask. Mom. How does Grandma spell her name. Oh yeah. Right. I couldn't remember whether *Fallen's* spelled with one *l* or two. And he's Otis, right. Like Ote. Like your brother Big Otis and my brother. Otis. Only my brother Otis Eugene goes by Gene now. And my sister. I never can get her name straight either. She converted to her second husband's religion, the American Moorish Church. Exchanged both names I knew her by. And added a few extra. My father subtracted names, gave his as Edgar Lawson when he was picked up by the cops in raids on those joints where he drank and gambled after hours. He told them the truth. Those were in fact his names. He just left off the Wideman part. My brother Robby became a Muslim. In the joint lots of inmates have never heard of a Robert Wideman. He's Farouk. Another name I couldn't spell till I checked it out. When I published my first novel, I wanted my father's name to be part of the record so I was John Edgar Wideman on the cover. Now the three names of my entitles sound pretentious to me, stiff and old-fashioned. I'd prefer to be just plain John Wideman, but can't shake the Edgar. It's my trademark, my brand name in the book trade. Is my grandmother's name Martha Irene Rutledge-Lawson-Wideman-Overton-Morehead-Fallen. Does she drag that dragon-tail baggage wherever she goes.

Hannibal Wideman, my grandfather from Greenwood, South Carolina, changed his name to Harry when he migrated north. Who had named him originally, whose sense of history included the memory of the Carthaginian general, African conqueror of Rome. Ironic that such a name would become an encumbrance as Harry crossed his Alps, south to north, an elephant of a name he shrunk, discarded, refused, seeking anonymity, ordinariness. Didn't pay for a black workingman to stick out, to draw attention to himself in Pittsburgh in 1901. A fancy name would brand him, clearly as his accent, as a down-home country boy fresh to the city. What happened to the history inscribed in *Hannibal*, its power to connect Harry Wideman to the past and assist in forging, determining a future.

My grandmother's last husband, Otis Fallen (my mother always claimed poor Otis so old and befuddled he never actually realized he was married again), pronounced his last name so it rhymed with "Allen." On paper it reads like the adjective meaning to have dropped, tumbled, etc., "fallen." Fallen, Martha.

She anointed me with many names. Each one appropriate for a particular time, place, occasion. *Spank. Doot. Spanky. John-Edgar. John. Doodlebug. Mr. Wideman.* She employed them with an exactitude that matched the perfectly formed letters of her handwriting. Part of the game was slipping up on purpose. Calling me Spanky, my name inside the family, in front of people who weren't family. Spanky . . . I mean *John*, her eyes twinkling, her face suddenly sixty, seventy, eighty years younger, a teasing little-girl smile and she's Martha Lawson again, back in Wrightsville, Pa.

What did you call me at the end. Your grandson half a century old now himself. Did you believe in that mannish *John* name yet or would there always be a tongue-in-cheek grin tucked away somewhere within that sound when it issued from your lips. Toward the end I couldn't gauge how much Grandma actually heard. We all learned to speak louder, to face her so she could read our lips as well as pick up sound. In a crowd she'd settle into herself and seem to drift away from the conversations rattling around her. Sometimes I thought it wasn't so much her difficulty in hearing as it was the prerogative she granted herself to hear what she wanted to hear, ignore the rest. She'd earned the right. Listening so long to the snow of words that never seems to diminish. People always needing someone to listen, to say something. Words, words, words, never an end in sight. She'd sit, slightly slumped, hands in lap. Was she asleep. Was her chin sinking onto her chest. No. Right on time, on target, she'd perk up and snap into the flow of words. If my name happened to be in what she was contributing, it would be the correct name, the one that fit precisely unless she winked slyly at me and brought her hand up to shush her mouth. Doot . . . I mean *John*. Hamming up the corrective gesture for everyone to see, walnuts in her cheeks or balls of dough, a smooth hilly pouch under each eye when she smiles and covers her offending lips with her hands. My long-shanked hand, my brother Rob's lean fingers, my sister Tish's color, my father's thick veins, a sucked-in hollowness below the puffy cheeks that belongs exclusively to her, her age when her false teeth are out and the flesh collapses inward on emptiness. If you thought of me when you were in the hospital, what name did you think. When you asked after your missing eldest grandson, what was the name in your question. Do you know a name that stands for all the others.

One present when they are absent, one that existed before they were invented. Do you ever speak aloud the name of that place where all the names converge, become no name, nothing. Where I am known by you and only you, nameless, a place empty as a grave you decorated with names. Identities like seeds planted there. But you must remember the ground untilled, untouched, unbroken, unsown. When you played your name games with me, is that the place I felt solid under my feet. You possessed the power to land me there, take me back, free me. When I wasn't beside you at the end to grip your hand, what did you call the emptiness you patted and consoled.

This has been one of those Marches of interminable rain, grayness, clamminess, gusting winds. If winter is earth sleeping and spring a wakening, the transition has been fitful, violent, unsettling dreams prematurely ripping the land into consciousness. Alert, aching because sleep is ending without fulfilling its restorative function, without bestowing its bounty of rest and peace. A few days of Arctic blue sky. Too pure, too distant for the pale green shoots that are beginning to push up, no matter what. A vast chilling blue. Trees skeletal. A few dead leaves cling, tatter of meat on the bone. A scouring wind. Anything vertical shivers and ripples and you realize the invisible wind is a medium thick and dense as water, the earth a pebble plummeting through it. Seasons are not heavy, solid blocks of time abutting one another. They lean, sway. Seasons are the records of billions upon billions of infinitesimally minute particles, each one cycling through its changes, its weather of metamorphosis, transition, adjustment. They determine the larger patterns we observe. Little pictures seeming to mirror the big one, but correspondences are a measure of our lack of understanding of either. Middling creatures. Caught in the middle. What we know always the limiting factor in what else, how much, we can know. March is winter spring summer fall, the stripping bare of certainty, all seasons present no matter how convenient it would be for us to have it another middling way, for our categories to maintain their separate identities, our centers to hold.

Yesterday, Thursday, March 26, 1991, around eight thirty in the evening, my grandmother died. Now my bargain rate, advance purchase ticket to Pittsburgh will be used for her funeral, not a visit to the hospital. So it goes. I was on the phone with my father, letting him know my plan to arrive in Pittsburgh Friday. He was down, way down. Though he'd never admit it directly, I could tell, because his voice was low, uninflected. Childhood buddy of his had recently died. His girlfriend's mother had died. Uncle Dave, Grandma's last surviving brother, had died in California the week before. And of course his mother lay dying, no longer alert, no longer speaking or recognizing people or focusing her eyes. Occasionally she started awake, made noises, blinked her eyes. She'd drifted into a comatose state after the doctor had begun morphine injections. To ease her pain. But everyone had told me she hadn't complained of pain. Her doctors must have anticipated the discomfort of dehydration, the slow starvation that was inevitable since they applied no measures to force-feed her or irrigate her failing system. Why not. I wanted to know who made these decisions. Someone to hold responsible, to blame.

Of course I should have been there. Or tried to call her. But I refuse the luxury of guilt now. For whatever reason, I didn't do what I should have done. Buying a plane ticket to Pittsburgh a half-ass measure. As much wishful thinking as a serious attempt to get home before she died. The odd thing is I began to believe she'd stay alive till I got there. Just a few more days, Grandma. Then it will be convenient for me to come. Hold on till Friday. Then it will be OK for you to die. But hold on. Welcome me home. I was relying on the possibility that my schedule and Death's would mesh, be in step. Began to believe that's how things would happen. Till I got the call from my mother. She said Catherine had called her and Catherine was on her way to the hospital with her friend Lil and my father if she could reach him. Catherine hadn't been able to reach my father because he'd been on the phone with me when Catherine called him, hearing about my plan to arrive on the weekend. My plan to see my grandmother before it was too late.

For about a year while we were waiting for an apartment to open up at 702 Copeland, we lived on the third floor of my grandmother's house at 712 Copeland in Shadyside, an almost entirely white Pittsburgh neighborhood with good schools my father worked two and a half jobs to keep us in. That's when I saw her in the tub. We almost died in that house, my mother, myself, my four siblings, gassed by a leaky stove. Robby, the baby then, saved us when his crying woke my grandmother and she came to our rescue. I made love for the first time in that house, on the couch in the downstairs apartment. My first lover the daughter of the man who boarded on the first floor of my grandmother's house.

Wanda was visiting from Harlem, where she lived on Convent Avenue. She was a gift out of the blue, as truly heaven-sent as Harlem-sent. Harlem just added spice, danger. Small, perfect, clearer about what she was doing than I would ever be. She said she liked me because I wore my jeans low on my hips, the way the Spanish boys did back home in New York. Liking me, forget the reason, whatever reason, was blessing enough. And to like me enough to pull down her own tight, low-slung jeans and then step out of her panties and lie down beside me, kissing and hugging on the couch in a corner of Mr. Lennox's sitting room. Wow. Her daddy was a waiter, like my father, and wouldn't be home before midnight. Uncle Mac I'd lost track of. Grandma was upstairs, probably in bed, with no reason to return down the steps, so Uncle Mac was the only one who might enter the front door and catch us in the tiny anteroom off the main hall, Mr. Lennox's parlor with his radio where he listened to the Pirates' baseball games. We'd been warned that the rest of the apartment was out of bounds. Don't youall go back in there. If you need to sit up and make google eyes at each other, sit in the parlor. And don't stay up late. No locks or doors between us and whatever traffic passing in and out the front entrance. Maybe Mr. Mac was upstairs, maybe he was working late at the Ricks' or at the storefront church on Tioga Street where he was assistant sometime pastor. He could bust through the door any moment and see most of the couch from the hall. But Wanda liked me and was prepared to show me how much so I was prepared to risk shame or death.

What I wasn't really ready for was the way things speeded up and tangled up, her body with mine, mine with hers, legs, hair, fingers, touching and moaning, little increments of mixed-up back-and-forth sallies, then a landslide, stuff I'd only imagined or read in stolen paperbacks, or tried on myself locked in the bathroom or daydreamed under the covers when I thought my younger brother Otis had finally stopped flopping and farting for the night and was snoring himself to oblivion on his side of the bed. Her smells and wetness, squeezing, opening. Starting slowly inch by inch, amazed at what I was seeing, at how simple it was once you got started, and trying to prolong, imprint and hurry at the same time everything new and incredible and scaring the shit out of me while I enjoyed it to death. No. Huh uh. I wasn't ready for all that instant joy and pumping away with my bare behind mooning Uncle Mac if he happened to bust through the front door. It was like swing low sweet chariot, my buns lifted, her sweet gold buns—gold, gold is exactly how I remember her, gold, golden, her skin soft gold light of candle glow and honey—lifting me and sweeping me away and then I was someplace else, watching a cool minute, till I was caught up again in a whirling daze and didn't return to earth, didn't care if I ever returned, didn't think of returning till whipped to a frazzle, everything I owned squeezed out the needle's eye in one of those big bangs that jump-started the universe. I rolled my thighs off hers to recapture my bearings, get a good look at where I'd been, what had been causing all the excitement, and saw the half-dollar-size puddle of cum between us. She scooted back to prop her head against the couch's armrest. There it was. A dollop of custard. Did we do that. A little baby lying there between us wouldn't have surprised me more. And I half expected that creamy stuff to osmose itself into a mouth and start yelling. Where had it come from. Who did it belong to. How many days had we been lying naked from the hips down, cooling out, exposed to the world on this couch in my grandmother's house. And even if we'd managed to get away with something, wasn't all the evidence anybody'd need to find us out, convict and punish us, right here, indelible, plain as day. Wherever else I'd been, I was home again that quick. A boy who'd been given permission to visit Mr. Lennox's daughter. But don't stay late. And behave yourself. And don't youall dare go back in his apartment. I'd messed up. Ruined the couch and sure as night follows day somebody was going to pay.

Wanda mopped up with her underpants, balled them and stuffed them in the back pocket of her jeans, a place I couldn't imagine with room for anything more than the tight apple mounds of her cheeks.

Rest will dry right up, she smiled.

And it did. Nothing to worry about. Just a spot. Something to remember me by. Are you going to remember me when I'm gone. You gon keep being nice to me. I like you cause you're nice. Not like them nasty boys at home want you for just one thing. Will you write.

I didn't but she did. One or two letters, then a third one a year or so later:

Dear John . . .

My mother didn't say a word when I returned home that evening from my grandmother's couch. Next day I was up and out early. Where you going in such a hurry already this morning, boy. Don't bother answering. Your grandmother's house mighty popular all the sudden. Don't you go waking people up. You know Mr. Lennox works late.

Grandma's front door unlocked. Wanda and her father probably still asleep. Uncle Mac and Grandma gone by now. I crept in. Checked the couch for a spot. You could see it only if you were looking for it. Maybe still the slightest bit damp. I brushed the purplish nap. Blew on it. And since my nose was so close, inhaled what I could of her sweetness. A good thing, too, because that whiff was as close as I ever got to her again. Or loving again for two long years till I was fifteen and talked Tommy into the backseat of Uncle Mac's rusty Lincoln Continental in the alley yard behind my grandmother's house.

What He Saw

I have a photo of a man whose name I don't know. A black South African man, gut-shot, supported on either side by women, large, turbaned black women whose dark faces bear the man's pain, the shock of his sudden, senseless injury as clearly as they carry the weight of his body slumped against them. A black-and-white picture. The light is flat and merciless. Distorted by the angle at which the camera was held to snap this image, the man's face dominates. A lean face, though the elongated forehead bulges, again an effect of camera position. The brow of a Benin bronze mask, one might say of it, swollen as a sail full of wind. A comparison like that might be appropriate if the man weren't dying, if his dazed expression and vacant eyes, the women's sorrow and fear, weren't real, a few feet away from the van in which we are sitting.

In this settlement called Crossroads some streets are wide for the same reason they say the boulevards of Paris are broad and straight. Within the grid of highway-sized main drags, an aimless, endless sprawl of dwellings. Acres of shanties, shacks, lean-tos, tents, shelters so mean and bizarre they take me back to the vacant lots of Pittsburgh, the clubhouses my gang of ten-year-olds jerry-rigged from whatever materials we could scavenge and steal. Only these habitations stretching as far as I could see in every direction were not the playhouses of kids acting out fantasies of escape and independence. In this jumble whole families slept in makeshift shelters, woke up every morning, concocted meals, moved their bowels, made love, watched one another, separated only by inches, day after day performing the primal tasks that enable a unit of human beings to survive.

Wide streets with little or no traffic. But we were lost. Our driver had pulled off on a shoulder, out of the way of the nonexistent vehicles this street or highway or whatever was built to accommodate. Our van and another following us had been separated from the press caravan inspecting Crossroads. We decided to stay put while the second van backtracked. We didn't know whether the way out of the settlement was ahead or behind us, right or left at the next yawning intersection.

The scale of this so-called squatters' camp had struck me first. Then the permanence of the roads that cordoned and defined it. Tarmac the last solid surface beneath your feet if you stepped from these runways onto the areas where people lived. Clatter and crunch of gravel then the pitch and slippage of loose, rutted earth under the van's tires after the lead car had diverted the caravan onto a side road. At first this byway had seemed as deserted as the main arteries. Then children began appearing. You saw them in groups of two or three in front of you or along the sides of the path. A scattering of curious kids checking out this invasion of their turf. Then I happen to glance out the back windows and see we'd gathered a crowd, hundreds of young people had materialized in our wake, the brothers and sisters of the bold ones whose stares had met us first. Empty. Full. A country immense enough to try and hide its secrets. Millions of black people who don't seem to be around until the whites summon them by ones or twos or a handful when there's a job to be done. Until—and this is a phenomenon mirroring the unpredictability of the land itself where you never know what's coming next, veldt or mountainscape, forest or desert—you turn a bend and you're surrounded by all the missing people, the black sea always more and less than the next step away.

Vehicles ahead of us had stopped in an open area and we pulled up next to them and parked. Barely a quarter mile from the turnoff, but no doubt we were in a different world. Row after row of dwellings with footpaths in between meandered in every direction. No discernible plan, no logic except the contours of the land, an eroded gully or outcropping of naked rock, the fact that a spot was already occupied, had dictated where the next dwelling would be erected. A crazy quilt patchwork of sculpted carpet spreading over the ground, covering, burying the earth. A dense fabric changing texture square by square. Or segment by segment since there were no straight lines, no right angles anywhere. Houses supporting one another, fragile embellishments of porch, roof, fenced yards all leaning against an adjacent structure and that structure leaning on its neighbor and the neighbor sharing an arrangement of stakes and ropes that shore up a common wall, the common wall at one end abutting a sheet of corrugated tin siding, vaguely perpendicular, that holds the wall's weight while wall sustains tin's verticality. A good wind and whole blocks would topple like dominos. I'd watched footage of a bulldozer scraping away a squatter camp. Plowing straight ahead, little or no resistance offered by the dozens of shelters it levels in a single charge. An hour or so and all that remains a pall of dust and mounds of rubble neatly heaped at measured intervals. Full. Empty. Before the smashing starts black people slip away, disappear into the immensity of the land, travel secret routes as ancient and deeply understood in the blood as the instinctual knowledge of migrating birds. Moving where they must, how they must, to satisfy imperatives of survival, renewal. Keeping on keeping on, we called it at home. If you start with nothing you have nothing to lose and you keep losing it but you keep starting again and carry that nothing, burden and gift, with you on the journey that is all the life you have. In Georgia, Mississippi, South Carolina uprooted even after we're dead. Blades dig up our ancestors' bones, crush them, scatter our cemeteries to clear the way for shopping malls, parking lots.

I hang back. There is smoke in my eyes. Coal burned here for cooking and heat. A thousand points of light. Fires kept alive in perforated oil drums. Smoldering fires, fire that leaps and dances and throws off sparks. Small children ring the women who tend the fire drums, women with babies slung on their backs, bellies, hips, shoulders, like the cameras and battery packs girding the European women in our party. Laughter, the babble of many excited languages in these dusty streets when the vans spill their cargo. Ground the color of thorns. Rocks everywhere. A munitions dump of rocks. Dogs, chickens, children underfoot. Houses on either side of the footpath are protected by exotic fences. Any material will do for fencing—boards, chicken wire, concrete blocks, string, brick, aluminum siding, pipe, plywood panels, bottles, broken bits of furniture, whatever can be combined, aligned, stuck in the ground to suggest the ancient idea of the African compound, preserve the sacred space of family, the fences a link with the ways of the ancestors in this shriven place that devours everything. Memory in these fences and skimpy yards, a conscious or unconscious continuity with the past and also the practical, immediate necessity of protection. Gangs prey

on the weak, the isolated, the stray. Thieves on everyone. Precious little new
wealth comes into the community, so what exists must be cycled and recycled ingeniously, brutally, till it's exhausted, tossed on the trash heap. True
of things, of people.

An old woman sweeping the stones in front of the canvas flap door of her
dwelling tells me how sorry she is for the newcomers in the low-lying areas
whose tents are inundated by red rivers of mud when it rains. How blessed
she feels, how happy to share her dry space with a family from over there
when they must flee to higher ground. A comrade pulls me aside, complains
in a whisper about dope dealers operating in broad daylight, cops white and
black on the take, kids addicted, violence intensified as the trade spreads.

I imagine night falling, a foul night wind. Shit, piss, rancid garbage, acrid
smoke. Loud talk, the inevitable squabbles and pitched fights. Night noises
magnified by a tin roof buckling in a gust of wind. Walls flutter, doors, when
there is a door, flap, wind shuttles through chinks and cracks, whining, whistling.
The crackle of fire, a dream of awakening in the middle of a furnace. Dogs howl,
babies shriek, chickens cackle. A mad rooster announces dawn every hour. Blazing midday light now but I can't help envisioning darkness at its center.

We stroll and gawk and snap. Some visitors pat the shaved heads of the
children. Peer into the dark interiors of their homes. One is open for in-
spection. A government official supervises the photo opportunity. Only
room inside for four camera people at a time. The official clocks each group.
Smiles as he counts down the last ten seconds, 3 . . . 2 . . . 1. That's all folks.
Hurries in the next crew.

Toward the far end of the footpath an invisible barrier none of the journalists
crosses. I watch a number of them approach it and retreat. Beyond the barrier
the path's deserted. No one's tempted to retrieve the story that might be lurking
there. We understand we must not spread ourselves too thin. A fragile strength
in numbers. Perhaps we're already infected by the laager mentality. Circle the
wagons. Move in a swarm. The heat and noise of each of us exciting, embold-
ening the others. But beyond that knot in which we are casual and self-assured,
another world begins. A larger, threatening presence palpable as the sullen coal
smoke that poisons the air. The presence is barely a whisper when the faces are
like your face, the voices your voice, the words in your language, the clothes
purchased from stores where you bought yours, a whisper then, a murmur
defeated by the buzzing certainty of your kind. But the whisper explodes to a

shout, a deafening roar—*Go back, go back; you do not belong here*—the instant you stray one inch beyond the safety zone. An invisible line cuts you off. On one side a whisper. On the other side a wind hurling you back. I pretend the color of my skin grants me license to pass beyond the point my colleagues stop.

To my left and slightly behind, a horse-drawn wagon trundles into view, stops on a vacant rise in front of crowded ranks of tents. Gunnysacks of coal stacked on the wagon. Coal dust has blackened its slatted sides. The horse's ribs sooty and distinct as the slats. The bare-chested, coveralled driver sootier. Kids try to climb up where the driver sits. He shoos them. They squeal at him. He hoots back, shakes his fist, but everybody's smiling. Where there should be a slit of gleaming white in the man's grimy face are dark gums, a cavernous emptiness. His body is taut and lean, wide shoulders bulk under his overalls' loose straps. Not more than twenty, a young man with an old man's mouth, he grins, toothless Pied Piper to the drove of kids who have been prancing behind his wagon, surrounding him and his horse now that the wagon's halted. More kids flying from everywhere, drawn by the shouting, the coal vendor's chant, the playful threats. Doesn't take much to make the young ones happy. Split high in the crotch, they gallop, dance. Quarter-miler's strides. Streamlined to black splinters of elegant bone. Cropped round heads like fists on stalks. Stick drawings animated. The gait of antelopes. Nervous as sparrows.

I stroll two hundred yards or so farther, beyond the invisible barrier, toward a distant glint on the horizon that turns out to be railroad tracks. A kind of shallow valley lushly green dips between the rail embankment and parched plain on which Crossroads has formed. What pulled me down the path, beyond the corridor of houses, many no wider across than the span of my arms, no deeper than three medium strides, down through the phantasmagoric architecture of yards, fences, second stories, porches, toward the emptiness on the far side of the invisible wall was the great, booming explosion of a tree, or island of trees, whose arching crowns towered at least a hundred feet over the broken horizon line of roofs. Trees the oldest living things around. Green, enduring. How had they survived whatever was imposing itself on the land, whatever was draining life out of the soil, the people. A green shock in the sky, a place I could fix my eyes upon, my thoughts, and vault over the question of what the hell were we doing here, tourists and squatters, visitors and prisoners.

A softness, a lushness at the base of these giant trees, a reminder of what Africa may have been once. Thick grass, grazing animals. From the mini-valley's floor, a man climbs toward a ridge where another ragged screen of shanties begins.

I was cheating, romanticizing this green remnant while Crossroads howled at my back for attention. The man climbed slowly, absorbed in what he was doing. A long stick in his hand he planted like a Swiss mountaineer, boosting himself up the slope. A few hairy, miniature water-buffalo-looking creatures with fluted horns nuzzled each other on the valley bottom, ghostly where the grass was thickest. I picked out three spotted goats, a horse, wondered if they belonged to the climber, wondered if anybody remembered this African postcard here, right next door to the desolation my colleagues were documenting.

Crossroads today. Yesterday Soweto. The grand tour. Rolling into Soweto in a column of combies trailing a gold, bulletproof Mercedes. Have you ever seen a car window two inches thick. Armor plating sinks the Mercedes low on its springs. It drags over the smallest bumps, groans like a wounded animal. What is our business. What in the world are we doing here. Later that night after the Soweto rally, the rowdy dinner, a sobering interview with one of the detainees freed after twenty-two years in prison, we tried to figure it out. At the top of the Carlton, Jo'burg's international hotel where white and black have been permitted to fraternize long before the current relaxation of apartheid, we had tried to begin at the beginning. Discussed our introduction to Soweto. A kid shitting, staring into the road that runs past the garbage-strewn berm which he'd chosen as a private place. Which suddenly wasn't as our convoy steamed past.

The question we bounced back and forth over our last drinks that evening in the very English, very Victorian, clubby, clubby Clubroom Bar of the Carlton was this: Why did some people shoot the boy and some not. Hey, I got him good. I saw the shot, too, dude. Everybody saw it, but I didn't take it. I could have, but I didn't. You make me feel good about you, man. I mean, you know, you had the sensitivity in a split second to decide not to shoot. I like that in you. I didn't really think about it. Saw him. Knew the picture was there. He was mine if I wanted him, but I didn't pull the trigger. Could you say why, now. Was it privacy. You didn't want to violate his privacy. Something like that. Privacy, dignity. But not exactly. Just knew I didn't want the picture. Something was wrong. I disagree. To me the kid said it all. Soweto. Goddamn Soweto. Little kid having to creep outside, over the hill through all that filth to do his business. These people don't have anything. Nothing, man. We got to tell their story. The dirty drawers got to me. Coal black. Least he had drawers. Lots don't. You dudes should have just left the little guy alone. How'd you feel trying to take a crap and half the press corps of southern Africa clicking away at you.

Let me propose something, gents. The speaker was a good kid, a relative of one of the trip's organizers and full of vodka so we let him go on. We have a print journalist, photographers, a video person, a fiction writer. I'd like to hear how each of you folks come at this from the perspective of your art.

We half-ass attempted to sort it out, but without much energy or luck. It was late. We wandered off into abstractions then silliness, teasing, flirting with the one woman present, something about different folks and different strokes degenerating into swimming against the tide, breast strokes. We were growing tired of one another's company. Needed the people at home we were missing. It had been a long day. With an early rise next morning. And each of us a little tired of himself, herself. We couldn't make sense of the boy. Emblem. Symbol. Mirror. Ourselves. What the hell were we doing.

Full. Empty. The African trick of disappearing a means perhaps of reclaiming the land. Of being present when not seen. Of being everywhere that is just out of view. Around a bend, folded into the cleft of a valley, concealed in high wavering grass, in a dark alleyway between tall buildings, lurking in the dreamscape that materializes once the eyes close for sleep. Everywhere. And just in case you forget, or don't believe they're out there anymore, the unexpected popping up of one leads your eyes to another, another, and then the whole noisy trekking multitude swarming. Like that marching fence of young people toi-toi-ing, singing the throat-deep tribal war songs, bodies stretched across the horizon, darkening it, animating it as they danced closer toward you, engulfing the narrow dirt path in Soweto where you and your colleagues were stopped short by this tidal wave of chanting, fist-thrusting, hip-hopping Africans that seemed for a righteous moment coming not to greet you, welcome you, but to sweep this bad joke of a place for human habitation away. And you with it.

We are lost. Lost in that moment when the wave blocked the path, cresting, gathering force for the fatal blowout. Lost now at the edge of this landing strip roadway, our last companion van gone. Guts of this settlement as foreign, after all, to our colored drivers as to us. We'd heard gunfire just moments before. Single shots followed by the popping of automatic weapons. Not a soul visible in the melee of houses recessed fifty yards or so from the road's edges. Does everyone except us know the bulldozers are coming. Or the helicopter gunships and paratroopers dropping from the sky. Or the rockets and bombs.

The shots had come from behind us, the direction the other van was backtracking for a way out. Finney was up on his knees, his video camera trained through the rear window, his face pressed into the eyepiece. As far as I could see down the road, nothing was moving. Only heat devils shimmering at the vanishing point of the flat, flat expanse. Unless those colors bleeding into the bluish shimmer were people darting across the road, fleeing gunfire.

What can you see, Finney.

Not much, man. Not much. But those were AK-47 sounds a minute ago. Beirut. Heard enough of them pop pop pop motherfuckers last me a lifetime.

Uh huh. No mistaking that sound.

All you guys are vets and war heroes, I know. But I'm scared. I ain't never heard nothing but my very own little Lone Ranger cap pistol.

Pam. You OK, Pam.

I'm OK. I just don't think we ought to be here.

Calvin the driver is sidesaddle in his seat. Speaking back at us. Pam's right. This is just the kind of business we hoped to avoid. We should have stuck with the caravan.

Loverboy here said turn left. A shortcut. Some fucking shortcut.

Well, now we have to wait for Erroll's van. We agreed we'd stick together. They'll return here looking for us.

We don't know where they are or what happened to them.

They've only been gone five minutes.

Don't even want to think about those shots, man. That's the way Erroll and them went. Where those shots came from.

They may have run into some bad shit and split.

Erroll wouldn't abandon us.

Well, he may not have had a choice. Who knows who was shooting at what.

If anything's happened to the other van, that's even more reason to stay put. Where would we go anyway. The reason we stopped is we don't know the way out.

Hey, man. Following any one of these big streets to the end's bound to get us out.

But where? Didn't you hear the dude say some go for miles. End in the middle of nowhere.

Listen, everybody. Even if I knew the way, I wouldn't desert the other van. You're responsible for us, too.

I know. I know. And I'm terribly sorry I've lost us.

People coming this way. Whole mess of people haul-assing.

I can barely make them out. Distinct bits of color, dark flashes. Pop pop popping again and the road's wiped clean.

A few still coming. Slowly. I think somebody's hurt. Yeah. They're carrying a wounded guy. Bunch of women and a wounded man.

The tableau wobbles into focus. I see them clearly, then the image is smeared intermittently as they weave in and out of what seems to be sheets of flame leaping from the surface of the tarmac.

Let me look through the zoom.

Pam repeats to us what Finney has been relaying. He shoos her and jams the machine into his forehead again.

I'm getting some amazing shit, man. Hot. Hot. The guy's bleeding. Blood all over his shirt.

A white shirt crackling in the heat haze.

Snatches of moaning reach us, the women's voices shredded, detached fragments in the heat-driven wind, so we hear them before we can really listen to whatever it is they might be saying. If it's words they're saying. Are they crying out for help. Or injured, too, in ways we can't tell.

We sure can't leave now.

No way. This is network shit, man. Six o'clock national news.

Please. I'm responsible for your safety.

This is our job.

Van wasn't going nowhere anyway, right. White and Cheers are loading up. Cheers festooned with cameras and film cartridges in belts that crisscross and circle his body like bandoliers. White wears a camouflage tunic with a thousand bulging pockets. Cheers has declared at least five times in my hearing, I'm gonna get me one of those. Or steal yours. They are scrambling, clanking out the van's sliding door. Calvin's arm waves at them, miming a gesture that could be barring or locking the door, though he's really not attempting to reach it. White and Cheers hit the tarmac running. In a second Finney's humping his gear through the door, getting it balanced on his shoulder in a wobbly little hitch as he lands and straightens up. A few bounds and he's caught the others. Three blind mice, I think, each one with a camera stuck in front of his face.

Those fools are crazy.

Probably no safer in here than out there.

You mean you're going, too. If you do, you're crazy, too. And don't even have the excuse of a camera.

We should all stay in the combi. First rule is stay with the vehicle in an emergency.

I miss the second rule. Yell over my shoulder. I'll try to bring them back. Keep them close at least.

Though she is only a few yards away I still can't decipher what the woman is saying. She's speaking more than one language. From the evidence confronting us, the cries and gestures, what's happened is clear. Shots fired into the crowd after the rally ended, after guest celebrity, news cameras, and foreigners had split. Many wounded and down. They were trying to find help for this victim. He's in shock, White said. White had seen shock before. Wagged his head like poor bastard's not going to make it. Half the white shirt dyed black. Light stunning away color. Preparing me for the photo Cheers would send later. Black and white, stark contrast, no middle ground. Black face, black blood. Shirt blazing as if it has been scrubbed and scrubbed to the threshold of incandescence. This photo in my hand today. That day an exact copy of the representation Cheers captured. The glare causing him, he said, to see nothing for a second. A blind plunge into the machine's vision. Arm extended overhead, he snapped what he didn't see. The day screaming in, streaming out the lens.

Calvin assumes authority again. Corrals us closer to the van. I climb in. Pam, nearly in tears, squeezes my hand. The women, who are all that remain of the cortege, gather alongside the van. The man reclines against two of them. Another leans over his face, cooing, fanning. The fourth woman converses with Calvin. Calvin fills us in. He's slid over to the passenger's seat, talking out the window. Translates back to us the language scatted like reggae, studded with almost familiar words. No way, no way he says he can take responsibility for transporting the man to hospital. You are foreigners. You don't understand. I must live here after you've gone home to America. No, no, no. No way. None of us should interfere. We would be committing serious crimes. Be arrested. His first duty is to us. The struggle. And to his family. We must understand his position. He is no coward, but we must let these people go their way. Larger issues at stake. The woman must have been made to understand this also because she breaks off abruptly, points to the intersection, a flatbed cart halted on the near corner. All four women begin shouting to get the cart driver's attention. The speaker double-times, squat and efficient, toward the corner and the others drape the man as best, as gently as they can, so his limp body is a litter now in their grasp as they inch forward.

Was the man a son, a brother, husband, father, lover of one of the women. Did they all belong to one family, one clan. I'd studied them through the van's open door. The women were approximately the same age. What exact age, I had no clue. Not young, not old. Their deep black skin suffered no aging in this light. Round, broad faces. High cheekbones. A tarry sheen, plushness and resiliency. Thick, work-hardened women, but supple, light on their feet. I'd thought of Slavic peasants. Women similarly featured, stamped from the same sturdy mold. Wearing babushkas. We used to call them hunkies. Eastern European women picking through secondhand clothes when I was a boy and tagged along with my mother and aunts to the rummage sales on Homewood Avenue. These South African women also had their heads wrapped, turbans, kerchiefs. Strong, bulky in the shoulders, wide-keeled, unbowed by the man's weight they eased toward the intersection.

The picture takers had fastened themselves again to the wounded man and his rescuers. Cheers whipped ahead of everybody. In the lead now, backpedaling. His shots would catch the whole party. Africans, the black video guy and still cameramen. Pictures of their picture-taking. A frame. A statement.

He never saw the hole that took him down. Clean as a bullet between the eyes. One second he's cock of the walk, high on the advantage he'd gained over the other photographers, busily scooting side to side to orchestrate them into what he was shooting, in front, in command, backing toward the corner. Then he disappears. Lucky he didn't break his neck. A hole cut out of the road, no warning posted, a neat, shallow rectangular ditch and he'd tumbled backward into it.

Did one of the other photographers catch the surprise on his face. The astonished sayonara as Cheers suddenly backflipped off the edge of the world. Would we all giggle one day at the Kilroy snapshot of him, embarrassed, pants down, sheepishly exiting the hole. Would Finney or White digress a moment to document Cheers's writhing, the sickening angle of one leg bent under him, buried in a ditch like Pharaoh with his ten thousand dollars' worth of equipment scattered around him. No. The luck of innocents and babes was with Cheers. He refused the hands stretched out to help, emerged sputtering, wiping himself off, frowning, checking his stuff, motioning ahead to the women, who had detoured the hole and him in it without losing a step, the real story we all pursued. Lucky as a sleepwalker.

Light pools on black faces, drips in glistening claw marks. Black skin absorbs the sun and radiates warmth long after nightfall from soft bosoms and cheeks, the muscled, high butts. Each bearer everywoman to the man. Daughter mother wife. Safer to view them that way. Not give them names, ages. In a few moments they'd be gone. The man would live or die. The women would mourn him or nurse him back to health. I'd be oceans away. Receive one day in the mail this black-and-white photo from Cheers. A black South African man lifted down off his cross by his women. The sorrowful progress stopped in time, emptied of time, time painted over by an image that proclaims nothing else will happen, this moment is all that matters.

A military-looking canvas-covered snub-backed truck blocks the intersection. Disgorges a squad of black boys in slouch hats, blue coveralls. The ghetto comrades call them *instant cops*. Ignorant kids recruited from the poorest, rawest quarters, their loyalty purchased by three square meals a day, a barracks roof over their heads, coveralls, boots, two weeks of indoctrination that transforms them from street punks going nowhere to bullies with guns and power who can push other black people around. I'd seen these paramilitary keepers of order before. Always in pairs or groups. In kiosk checkpoints along the wide streets. I knew they patrolled here. Which meant sauntering along the bare peripheries of the settlement, gun cradled in one arm, hat cocked at a hip angle. They bother the girls, I'd been told. Harass comrades.

Shoot when they feel like shooting. We kill them when we can. All the above flashing back as I stop beside the booby trap that had upended Cheers. Wonder about its utility as a foxhole when the shooting starts. Because the procession is frozen as I am in its tracks. The instant cops have formed into a phalanx blockading the road. Rifles up and trained at our hearts. I want to believe I will have time to react once the firing commences. Plenty of targets between me and guns. Should I drop into the hole. Try to sprint back to the van. Would the van be safe. Isn't it as much the enemy as I am.

An officer leaps from the truck's cab and screams a command. Rifle butts thump the ground. I'm grateful for the two weeks of training. The men relax into a kind of shambling, shifty-eyed parade rest alert. I'm close enough to see they're scared, too. And that scares me more.

The officer beckons the women and their burden forward. I begin to retreat, slowly, hoping no one is paying attention to me. Hoping the officer's orders didn't include me, remembering Cheers poleaxed, dropping out of sight, expecting a land mine under my heels, the earth to open and swallow me whole. But determined to back away, back, back.

Right on time the women explode in a volley of shouts, cries, pleadings, outrage. Beat their chests, pull at turbaned hair. One is doubled over, pounds the ground as if she, too, is afflicted with a grievous stomach wound. One points to the wounded man. Flails at heaven, then, head bowed, folds her arms across her chest, swaying, moaning. I can't be sure what anything means. Are the women attacking, begging, demanding. Whatever else it accomplishes, the storm they crank up allows me to sidle more quickly to the van and slip into the open door. Cheers, White, and Finney aren't too far behind. I'd seen the officer karate-chop the air. Cheers, White, and Finney aren't completely nuts. They'd instantly obeyed his unambiguous signal to cease and desist, dropped cameras to their sides, retreated. Guilty schoolboys.

Those motherfuckers weren't playing, man.

That was close, real close. Could have gone either way. I don't think those cats decided till the last minute whether they were going to cap us or not.

Let's hope they keep deciding not to.

I believe it's over. They're letting them lay him on the cart.

Still leaves *us*. We's a whole nother story, man.

The police won't want an incident. Not with foreign press involved. If we just sit tight, they'll probably bugger off and we'll be okay.

You're the man, Calvin.

They may come confiscate your film.

Naw. Not my pictures. I'll fight those assholes for my pictures.

You and what army, fool.

Finney be all up in the dude's face in a minute. Here, Cap'n Boss. Take my tape and the camera, too. I didn't mean no harm. Lemme do a picture of you in your nice uniform for your wife and kiddies.

What do you think will happen to the wounded man.

They'll let him go to hospital, probably. What will happen then is anybody's guess. The hospital here is very poor. And the unlucky devil seems seriously hurt.

Be gone before dark.

You still determined to wait for the other van.

Things are different now. We don't want the police to think we're skulking about. We'd better leave right after they do. We'll just have to feel our way out.

Try the first left, Calvin.

Shut up, man. You the one fucked us up with your shortcut.

Just didn't go far enough. We needed to drive a little farther and I would have recognized the way out. Guarantee it.

I wonder where the others are.

They may have been escorted out. The police are about now. They'll be clearing the area. Impose an early curfew. You won't see anyone. When the shooting starts these people know to hide.

But the rally was peaceful. It was over. Who was shooting.

Of course I'm not positive. But most likely blue behinds like these. Letting people know the rally annoyed them. They didn't approve of the rally so they killed a few who attended.

That's horrible, Calvin.

We're working to change things in my country. I'll continue the fight after you leave. I know the police. I'm not afraid of them, but I must answer to them in ways you don't. That's why you must listen to me.

Sorry, Calvin. But we got a job, too. You know. In a couple hours, if we ever get out of here, this shit I copped be on TV all over the world.

Shooting people minding their own business. People trying to go home. Damn.

Home. You call this junkyard home.

White's got his camera up, shielded by his body. A sneak thief furtively snapping something he's seen down the long, flat road. Twisting heat mirages. An abandoned dugout and the scrap of rag on a stick that must have once been its roof. The dust-colored dog rooting in gravel. I wonder what's caught his attention. If he copped it. If I'll open an envelope one day and it will all unfurl again again and again.

Newborn Thrown in Trash and Dies

They say you see your whole life pass in review the instant before you die. How would *they* know. If you die after the instant replay, you aren't around to tell anybody anything. So much for they and what they say. So much for the wish to be a movie star for once in your life because I think that's what people are hoping, what people are pretending when they say you see your life that way at the end. Death doesn't turn your life into a five-star production. The end is the end. And what you know at the end goes down the tube with you. I can speak to you now only because I haven't reached bottom yet. I'm on my way, faster than I want to be traveling and my journey won't take long, but I'm just beginning the countdown to zero. Zero's where I started also so I know a little bit about zero. Know what they say isn't necessarily so. In fact the opposite's true. You begin and right in the eye of that instant storm your life plays itself out for you in advance. That's the theater of your fate, there's where you're granted a preview, the coming attractions of everything that must happen to you. Your life rolled into a ball so dense, so superheavy it would drag the universe down to hell if this tiny, tiny lump of whatever didn't dissipate as quickly as it formed. Quicker. The weight of it is what you recall some infinitesimal fraction of when you stumble and crawl through your worst days on earth.

Knowledge of what's coming gone as quickly as it flashes forth. Quicker. Faster. Gone before it gets here, so to speak. Any other way and nobody would stick around to play out the cards they're dealt. No future in it. You begin forgetting before the zero's entirely wiped off the clock face, before the next digit materializes. What they say is assbackwards, a saying by the way, assbackwards itself. Whether or not you're treated to a summary at the end, you get the whole thing handed to you, neatly packaged as you begin. Then you forget it. Or try to forget. Live your life as if it hasn't happened before, as if the tape has not been prepunched full of holes, the die cast.

I remember because I won't receive much of a life. A measure of justice in the world, after all. I receive a compensatory bonus. Since the time between my wake-up call and curfew is so cruelly brief, the speeded-up preview of what will come to pass, my life, my portion, my destiny, my career, slowed down just enough to let me peek. Not slow enough for me to steal much, but I know some of what it contains, its finality, the groaning, fatal weight of it around my neck.

Call it a trade-off. A standoff. Intensity for duration. I won't get much and this devastating flash isn't much either, but I get it. Zingo.

But the future remains mysterious. Even if we all put our heads together and become one gigantic brain, a brain lots smarter than the sum of each of our smarts, an intelligence as great as the one that guides ants, whales, or birds, because they're smarter, they figure things out not one by one, each individual locked in the cell of its head, its mortality, but collectively, doing what the group needs to do to survive, relate to the planet. If we were smarter even than birds and bees, we'd still have only a clue about what's inside the first flash of being. I know it happened and that I receive help from it. Scattered help. Sometimes I catch on. Sometimes I don't. But stuff from it's being pumped out always. I know things I have no business knowing. Things I haven't been around long enough to learn myself. For instance, many languages. A vast palette of feelings. The names of unseen things. Nostalgia for a darkness I've never experienced, a darkness another sense I can't account for assures me I will enter again. Large matters. Small ones. Naked as I am I'm dressed so to speak for my trip. Down these ten swift flights to oblivion.

Floor Ten. Nothing under the sun, they say, is new. This time they're right. They never stop talking so percentages guarantee they'll be correct sometimes. Especially since they speak out of both sides of their mouths at once: *Birds of a feather flock together. Opposites attract.* Like the billion billion monkeys at typewriters who sooner or later will bang out this story I think is uniquely mine. Somebody else, a Russian, I believe, with a long, strange-sounding name, has already written about his life speeding past as he topples slow-motion from a window high up in a tall apartment building. But it was in another country. And alas, the Russian's dead.

Floor Nine. In this building they shoot craps. One of many forms of gambling proliferating here. Very little new wealth enters this cluster of buildings that are like high-rise covered wagons circled against the urban night, so what's here is cycled and recycled by games of chance, by murder and other violent forms of exchange. Kids do it. Adults. Birds and bees. The law here is the same one ruling the jungle, they say. They say this is a jungle of the urban asphalt concrete variety. Since I've never been to Africa or the Amazon I can't agree or disagree. But you know what I think about what they say.

Seven come eleven. Snake eyes. Boxcars. Fever in the funkhouse searching for a five. Talk to me, baby. Talk. Talk. Please. Please. Please.

They cry and sing and curse and pray all night long over these games. On one knee they chant magic formulas to summon luck. They forget luck is rigged. Some of the men carry a game called Three Card Monte downtown. They cheat tourists who are stupid enough to trust in luck. Showmen with quick hands shuffling cards to a blur, fast feet carrying them away from busy intersections when cops come to break up their scam or hit on them for a cut. Flimflam artists, con men who daily use luck as bait and hook, down on their knees in a circle of other men who also should know better, trying to sweet-talk luck into their beds. Luck is the card you wish for, the card somebody else holds. You learn luck by its absence. Luck is what separates you from what you want. Luck is always turning its back and you lose.

Like other potions and powders they sell and consume here luck creates dependency. In their rooms people sit and wait for a hit. A yearning unto death for more, more, more till the little life they've been allotted dies in a basket on the doorstep where they abandoned it.

The Floor of Facts. Seventeen stories in this building. The address is 2950 West 23rd Street. My mother is nineteen years old. The trash chute down which I was dropped is forty-five feet from the door of the apartment my mother was visiting. I was born and will die Monday, August 12, 1991. The small door in the yellow cinder block wall is maroon. I won't know till the last second why my mother pushes it open. In 1990 nine discarded babies were discovered in New York City's garbage. As of August this year seven have been found. 911 is the number to call if you find a baby in the trash. Ernesto Mendez, forty-four, a Housing Authority caretaker, will notice my head, shoulders, and curly hair in a black plastic bag he slashes open near the square entrance of the trash compactor on the ground floor of this brown-brick public housing project called the Gerald J. Carey Gardens. Gardens are green places where seeds are planted, tended, nurtured. The headline above my story reads "Newborn Is Thrown in Trash and Dies." The headline will remind some readers of a similar story with a happy ending that appeared in March. A baby rescued and surviving after she was dropped down a trash chute by her twelve-year-old mother. The reporter, a Mr. George James who recorded many of the above facts, introduced my unhappy story in the Metro section of *The New York Times* on Wednesday, August 14, with this paragraph: "A young Brooklyn woman gave birth on Monday afternoon in a stairwell in a Coney Island housing project and then dropped the infant down a trash chute into a compactor ten stories below, the police said yesterday." And that's about it. What's fit to print. My tale in a nutshell followed by a relation of facts obtained by interview and reading official documents. Trouble is I could not be reached for comment. No one's fault. Certainly no negligence on the reporter's part. He gave me sufficient notoriety. Many readers must have shaken their heads in dismay or sighed or blurted, Jesus Christ, did you see this, handing the Metro section across the breakfast table or passing it to somebody at work. As grateful as I am to have my story made public you should be able to understand why I feel cheated, why the newspaper account is not enough, why I want my voice to be part of the record. The awful silence is not truly broken until we speak for ourselves. One chance to speak was snatched away. Then I didn't cry out as I plunged through the darkness. I didn't know any better. Too busy thinking to myself, *This is how it is, this is how it is, how it is* . . . accustoming myself to what it seemed life brings, what life is. Spinning, tumbling, a breathless rush, terror, exhilaration and wonder, wondering is this it, am I doing it right. I didn't know any better. The floors, the other lives packed into this building were going on their merry way as I flew past them in the darkness of my tunnel. No one waved. No one warned me. Said hello or goodbye. And of course I was too busy flailing, trying to catch my breath, trying to stop shivering in the sudden, icy air, welcoming almost the thick, pungent draft rushing up at me as if another pair of thighs were opening below to replace the ones from which I'd been ripped.

In the quiet dark of my passage I did not cry out. Now I will not be still. *A Floor of Questions.* Why.

A Floor of Opinions. I believe the floor of fact should have been the ground floor, the foundation, the solid start, the place where all else is firmly rooted. I believe there should be room on the floor of fact for what I believe, for this opinion and others I could not venture before arriving here. I believe some facts are unnecessary and that unnecessary borders on untrue. I believe facts sometimes speak for themselves but never speak for us. They are never anyone's voice and voices are what we must learn to listen to if we wish ever to be heard. I believe my mother did not hate me. I believe somewhere I have a father, who if he is reading this and listening carefully will recognize me as his daughter and be ashamed, heartbroken. I must believe these things. What else do I have. Who has made my acquaintance or noticed or cared or forgotten me. How could anyone be aware of what hurtles by faster than light, blackly, in a dark space beyond the walls of the rooms they live in, beyond the doors they lock, shades they draw when they have rooms and the rooms have windows and the windows have shades and the people believe they possess something worth concealing.

In my opinion my death will serve no purpose. The streetlamps will pop on. Someone will be run over by an expensive car in a narrow street and the driver will hear a bump but consider it of no consequence. Junkies will leak out the side doors of this gigantic mound, nodding, buzzing, greeting their kind with hippy-dip vocalizations full of despair and irony and stylized to embrace the very best that's being sung, played, and said around them. A young woman will open a dresser drawer and wonder whose baby that is sleeping peaceful on a bed of dishtowels, T-shirts, a man's ribbed sweat socks. She will feel something slither through the mud of her belly and splash into the sluggish river that meanders through her. She hasn't eaten for days, so that isn't it. Was it a deadly disease. Or worse, some new life she must account for. She opens and shuts the baby's drawer, pushes and pulls, opens and shuts.

I believe all floors are not equally interesting. Less reason to notice some than others. Equality would become boring, predictable. Though we may slight some and rattle on about others, that does not change the fact that each floor exists and the life on it is real, whether we pause to notice or not. As I gather speed and weight during my plunge, each floor adds its share. When I hit bottom I will bear witness to the truth of each one.

Floor of Wishes. I will miss Christmas. They say no one likes being born on Christmas. You lose your birthday, they say. A celebration already on

December 25 and nice things happen to everyone on that day anyway, you give and receive presents, people greet you smiling and wish you peace and goodwill. The world is decorated. Colored bulbs draped twinkling in windows and trees, doorways hung with wild berries beneath which you may kiss a handsome stranger. Music everywhere. Even wars truced for twenty-four hours and troops served home-cooked meals, almost. Instead of at least two special days a year, if your birthday falls on Christmas, you lose one. Since my portion's less than a day, less than those insects called ephemera receive, born one morning dead the next, and I can't squeeze a complete life cycle as they do into the time allotted, I wish today were Christmas. Once would be enough. If it's as special as they say. And in some matters we yearn to trust them. Need to trust something, someone, so we listen, wish what they say is true. The holiday of Christmas seems to be the best time to be on earth, to be a child and awaken with your eyes full of dreams and expectations and believe for a while at least that all good things are possible—peace, goodwill, love, merriment, the raven-maned rocking horse you want to ride forever. No conflict of interest for me. I wouldn't lose a birthday to Christmas. Rather than this smoggy heat I wish I could see snow. The city, this building snug under a blanket of fresh snow. No footprints of men running, men on their knees, men bleeding. No women forced out into halls and streets, away from their children. I wish this city, this tower were stranded in a gentle snowstorm and Christmas happens day after day and the bright fires in every hearth never go out, and the carols ring true chorus after chorus, and the gifts given and received precipitate endless joys. The world trapped in Christmas for a day dancing on forever. I wish I could transform the ten flights of my falling into those twelve days in the Christmas song. *On the first day of Christmas my true love said to me* . . . angels, a partridge in a pear tree, ten maids a milking, five gold rings, two turtledoves. I wish those would be the sights greeting me instead of darkness, the icy winter heart of this August afternoon I have been pitched without a kiss through a maroon door.

Floor of Power. El Presidente inhabits this floor. Some say he owns the whole building. He believes he owns it, collects rent, treats the building and its occupants with contempt. He is a bold-faced man. Cheeks slotted nose to chin like a puppet's. Chicken lips. This floor is entirely white. A floury, cracked white some say used to gleam. El Presidente is white also. Except for the pink dome of his forehead. Once, long ago, his flesh was pink head to toe. Then he painted himself white to match the white floor of power. Paint ran out just after the brushstroke that permanently sealed his eyes. Since El Presidente is cheap and mean he refused to order more paint. Since El Presidente is vain and arrogant he pretended to look at his unfinished self in the mirror and proclaimed he liked what he saw, the coat of cakey white, the raw pink dome pulsing like a bruise.

El Presidente often performs on TV. We can watch him jog, golf, fish, travel, lie, preen, mutilate the language. But these activities are not his job; his job is keeping things in the building as they are, squatting on the floor of power like a broken generator or broken furnace or broken heart, occupying the space where one that works should be.

Floor of Regrets. One thing bothers me a lot. I regret not knowing what is on the floors above the one where I began my fall. I hope it's better up there. Real gardens perhaps or even a kind of heaven for the occupants lucky enough to live above the floors I've seen. Would one of you please mount the stairs, climb slowly up from floor ten, examine carefully, one soft, warm night, the topmost floors and sing me a lullaby of what I missed.

Floor of Love. I'm supposed to be sleeping. I could be sleeping. Early morning and my eyes don't want to open and legs don't want to push me out of bed yet. Two rooms away I can hear Mom in the kitchen. She's fixing breakfast. Daddy first, then I will slump into the kitchen Mom has made bright and smelling good already this morning. Her perkiness, the sizzling bacon, water boiling, wheat bread popping up like jack-in-the-box from the shiny toaster, the Rice Krispies crackling, fried eggs hissing, the FM's sophisticated patter and mincing string trios would wake the dead. And it does. Me and Daddy slide into our places. Hi, Mom. Good morning, Dearheart. The day begins. Smells wonderful. I awaken now to his hand under the covers with me, rubbing the baby fat of my tummy where he's shoved my nightgown up past my panties. He says I shouldn't wear them. Says it ain't healthy to sleep in your drawers. Says no wonder you get those rashes. He rubs and pinches. Little nips. Then the flat of his big hand under the elastic waistband wedges my underwear down. I raise my hips a little bit to help. No reason not to. The whole thing be over with sooner. Don't do no good to try and stop him or slow him down. He said my mama knows. He said go on fool and tell her she'll smack you for talking nasty. He was right. She beat me in the kitchen. Then took me into their room and he stripped me butt-naked and beat me again while she watched. So I kinda hump up, wiggle, and my underwear's down below my knees, his hand's on its way back up to where I don't even understand how to grow hairs yet.

The Floor That Stands for All the Other Floors Missed or Still to Come. My stepbrother Tommy was playing in the schoolyard and they shot him dead. Bang. Bang. Gang banging and poor Tommy caught a cap in his chest. People been in and out the apartment all day. Sorry. Sorry. Everybody's so sorry. Some brought cakes, pies, macaroni casseroles, lunch meat, liquor. Two Ebony Cobras laid a joint on Tommy's older brother who hadn't risen from the kitchen chair he's straddling, head down, nodding, till his boys bop through the door. They know who hit Tommy. They know tomorrow what they must do. Today one of those everybody-in-the-family-and-friends-in-dark-clothes-funeral days, the mothers, sisters, aunts, grandmothers weepy, the men motherfucking everybody from god on down. You can't see me among the mourners. My time is different from this time. You can't understand my time. Or name it. Or share it. Tommy is beginning to remember me. To join me where I am falling unseen through your veins and arteries down down to where the heart stops, the square opening through which trash passes to the compactor.

Welcome

At this time of the year she could not help thinking of the daughter given then so quickly taken away. Not daughter. She didn't think daughter. She thought Njeri. Who had been her, living inside her, unseparate, her blood breath and heart beating then Njeri for a spring summer and fall and then when the streets again were full of snow not full really but rags and tags of old snow everywhere and blistered skins of ice and the hawk under your clothes the instant you step out the door, then in a haze of sedation that quieted the howling pain Njeri had slipped away, her own pain an afterthought recalled days years later howling as if God or the Devil himself were entering or leaving her Njeri's breathing something she could watch but could not do yes it was that simple you could not do it for her that simple you lay down one day and just about died and then a child was born and you were in two places two pieces always the inside outside outside inside the cold raw your skin cracks and shatters the whole world one crisp frozen sheet of glass a strong wind could break everything the lighted windows like ornaments hung on buildings the music in the aisles of department stores this season fresh each time it comes she comes the first time again dancing her brother Njeri in his arms to the Brothers Johnson *I'll be good to you good to you good to you* beside a glittering tree and then the next Christmas Njeri is gone. She cannot help thinking and then she sees through the lines of the carols, the songs that always were to her packages wrapped neatly, carefully, lovingly wrapped in beautiful paper, stars, bells, trees, stripes of luminous ribbon, swirls of ribbon flowers, someone had spent hours decorating what was precious inside to save it, give it away, those carols each held Njeri, her smell, her eyes, the words she'd begun to chatter.

She would be twelve now. A dozen candles on the cake to count. 1—2—3—4—5 . . . and her chipmunk cheeks bell to puff them all out in a single breath. No one had said one word last birthday. She'd waited for her mother to call and when she finally did neither of them mentioned the day, the day Njeri had come here or the day one year plus eleven days more when she'd left. She tried to remember what they did say. What else could they have talked about? Her mother knew the birth day, the death day. How in this season those days would drop like something heavy shot from the sky. A soundless explosion, the sky screams, the earth buckles as something that had been flying lands with all the weight of things broken that will not rise again. Perhaps they'd talked about the grandkids, what each one wanted, what they were going to get and not get. Lines in the stores. Layaways. Snapshots with tacky Santas the wrong color. Dolls that pee. Machines that talk and count and shoot and how many batteries needed to make them run. How much it cost and how in God's name was anybody ever going to pay for it all in January when the bills came due. What else could they have talked about? And had her mother sighed after she hung up the phone, happy or not happy she'd avoided mentioning Njeri? Had her mother been trying to take all the weight upon herself the way she decided sometimes to spare her children and be the strong one, the one who could bear the suffering meant for all of them, willing herself to stand alone in the rain, as if she could will the rain to fall on her and no one else? How much had her mother wanted to say Njeri's name? How many times did her mother need to say it to herself as she gripped the phone and said other words into it? She had not said Njeri either. Always other things to talk about. Sometimes on the phone with her mother she wouldn't know who was doing the talking and who the listening. Conversation weaves back and forth. Whose turn to answer? Whose turn to start a new topic? Or listen? Who'd attended the Community Council meeting Tuesday night at the center? Was she there or had her mother told her about it and who'd heard Delia Goins tell that big lie on Willa Mae who'd never even been to Cleveland? Or did Willa follow her up and down the aisles of the A&P whispering in her ear and then she passed Willa's tale to her mother and she could tell her mother was nodding uh huh, uh huh at the other end of the line, hold on a minute water's boiling and in the quiet, the crackle of the wait, Njeri's name over and over as if they both understood space must be allowed for it so something would say it get it over with and say it again and again since they wouldn't since they couldn't bring themselves to say it, they must make space to let something else say it so both of them could stop holding their breath, let it out, the sinus bursting pressure in ears and throat and behind the eyes, let it out.

I put water on for coffee before I dialed you. Can't keep anything in my brain anymore. Afraid I'm going to leave the stove on when I go to bed one night and burn down the house.

Always terrible fires around Christmas. Every Christmas you hear about babies and old folks burning up. Whole families.

Dry trees and hot lights. Kids playing around all those wires. Do you have your tree yet?

Mom. You know we don't get trees anymore.

Of course I do. Talking to myself, I guess. I've been putting off and putting off getting a tree. What it is I think I don't really want the bother. Nobody here now but me. What do I need with a Christmas tree?

She could hear how the talk went but could not remember really whether it was last year or any particular year. Two women talking. During the holiday season. One was her mother. She was the other. The woman's daughter who was now a woman herself. Who'd had children of her own. Children getting big now who she'd make Kwansa for. Grandchildren. Faces and names more familiar than her own. Not separate from her own. Their sicknesses. Their smiles. Shopping to find a gift for Grandma. A daughter. She was her mother's daughter and her kids were gifts, her children herself returning to her mother's house for an old-fashioned Christmas. Bright boxes under the tree. One missing. One lost. But let's not talk about that this afternoon. Even if it just about kills us both.

Hello hi good morning how are you haven't heard from you oh I'm fine everybody here's OK on my way to Homewood Avenue to get some last-minute shopping done how you doing same ole same ole I you she said did you hear . . .

Have you talked to Tom lately?

He's on the road. I worry so when he's on the road.

Mom, you worry when he's sitting at the dinner table beside you.

I know. I know. I'm terrible.

No. You're not terrible. Worrying's your job. Wouldn't be you if you weren't lying in bed with one eye open waiting for whichever one of us out partying to come tipping up the stairs. I knew you'd be awake. Whatever time I dragged in. Why'd I always try to creep up those big-mouth steps. Like they wouldn't moan and groan no matter how quiet I tried to be. Like you wouldn't be in your room listening, waiting. Zat you, sis.

Your brother's changed.

She sees him in a plane over New York City. It is Sunday morning, early. She looks down on bridges, highways, houses laid out like a crowded cemetery. Haze hangs over the skyline. Flat low-lying stretches of land are sweat-stained where the ocean has come and gone. Most of the sky a blue sigh. Except for brown smearing the tops of the tallest buildings. Except for snowy swipes of cloud here and there that help her know how high she is, how far she can see. He is over New York or some other city she's met only in movies or in her dream of escape. She knows he's flying to some fabulous place and knows he won't stay long. He'll be home for the holidays. He'll tell her it's best here at home when the family's all together. When you travel to a place and don't really know anybody there, it gets old pretty quick. I used to love it, he says, but now I think of myself falling down in the street. Strangers stepping past and stepping over and a cold white room with no visitors, no one who understands I wasn't always the wreck they see now. She listens and thinks how impossible it is to be in another place, how difficult it is to imagine herself landing in another place, visiting, staying, having another life. She envies her brother. She's glad he does what he does so she doesn't need to bother.

From some faraway city he'd sent them that nice card the Christmas Njeri came.

> *Thou were born of a mayden mylde*
> *Upon a day, so it befelle*
> *There fore we say, bothe man and childe*
> *"Thou arte welcum with us to dwelle."*

He's older. We're all older, Mom. All changed.

Yes. God knows that's true, but he's different, changed in ways that make me worry about him.

After all that's happened these past few years, it's a wonder he's not crazy. Wonder we're not all stone crazy.

Sometimes I believe we're being tested.

Well, I wish whoever's conducting the damned test would get it the hell over with. Enough's enough.

You sound like him now.

He's my brother.

And my son. Youall are what I live for now. The only thing that keeps me going.

C'mon, lady. Don't talk that mess. Make yourself sound like some dried-up prune piece of something.

Listen at you. Listen how you talk to your poor sick pitiful old mother.

We're all poor. But I ain't buying the rest. You heard what the doctor said. You're a healthy woman with lots of life left.

Except.

We're taking care of the except. And you're coming along just fine.

It's a pretty big except. Big. Big. All my hair's gone. And how those treatments make me feel is a long way from fine, but let's leave the doctors out of this. I'm not the one I'm worried about now. I'm worried about Tom.

Looked good to me last time he was home. Same old big brother as far as I could tell. A little thinner maybe, but still eats like a horse. Nothing wrong with that man's appetite. And he still loves to tease.

He's not himself.

What do you expect, Mom? Nobody could live through what he did, what we all did, and not come out changed.

I know what it is.

What?

It hasn't hit him yet. Not really. He's walking around talking and doing what he thinks he needs to do and I don't believe he's let it hit him yet. He thinks he's faced it down and now he's going on with his life, but it's still out there somewhere waiting and he won't be ready, he won't know what to do when it hits him.

Mom.

You were that way with Njeri, bless her soul. Youall are my children and I know how you are. My Hard-Hearted Hannah pour water on a drowning man. But then she goes off somewhere and drowns her own self.

He's been through a lot. He's coping the best he can. Better than most people would as far as I can tell.

Oh. He's tough, all right. You're all tough. My tough-as-nails children. Tell me about it. I got the scars to prove it. But each and every one has that soft spot, too. Under all the ice. Deep under there, deep, deep, but not so deep it can't be reached. I've seen that, too. Got the scars behind that, too.

She tells a story about her brother. An old one she doesn't have to work too hard at. One her mother can jump in and finish with her. Then a tidbit about Keesha, the youngest, the last gift, not to replace Njeri but give her lost daughter another chance, this time in the strong brown arms and legs and healthy lungs of her sister, baby sister who knows Njeri as a photograph on the mantel. That's Njeri, baby, your sister. Yes, she used to live here. She still lives here in Mama's heart. Yes. Inside. You can't see her but she's there. Always. Beside you and Staci and Tanya. Yes. Plenty room for all of you, don't worry. You can't touch her or see her, but here's what she looked like. Her picture. You would be her little sister. Uh huh. That's right. Yes. She's a baby still in the picture because she didn't have a chance to grow up and be a big girl like you. Mama's big girl. But she's here. You're both here. All my babies, all my big girls.

Faver. You know how Keesh says *father*. Faver, I don't care if it good I'm not going to drink this goddamn juice. And Faver just about fell out his chair. Trying his best not to laugh. Hand all up in front of his mouth. Bout strangled hisself. Coughing, you know. Trying not to laugh.

What did you say? Still had his hand up. You know. He could barely talk. Trying to get together his proper father voice.

Where'd you hear that word, young lady?

What goddamn word, Faver?

Then I'm rolling. I had to leave the table. Let Faver handle this one, I'm thinking. I'm out of here. Time to go to work.

She stares at the phone. Her mother's voice no longer in there. A little death. If she lifts the receiver it will buzz and then a voice comes on and then it will beep and then silence. Not her mother's voice. A woman's voice but no woman she knows. Once she'd been sure she'd never touch a phone again. Not after she'd called her mother and cried into the receiver and couldn't say one word except *Mom . . . Mom*. Three times if she's remembering right, standing at a bank of phones in the hospital lobby, reading numbers and messages scratched on the partition that screened her face but not her voice from the caller next to her. How could you do so many things at once? Dial and read and say *Mom* three times and hate to be where you are so public and so sorry sorry you are hurting your mother and making a fool of yourself sobbing like a baby and none of it does a damn bit of good because you can also hang like a spider from the dirty ceiling and pity yourself and see none of it doing any good because your baby is still dead upstairs on a metal cart wrapped up in hospital blankets wherever they'd taken her.

You could lose a child in an instant that way and for a long time after feel each lurch forward of the hands of the clock, as if you were stuck there like a naked chicken turning on a spit but you didn't turn you ticked one click at a time so time didn't change night into day one hour into the next one minute passing to another minute, time stopped then had to start up again, again and again. You wondered why anybody wanted to continue, how others could pretend to keep going. Your children. Why were they such noisy survivors? As if only she could remember. Till their eyes, their demands shocked her into speeding up again, matching herself to the business around her so she can step again into the frantic pace of those who were not skewered as she was, who were not clicking as she was, miles between clicks, lifetimes between each tiny lunge forward.

You could lose a child like that, once and for always in an instant and walk around forever with a lump in your throat, with the question of *what might have been* weighing you down every time you measure the happiness in someone else's face. Or you could lose a child and have him at the same time and how did this other way of losing a child in prison for life change her brother.

Her brother had said: No matter how much you love them you only get one chance, so if something happens and you lose one, no matter how, no matter who's to blame, you're guilty forever because you had that one chance, that precious life given to you to protect, and you blew it. I know you must understand, sis. And she did and didn't and reached out to touch him, but he wasn't asking for that. His eyes in another country that quick.

She feels the pull of that slow slow time on her shoulders. Shrugs it off and squeezes her arms into her coat. I could stand here all day, she thinks, and says aloud Huh uh to the silence in the empty house as she slams the door behind her and steps into the winter street.

Tom, Tom the piper's son / Stole a pig and away he run.

She is staring at her boots. Hears tinkling of a bell. The old man's propped on a box on a grate just beyond the corner of Hamilton and Homewood in front of the little store where people are lined up to buy lottery tickets. The man's beard is not white. He's not wearing a red suit trimmed in milky white fur. No shiny black leather boots on his feet but on his head an elf's tassel cap, many colors, earflaps like those Eskimo reindeer people wear. The jingle bell, then rattle of change in his tin cup. People in the store bob up and down, blow on their hands and hug themselves and shiver as if it's just as cold inside as outside. She can only see them from the shoulders up in the partially painted-over window. They are real now. Like fish constantly swimming in their glass tanks, they must move to live. They are bumping into each other. Huddling. Exchanging news, lies, yesterday's numbers. She didn't believe in luck. If she was supposed to win some huge pot of money, she'd know it, she'd be told when, where and how to collect it. It wouldn't just happen. Nothing just happened. It was already out there waiting. She hadn't known she was staring at her feet until she heard the bell and saw the old man staring at his crusty high-top sneakers. One reason he was over that grate begging pennies was so she could see his old face, remember her grandfather's in it, her brother's in that. Another reason was to chase her eyes from the pavement, remind her she could not walk these Homewood streets in a dream.

He was blind. Blind. Old crippled blind Solomon. She needed to say the word before she could remember he was blind as a stone. And there were no legs in that mound of rags draping the crate. No feet in his used-to-be-sky-blue Connies. Someone had pulled him in a kid's wagon to this warm spot over the grate. Wagon nowhere in sight. Probably hauling groceries home for the shoppers at the A&P. Same one who pulled Solomon here be hustling groceries now. She can hear the wagon wheels bumping over the broken streets. She's digging in her purse for a quarter. Maybe two quarters since it's the holiday season. To give a boy who sets her bags on the stoop. To drop in Solomon's tin cup. She studies the lines of his face, thinks of swirls of barbed wire that would tear up your hand if you tried to pat his cheeks.

Her grandfather shaved clean everyday, chin clean as his clean bald head till his heart stopped the first time and he was a prisoner in the big chair in the living room. When their father left them they'd stay at Grandma's house and play around their grandfather's feet and he'd cough into his huge red handkerchief the only sound from him for days except sometimes when they were in the middle of a game his voice would begin a conversation with nobody they could see and the words float down to the floor so they'd stop what they were doing, freeze and listen to words only half understood, half hummed, whistled, whispered, Sunshine you are my sunshine or Froggy went a courtin and he did ride or Tom Tom the piper's son the song with his name a name they never called him everybody called him DaddyTom except Grandma, who said Thomas, Thomas, and shook his arm when the snoring got too loud she couldn't hear her stories on the radio or when she took the snot rag from his hand all nasty and bloody in two fingers the way Mom would carry traps with mouse crushed in them when we lived in that basement on Bellefonte Street Tom Tom he'd sing little half songs and we'd be down there nailed to the floor wondering what he might say next and who was up there with him talking back. Little pickaninnies he'd call us and pat our heads and tickle us with his funny-looking nub of crooked thumb and find us pennies in the pocket of his flannel shirt and then he'd be gone again days and days no sound but the coughing till spooky talk begins again out of nowhere and we'd pay attention as if our lives depended on not missing one word. After his heart stopped the second time bristle grew on his cheeks, all the color drained from him but his cheeks turned comic-book hairy blue and lines like blind Solomon's deep black cut the dough of his skin into a thousand pieces. Coughing and snoring and the bad smell of his feet, he spent most days in bed but when he's downstairs we'd play a little farther away from his chair than we used to, farther from his silence, his wordlessness except once or twice as if we all heard a signal we'd scoot closer, stop and listen even though we knew DaddyTom was finished long ago saying whatever it was he needed to tell us. DaddyTom didn't look back when we looked at him. His noises made him wet. Grandma wiped him with towels. Solomon lets me study his face. Then does something he shouldn't be able to do. Returns my stare so I know he knows I'm there in front of him and he also lets me know enough's enough he's tired of me leaning my eyeballs on him so I'm a little ashamed when I turn away until I remember what he's sitting there for. Not to be worn out by my staring, but to be a way I can begin to learn my brother's pain.

My brother who is Tom. Named for our grandfather. My brother Tom who named his lost son after Will, our handsome father who shaved every morning and sang, too. Crooned gospel songs and love songs before he deserted us. Sweet music at the mirror Sunday morning while he shaved and dressed.

When people come out the store they are smiling. A few drop coins in Solomon's cup for luck. Luck no one should believe they can beg or buy. Not with buckets of tears or shovelfuls of gold dumped in a cup big enough to hold Solomon and his box and the whole damn corner store. Luck is what you wish for. And as long as you're wishing you sure don't have it. So you sure should shut up and go on about your business and something will tell you soon enough what happens next. What always happens next in its own peculiar way in its own sweet time because there's nothing else. Only that.

Doctor said there's nothing else we can do, Mrs. Crawford. I'm sorry, Mrs. Crawford. And he was. A sorry-ass bringer of bad news and nothing else he could do. Nobody to blame. Just that sorry moment when he said Njeri had to die and nobody's fault nobody could do anything more and because he was sorry there in front of her bringing the sorry news why shouldn't she strike him down tear up his sorry white ass just because there was nothing else she could do nobody could do nobody to blame just knock him down and stomp on his chest and grind those Coke-bottle glasses into his soft sorry face.

Sunshine. My only sunshine.

She'll say it's good to see you. And her brother will grin back at her. Hug each other close as they've learned to do these last dozen years. How are you?

Kiss. Kiss me. My cheeks. My lips. Do it. Don't say a word.

I'm fine. Everybody's fine.

The lives we live lead to this. You are my brother. I'm your sister. We will spend most of our time apart then on holidays we'll hug, cling. When we let go, what I'll truly want to know is everything about you.

Do you remember DaddyTom singing?

Did you hold your breath the whole time like I did? Did it snow while we were holding our breath? Did the seasons change? Did Christmas come?

I'm OK. Terry and the kids send love.

Too bad they couldn't make it.

They're very disappointed. But Terry had to stay close to her father, sick as he is. So it's just me. In and out quick. I want to be back with Terry and the kids Christmas morning. Maybe we can all get here Easter.

I feel so badly for her father. He's a good man. A year since youall've been here, I bet. Kids grow so fast. I won't recognize your youngest.

She's prettier every day. Like your Keesha.

Hey, Keesha. Look at you. You're getting tall, girl. Come over here and give your uncle some sugar, sugar pie.

It doesn't take long, does it?

In his face I see whatever he's put there for me. I will let him go. The moment will pass. He will bend down to kiss Keesha, then lift her high in his arms. He asks about my whole life as I ask about his in the singsong questions. If he stays long enough to catch him a second time, alone, then's when I'll ask about my nephew, his son, who's not dead and gone in an instant, but who's lost to him, to us in ways none of us knows words for. None of us can say except in the silence this old toothless man was set on a corner to break with his cup his bell his silence all of him that's missing under rags that are blankets blankets blankets.

When I do finally catch him he tells me how hard it is to face these Homewood streets. Like the world is washed fresh after rain, right, and when you step out in the sunshine everything is different, sis, anything seems possible, well, think of just the opposite. Of flying or driving for hours on the turnpike and getting off in Monroeville then the parkway and already the dread starting, the little-boy feeling of fear I used to have when I'd leave home to deliver newspapers in Squirrel Hill and all the houses up there big and set back from the curb and wide spaces between them and green lawns, fat trees and nothing but white people in those huge houses. I'd walk softly no place up there really to put my feet afraid my big black footprints would leave a trail anywhere I stepped. That kind of uneasiness, edginess till the car crosses Braddock Avenue. Then blam. The whole thing hits me. I'm home again and it's the opposite of a new shiny world because I feel everything closing down. Blam. I know nothing has changed and never will, these streets swallow me alive and hate everybody and that's how it's going to be. Takes me a day at least to get undepressed behind that feeling of being caught up again and unable to breathe and everybody I love in some kind of trouble that is past danger worse than danger, a state I don't want to give a name to, can't say because I don't want to hear it. Then I sort of gradually settle in. Youall remind me of what's good here. Why I need to come back. How this was home first and always will be.

Last night I was driving to cop some chicken wings you know how I love them salty and greasy as they are I slap on extra hot sauce and pop a cold Iron City pour it over ice hog heaven you know so I'm on my way to Woodside Bar-B-Que and I see a man and a little boy on the corner at the bus stop on Frankstown at the bottom of the hill across from Mom's street. It's cold cold cold. I'm stopped at the light. So I can see the little boy's upset and crying. His father's standing there looking pissed off, helpless and lost. Staring up the hill for a bus that probably ain't coming for days this late on a weekend. Daddy a kid himself and somehow he finds himself on a freezing night with an unhappy little boy on a black windy corner and no bus in sight no soul in sight like it's the end of the world and I think, Damn, why are they out there in this arctic-ass weather, the kid shivering and crying in a skimpy K Mart snowsuit, the man not dressed for winter either, a hooded sweatshirt under his shiny baseball jacket and I see a woman somewhere, the mother, another kid really, already split from this young guy, a broken home, the guy's returning the boy to his mother, or her mother or his and this is the only way, the best he can do and the wind howls the night gets blacker and blacker they'll find the two of them, father son man and boy frozen to death, icicles in the morning on the corner.

I think all that in a second. The whole dreary story line. Characters and bad ending waiting for the light to change on my way for chicken wings. On my way back past that same corner I see the father lift his son and hug him. No bus in sight and it's still blue cold but the kid's not fidgeting and crying anymore he's up in his daddy's arms and I think, Fuck it. They'll make it. Or if they don't somebody else will come along and try. Or somebody else try. To make kids. A home. A life. That's all we can do. Any of us. And that's why Homewood's here, because lots of us won't make it but others will try and keep on keeping on. And if I'd had just one wish in the world then, it would have been to be that father or that son hugging that moment when nothing could touch them.

One more thing and then I'll shut up. But I need to tell you one more thing because that's how it happened. Just little things one after another prying me open. Tears in my eyes when I got back to that corner because there was this fat girl in the Woodside. No, not fat. A big girl, solid, pretty, light on her feet, a large pretty big-eyed brown girl thirteen or fourteen with black crinkly hair and smooth kind of round chubby cheek babydoll face who served me my chicken wings through the iron bars they have on the counter at the Woodside. And while she was using tongs to dig my dozen wings out the bin she was singing. Singing while she wrapped them in wax paper and stuffed them in a bag. Bouncing on her toes and in the sweetest, purest, trilling soprano singing little riffs in another language of something for this time of year, something old like Bach with Christ's name in it and hallelujah hallelujah you know and it sounded so fine I hoped she'd never stop singing and my eyes clouded up for no good reason right there standing in the Woodside. I'm no crier, sis. You know me. But I couldn't stop all the way home till I saw those two on the corner again and knew how much I was missing Will, and then I had to cry some more.

God's Gym
(2005)

Weight

My mother is a weightlifter. You know what I mean. She understands that the best-laid plans, the sweetest beginnings, have a way of turning to shit. Bad enough when life fattens you up just so it can turn around and gobble you down. Worse for the ones like my mother who life keeps skinny, munching on her daily, one cruel little needle-toothed bite at a time so the meal lasts and lasts. Mom understands life don't play so spends beaucoup time and energy getting ready for the worst. She lifts weights to stay strong. Not barbells or dumbbells, though most of the folks she deals with, especially her sons, act just that way, like dumbbells. No. The weights she lifts are burdens—her children's, her neighbors', yours. Whatever awful calamities arrive on her doorstep or howl in the news, my mom squeezes her frail body beneath them. Grips, hoists, holds the weight. I swear sometimes I can hear her sinews squeaking and singing under a load of invisible tons.

I ought to know, since I'm one of the burdens bowing her shoulders. She loves heavy, hopeless me unconditionally. Before I was born, Mom loved me, forever and ever till death do us part. I'll never be anyone else's darling, darling boy, so it's her fault, her doing, isn't it, that neither of us can face the thought of losing the other. How could I resist reciprocating her love. Needing her. Draining her. Feeling her straining underneath me, the pop and crackle of her arthritic joints, her gray hair sizzling with static electricity, the hissing friction, tension, and pressure as she lifts more than she can bear. Bears more than she can possibly lift. You have to see it to believe it. Like the Flying Wallendas or Houdini's spine-chilling escapes. One of the greatest shows on earth.

My mother believes in a god whose goodness would not permit him to inflict more troubles than a person can handle. A god of mercy and salvation. A sweaty, bleeding god presiding over a fitness class in which his chosen few punish their muscles. She should wear a T-shirt: *God's Gym*.

In spite of a son in prison for life, twin girls born dead, a mind-blown son who roams the streets with everything he owns in a shopping cart, a strung-out daughter with a crack baby, a good daughter who miscarried the only child her dry womb ever produced, in spite of me and the rest of my limp-along, near-to-normal siblings and their children—my nephews doping and gangbanging, nieces unwed, underage, dropping babies as regularly as the seasons—in spite of breast cancer, sugar diabetes, hypertension, failing kidneys, emphysema, gout, all resident in her body and epidemic in the community, knocking off one by one her girlhood friends, in spite of corrosive poverty and a neighborhood whose streets are no longer safe even for gray, crippled-up folks like her, my mom loves her god, thanks him for the blessings he bestows, keeps her faith he would not pile on more troubles than she could bear. Praises his name and prays for strength, prays for more weight so it won't fall on those around her less able to bear up.

You've seen those iron-pumping, muscle-bound brothers fresh out the slam who show up at the playground to hoop and don't get picked on a team cause they can't play a lick, not before they did their bit, and sure not now, back on the set, stiff and stone-handed as Frankenstein, but finally some old head goes on and chooses one on his squad because the brother's so huge and scary-looking sitting there with his jaw tight, lip poked out, you don't want him freaking out and kicking everybody's ass just because the poor baby's feelings is hurt, you know what I mean, the kind so buff looks like his coiled-up insides about to bust through his skin or his skin's stripped clean off his body so he's a walking anatomy lesson. Well, that's how my mom looks to me sometimes, her skin peeled away, no secrets, every taut nerve string on display.

I can identify the precise moment when I began to marvel at my mother's prodigious strength, during a trip with her one afternoon to the supermarket on Walnut Street in Shadyside, a Pittsburgh, Pennsylvania, white community with just a few families of us colored sprinkled at the bottom ends of a couple of streets. I was very young, young enough not to believe I'd grow old, just bigger. A cashier lady who seemed to be acquainted with my mother asked very loudly, Is this your son, and Mom smiled in reply to the cashier's astonishment, saying calmly, Yes, he is, and the doughy white lady in her yellow Krogers smock with her name on the breast tried to match my mother's smile but only managed a fake grin like she'd just discovered shit stinks but didn't want anybody else to know she knew. Then she blurted, He's a tall one, isn't he.

Not a particularly unusual moment as we unloaded our shopping cart and waited for the bad news to ring up on the register. The three of us understood, in spite of the cashier's quick shuffle, what had seized her attention. In public situations the sight of my pale, Caucasian-featured mother and her variously colored kids disconcerted strangers. They gulped. Stared. Muttered insults. We were visible proof somebody was sneaking around after dark, breaking the apartheid rule, messy mulatto exceptions to the rule, trailing behind a woman who could be white.

Nothing special about the scene in Krogers. Just an ugly moment temporarily reprieved from turning uglier by the cashier's remark, which attributed her surprise to a discrepancy in height, not color. But the exchange alerted me to a startling fact—I was taller than my mother. The brown boy, me, could look down at the crown of his light-skinned mother's head. Obsessed by size, like most adolescent boys, size in general and the size of each and every particular part of my body and how mine compared to others, I was always busily measuring and keeping score, but somehow I'd lost track of my mother's size, and mine relative to hers. Maybe because she was beyond size. If someone had asked me my mother's height or weight, I probably would have replied, *Huh. Ubiquitous*, I might say now. A tiny skin-and-bone woman way too huge for size to pin down.

The moment in Krogers is also when I began to marvel at my mother's strength. Unaccountably, unbeknown to me, my body had grown larger than hers, yes, and the news was great in a way, but more striking and not so comforting was the fact that, never mind my advantage in size, I felt hopelessly weak standing there beside my mom in Krogers. A wimpy shadow next to her solid flesh and bones. I couldn't support for one hot minute a fraction of the weight she bore on her shoulders twenty-four hours a day. The weight of the cashier's big-mouthed disbelief. The weight of hating the pudgy white woman forever because she tried to steal my mother from me. The weight of cooking and cleaning and making do with no money, the weight of fighting and loving us iron-headed, ungrateful brats. Would I always feel puny and inadequate when I looked up at the giant fist hovering over our family, the fist of God or the Devil, ready to squash us like bugs if my mother wasn't always on duty, spreading herself thin as an umbrella over our heads, her bones its steel ribs keeping the sky from falling.

Reaching down for the brass handle of this box I must lift to my shoulder, I need the gripping strength of my mother's knobby-knuckled fingers, her superhero power to bear impossible weight.

Since I was reading her this story over the phone (I called it a story but Mom knew better), I stopped at the end of the paragraph above that you just completed, if you read that far, stopped because the call was long distance, daytime rates, and also because the rest had yet to be written. I could tell by her silence she was not pleased. Her negative reaction didn't surprise me. Plenty in the piece I didn't like either. Raw, stuttering stuff I intended to improve in subsequent drafts, but before revising and trying to complete it, I needed her blessing.

Mom's always been my best critic. I depend on her honesty. She tells the truth yet never affects the holier-than-thou superiority of some people who believe they occupy the high ground and let you know in no uncertain terms that you nor nobody else like you ain't hardly coming close. Huh-uh. My mother smiles as often as she groans or scolds when she hears gossip about somebody behaving badly. *My, my, my*, she'll say, and nod and smile and gently broom you, the sinner, and herself into the same crowded heap, no one any better than they should be, could be, absolute equals in a mellow sputter of laughter she sometimes can't suppress, hiding it, muffling it with her fist over her mouth, nodding, remembering how people's badness can be too good to be true, *My, my, my.*

Well, my story didn't tease out a hint of laugh, and forget the 550 miles separating us, I could tell she wasn't smiling either. Why was she holding back the sunshine that could forgive the worst foolishness. Absolve my sins. Retrieve me from the dead-end corners into which I paint myself. Mama, please. Please, please, please, don't you weep. And tell ole Martha not to moan. Don't leave me drowning like Willie Boy in the deep blue sea. Smile, Mom. Laugh. Send that healing warmth through the wire and save poor me.

Was it the weightlifting joke, Mom. Maybe you didn't think it was funny.

Sorry. Tell the truth, I didn't see nothing humorous about any of it. *God's T-shirt.* You know better. Ought to be ashamed of yourself. Taking the Lord's name in vain.

Where do you get such ideas, boy. I think I know my children. God knows I should by now, shouldn't I. How am I not supposed to know youall after all you've put me through beating my brains out to get through to you. *Yes, yes, yes.* Then one youall goes and does something terrible I never would have guessed was in you. Won't say you break my heart. Heart's been broke too many times. In so many little itty-bitty pieces can't break down no more, but youall sure ain't finished with me, are you. Still got some new trick in you to lay on your weary mother before she leaves here.

Guess I ought to be grateful to God an old fool like me's still around to be tricked. Weightlifter. Well, it's different. Nobody ain't called me nothing like weightlifter before. It's different, sure enough.

Now here's where she should have laughed. She'd picked up the stone I'd bull's-eyed right into the middle of her wrinkled brow, between her tender, brown, all-seeing eyes, lifted it and turned it over in her hands like a jeweler with a tiny telescope strapped to his skull inspecting a jewel, testing its heft and brilliance, the marks of God's hands, God's will, the hidden truths sparkling in its depths, multiplied, splintered through mirroring facets. After such a brow-scrunching examination, isn't it time to smile. Kiss and make up. Wasn't that Mom's way. Wasn't that how she handled the things that hurt us and hurt her. Didn't she ease the pain of our worst injuries with the balm of her everything's-going-to-be-all-right-in-the-morning smile. The smile that takes the weight, every hurtful ounce, and forgives, the smile licking our wounds so they scab over and she can pick them off our skin, stuff their lead weight into the bulging sack of all sorrows slung across her back.

The possibility that my wannabe story had actually hurt her dawned on me. Or should I say bopped me upside my head like the Br'er Bear club my middle brother loads in his cart to discourage bandits. I wished I was sitting at the kitchen table across from her so I could check for damage, her first, then check myself in the mirror of those soft, brown, incredibly loving mother's eyes. If I'd hurt her even a teeny-tiny bit, I'd be broken forever unless those eyes repaired me. Yet even as I regretted reading her the clumsy passage and prepared myself to surrender wholly, happily to the hounds of hell if I'd harmed one hair on her frail gray head, I couldn't deny a sneaky, smarting tingle of satisfaction at the thought that maybe, maybe words I'd written had touched another human being, mama mia or not.

Smile, Mom. It's just a story. Just a start. I know it needs more work. You were supposed to smile at the weightlifting part.

God not something to joke about.

C'mon, Mom. How many times have I heard Reverend Fitch cracking you up with his corny God jokes.

Time and a place.

Maybe stories are my time and place, Mom. You know. My time and place to say things I need to say.

No matter how bad it comes out sounding, right. No matter you make a joke of your poor mother . . .

Poor mother's suffering. You were going to say, *Poor mother's suffering,* weren't you.

You heard what I said.

And heard what you didn't say. I hear those words too. The unsaid ones, Mom. Louder sometimes. Drowning out what gets said, Mom.

Whoa. We gon let it all hang out this morning, ain't we, son. First that story. Now you accusing me of *your* favorite trick, that muttering under your breath. Testing me this morning, aren't you. What makes you think a sane person would ever pray for more weight. Ain't those the words you put in my mouth. More weight.

And the building shook. The earth rumbled. More weight descended like God's fist on his Hebrew children. Like in Lamentations. The book in the Bible. The movie based on the book based on what else, the legend of my mother's long-suffering back.

Because she had a point.

People with no children can be cruel. Had I heard it first from Oprah, the diva of suffering my mother could have become if she'd pursued show biz instead of weightlifting. Or was the damning phrase a line from one of Gwen Brooks's abortion blues. Whatever their source, the words fit, and I was ashamed. I do know better. A bachelor and nobody's daddy, but still my words have weight. Like sticks and stones, words can break bones. Metaphors can pull you apart and put you back together all wrong. I know what you mean, Mom. My entire life I've had to listen to people trying to tell me I'm just a white man in a dark skin.

Give me a metaphor long enough and I'll move the earth. Somebody famous said it. Or said something like that. And everybody, famous or not, knows words sting. Words change things. Step on a crack, break your mother's back.

On the other hand, Mom, metaphor's just my way of trying to say two things, be in two places at once. Saying goodbye and hello and goodbye. Many things, many places at once. You know, like James Cleveland singing our favorite gospel tune, "I Stood on the Banks of the Jordan." Metaphors are very short songs. Mini-mini-stories. Rivers between, like the Jordan where ships sail on, sail on and you stand and wave goodbye-hello, hello-goodbye.

Weightlifter just a word, just play. I was only teasing, Mom. I didn't mean to upset you. I certainly intended no harm. I'd swallow every stick of dynamite it takes to pay for a Nobel prize before I'd accept one if it cost just one of your soft, curly hairs.

Smile. Let's begin again.

It's snowing in Massachusetts / The ground's white in O-hi-o. Yes, it's snowing in Massachusetts / And ground's white in O-hi-o. / Shut my eyes, Mr. Weatherman / Can't stand to see my baby go.

When I called you last Thursday evening and didn't get an answer I started worrying. I didn't know why. We'd talked Tuesday and you sounded fine. Better than fine. A lift and lilt in your voice. After I hung up the phone Tuesday, said to myself, Mom's in good shape. Beat-up but her spirit's strong. Said those very words to myself more than once Tuesday. *Beat-up but her spirit's strong.* The perkiness I sensed in you helped make my Wednesday super. Early rise. Straight to my desk. Two pages before noon and you know me, Mom. Two pages can take a week, a month. I've had two-page years. I've had decades dreaming the one perfect page I never got around to writing. Thursday-morning reams of routine and no pages but not to worry, I told myself. After Wednesday's productivity, wasn't I entitled to some down time. Just sat at my desk, pleased as punch with myself till I got bored feeling so good and started a nice novel, *Call It Sleep.* Dinner at KFC buffet. Must have balled up fifty napkins trying to keep my chin decent. Then home to call you before I snuggled up again with the little Jewish boy, his mama, and their troubles in old NYC.

Let your phone ring and ring. Too late for you to be out unless you had a special occasion. And you always let me know well ahead of time when something special coming up. I tried calling a half-hour later and again twenty minutes after that. By then nearly nine, close to your bedtime. I was getting really worried now. Couldn't figure where you might be. Nine fifteen and still no answer, no clue what was going on.

Called Sis. Called Aunt Chloe. Nobody knew where you were. Chloe said she'd talked with you earlier, just like every other morning. Sis said you called her at work after she got back from lunch. Both of them said you sounded fine. Chloe said you'd probably fallen asleep in your recliner and left the phone in the bedroom or bathroom and your hearing's to the point you can be wide awake but if the TV's on and the phone's not beside you or the ringer's not turned to high, she said sometimes she has to ring and hang up, ring and hang up two, three times before she catches you.

Chloe promised to keep calling every few minutes till she reached you. Said, They have a prayer meeting Thursdays in your mother's building and she's been saying she wants to go and I bet she's there, honey. She's all right, honey. Don't worry yourself, okay. We're old and fuddle-headed now, but we're tough old birds. Your mother's fine. I'll tell her to call you soon's I get through to her. Your mom's okay, baby. God keeps an eye on us.

You know Aunt Chloe. She's your sister. Five hundred miles away and I could hear her squeezing her large self through the telephone line, see her pillow arms reaching for the weight before it comes down on me.

Why would you want to hear any of this. You know what happened. Where you were. You know how it all turned out.

You don't need to listen to my conversation with Sis. Dialing her back after we'd been disconnected. The first time in my life I think my sister ever phoned me later than ten o'clock at night. First time a lightning bolt ever disconnected us. Ever disconnected me from anybody ever.

Did you see Eva Wallace first, Mom, coming through your door, or was it the busybody super you've never liked since you moved in. Something about the way she speaks to her granddaughter, you said. Little girl's around the building all day because her mother's either in the street or the slam and the father takes the child so rarely he might as well live in Timbuktu so you know the super doesn't have it easy and on a couple of occasions you've offered to keep the granddaughter when the super needs both hands and her mind free for an hour. You don't hold the way she busies up in everybody's business or the fact the child has to look out for herself too many hours in the day against the super, and you're sure she loves her granddaughter, you said, but the short way she talks sometimes to a child that young just not right.

Who'd you see first pushing open your door. Eva said you didn't show up after you said you'd stop by for her. She waited a while, she said, then phoned you and got no answer and then a friend called her and they got to running their mouths and Eva said she didn't think again about you not showing up when you were supposed to until she hung up the phone. And not right away then. Said as soon as she missed you, soon as she remembered youall had planned on attending the Thursday prayer meeting together, she got scared. She knows how dependable you are. Even though it was late, close to your bedtime, she called you anyway and let the phone ring and ring. Way after nine by then. Pulled her coat on over her housedress, scooted down the hall, and knocked on your door cause where else you going to be. No answer so she hustled back to her place and phoned downstairs for the super and they both pounded on your door till the super said, We better have a look just in case, and unlocked your apartment. Stood there staring after she turned the key, trying to see through the door, then slid it open a little and both of them, Eva said, tiptoeing in like a couple of fools after all that pounding and hollering in the hall. Said she never thought about it at the time but later, after everything over and she drops down on her couch to have that cigarette she knew she shouldn't have with her lungs rotten as they are and hadn't smoked one for more than a year but sneaks the Camel she'd been saving out its hiding place in a baggie in the freezer and sinks back in the cushions and lights up, real tired, real shook up and teary, she said, but couldn't help smiling at herself when she remembered all that hollering and pounding and then tipping in like a thief.

It might have happened that way. Being right or wrong about what happened is less important sometimes than finding a good way to tell it. What's anybody want to hear anyway. Not the truth people want. No-no-no. People want the best-told story, the lie that entertains and turns them on. No question about it, is there. What people want. What gets people's attention.

What sells soap. Why else do the biggest, most barefaced liars rule the world.

Hard to be a mother, isn't it, Mom. I can't pretend to be yours, not even a couple minutes' worth before I go to pieces. I try to imagine a cradle with you lying inside, cute, miniature bedding tucked around the tiny doll of you. I can almost picture you asleep in it, snuggled up, your eyes shut, maybe your thumb in your mouth, but then you cry out in the night, you need me to stop whatever I'm doing and rush in and scoop you up and press you to my bosom, lullaby you back to sleep. I couldn't manage it. Not the easy duty I'm imagining, let alone you bucking and wheezing and snot, piss, vomit, shit, blood, you hot and throbbing with fever, steaming in my hands like the heart ripped fresh from some poor soul's chest.

Too much weight. Too much discrepancy in size. As big a boy as I've grown to be, I can't lift you.

Will you forgive me if I cheat, Mom. Dark-suited, strong men in somber ties and white shirts will lug you out of the church, down the stone steps, launch your gleaming barge into the black river of the Cadillac's bay. My brothers won't miss me not handling my share of the weight. How much weight could there be. Tiny, scooped-out you. The tinny, fake wood shell. The entire affair's symbolic. Heavy with meaning, not weight. You know. Like metaphors. Like words interchanged as if they have no weight or too much weight, as if words are never required to bear more than they can stand. As if words, when we're finished mucking with them, go back to just being words.

The word *trouble*. The word *sorrow*. The word *by-and-by*.

I was wrong and you were right, as usual, Mom. So smile. Certain situations, yours for instance, being a mother, suffering what mothers suffer, why would anyone want to laugh at that. Who could stand in your shoes a heartbeat—*shoes, shoes, everybody got to have shoes*—bear your burdens one instant and think it's funny. Who ever said it's OK to lie and kill as long as it makes a good story.

Smile. Admit you knew from the start it would come to this. Me trembling, needing your strength. It has, Mom, so please, please, a little-bitty grin of satisfaction. They say curiosity kills the cat and satisfaction brings it back. Smiling. Smile, Mom. Come back. You know I've always hated spinach but please spoonfeed me a canful so those Popeye muscles pop in my arms. I meant shapeshifter, not weightlifter. I meant the point of this round, spinning-top earth must rest somewhere, on something or someone. I meant you are my sunshine. My only sunshine.

The problem never was the word *weightlifter*, was it. If you'd been insulted by my choice of metaphor, you would have let me know, not by silence but by nailing me with a quick, funny, signifying dig, and then you would have smiled or laughed and we'd have gone on to the next thing. What must have bothered you, stunned you, was what I said into the phone before I began reading. Said this is about a man scared he won't survive his mother's passing.

That's what upset you, wasn't it. Saying goodbye to you. Practicing for your death in a story. Trying on for size a world without you. Ignoring, like I did when I was a boy, your size. Saying aloud terrible words with no power over us as long as we don't speak them.

So when you heard me let the cat out the bag, you were shocked, weren't you. Speechless. Smileless. What could you say. The damage had been done. I heard it in your first words after you got back your voice. And me knowing your lifelong, deathly fear of cats. Like the big, furry orange tom you told me about, how it curled up on the porch just outside your door, trapping you a whole August afternoon inside the hotbox shanty in Washington, D.C., when I lived in your belly.

Why would I write a story that risks your life. Puts our business in the street. I'm the oldest child, supposed to be the man of the family now. No wonder you cried, Oh Father. Oh Son. Oh Holy Ghost. Why hast thou forsaken me. I know you didn't cry that. You aren't Miss Oprah. But I sure did mess up, didn't I. Didn't I, Mom. Up to my old tricks. Crawling up inside you. My weight twisting you all out of shape.

I asked you once about the red sailor cap hanging on the wall inside your front door. Knew it was my brother's cap on the nail, but why that particular hat, I asked, and not another of his countless fly sombreros on display. Rob, Rob, man of many lids. For twenty years in the old house, now in your apartment, the hat a shrine no one allowed to touch. You never said it, but everybody understood the red hat your good-luck charm, your mojo for making sure Rob would get out the slam one day and come bopping through the door, pluck the hat from the wall, and pull it down over his bean head. Do you remember me asking why the sailor cap. You probably guessed I was fishing. Really didn't matter which cap, did it. Point was you chose the red one and why must always be your secret. You could have made up a nice story to explain why the red sailor cap wound up on the nail and I would have listened as I always listened, all ears, but you knew part of me would be trying to peek through the words at your secret. Always a chance you might slip up and reveal too much. So the hat story and plenty others never told. The old folks had taught you that telling another person your secret wish strips it of its power, a wish's small, small chance, as long as it isn't spoken, to influence what might happen next in the world. You'd never tell anyone the words sheltered in the shadow of your heart. Still, I asked about the red sailor cap because I needed to understand your faith, your weightlifting power, how you can believe a hat, any fucking kind of hat, could bring my baby brother home safe and sound from prison. I needed to spy and pry. Wiretap the telephone in your bosom. Hear the words you would never say to another soul, not even on pain of death.

How would such unsaid words sound, what would they look like on a page. And if you had uttered them, surrendered your stake in them, forfeited their meager, silent claim to work miracles, would it have been worth the risk, even worth the loss, to finally hear the world around you cracking, collapsing, changing as you spoke your little secret tale.

Would you have risen an inch or two from this cold ground. Would you have breathed easier after releasing the heaviness of silent words hoarded so unbearably, unspeakably long. Let go, Mom. Shed the weight just once.

Not possible for you, I know. It would be cheating, I know. The man of unbending faith did not say to the hooded inquisitors piling a crushing load of stones on his chest, *More light. More light.* No. I'm getting my quotes mixed up again. Just at the point the monks thought they'd broken his will, just as spiraling fractures started splintering his bones, he cried, *More bricks. More bricks.*

I was scared, Mom. Scared every cotton-picking day of my life I'd lose you. The fear a singsong taunt like tinnitis ringing in my ear. No wonder I'm a little crazy. But don't get me wrong. Not your fault. I don't blame you for my morbid fears, my unhappiness. It's just that I should have confessed sooner, long, long ago, the size of my fear of losing you. I wish you'd heard me say the words. How fear made me keep my distance, hide how much I depended on your smile. The sunshine of your smiling laughter that could also send me silently screaming out the room in stories I never told you because you'd taught me as you'd been taught, not to say anything aloud I didn't want to come true. Nor say out loud the things I wished to come true. Doesn't leave a hell of a lot to say, does it. No wonder I'm tongue-tied, scared shitless.

But would it be worth the risk, worth failing, if I could find words to tell our story and also keep us covered inside it, work us invisibly into the fret, the warp and woof of the story's design, safe there, connected there as words in perfect poems, the silver apples of the moon, golden apples of the sun, blue guitars. The two of us like those rhyming pairs *never* and *forever*, *heart* and *part*, in the doo-wop songs I harmonized with the fellas in the alley around the corner from Henderson's barbershop up on Frankstown Avenue, first me, then lost brother Sonny and his crew, then baby brother Rob and his cut-buddy hoodlums rapping, and now somebody else brown and young and wild and pretty so the song lasts forever and never ever ends even though the voices change back there in the alley where you can hear bones rattling in the men's fists, *fever in the funkhouse looking for a five*, and hear wine bottles exploding and the rusty shopping cart squeaking over the cobblestones of some boy ferrying an old lady's penny-ante groceries home for a nickel once, then a dime, a quarter, four quarters now.

Would it be worth the risk, worth failing.

Shouldn't I try even if I know the strength's not in me. No, you say. Yes. Hold on, let go. Do I hear you saying, Everything's gonna be all right. Saying, Do what you got to do, baby, smiling as I twist my fingers into the brass handle. As I lift.

The Silence of
Thelonious Monk

One night years ago in Paris, trying to read myself to sleep, I discovered that Verlaine loved Rimbaud. And in his fashion Rimbaud loved Verlaine. Which led to a hip-hop farce in the rain at a train station. The Gare du Nord, I think. The two poets exchanging angry words. And like flies to buttermilk a crowd attracted to the quarrel, till Verlaine pulls a pistol. People scatter and Rimbaud, wounded before, hollers for a cop. Just about then, at the moment I began mixing up their story with mine, with the little I recall of Verlaine's poetry—*Il pleut dans mon coeur / Comme il pleut sur la ville*, lines I recited to impress you, lifetimes ago, didn't I, the first time we met—just then, with the poets on hold in the silence and rain buffeting the train station's iron roof, I heard the music of Thelonious Monk playing somewhere. So softly it might have been present all along as I read about the sorry-assed ending of the poets' love affair—love offered, tasted, spit out, two people shocked speechless, lurching away like drunks, like sleepwalkers, from the mess they'd made. Monk's music just below my threshold of awareness, scoring the movie I was imagining, a sound track inseparable from what the actors were feeling, from what I felt watching them pantomime their melodrama.

Someone plays a Monk record in Paris in the middle of the night many years ago and the scratchy music seeping through ancient boardinghouse walls a kind of silent ground upon which the figure of pitter-pattering rain displays itself, rain in the city, rain Verlaine claimed he could hear echoing in his heart, then background and foreground reverse and Monk the only sound reaching me through night's quiet.

Listening to Monk, I closed the book. Let the star-crossed poets rest in peace. Gave up on sleep. Decided to devote some quality time to feeling sorry for myself. Imagining unhappy ghosts, wondering which sad stories had trailed me across the ocean ready to barge into the space that sleep definitely had no intention of filling. Then you arrived. Silently at first. You playing so faintly in the background it would have taken the surprise of someone whispering your name in my ear to alert me to your presence. But your name once heard, background and foreground switch. I'd have to confess you'd been there all along.

In a way it could end there, in a place as close to silence as silence gets, the moment before silence becomes what it must be next, what's been there the whole time patiently waiting, part of the silence, what makes silence speak always, even when you can't hear it. End with me wanting to tell you everything about Monk, how strange and fitting his piano solo sounded in that foreign place, but you not there to tell it to, so it could/did end, except then as now you lurk in the silence. I can't pretend not to hear you. So I pretend you hear me telling what I need to tell, pretend silence is you listening, your presence confirmed word by word, the ones I say, the unspoken ones I see your lips form, that form you.

Two years before Monk's death, eight years into what the critic and record producer Orrin Keepnews characterized as Monk's "final retreat into total inactivity and seclusion," the following phone conversation between Monk and Keepnews occurred:

Thelonious, are you touching the piano at all these days?

No, I'm not.

Do you want to get back to playing?

No, I don't.

I'm only in town for a few days. Would you like to come and visit, to talk about the old days?

No, I wouldn't.

Silence one of Monk's languages, everything he says laced with it. Silence a thick brogue anybody hears when Monk speaks the other tongues he's mastered. It marks Monk as being from somewhere other than wherever he happens to be, his off-beat accent, the odd way he puts something different in what we expect him to say. An extra something not supposed to be there, or an empty space where something usually is. Like all there is to say but you don't say after you learn in a casual conversation that someone precious is dead you've just been thinking you must get around to calling one day soon and never thought a day might come when you couldn't.

I heard a story from a friend who heard it from Panama Red, a conk-haired, redbone, geechee old-timer who played with Satchmo way back when and he's still on the scene, people say, sounding better and better the older he gets, Panama Red who frequented the deli on Fifty-seventh Street Monk used for kosher.

One morning numerous years ago—story time always approximate, running precisely by grace of the benefit of the doubt—Red said, How you doing, Monk.

Uh-huh, Monk grunts.

Good morning, Mr. Monk. How you do-ink this fine morning, Sammy the butcher calls over his shoulder, busy with a takeout order or whatever it is that keeps his back turned.

If a slice of dead lunch meat spoke, it would be no surprise at all to Sammy compared to how high he'd jump, how many fingers he'd lose in the slicer if the bearish, bearded schwartze in a knitted kufi returned his *Good morning*.

Monk stares at the white man in white apron and white T-shirt behind the white deli counter. At himself in the mirror where the man saw him. At the thin, perfect sheets that buckle off the cold slab of corned beef.

Red holds his just-purchased, neat little white package in his hand and wants to get home and fix him a chopped liver and onion sandwich and have it washed down good with a cold Heineken before his first pupil of the afternoon buzzes, so he's on his way out when he hears Sammy say, Be with you in a moment, Mr. Monk.

Leave that mess you're messing wit alone, nigger, and get me some potato knishes, the story goes, and Panama Red cracking up behind Monk's habit of niggering white black brown red Jew Muslim Christian, the only distinction of color mattering the ivory or ebony keys of his instrument and Thelonious subject to fuck with that difference too, chasing rainbows.

Heard the story on the grapevine, once, twice, and tried to retell it and couldn't get it right and thought about the bird—do you remember it—coo-cooing outside the window just as we both were waking up. In the silence after the bird's song I said Wasn't that a dainty dish to set before the king, and you said, Don't forget the queen and I said Queen doesn't rhyme with sing and you said It wasn't a blackbird singing outside and I said I thought it was a mourning dove and then the bird started up again trying to repeat itself, trying, trying, but never quite getting it right it seemed. So it tried and tried again as if it had fallen in love with the sound it had heard itself coo once perfectly.

Il pleut dans la ville. Rain in the city. When the rain starts to falling / my love comes tumbling down / and it's raining teardrops in my heart. Rain a dream lots of people are sharing and shyly Monk thinks of how it might feel to climb in naked with everybody under the covers running through green grass in a soft summer shower. Then it's windshield wipers whipping back and forth. Quick glimpses of the invisible city splashing like eggs broken against the glass. I'm speeding along, let's say the West Side Highway, a storm on top, around, and under. It feels like being trapped in one of those automatic car washes doing its best to bust your windows and doors, rapping your metal skin like drumsticks. I'm driving blind and crazed as everybody else down a flooded highway no one with good sense would be out on on a night like this. Then I hit a swatch of absolute quiet under an overpass and for a split second anything is possible. I remember it has happened before, this leap over the edge into vast, unexpected silence, happened before and probably will again if I survive the furious storm, the traffic and tumult waiting to punish me instantly on the far side of the underpass. In that silence that's gone before it gets here good I recalled exactly another time, driving at night with you through a rainstorm. Still in love with you though I hadn't been with you for years, ten, fifteen, till that night of dog-and-cat rain on an expressway circling the city after our eyes had met in a crowded room. You driving, me navigating, searching for a sign to Woodside you warned me would come up all the sudden. There it is. There it is. You shouted. Shit. I missed it. We can get off the next exit, I said. But you said no. Said you didn't know the way. Didn't want to get lost in the scary storm in a scary neighborhood. I missed the turn for your apartment and you said, It's late anyway. Too late to go back and you'd get hopelessly lost coming off the next exit, so we continued downtown to my hotel where you dropped me after a good-night, goodbye-again peck on the cheek. Monk on the radio with a whole orchestra rooty-tooty at town hall, as we raced away from the sign I didn't see till we passed it. Monk's music breaking the silence after we missed our turn, after we hollered to hear each other over the rain, after we flew over the edge and the roof popped off and the sides split and for a moment we were suspended in a soundless bubble where invisible roads crisscrossed going nowhere, anywhere. Airborne, the tires aquaplaning, all four hooves of a galloping horse simultaneously in the air just like Muybridge, your favorite photographer, claimed, but nobody believed the nigger, did they, till he caught it on film.

Picture five or six musicians sitting around Rudy Van Gelder's living room, which is serving as a recording studio this afternoon. Keepnews is paying for the musicians' time, for Van Gelder's know-how and equipment, and everybody ready to record but Monk. Monk's had the charts a week and Keepnews knows he's studied them from comments Monk muttered while the others were sauntering in for the session. But Monk is Monk. He keeps fiddle-faddling with a simple tune, da, da, da, da, plunks the notes, stares into thin air as if he's studying a house of cards he's constructed there, waiting for it to fall apart. Maybe the stare's not long in terms of minutes (unless you're Keepnews, paying the bill) but long enough for the other musicians to be annoyed. Kenny Clark, the drummer, picks up the Sunday funnies from a coffee table. Monk changes pace, backpedals mid-phrase, turns the notes into a signifying riff.

K.C., you know you can't read. You drum-drum dummy. Don't be cutting your eyes at me. Ima ABC this tune to death, Mister Kenny Clark. Take my time wit it. Uh-huh. One-and-two and one-and-two it to death, K.C. Don't care if your eyes light up and your stomach says howdy. One anna two anna one anna we don't start till I say start. Till I go over it again. Pick it clean. All the red boogers of meat off the bone then belch and fart and suck little strings I missed out my teefs and chew them last, salty, sweet gristle bits till the cows come home, and then, maybe then it might be time to start so stop bugging me with your bubble eyes like you think you got somewhere better to go.

Once I asked Monk what is this thing called love. Bebop, hip-hop, whatever's good till the last drop and you never get enough of it even when you get as much as you can handle, more than you can handle, he said, just as you'd expect from somebody who's been around such things and appreciates them connoisseurly but also with a passionate innocence so it's always the first time, the only time love's ever happened and Monk can't help but grunt uh-huh, uh-huh while he's playing even though he's been loved before and it ain't no big thing, just the only thing, the music, love, lifting me.

Monk says he thinks of narrow pantherish hips, the goateed gate to heaven, and stately, stately he slides the silky drawers down, pulls them over her steepled knees, her purple-painted toes. Tosses the panties high behind his back without looking because he knows Pippen's where he's supposed to be, trailing the play, sniffing the alley-oop dish, already slamming it through the hoop so Monk can devote full attention to sliding both his large, buoyant hands up under the curve of her buttocks. A beard down there trimmed neat as Monk trims his.

Trim, one of love's names. Poontang. Leg. Nooky. Cock.

Next chorus also about love. Not so much a matter of mourning a lost love as it is wondering how and when love will happen next or if love will ever happen again because in this vale of Vaseline and tears, whatever is given is also taken away. Love opens in the exact space of wondering what my chances are and figuring the hopeless odds against love. Then, biff, bam. Just when you least expect it, Monk says. Having known love before, I'm both a lucky one, ahead of the game, and also scared to death by memories of how sweet it is, how sad something that takes only a small bit of anybody's time can't be found more copiously, falling as spring rain or sunlight these simple things remind me of you and still do do do when Monk scatters notes like he's barefoot feeding chickenfeed to chickens or bleeding drop by drop precious Lord in the snow.

I believe when we're born each of us receives an invisible ladder we're meant to climb. We commence slowly, little baby shaky steps. Then bolder steps as we get the hang of it. Learn our powers, learn the curious construction of these ladders leaning on air, how the rungs are placed irregularly, almost as if they customize themselves to our stepping sometimes, so when we need them they're there or seem to be there solid under our feet because we're steady climbing and everybody around us steady climbing till it seems these invisible ladders, measure by measure, are music we perform as easily as breathing. Playing our song, we smile shyly, uneasily, the few times we remember how high and wide we've propelled ourselves into thin air step by step on rungs we never see disappearing behind us. And you can guess the rest of that tune, Monk says.

You place your foot as you always do, do, do, one in front of the other, then risk as you always do, do, do your weight on it so the other foot can catch up. Instead of dance music you hear a silent wind in your ears, blood pounding your temples, you're inside a house swept up in a tornado and it's about to pop, you're about to come tumbling down.

When your love starts to falling. Don't blame the missing rung. The ladder's still there. A bridge of sighs, of notes hanging in the air. A quicksilver run down the piano keys, each rib real as it's touched, then gone, wiped clean as Monk's hand flies glissando in the other direction.

One night in Paris trying to read myself to sleep, I heard the silence of rain. You might call silence a caesura, a break in a line of verse, the line pausing naturally to breathe, right on time, on a dime. But always a chance the line will never finish because the pause that refreshes can also swallow everything to the right and left of it.

Smoke curls from a gun barrel. The old poet, dissed by his young lover, shoots him, is on his way to jail. Rimbaud recovers from the wound, heads south toward long, long silence. Standing on a steamer's deck, baseball cap backward on his head, elbows on the rail, baggy pants drooping past the crack of his ass, Rimbaud sees the sea blistered by many dreamers like himself who leap off ships when no one's looking, as if the arc of their falling will never end, as if the fall can't be real because nobody sees it or hears it, as if they might return to their beginnings and receive another chance, as if the fall will heal them, a hot torch welding shut the black hole, the mouth from which silence issues thick as smoke from necklaces of burning tires.

Monk speaks many languages. The same sound may have different meanings in different languages. (To say = *tu sais* = you know.) And the same sound may also produce different silences. To say nothing is not necessarily to know nothing. The same letters can represent different sounds. Or different letters equal the same sound (pane, pain, payne). In different languages or the same. A lovers' quarrel in the rain at the train station. The budding poet seals his lips evermore. The older man trims his words to sonnets, willed silence caging sound. Their quarrel echoes over and over again, what was said and not said and unsaid returns. The heart (ancient liar/lyre) hunched on its chair watching silent reruns, lip-synching new words to old songs.

Monk's through playing and everybody in the joint happy as a congregation of seals full of fish. He sits on the piano bench, hulking, mute, his legs chopped off at the knees like a Tutsi's by his fellow countrymen, listening in the dark to their hands coming together, making no sound. Sits till kingdom come, a giant sponge or ink blotter soaking up first all the light, then the air, then sucking all sound from the darkness, from the stage, the auditorium. The entire glittering city shuts down. Everything caves in, free at last in this bone-dry house.

Silence. Monk's. Mine. Yours. I haven't delved into mine very deeply yet, have I, avoid my silence like a plague, even though the disease I'm hiding from already rampant in my blood, bones, the air.

Where are you? How far to your apartment from the Woodside exit? What color are your eyes? Is your hair long or short? I know your father's gone. I met a taxi driver who happened to be from your hometown, a friendly, talkative brother about your father's age, so I asked him if he knew your dad, figuring there would have been a colored part of your town and everybody would sort of know everybody else the way they used to in the places where people like our parents were raised. Yeah, oh yeah. Course I knew Henry Diggs, he said. Said he'd grown up knowing your dad and matter of fact had spoken with him in the American Legion Club not too long before he heard your father had died. Whatever took your father, it took him fast, the man said. Seemed fine at the club. Little thin maybe but Henry always been a neat, trim-looking fellow and the next thing I heard he was gone. Had that conversation with a cabdriver about five years ago and the way he talked about your dad I could picture him neat and trim and straight-backed, clear-eyed. Then I realized the picture out-of-date. Twenty years since I'd seen your father last and I hadn't thought much about him since. Picture wasn't actually a picture anyway. When I say picture I guess I mean the taxi driver's words made your father real again by shaking up the silence. Confirmed something about your dad. About me. The first time I met your father and shook his hand, I noticed your color, your cheekbones in his face. That's what I'd look for in his different face if someone pointed out an old man and whispered your father's name. You singing in his silent features.

Picturing you also seems to work till I try to really see the picture. Make it stand still, frame it. View it. Then it's not a picture. It's a wish. A yearning. Many images layered one atop the other, passing through one another, each one so fragile it begins to fade, to dance, give way to the next before I can fix you in my mind. No matter how gently I lift the veil, your face comes away with it . . .

James Brown the hardest worker in show biz, drops down on one knee.

Please. Please. Please. Don't go. A spotlight fixes the singer on a darkened stage. You see every blister of sweat on his glistening skin, each teardrop like a bedbug crawling down the black satin pillowcase of his cheeks. Please. Please. Please. But nobody answers. Cause nobody's home. She took his love and gone. J.B. dies a little bit onstage. Then more and more. His spangled cape shimmers where he tossed it, a bright pool at the edge of the stage where someone he loves dived in and never came up.

Silence a good way of listening for news. Please. Please. Is anybody out there? The singer can't see beyond the smoking cone of light raining on his shoulders, light white from outside, midnight blue if you're inside it. Silence is Please. Silence is Please Please Please hollered till it hurts. Noise no one hears if no one's listening. And night after night evidently they ain't.

Who wants to hear the lost one's name? Who has the nerve to say it? Monk taps it out, depressing the keys, stitching messages his machine launches into the make-believe of hearts. Hyperspace. Monk folded over his console. Mothership. Mothership. Beam me up, motherfucker. It's cold down here.

Brother Sam Cooke squeezed into a phone booth and the girl can't help it when she catches him red-handed in the act of loving somebody else behind the glass. With a single shot she blows him away. But he's unforgettable, returns many nights. Don't cry. Don't cry. No, no, no—no. Don't cry.

My silence? Mine. My silence is, as you see, as you hear, sometimes broken by Monk's music, by the words of his stories. My silence not like Monk's, not waiting for what comes next to arrive or go on about its goddamned business. I'm missing someone. My story is about losing you. About not gripping tight enough for fear my fingers would close on air. Love, if we get it, as close to music as most of us get, and in Monk's piano solos I hear your comings and goings, tiptoeing in and out of rooms, in and out of my heart, hear you like I hear the silence there would be no music without, the silence saying the song could end at this moment, any moment silence plays around. Because it always does, if you listen closely. Before the next note plays, silence always there.

Three thirty in the a.m. I'm wide awake and alone. Both glow-in-the-dark clocks say so—the square one across the room, the watch on the table beside the bed, they agree, except for a ten-minute discrepancy, like a long-standing quarrel in an old marriage. I don't take sides. Treat them both as if there is something out there in the silence yet to be resolved, as if the hands of these clocks are waiting as I am for a signal so they can align themselves perfectly with it.

I lie in my bed a thousand years. Aching silently for you. My arms crossed on my chest, heavy as stones, a burden awhile, then dust trickling through the cage of ribs, until the whole carcass collapses in on itself, soundlessly, a heap of fine powder finally the wind scatters, each particle a note unplayed, returned perfectly intact, back where it came from.

When Monk finishes work it's nearly dawn. He crosses Fifty-seventh Street, a cigarette he's forgotten to light dangling from his lower lip.

What-up, Monk.

Uh-huh.

Moon shines on both sides of the street. People pour from lobbies of tall hotels, carrying umbrellas. Confetti hang-glides, glittery as tinsel. A uniformed brass band marches into view, all the players spry, wrinkled old men, the familiar hymn they toot and tap and whistle and bang thrashes and ripples like a tiger caught by its tail.

Folks form a conga line, no, it's a second line hustling to catch up to Monk, who's just now noticed all the commotion behind him. The twelve white horses pulling his coffin are high steppers, stallions graceful, big-butted, and stylized as Rockettes. They stutter-step, freeze, raise one foreleg bent at the knee, shake it like shaking cayenne pepper on gumbo. The horses also have the corner boys' slack-leg, drag-leg pimp strut down pat and perform it off-time in unison to the crowd's delighted squeals down Broadway while the brass band cooks and hordes of sparrow-quick pickaninnies and rump-roast-rumped church ladies wearing hats so big you think helicopter blades or two wings to hide their faces and players so spatted and chained, ringed and polished, you mize well concede everything you own to them before the game starts, everybody out marching and dancing behind Mr. Monk's bier, smoke from the cigarette he's mercifully lit to cut the funk drifting back over them, weightless as a blessing, as a fingertip grazing a note not played.

In my dream, we're kissing goodbye when Monk arrives. First his music, and then the great man himself. All the air rushes from my lungs. Thelonious Apoplecticus, immensely enlarged in girth, his cheeks puffed out like Dizzy's. He's sputtering and stuttering, exasperated, pissed off as can be.

Squeaky chipmunk voice like a record playing at the wrong speed, the way they say Big O trash-talked on the b-ball court or deep-sea divers squeak if raised too rapidly from great depths. Peepy dolphin pip pip peeps, yet I understand exactly.

Are you crazy, boy. Telling my story. Putting mouth in my words. Speechless as my music rendered your simple ass on countless occasions, what kind of bullshit payback is this? Tutti-frutti motherfucker. Speaking for me. Putting your jive woogie in my boogie.

Say what, nigger? Who said I retreated to silence? Retreat hell. I was attacking in another direction.

The neat goatee and mustache he favored a raggedy wreath now, surrounding his entire moon face. He resembles certain Hindu gods with his nappy aura, his new dready cap of afterbirth in flames to his shoulders. Monk shuffles and grunts, dismisses me with a wave of his glowing hand. When it's time, when he feels like it, he'll play the note we've been waiting for. The note we thought was lost in silence. And won't it be worth the wait.

Won't it be a wonder. And meanwhile, love, while we listen, these foolish things remind me of you.

Are Dreams Faster Than the Speed of Light

He'd played those idle, whistling-in-the-dark games with friends. If you had to choose, which would you rather be, blind or deaf. Lose your arms or legs. With only twenty-four hours to live, how would you spend your last day. Well, someone not playing games had turned the games real. The doctors couldn't tell him exactly how long he'd live but could estimate plus or minus a couple months how long it would be before he'd want to die. A long or short year from today, they said, he'd enter final storms of outrageous suffering and the disease he wouldn't wish on a dog that had just bitten a hole in his ass, the disease he calls X cause its name's almost as ugly as its symptoms, would shrink his muscles into Frito corn curls and saw through one by one, millimeter by millimeter, with excruciating slowness all the cords stringing him along with the illusion he's the puppet master of his limbs, and dry up his lungs so they harden, burn, and crumble and he'll cough them up in great heaving spasms of black-flecked phlegm. No one knew the precise day or hour but sure as shit, given his symptoms—the jiggle in his legs, spiraling auras wiggling through the left side of his field of vision, numbness of tongue, fasciculations everywhere rippling like a million snakes under his skin, bone-aching weariness totally out of proportion to the minimal bit of physical activity required to survive day by day—the specialists agreed unanimously his ass was grass, maybe he'd last one more Christmas, if lucky, just in time to beg Santa for death if death hadn't already come creeping and smirking into his room.

The riot of pain the doctors promised doesn't scare him. Drugs will dull most of it, won't they. He just hates the anticipation. Always prided himself on being the kind of guy who liked to bull-rush the enemy, get it on, get it over. As long as he had a chance to fight back, he could handle whatever. From day one, his color plus a jock mentality had turned every encounter into a contest. Even the smallest choices. For the past year he'd believed the tremor in his hands a symptom of his crazy habit of always needing to win. You reach for the pepper and at the last instant, because your mind's still debating the pluses and minuses of whether to sprinkle pepper or salt on your pasta, your hand hesitates, flutters in the air above the nearly identical shakers. Sometimes you knock over stuff. Sometimes you laugh at yourself. Sometimes you want to scream. To kill. Or die. Each decision a drama. Your fate and the future of Western civilization hinge on whether you top your coffee with a dab of half-and-half or a dollop of skim milk.

Now it turns out the problem is not indecision, not fear of doing the wrong thing and losing. No. Not his wacky mind causing his hands to tremble. His body's wacky. Loose connections in the circuitry of nerves. Connections blocked by inflamed tissue and arthritic bones. Simple motions frustrated by lack of information. Muscles atrophying because they don't receive enough love from the brain. They forget how to contract or stretch. All the switchboard operators sprawled dead or dying after a terrorist raid.

When his eyes slink open in the morning he tells himself, You're still here, nothing's different. Nothing to worry about, anyway. Over is over. Once gone, you're really gone. It's the air conditioner, the fridge, stupid, not death droning in your ear. Crowds amaze him. Busy swarms of people who haven't heard the news. Hey, he wants to shout. Listen up, everybody. It ain't just about me. Each and every one of you has got to go. For sure. Damned sure. Maybe the woman scowling into her paperback or that guy propped half asleep against the pole will be gone before this year's up. How would the others packed at this particular moment into this particular subway car behave if they knew what he knew. Knew their score. A week, ten days, a long or short year. Would their hearts beat faster when they tried to figure out what to do next, tried to figure out what this time means, this minute or day or month remaining. Everything and nothing. Would they hear each click of a faceless clock counting down what's left of their lives. Would they understand they'd never understand. Not even this simplest thing about being on the earth. Caught in a net that's nothing but holes.

The doctors say his time's almost up and suddenly he's old, just about as old as he'll ever get. An old man, all the people who once mattered long gone so the death sentence a fresh start too. He owes nothing to anyone. Owns the little time left. Though he can't afford to waste a second, no rush either. Size doesn't matter. Everybody gets a whole life—beginning, middle, end—no matter how quickly it's over. Like those insects *ephemerids* he'd read about, their entire life cycle squeezed into an hour of a May afternoon. Like his siblings, the twin boy and girl who couldn't stick around long enough to receive names, dying a few hours after birth, taking his sweet, sweet mother with them.

How long does it take to die. Well . . . that, of course, depends on many factors . . . He watches the doctor's face, watches himself lean forward, and in a weird way he's watcher and watched, patient and doctor, weather and weatherman. The doc's gleaming brow reassures, sleek flesh befitting his whopping fees, the location of his office, the trust you must invest in his words, healthy sheen, vacation tan. Tiny ellipsoid spectacles slide down his nose a smidgen as he closes a smidgen the distance between you, kisser and kissed. He's seen the same commercials you have, represents just this side of convincingly the actor acting like a doctor, this doc with big hands and big face and a habit of staring offstage at the imponderably heavy-duty shit always lurking just beyond the high-definition scene in which the two of you are engaged in delicate conversation about fate—your fate, not his, because this doctor's a permanent member of the cast, always available to move the plot along, advise, console, subtle as a brick revealing the brutal verdict. I've never figured out how to inform the patient, he confides. Fortunately, I don't see cases like yours very often. What can I say, except it's one of those things in life we must adjust to as best we can. Nobody ever said it was going to be easy. It's a job and somebody has to do it, somebody's got to die. Did the doc really say that. Was he complaining about his tough job or commiserating with his patient. Does it matter. He steals the doctor's voice again, pipes it through the plane. This is your captain speaking . . . We are experiencing an emergency. Please remove the oxygen mask of the helpless passenger beside you before you remove yours.

He'd begun compiling a list of chores, necessary things to do to prepare for the end. A notebook page full before he realized the list was about expecting time, using time, filling time, about plans, control, the future, wishful thinking, as if time were at his disposal. As if he possessed the power to choose—blind or deaf—as those silly scare games proposed. As if he weren't already eyeless, crippled, helpless, just about out of time. Next move always the last move. When he switched the list to *must do*, he was relieved by its shortness. Only two items: he must die, and before his time's up he must end the bad ending of his father's life. Couldn't leave his poor daddy behind to suffer any longer—how long, how long. He must take his father's life.

An unimaginable thought at first. How in hell could you kill murder whack terminate snuff your own father. Ashamed of the thought, then guilty when he doesn't act. If he loves his father, why allow him to suffer. Somebody needs to step up to the plate. Who, if not him. In the limbo of the veterans' hospital his father's shrinking body, in spite of its skinny frailty, of the burden of its diseased mind, might not fail for years. Meaningless years in terms of quality of life his father could expect, meaningless except for whatever it means when a fatally wounded animal suffers, means when an intensely proud, private man whose major accomplishment in life was maintaining a fierce independence winds up on display, naked, paddling around in his own shit. Cruel years of pointless hanging on. Years the son does not have now, thus different now, on his mind daily, monopolizing the little time, his only time remaining.

The father so present dying, so absent alive. For years, decades, starting even before his daddy had passed him to his grandmothers and aunts to raise, they'd been losing touch, becoming two men who see each other infrequently, not exactly strangers, more like long-standing acquaintances who hook up now and then in restaurants or bars, talk ball games, politics, an easy, no-strings-attached fondness. They observe an almost courtly politeness and restraint, as if questions about the other's personal life would be not only prying but breaking the rules, a kind of betrayal even, an admission of desiring more than the other so far had given and thus a rebuke, whiny dissatisfaction, after all these years, with an arrangement formed by mutual consent that had seemed to serve them both well enough.

Since he wasn't God and couldn't simply will his father's death and be done with it, killing his father necessitated tending to messy details. A weapon, for instance. And words, his unreliable weapon of choice, wouldn't suffice in this crisis, either. Wouldn't buy more time. Or finish his father's time. Yet a word, *hemlock*, popped into his mind, clarified options. A quick, lethal does of poison no doubt the most efficient, practical means

of accomplishing the dirty work. *Hemlock* shorthand for his plan, code word for whatever poison he might procure. Hemlock certainly sounded nicer than strychnine, anthrax, arsenic, cyanide, cyclone B—poisons he associated with murder mysteries, pest exterminators, concentration camps. After repeating the word to himself many times, it took on a life of its own: Hemlock, a cute, sleepy-eyed little turtle. Hemlock finally because it reminded him of the painting.

During its first year, when the veterans' hospital was overstaffed and underused, only a small group of patients occupied the locked-down seventh-floor ward, and walking the brand-new halls with his father, he'd been reassured without realizing it by an illusion of spaciousness and tranquillity some clever architect had contrived with high ceilings, tall windows, gleaming floor tiles, unadorned planes of wall like a gallery stripped for the next exhibition. Almost as if he strolled with his father through that familiar classic painting, the one whose title he couldn't recall then or now, *The Academy of So-and-so at Somewhere*, he thinks, remembering a slide from a college survey of art, philosophers in togas, their elegant postures, serious demeanors, a marble dome, sky-roofed arcades, a scene, said the voice-over, embodying intricate thought, calm speculation, the slow, careful accumulation of beads of truth on invisible threads connecting Socrates to Plato, Plato to Aristotle, Aristotle to Virgil or Dante or the pope, whoever these bearded, antique figures populating the painting were supposed to depict, wherever the idyllic version of Greece or Rome was supposed to exist, living and dead in earnest conversation—maybe it's heaven, the strollers immortals, maybe he had needed to flee that far away from the nearly empty, spic-and-span-scrubbed corridors of the seventh-floor ward to feel what he felt then and wishes he could feel again: the peace, false or not, of those first walks now that everything has changed, very aware now, mainly because it's missing and irretrievable, of the comforting illusion he'd once enjoyed, the sense of order and safety impossible today beside his father in a traffic jam of shambling, drugged, dull-eyed, muttering men in aqua pajamas, father and son slowly shuffling back and forth along corridors where windows begin above their shoulders and ascend to the top of high off-white walls, giant glass panels cloning light but allowing no one to see in, no one to see out.

Did the building in the painting have a basement, underground kennels the artist chose not to include. Where were the people who clean and polish

the marble. Where were the sick and dying. The maimed in body and spirit. Where were the good citizens with brown faces who look like us, Daddy, who are doomed like us, Daddy.

Are dreams faster than the speed of light. Should he ask his father. Wouldn't his daddy know all the answers now, the whole truth and nothing but the truth tucked away in his silence, silence deep as the painting's, his father mute like those white-robed sages frozen beneath a canopy of marble arches, all the time in the world on their hands, the ever blue Mediterranean sky at bay above their heads.

He stands pressed into a tall corner watching his father, a brown, wooden man on the barber's wooden stool. Next to his father on a folding chair another aqua-pajamaed man, face pale as the ghostly philosophers', a dentist they say in his other life, babbles nonstop, cracking himself up, ha-ha-ha-ha as if he's still the life of the party, entertaining a captive audience of dental technicians and patients in the tooth-pulling parlor where he reigns until it's his turn on the stool.

The barber, who comes on Tuesdays and Thursdays to the VA hospital and sets up shop in an alcove near the nurses' station so he can holler for help if a patient gets unruly, snips, snips, snips, scissors snipping like a patient swarm of insects darting around his father's head. A crown of snips if you drew lines from one snip to the next. The black-handled scissors restore the handsome, well-groomed man his father has always been, disguise the madness lying in wait to seize his features. Scissors snip, snip, snipping, the barber intent as Babo in Melville's *Benito Cereno*, as Michelangelo coaxing the sleeping David from a block of marble, like the voice trimming and snipping these words, these words words words snipping, killing, drifting away, white hairs, brown hairs, gray hairs, little commas and tightly curled spirals that accumulate on the cloth draping his father's shoulders, hairs that have grown too long and wild, telling tales *Beware, beware, his flashing eyes and floating hair* on the tight-lipped, vacant-eyed man shuffling toward you in one of the corridors radiating like spokes from the panopticon hub of the nurses' station.

His father's face looking good, holding on in spite of scalding daylight powering from the window above the alcove. Still a striking face, a brown-eyed, handsome man, uh-huh, *he was a brown-eyed handsome man*, this pretty daddy who stares without blinking at a landscape only he's able to

see, a place elsewhere demanding more and more of his attention until one day his father had shrugged his shoulders and let the weight of this world slip off his back. As simple as that. As simple and quick as standing up when the barber finishes and letting the white cloth drop behind you onto the empty stool.

Are dreams faster than the speed of light. He had asked himself the question after Lisa related a story about a Chinese physicist at Cal Tech or Berkeley or UCLA, he doesn't remember which university, just the fact it was a West Coast school because he recalls imagining out loud a life for the scientist, how the guy winds up in charge of a world-class experimental physics lab after being born in an internment camp out west. Would a spotless lab coat, a droptop BMW erase memories of almost starving to death, a nisei father killed defending American interests in the Pacific, the bittersweet day of release from the camp, his mother's tears, her brown hands eternally cracked from trying to grow food in Arizona sand, wait a minute Lisa interrupts in the middle of my riff, *Chinese* not *Japanese*, she says, but who cares about such fine distinctions when war fever's high, he says. A chink's a chink. Yellow peril. Yellow menace. This article's about today, not World War Two, stupid, so stop raving, she says, waving in his face a clipping from the *Times* that describes an experiment a Chinese scientist conducted and experts from around the world either hailed enthusiastically or dissed as a crock of inscrutable shit, the division of opinion duly noted and quoted so discriminating readers of the science section could decide for themselves.

Something about light waves behaving weirdly when superheated in a bath of cesium. Light wave/particles accelerated till they're simultaneously here and there, present and absent, moving faster than light's supposed to move, faster than 186,000 miles per second, the speed everybody agreed till now nothing can move faster than. About kung fu a Chinese physicist performed with microwaves, mirrors, and lasers, a trick comparable to marking and releasing a rat before it's been captured. The scientist proving with measurements of before and after that no reliable measurements of before and after exist, since the rat/light breaks free on the far side of the labyrinth at precisely the instant it's about to enter. One impossibility—motion faster than the speed of light—proving another impossibility possible. You know, like a unicorn's mother appearing on *Oprah* with a photo of the son she's begging viewers to help her locate.

Wow. Flying faster than the speed of light you could travel through time, Lisa hollers. And then, as if the news too urgent to wait till she finishes showering, she shouts through the bathroom door, A person could be in two places at once.

I'm always in two places, he almost shouts back. Too goddamned many different places at once, thinking of himself dispersed as data on some marketing consultant's spreadsheet or as a blip on a Pentagon doomsday planner's screen estimating acceptable first-strike losses. His mom in heaven, smiling down on him. Hungry worms slithering in the mud smiling up. Here. There. Everywhere. In a different place from Lisa, as usual. Locked up in one of America's concentration camps while she hitchhikes through history.

Do you think this advance in science will prevent roundups of civilians, rape, torture, mass exterminations in the next world war, my sweet.

C'mon. Stop being a grouch, Lisa says. And he decides to let her enthusiasm infect him, especially since she's standing beside the bed naked. Why worry about his looming death. Why not thank goodness no world war at present. None he's aware of, at least. Lots of small flare-ups, police actions, rebels in the hills, terrorists, spasms of ethnic cleansing, etc., but no knock-down-drag-out global conflict, unless Big War too has learned to be in many places at once, no place and everywhere, like the rat, the particles. Like him.

He intended to keep the clipping, can't remember if he did or where he might have stashed it, but recalls they'd made love not war that night. Lisa moist and warm from her shower, his hand running up and down her thigh, fingertips tickling her hipbone, the smooth hollow of her flank, his hand sliding around and up to sample the flat, limber strength above her butt's *mmmmm good*, buttery curve.

Your father's a fine-looking man, sir, the barber says, stepping back from the stool to admire his handiwork. Does he expect a tip. Where's the motor-mouth dentist who was next.

No sign his father heard the barber. No sign his father still on the planet except for the shell of body abandoned on the stool.

Hey. Yo. You. Mr. brown-eyed, handsome Bojangles man, the barber turned you into a movie star, mister. All the ladies swoon, they see you struttin' down the avenue.

Does the man on the stool respond with the slightest of twinkles, a tiny, teasy pursing upturn of one corner of his mouth, Daddy's way, his way. Do the man's eyeballs roll toward the ceiling because his son's talking trash, or is he remembering scissors, remembering he must sit very still to avoid danger in the air above his head, the helicopter blades still up there snip-snipping, clipping away hair, bone, brain if you're not careful. If you make a sudden wrong move.

Later, walking the ward, fingers pinching his father's blue-green sleeve, he thinks you could call it a freak show—that one's glare, this one's wailing, that poor soul sitting on the side of the bed diddling himself, pajama bottoms down around his ankles—or just concede craziness its due, let craziness convince, let it suck you in or the effort of resisting can make you crazy. When it comes to reality, one man, one vote. Purest democracy on the seventh floor. Equal opportunity votes for men who believe they're women. Only the doctors and staff try to convert. But no sudden turnabouts here. No compromises, deals, consensus. Each aqua fish swims in a different sea. Even when they bump or fight or scream at each other, the water's different for each one. Different bumps, different fights. Real craziness is believing otherwise.

On the seventh floor the sensible question always *why not*. Why isn't his father's tale of a nurse fondling him a possibility. Not a tale exactly. His father couldn't string enough words together to construct a tale. A kind of sweet wonderment, a bedazzled grogginess in his father's voice and movements, pleasure expressed with body language, winks, sighs, exclamations, his large, knotty hands eloquently molding shapes out of thin air. Signs of a very intimate encounter a slightly embarrassed son must witness. Maybe an incident earlier this morning. Or days before or weeks or never. For sure it's happening now. A minidrama staged on the screen of his daddy's face. Is his father frowning because he's suddenly been deserted by his angel, required to speak to the figure beside him, a figure bewildering till it morphs again into a woman with soft, curious hands, her warmth, her perfume melting him, lifting him, then the beam of her dissolves to his son and he wants the son to meet this nice lady, the pretty woman he can't say with words, who breaks apart and floats away when he reaches for her, for the next word, for a way to keep her or let her go while he explains her to this ghost who claims to be his son.

As if I know. *As if I'll ever know. As if anybody ever knows.* Hard enough to live in his own dreams. A nightmare of emaciated naked people passing by in an endless line. His job hosing them down before they vanish in roiling clouds of disinfectant that's also poisonous gas. Then he's knee-deep in piles of bloody, contorted corpses he must untangle, arrange in neat rows according to gender color age size. A nightmare equal parts Holocaust and Middle Passage and him equal parts victim and executioner. The whole evil concoction like a program he's watching on the History Channel, safe until it snatches him inside and the images on the screen are his memories, his heart pounding because he knows his father's lollipop head will scroll by on one of those stick people, his father's face, his own, face after familiar face asking why, why, why are we here and you there, why are you combing through heaps of mangled dead bodies searching for us when we're beside you, right here in front of your eyes.

Maybe a routine wash-up his father is embellishing. An aide's daily chore to change the soiled diaper, scrub the old man clean, shave him, perhaps oil and talc his skin. A particularly kind nurse reminded of a father or husband or son or lover by this good-looking, helpless brown-skinned man, gentle, gentle as a newborn on his good days. An extra portion of TLC administered. Her soft, firm hands massage bare shoulders and back. His father amazed. Reminded of the truth of himself. Of desire belonging to him, the terrifying, demanding return of focus when the fog is pierced and a bright, solid world of haunting clarity streams through the needle's eye *faster than the speed of light.*

Tell me again, son. I hate to keep asking you to repeat things but it's getting harder and harder for your old father to keep it all straight. Play my numbers in the tobacco shop over by where Sears used to be, you know, over there on Hiland Avenue. Walk out the tobacco shop and half-hour later can't remember whether I played my goddamn figures or not. It's vexing, vexing. Standing there on the sidewalk not knowing what I did or didn't do. Come next morning I think about putting my numbers in and damn, realize I ain't checked what hit yesterday. Forget to check, forget if I played or not, forget there's a goddamn lottery, forget all that money white people owe me. What I'm trying to say is I know you already told me once, but I can't keep nothing straight in this feeble-ass mind of mine anymore. So tell me again, son. Why do I have to die. Why you have to kill me.

The academy's retractable roof opens and warm starlight bathes father and son. Lutes strum just loud enough to be heard, not exactly breaking the silence, more a reminder of silence, a pulse within night's quiet, this night with qualities of day exhaling the freshly scrubbed breath of dawn. His father's face glows. A zigzag vein pulses in his temple. His proud, high forehead imposing as the brows of Benin nobles sculpted in bronze.

Levitating like Yoruba priests he'd read about, they float two or three inches above the treadmill looping of a path contrived to convince you you're strolling or running or flying faster than the speed of light and the sham works until a moment like this one beside his father, when he peers down and observes the peculiar laxness of their ankles, their dangling feet not quite brushing the path that revolves beneath them, feet supple as fins, as the naked, boneless feet of blond angels hovering and strumming lutes in the ether of medieval illuminations. Not very high but sufficiently high to understand they are being taken for a ride, each step forward on the rotating path also a step in place, a step backward, the world surrounding them a painted backdrop or dancing shadows on a screen, you know, the way a filmstrip projected behind stationary actors animates Hollywood scenes, just mirrors and shuck and jive, the son understands, gazing down past his father's mashed-back slippers, his own clownish, overbuilt, winged sneakers, shoes tied to feet tied to ankles limp as a lynched man, shoes freed of the body's weight, trussed-up feet going nowhere fast, a mountain of empty shoes, shoes, shoes, late and soon.

It's about me, Daddy. Not you. Something awful's happening to me. The doctors say I have just a little time left. And some of it will be bad, very bad. The disease killing me will kick up its heels and party hearty. Oh-la-la, Daddy. I'm not scared for myself, but I'm scared for you. Don't want to leave you behind to suffer.

His father's head droops. Perfect haircut, courtesy of the state, intact. He could be nodding or he could be ratcheting down one notch farther into Zombieville.

Why his father and no one else. Why did he confess the dirty secret of the disease only to his father. If Lisa was as helpless as his father, would he have shared the news of his death with her. The huge, trifling news. All these years assiduously looking out for himself as if he'd been entrusted with a project of cosmic significance. Hmmmm. Not much to him after all. Maybe that's why he hoarded his news. No news, really. No big thing. Everyone dies sooner or later and oop-poop-a-doop, surprise—surprise—one less monkey don't stop no show. Did he believe withholding his little secret would inflate it into big news. Wasn't he like those homeless particle waves flying faster than the speed of light—gone, gone before he even got here.

Only once, when she was leaning over the sink, intent on cleaning up a mess they'd made, her thin back looking even smaller with her little girl's shoulders hunched forward, both arms invisible from where he sat, only that once had he almost said to anyone other than his father, I'm going to be very sick and soon after that I'll die. Dressed for court in elegant business suits with short skirts and double-breasted jackets, shiny panty hose encasing shapely legs, black hair precisely bobbed, Lisa could transform herself into a cartel-busting, justice-for-the-wretched-of-the-earth, petite Abrams tank. He'd feel proud of her glamour, her gleaming impenetrability and incorruptibility. When she smiled at him, testing him one last time on the intricate maneuvers required to mesh and unmesh his sloth with her complicated schedule that particular day, he loved her, loved how full of herself, how undaunted she could be, marveled at the distance between them, distance they sometimes miraculously closed, but distance that also stunned him each morning. Would he matter enough to woo her back. Slouched in the fat chair, staring at the stalled novel in his notebook, he'd exhale a sigh of relief after the door closed behind her slim, perfect hips, hopelessly missing her, but also glad she was gone so he could get on with the rest of his life.

After the phone rings, in the instant between recognizing Lil Sis's voice and listening to what Lil Sis is saying, he wonders why he hadn't thought of her, isn't Lil Sis the perfect person to tell the news of his death, this stranger, this half-sister, strangely closer now because the father they share, a stranger during his life to both of them, is dying. Should he tell her about hemlock too.

Hate to call with bad news, but Daddy's had a fall. Doesn't sound too good. The doctor wants to operate right away.

A fall.

That's what they claim. But you know as well as I do the rough stuff goes on at the VA. They say one of the nurses found him lying on the floor and Daddy couldn't get up. Sounds like his hip busted up really badly. In splinters, they say. Lots of bleeding inside the joint and that's why they have to operate quick, before it gets infected. I want to know how in hell he wound up on the floor. But Daddy can't tell us, so I guess we'll never find out, will we.

Operate how soon.

If we say okay, they'll try to schedule him for tomorrow morning.

After he hangs up the phone, he thinks he should have said no. Let nature take its goddamn course. Out of it as his father already is, he'll be worse after surgery. Old people can't deal with anesthesia. His grandfather never the same after they knocked him out and cut on him.

But you can't just let a person rot. Surgery or not, his own rot-smart bones whisper, this mugging will finish off your father. Is he just a tiny bit disappointed he's lost the chance to play hero. After all the agonizing, rationalizing, and fighting with himself, finally, a rush of cool determination. Clarity at last. Yes, yes. Ready to purchase poison, activate the plan. A hemlocked vanilla milk shake the final solution. A special treat he'd bring to the hospital next Sunday. Vanilla milk shake my dad's favorite thing, folks. Sharing one with him for old time's sake. Father and son on the last train out of Dodge. A carefully drafted note in plain view on the bedside table explaining everything so nobody gets the wrong idea.

To top off the plan, he'd prepay a double funeral. Ride off with his daddy in a horse-drawn black hearse. A glorious New Orleans goodbye parade winding through the streets of Homewood. The Pittsburgh Rockets Drum and Bugle Corps leading the march. Shiny trumpets and tubas. Umpah-umpah. Ratta-tat-tat-tat. Tease of jive and boogie in their mournful playing, their precise highstepping. Barbequed kielbasa with red-hot sauce. Coolers full of icy Iron City. Hmmm. Oh, didn't we ramble, Daddy. Oh, didn't we.

You never know, do you.

The big-eared, retro phone smirks at him. So much ado about nothing. No opportunity, after all, to play God. Game called on account of rain. The coy old AME Zion deity working in his own good time his wonders to perform.

At the hospital, not counting his father, three of them in the room when a nurse breezes in to brief the family. Very sound reasons not to count his father, but how could you ever be sure. Introducing himself as Clarence, folks, the nurse flashes a silver-starred front tooth. In six months, if he lives that long, will his eyes still be able to read the tattoo on the nurse's hairy forearm. A posse of needles, tubes, gauges, pumps, suction, drips protects the bed. Virtual life puttering on forever in printouts, on screens, in beeping monitors, whether or not a glimmer of vitality in his father's eyes.

Of course, even now, at his dad's direst moment, at this sad, affecting denouement, the son flies elsewhere, faster than the speed of light, father forgotten, son dreaming ahead to what it will be like at his own miserable countdown. Shit, he's thinking. Shit. What's the point. What's the horseshit stinking point.

The nurse updates them.

We can't get Mr. Wideman to eat. Goes on to explain why it's important for patients to eat. Explains that patients die if we don't manage to start them eating post-op. Explains the options, mouthwise or IVs, folks, and how the mouthwise method is much preferred by doctors, staff, studies, you know. And next thing I know, after Lil Sis's husband and I crank up the bed, I'm standing beside my father waving a spoonful of vanilla ice cream (go figure) I'm supposed to coax, wheedle, beg, sneak, lever, ram down his throat. I try to steady my shaky hand. Inch the spoon closer, closer to cracked lips the exact shape and color of mine, lips I swam through like a fish when I was birthed a second time *John Edgar, John* my dead mother's dead father's name, *Edgar* my father's, both names chosen by my mother to bind me to the men she'd loved most in the world. *Entitles*, my South Carolina grandfather would have called the names my father whispered to Reverend Felder and the good reverend's bass intoned loudly to family and friends gathered around the baptismal font of Homewood AME Zion.

And dead as he is, as I am for all intents and purposes, I find myself touching my father's mouth, prying open a space between what dwells outside him and all that's indwelling, and then into the passage propped open by thumb and finger I attempt to slip a spoon, ease a spoon, pray a spoon the way I'd heard my mother on her knees pray, the entire congregation of Homewood AME Zion pray and chant Sunday mornings to a God I never could love, not even then, long ago when I was a boy, only fear, only address when I desired something very badly I knew I wasn't going to get anyway so why not ask, why not believe a different life possible, joining the other lives I daydreamed daily. Lives not in my father's house nor my mother's bosom nor God's bosom nor the streets of Homewood. Made-up lives like this one I try to save holding open my father's mouth.

His teeth chatter, his jaw twitches as uneven surges of air enter and leave. Losing most of the load maneuvering the spoon through a broken fence of snags anchored in corpse-foul gums, I keep Lil Sis busy wiping vanilla drool from our daddy's chin as I ladle what I can into him, down him, and nothing, nothing else matters.

Who Invented the
Jump Shot

The native American rubber-ball game played on a masonry court has intrigued scholars of ancient history since the Spaniards redefined the societal underpinnings of the New World.

—Scarborough and Wilcox,
The Mesoamerican Ballgame

The seminar room was packed. *Packed* as in crowded, *packed* as in a packed Supreme Court, *packed* as in a fresh-meat inmate getting his shit packed by booty bandits. In other words, the matter being investigated, "Who Invented the Jump Shot," (a) has drawn an overflow crowd of academics, (b) the fix is in, (c) I'm about to be cornholed without giving permission.

The title of the session let the cat out the bag. It advertised two false assumptions—that at some particular moment in time the jump shot had appeared, new and fully formed as Athena popping from the thigh of Zeus, and that a single individual deserved credit as inventor. "Who Invented the Jump Shot" will be a pissing contest. And guess who will win. Not my perpetually outnumbered, outvoted, outgunned side. Huh-uh. No way. My noncolored colleagues will claim one of their own, a white college kid on such and such a night, in such and such an obscure arena, proved by such and such musty, dusty documents, launched the first jump shot. Then they'll turn the session into a coming-out party for the scholar who invents the inventor. Same ole, same ole aggression, arrogance, and conspicuous consumption. By the end of the seminar's two hours they'll own the jump shot, unimpeachable experts on its birth, development, and death. Rewriting history, planting their flag on a chunk of territory because no native's around to holler, Stop, thief.

And here I sit, a colored co-conspirator in my lime-colored plastic con-
tour chair, my transportation, food, and lodging complimentary, waiting for
an answer to a question nobody with good sense would ask in the first place.
Even though I've fired up more jumpers than all the members of the Asso-
ciation for the Study of Popular Culture combined, do you think anybody
on the planning committee bothered to solicit my opinion on the shot's origins. With their linear, lock-step sense of time, their solipsism and bonehead
priorities, no wonder these suckers can't dance.

Let's quietly exit from this crowded hall in a mega–conference center in
Minneapolis and seek the origins of the jump shot elsewhere, in the darkness where my lost tribe wanders still.

Imagine the cramped interior of an automobile, a make and model
extant in 1927, since that's the year we're touching down, on a snowy night
inside, let's say, a Studebaker sedan humping down a highway, a car packed
with the bodies of five large Negroes and a smallish driver whose pale,
hairy-knuckled fingers grip the steering wheel. It's January 27, 1927, to be
exact, and we're on our way from Chicago to Hinckley, Illinois, population
3,600, a town white as Ivory Snow, to play a basketball game against Hinckley's best for money.

Though he's not an athlete, the driver wears a basketball uniform under his shirt, you know, the way some men who are not women sport a bra
and panties under their clothes, just in case. In any case, even if pressed into
playing because the referee fouls out one of us, the driver's all business, not
a player. A wannabe big-time wheeler-dealer but so far no big deal. Now
he's got a better idea. He's noticed how much money white people will pay
to see Negroes do what white people can't or won't or shouldn't but always
wanted to do, especially after they see Negroes doing it. Big money in the
pot at the end of that rainbow. Those old-time minstrel shows and medicine
shows a gold mine and now black-faced hoofers and crooners starring in
clubs downtown. Why not ball games. Step right up, ladies and gents. Watch
Jimbo Crow fly. Up, up, and away with the greatest of ease. Barnstorming
masters of thin air and striptease, of flim and flam and biff-bam-thank-you-
mammy jamming.

Not the world-renowned Globies quite yet, and the jump shot not the
killer weapon it will be one day, but we're on our way. Gotta start somewhere,
so Mr. Abe the driver has rounded up a motley squad and the Globies' first

tour has commenced humbly, if not exactly in obscurity, since we headed for Hinckley in daylight, or rather the dregs of daylight you get on overcast afternoons in gray, lakeside Chicago, 3:30 p.m. the time on somebody's watch when Pascal Rucker, the last pickup, grunts and fusses and stuffs his pivot man's bulk into the Studebaker's back seat and we're off.

Soon a flying highway bug *splat* invents the windshield. The driver's happy. Open road far as the eye can see. He whistles chorus after identical chorus, optimistically mangling a riff from a herky-jerky Satchmo jump. The driver believes in daylight. Believes in signing on the bottom line. Believes in the two-lane, rod-straight road, his sturdy automobile. He believes he'll put miles between Chicago and us before dark. Deliver his cargo to Hinckley on schedule. Mercifully, the whistling stops when giant white flakes begin to pummel us soundlessly. Shit, he mutters, shit, shit, then snorts, then announces, No sweat, boys. I'll get us to Hinckley. No sweat. Tarzan Smith twists round from the front seat, rolls his lemur eyes at me, *Right*, and I roll my eyes back at him, *Right*.

The Studebaker's hot engine strains through a colder than cold night. Occasional arrhythmic flutter-*fluups* interrupt the motor's drone, like the barely detectable but fatal heart murmurs of certain athletes, usually long, lean Americans of African descent who will suddenly expire young, seemingly healthy in the prime of their careers, a half-century later. *Fluups* worrying the driver, who knows the car's seriously overloaded. Should he pull over and let it rest. Hell, no, lunkhead. Just let it idle a while on the shoulder. Cut off the goddamn motor and who knows if it'll start up again. The driver imagines the carful of them marooned, Popsicles stuck together till spring thaws this wilderness between Chicago and Hinckley. Slows to a creepy crawl. Can't run, can't hide. An easy target for the storm. It pounces, cuffs them from side to side of the highway, pisses great, sweeping sheets of snow spattering against the tin roof. How will he hear the next *fluup*. His head aches from listening. Each mile becomes minutes and minutes hours and hours stretch into an interminable wait between one *fluup* and the next. Did he hear the last one or imagine it. If *fluup*'s the sound of doom, does he really want to hear it again.

Some ungenerous people might suggest the anxious person hunched over the steering wheel obsesses on *fluup*s to distract himself from the claustrophobia and scotophobia he can't help experiencing when he's the only white man stuck somewhere in the middle of nowhere with these colored guys he gets along with very well most of the time. C'mon. Give the driver a break. He rides, eats, drinks with them. To save money he'll sleep in the same room, the same bed, for Chrissakes, with one of them tonight. He'll be run out of godforsaken little midwestern towns with the players after they thump the locals too soundly. Nearly lynched when Foster grins back at a white woman's lingering Chessy-cat grin. Why question the driver's motives. Give the man the benefit of the doubt. Who are you, anyway, to cast the first brick.

Who handed you a striped shirt and whistle. In the driver's shoes—one cramping his toes, the other gingerly tapping the accelerator—you'd listen too. Everybody crazy enough to be out on the road tonight driving way too fast. As if pedal to the metal they can outrun weather, outrun accidents. You listen because you want to stay alive.

Or try to listen, try to stay alert in the drowsy heat of the car's interior, your interior hot and steamy too, anticipating a rear-end assault from some bootlegger's rattling, snub-nosed truck. Does he dare stomp harder on the gas. Can't see shit. The windshield ice-coated except for a semiclear, half-moon patch more or less the size of his soon-to-be-roommate Smith's long bare foot. The driver leans forward, close enough to kiss the glass. Like looking at the world through the slot of one of those deep-sea diving helmets. Squinting to thread the car through the storm's needle eye makes his headache worse. Do his players believe he can see where he's going. Do they care. Two guys in the front seat trade choruses of snores. Is anybody paying attention. Blind as he is peering through snow-gritty glass, he might as well relax, swivel around, strike up a conversation if somebody's awake in the back.

It's fair to ask why, first thing, I'm inside the driver's head. Didn't we start out by fleeing a conference hall packed with heads like his. A carful of bloods and look whose brains I pick to pick. Is my own gray matter hopelessly whitewashed. Isn't the whole point of writing to escape what people not me think of me. In my defense I'll say it's too easy to feel what the players feel. Been there, done that. Too easy, too predictable. Of course not all players alike. Each one different from the other as each is different from the driver. But crammed in the Studebaker with someone not one of them at the wheel, players share a kind of culture, cause when you get right down to it, the shit's out of your hands, anybody's hands, ain't nowhere to go but where you're going so kick back and enjoy the ride. Or ignore the ride. Hibernate in your body, your good, strong, hungry player's body. Eat yourself during the long ride. Nourish your muscle with muscle, fat with fat, cannibalizing yourself to survive. Cause when the cargo door bangs open you better be ready to explode out the door. Save yourself. Hunker down. Body a chain and comfort. Body can be hurt, broken, disappear as smoke up a chimney, but because we're in this together, there's a temporary sense of belonging, of solidarity and weight while we anticipate the action we know is coming. Huge white flakes tumbling down outside, but you crouch warm inside your body's den, inside this cave of others like you who dream of winning or losing, of being a star or a chump, inventing futures that drift through your mind, changing your weatherscape, tossing and turning you in the busy land of an exile's sleep. If it ain't one thing it's another, raging outside the window, my brothers. Let it snow, let it snow, let it snow.

Whatever I pretend to be, I'm also one of them. One of us riding in our ancient, portable villages. Who's afraid of insane traffic, of howling plains, howling savages. *Howling. Savages.* Whoa. Where did those words come from. Who invented them. Treacherously, the enemy's narrative insinuates itself. Takes over before you realize what's going on. Howling savages. It's easy to stray. Backslide. Recycle incriminating words as if you believe the charges they contain. Found again. Lost again. *Howling savages.* Once you learn a language, do you speak it or does it speak you. Who comes out of your mouth when you use another's tongue. As I pleaded above, the mystery, the temptation to be other than I am disciplines me. Playing the role of a character I am not, and in most circumstances would not wish to be, renders me hyperalert. Pumps me up, and maybe I'm most myself not playing myself.

Please. If you believe nothing else about me, please believe I'm struggling for other words, my own words, even if they seem to spiral out of a mind, a mouth, like the driver's, my words, words I'm trying to earn, words I'm bound to fall on like a sword if they fail me. In other words I understand what it's like to be a dark passenger and can't help passing on when I speak the truth of that truth. What I haven't done, and never will, is be him, a small, pale, scared hairy mammal surrounded by giant carnivores whose dark bodies are hidden by darkness my eyes can't penetrate, fierce predators asleep or maybe prowling just inches away and any move I make, the slightest twitch, shiver, sneeze, *fluup* it's my nature to produce, risks awakening them.

Imagine a person in the car that snowy night, someone at least as wired as the driver, someone as helplessly alert, eyes hooded, stocking-capped hair hidden by a stingy brim, someone who has watched night fall blackly and falling snow mound in drifts taller than the Studebaker along fences bordering the highway, imagine this someone watching the driver, trying to piece together from the driver's movements and noises a picture of what the man at the wheel is thinking. Maybe the watcher's me, fresh from the Minneapolis conference, attempting to paint a picture of another's invisible thoughts. Or perhaps I'm still in my lime chair inventing a car-chase scene. You can't tell much by studying my face. A player's face disciplined to disguise my next move. Player or not, how can you be sure what someone else is thinking. Or seeing. Or saying. A different world inside each and every head, but we also like to believe another world's in there, a reasonably reliable facsimile of a reality we agree upon and pursue, a world the same for everyone, even though no one has been there or knows for sure if it's there. Who knows. Stories pretend to know. Stories claiming to be true. Not true. Both. Neither. Claiming to be inside and outside. Real and unreal. Stories swirling like the howling, savage storm pounding the Studebaker. Meaning what. Doesn't meaning always sit like Hinckley, nestled in darkness beyond the steamed peephole, meaning already sorted, toe-tagged, logged, an accident waiting for us to happen.

Since I've already violated Poe's rules for inventing stories, I'll confess this fake Studebaker's interior is a site suspiciously like the inside of whatever kind of car my first coach, John Cinicola, drove back in the day when he chauffeured us, the Shadyside Boys Club twelve-and-under hoop team, to games around Pittsburgh, Pennsylvania, fifty years ago, when *fluups* not necessarily warnings of a bad heart or failing motor but farts, muted and discreet as possible in the close quarters of anywhere from seven to ten boy bodies crammed in for the ride, farts almost involuntary yet unavoidable, scrunched up as our intestines needed to be to fit in the overpacked car. Last suppers of beans and wieners didn't help. Fortunately, we shared the same low-rent, subsistence diet and our metabolisms homogenized the odor of the sneaky, invisible pellets of gas nobody could help expelling, grit your teeth, squirm, squeeze your sphincter as you might. Might as well ask us to stop breathing or snoring. Collectively we produced a foul miasma that would have knocked you off your feet if you were too close when the

Studebaker's doors flung open in Hinckley, but the smell no big deal if you'd made the trip from Chicago's South Side. A thunderhead of bad air, but our air, it belonged to us, we bore it, as we bear our history, our culture, just as everybody else must bear theirs.

In other words stone funky inside the car, and when the driver cracks the window to cop a hit of fresh air, he's lying if he says he ain't mixed up in the raunchiness with the rest of us. Anyway not much happening in the single-wagon wagon train crossing barren flatlands west of Chicago, its pale canvas cover flapping like a berserk sail, the ship yawning, slapped and bruised by roaring waves that crest the bow, blinding surges of spray, foamy fingers of sea scampering like mice into the vessel's every nook and cranny. A monumental assault, but it gets old after a while, even though our hearts pump madly and our throats constrict and bowels loosen, after a while it's the same ole, same ole splish-splash whipping, ain't it so, my sisters and brothers and we steel ourselves to outlast the storm's lashing, nod off till it whips itself out. Thus we're not really missing much if we break another rule and flash forward to Hinckley.

One Hinckley resident in particular anxiously awaits our arrival. A boy named Rastus whose own arrival in town is legendary. They say his mama, a hoboing ho like those Scottsboro girls, so the story goes, landed in Hinckley just before her son. Landed butt first and busted every bone in her body when the flatcar she'd hopped, last car of a mile-long bluesy freight train, zigged when she thought it would zag, whipping her off her feet, tossing her ass over elbows high in the air. Miraculously, the same natural-born talent that transforms Negroes into skywalkers and speed burners enabled this lady to regain her composure while airborne and drop like an expertly flipped flapjack flat on her back. In spite of splitting her skull wide open and spilling brain like rotten cantaloupe all over the concrete platform of Hinckley station, her Fosbury flop preserved the baby inside her. Little Rastus, snug as a bug on the rug of his mama's prodigiously padded booty, sustained only minor injuries—a slight limp, a lisp, a sleepy IQ.

Poor orphaned Rastus didn't talk much and didn't exactly walk nor think straight either, but the townsfolk took pity on the survivor. Maybe they believed the good luck of his sunny-side-up arrival might rub off, because they passed him house to house until he was nine years old, old enough to earn his keep in the world, too old to play doctor and nurse in backyards with the town's daughters. Grown-up Rastus a familiar sight in Hinckley, chopping, hauling, sweeping. A hired boy you paid with scraps from the table. Rastus grateful for any kind of employment and pretty reliable too if you didn't mind him plodding along at his lazy pace. Given half a chance, Rastus could do it all. If somebody had invented fast-food joints in those days, Rastus might have aspired to assistant-manage one. Rastus, Hinckley's pet. Loved and worked like a dog. No respect, no pussy, and nothing but the scare-crow rags on his back he could really call his own, but Rastus only thirty-six. There's still time. Time Rastus didn't begin to count down until the Tuesday he saw on a pole outside Hinckley's only barbershop a flyer announcing the Harlem Globies' visit.

Of course Rastus couldn't read. But he understood what everybody else in town understood. The poster meant niggers coming. Maybe the word *Harlem*, printed in big letters across the top of the poster, exuded some distinctive ethnic scent, or maybe if you put your ear close to the poster you'd hear faint echoes of syncopated jazz, the baffled foot-tapping of Darktown strutters like ocean sound in seashells. Absent these clues, folks still get the point. The picture on the flyer worth a thousand words. And if other illiterates (the majority) in Hinckley understood immediately who was coming to town, why not Rastus. He's Hinckley if anybody's Hinckley. What else was he if he wasn't.

Rastus gazes raptly at the players on the flyer. He's the ugly duckling in the fairy tale discovering swans. Falls in love with the impossibly long, dark men, their big feet, big hands, big white lips, big white eyes, big shiny white smiles, broad spade noses just like his. Falls in love with himself. Frowns recalling the day his eyes strayed into a mirror and the dusty glass revealed how different from other Hinckley folks he looked. Until the mirror sneaked up, *Boo*, he had avoided thinking too much about what other people saw when they looked at him. Mostly people had seemed not to look. Or they looked through him. Occasionally someone's eyes would panic as if they'd seen the devil. But Rastus saw devils and beasts too. The world full of them, so he wasn't surprised to see the scary sign of one still sticking like a fly to flypaper on somebody's eyeballs.

After the mirror those devilish beasts and beastly devils horned in everywhere. For instance, in the blue eyes of soft-limbed, teasing girls who'd turn his joint to a fiery stone, then prance away giggling. He learned not to look too closely. Learned to look away, look away. Taught himself to ignore his incriminating image when it floated across fragments of glass or the surface of still puddles, or inside his thoughts sometimes, tempting him to drown and disappear in glowing beast eyes that might be his. Hiding from himself no cure, however. Hinckley eyes penetrated his disguise. Eyes chewing and swallowing or spitting him out wet and mangled. Beast eyes no matter how artfully the bearer shapeshifted, fooled you with fleshy wrappings make your mouth water.

Maybe a flashback will clarify further why Rastus is plagued by a negative self-image. One day at closing time his main employer, Barber Jones, had said, You look like a wild man from Borneo, boy. All you need's a bone through your nose you ready for the circus. Set down the broom and get your tail over here to the mirror, boy. I'ma show you a wild cannibal.

See yourself, boy. Look hard. See them filthy naps dragging down past your shoulders. People getting scared of you. Who you think you is. Don King or somebody. Damned wool stinks worse'n a skunk. I'ma do you a favor, boy.

Barber Jones yakkety-yakking as he yaks daily about the general state of the world, the state of Hinckley and his dick first thing in the morning or last thing at night when just the two of them in the shop. Yakkety-yak, only now the subject is Rastus, not the usual nonstop monologue about rich folks in charge who were seriously fucking up, not running the world, nor Hinckley, nor his love life, the way Barber Jones would run things if just once he held the power in his hands, him in charge instead of those blockheads who one day will come crawling on their knees begging him to straighten things out, yakking and stropping on the razor strop a Bowie knife he'd brought special from home for this special occasion, an occasion Rastus very quickly figures he wants no part of, but since he's been a good boy his whole life, he waits, heart thumping like a tom-tom, beside a counter-to-ceiling mirror while fat-mouth Jones sharpens his blade.

A scene from Herman Melville's *Benito Cereno* might well have flashed through Rastus's mind if he'd been literate. But neither the African slave Babo shaving Captain Delano nor the ironic counterpoint of that scene, blackface and whiteface reversed, playing here in the mirror of Jones Barbershop, tweaks Rastus's consciousness of who he is and what's happening to him. Mr. Melville's prescient yarn doesn't creep into the head of Barber Jones either, even though Rastus pronounces "Barber" as *baba*, a sound so close to *Babo* it's a dead giveaway. Skinning knife in hand, Baba Jones is too busy stalking his prey, improvising Yankee Doodle–like on the fly how in the hell he's going to scalp this coon and keep his hands clean. He snatches a towel from the soiled pile on the floor. He'll grab the bush with the towel, squeeze it in his fist, chop through the thick, knotty locks like chopping cotton.

Look at yourself in the mirror, boy. This the way you want to go round looking. Course it ain't. And stop your shakin. Ain't gon hurt you. You be thanking me once I'm done. Hell, boy, won't even charge you for a trim.

Lawd, lawd, am I truly dat nappy-haired ting in de mere. Am dat my bery own self, dat ugly ole pestering debil what don look lak nobody in Hinckley sides me. Is you me, Rastus. Lawd, lawd, you sho nuff tis me, Rastus confesses, confronting the living proof, his picture reversed right to left, left to right in the glass. Caged in the mirror like a prisoner in a cell is what he thinks, though not precisely in those words, nor does he think the word *panopticon*, clunkily Melvillean and thus appropriate for the network of gazes pinning him down to the place where they want him to stay. No words necessary to shatter the peace in Rastus's heart, to upset the détente of years of not looking, years of imagining himself more or less like other folks, just a slightly deformed, darker duck than the other ducks floating on this pond he'd learned to call Hinckley.

Boom. A shotgun blasts inside Rastus's brain, cold as the icy jolt when the driver cracks the Studebaker's window, as cold and maybe as welcome too, since if you don't wake up, Rastus, sleep can kill you. *Boom.* Every scared Hinckley duck quacks and flutters and scolds as it rises from the pond and leaves Rastus behind, very much alone. He watches them form neat, V-shaped squadrons high in the blue empyrean, squawking, honking, off to bomb the shit out of somebody in another country. You should have known long ago, should have figured it would happen like this one day. You all alone. Your big tarbaby feet in miring clay. You ain't them and they ain't you. Birds of a different feather. You might mistake them for geese flying in formation way up in the sky, but you sure ain't never heard them caw-caw, boy. Huh-uh. You the cawing bird and the shotgun aimed for you ain't gon miss next time. Your cover's busted, boy. Here come Baba Jones.

You sure don wanna go around looking just so, do you, boy.

Well, Rastus ain't all kinds of fool. He zip-coons outta there, faster than a speeding bullet. (Could this be *it*—not the instant the jump shot is invented, we know better than that, but one of many moments, each monumental, memorable in its own way, when Rastus or whoever chooses to take his or her game up another level—not a notch but a quantum leap, higher, hyper, hipper—decides to put air under her or his feet, jumpshoot-jump-start-rise-transcend, eschew the horizontal for the vertical, operating like Frantz Fanon when he envisioned a new day, a new plane of existence, a new reality, up, up, and away.) Maybe he didn't rise and fly, but he didn't Jim Crow neither. No turning dis way and wheeling dat way and jiggling up and down in place. Next time the baba seen him, bright and early a couple mornings later, Rastus had shaved his skull clean as a whistle. Gold chains draping his neck like Isaac Hayes. How Rastus accomplished such a transformation is another story, but we got enough stories by the tail feathers, twisted up in our white towel—count 'em—so let's switch back to the moment earlier in the story, later in Hinckley time, months after Rastus clipped his own wings rather than play Samson to Jones's Delilah.

Rastus still stands where we left him, hoodooed by the Harlem Globies' flyer. Bald, chained Rastus who's been nowhere. Doesn't even know what name his mother intended for him. Didn't even recognize his own face in the mirror till just yesterday, Hinckley time. Is the flyer a truer mirror than the one in the barbershop, the mirror Rastus assiduously keeps at his back these days as he sweeps, dusts, mops. He studies the grinning black men on the poster, their white lollipop lips, white circles around their eyes, white gloved fingers, his gaze full of longing, nostalgia, more than a small twinge of envy and regret. He doesn't know the Globies ain't been nowhere neither, not to Harlem nor nowhere else, their name unearned, ironic at this point in time. Like the jump shot, the Globies not quite invented yet. Still a gleam in the owner/driver's eye, his wishful thinking of international marketing, product endorsements, movies, TV cartoon, prodigious piles of currency, all colors, sizes, shapes promiscuously stacking up. Not Globies yet because this is the team's maiden voyage, first trot, first road game, this trek from Chicago to Hinckley. But they're on their way, almost here, if you believe the signs tacked and glued all over town, a rain, a storm, a blizzard of signs. If he weren't afraid the flimsy paper would come apart in his hands, Rastus would peel the flyer off the pole, sneak it into the barbershop, hold it up alongside his face so he could grin into the mirror with his lost brothers. Six Globies all in a row. Because, yes, in spite of signs of the beast, the players are like him. Different and alike. Alike and different. The circle unbroken. Yes. Yes. Yes. And *whoopee* they're coming to town.

Our boy Rastus sniffs opportunity knocking and decides—with an alacrity that would have astounded the townsfolk—to become a Globie and get the hell out of Hinckley.

As befits a fallen world, however, no good news travels without bad. The night of the game Rastus not allowed in the armory. Hinckley a northern town, so no Jim Crow laws turned Rastus away. Who needed a law to regulate the only Negro in town. Sorry, Rastus, just white folks tonight.

I neglected to mention an incident that occurred the year before Rastus dropped into Hinckley. The town's one little burnt-cork, burnt-matchstick tip of a dead-end street housing a few hard-luck Negroes had been spontaneously urban-removed, and its inhabitants, those who survived the pogrom, had disappeared into the night, the same kind of killingly cold night roughing up the Studebaker. That detail, the sudden exodus of all the town's Negroes, should have been noted earlier in story time, because it helps you understand Hinckley time. A visitor to Hinckley today probably won't hear about the abovementioned event, yet it's imprinted indelibly in the town's memory. Now you see it, now you don't, but always present. A permanent marker separating before and after. Hinckley truly a white man's town from that night on.

And just to emphasize how white they wanted their town to be, the night of the fires everybody wore sheets bleached white as snow, and for a giggle, under the sheets, blacked their faces. A joke too good to share with the Negroes, who saw only white robes and white hoods with white eyes in the eyeholes. We blacked up blacker than the blackest of 'em, reported one old-timer in a back issue of the Hinckley *Daily News*. Yes we did. Blacker than a cold, black night, blacker than black. Hauled the coloreds outdoors in their drawers and nightgowns, pickaninnies naked as the day they born. Told 'em, You got five minutes to pack a sack and git. Five minutes we's turnin these shacks and everythin in 'em to ash.

Meanwhile the wagons transporting the Globies into town have arrived, their canvas covers billowing, noisy as wind-whipped sails, their wooden sides, steep as clipper ships, splashed with colorful, irresistible ads for merchandise nobody in Hinckley has ever dreamed of, let alone seen. A cornucopia of high-tech goods and services from the future, Hinckley time, though widely available in leading metropolitan centers for decades. Mostly beads and baubles, rummage-sale trash, but some stuff packed in the capacious holds of the wagons extremely ancient. Not stale or frail or old-fashioned or used or useless. No, the oldest, deepest cargo consisted of things forgotten. *Forgotten?* Yes, forgotten. Upon which subject I would expand if I could, but forgotten means forgotten, doesn't it. Means lost. A category whose contents I'm unable to list or describe because if I could, the items wouldn't be forgotten. Forgotten things are really, really gone. Gone even if memories of them flicker, ghosts with more life than the living. Like a *Free Marcus* button you tucked in a drawer and lived the rest of your life not remembering it lay there, folded in a bloodstained head kerchief, until one afternoon as you're preparing to move the last mile into senior citizens' public housing and you must get rid of ninety-nine and nine-tenths percent of the junk you've accumulated over the years because the cubicle you're assigned in the high-rise isn't much larger than a coffin, certainly not a king-sized coffin like pharaohs erected so they could take everything with them—chariots, boats, VCRs, slaves, wives—so you must shed what feels like layers of your own tender skin, flaying yourself patiently, painfully, divesting yourself of one precious forgotten thing after another, toss, toss, toss. Things forgotten in the gritty bottom of a drawer and you realize you've not been living the kind of life you could have lived if you hadn't forgotten, and now, remembering, it's too late.

In other words, the wagons carried tons of alternative pasts—roads not taken, costumes, body parts, promises, ghosts. Hinckley folks lined up for miles at these canvas-topped depots crackling whitely in the prairie wind. Even poor folks who can't afford to purchase anything mob the landing, ooohing and ahhhing with the rest. So many bright lost hopes in the bellies of the schooners, the wagons might still be docked there doing brisk business a hundred years from now, the Globies in their gaudy, revealing uniforms showing their stuff to a sea of wide eyes, waving hands, grappling, grasping hands, but hands not too busy to clap, volleys of clapping, then a vast, collective sigh when clapping stops and empty hands drop to people's sides, sighs so deep and windy they scythe across the Great Plains, rippling mile after endless mile of wheat, corn, barley, amber fields of grain swaying and purring as if they'd been caressed when a tall Globie dangles aloft some item everybody recognizes, a forgotten thing all would claim if they could afford it, a priceless pearl the dark ballplayer tosses gratis into the crowd of Hinckleyites, just doing it to do it, and the gift would perform tricks, loop-de-looping, sparkling, airborne long enough to evoke spasms of love and guilt and awe and desire and regret, then disappear like a snowflake or a sentence grown too large and baroque, its own weight and ambition and daring and vanity ripping it apart before it reaches the earth. A forgotten thing twisting in the air, becoming a wet spot on fingers reaching for it. A tear inching down a cheek. An embarrassing drop of moisture in the crotch of somebody's drawers.

Wheee. Forgotten things. Floating through the air with the greatest of ease. Hang-gliding. Flip-flopping.

Flip-floppety-clippety-clop. The horse-drawn caravan clomps up and down Hinckley's skimpy grid of streets. Disappears when it reaches the abandoned, dead-end, former black quarter and turns right to avoid the foundation of a multiuse, multistory, multinational parking garage and amusement center, a yawning hole gouged deeper into the earth than the stainless steel and glass edifice will rise into the sky.

Is dat going to be the Mall of America, one of the Globie kids asks, peeking out from behind a wagon's canvas flap. A little Hinckley girl hears the little Globie but doesn't reply.

Then she's bright and chirrupy as Jiminy Cricket and chases after the gillies till she can't keep up, watching the last horse's round, perfect rump swaying side to side like Miss Maya's verse. Feels delicious about herself because she had smiled, managed to be polite to the small brown face poking out of the white sheet just as her mother said she must, but also really, basically, ignored it, didn't get the brown face mixed up with Hinckley faces her mother said it wouldn't and couldn't ever be. Always act a lady, honey. But be careful. Very careful. Those people are not like us. Warmed by the boy's soft voice, his long eyelashes like curly curtains or question marks, the dreamy roll of the horse's huge, split butt, but she didn't fall in love. Instead she chatters to herself in a new language, made up on the spot. *Wow. Gumby-o. Kum-bye-a. Op-poop-a-doop* . . . as if she's been tossed a forgotten thing and it doesn't melt.

She wishes she'd said yes to the boy, wishes she could share the good news.

Daddy said after the bulldozers a big road's coming, sweety-pie, and we'll be the centerpiece of the universe, the envy of our neighbors, Daddy said I can have anything I want, twenty-four seven, brother, just imagine, anything I want, cute jack-in-the-box, pop-up brown boys, a pinto pony, baby dolls with skin warm and soft as mine, who cry real tears. *Word. Bling-bling. Oop-poop-a-doop.*

After a dust cloud churned by the giant tires of the convoy settles, the little girl discovers chocolate drops wrapped in silver foil the chocolate soldiers had tossed her. In the noise and confusion of the rumbling vehicles, she'd thought the candies were stones. Or cruel bullets aimed at her by the dark strangers in canvas-roofed trucks her mother had warned her to flee from, hide from. Realizing they are lovely chocolate morsels, immaculate inside their shiny skins, she feels terrible for thinking ugly thoughts about the GIs, wants to run to the convoy and say *Danke, Danke* even though her mother told her, They're illiterate, don't speak our language. As she scoops up the surprises and stuffs them in her apron pocket, she imagines her chubby legs churning in pursuit of the dusty column. The convoy had taken hours to pass her, so it must be moving slowly. But war has taught her the treacherous distance between dreams and reality. Even after crash diets and aerobic classes her pale short legs would never catch the wagons, so she sits down, settles for cramming food into her mouth with both hands, as if she's forgotten how good food can be and wants to make up for all the lost meals at once. Licking, sucking, crunching, chewing. The melting, gooey drops smear her cheeks, hands, dimpled knees—chocolate stain spreading as the magic candy spawns, multiplies inside her apron pocket, a dozen new sweet pieces explode into being for every piece she consumes. She eats till she's about to bust, sweet chocolate coating her inside and out, a glistening, sticky tarbaby her own mother would have warned her not to touch. Eats till she falls asleep and keels over in the dusty street.

Dusty? What's up with this dusty. I thought you said it was snowing. A snowstorm.

Snowstorm. Oh yeah. Should have let you know that in expectation of a four-seasons mega-pleasure center, Hinckley domed itself last year.

Believe it or not, it's Rastus who discovers the girl. Since being refused entrance to the Globies' show, he's been wandering disconsolate through Hinckley's dark streets when suddenly, as fate would have it, he stumbles into her. Literally. Ouch.

Less painful than unnerving when Rastus makes abrupt contact with something soft and squishy underfoot. He freezes in his tracks. Instinctively his leg retracts. He scuffs the bottom of his shoe on the ground, remembering the parade earlier in the day, horses large as elephants. Sniffs the night air cautiously. Hopes he's wrong. Must be. He smells sugar and spice, everything nice, overlaid with the cloyingly sweet reek of chocolate. Another time and place he might have reared back, kicked the obstacle in his path, but tonight he's weak, depleted, the mean exclusion of him from the Globie extravaganza the final straw. Besides, what kind of person would kick a dog already down, and dog or cat's what he believes he'll see as he peers into the shadows webbing his feet.

Rastus gulps. His already overtaxed heart *fluups*. Chocolate can't hide a cherub's face, the Gerber-baby-plump limbs and roly-poly torso. Somebody's daughter lying out here in the gutter. Hoodooed. Stricken. Poor babygirl. Her frail—make up your mind—chest rises and falls faintly, motion almost imperceptible since they never installed streetlamps on this unpaved street when Negroes lived here, and now the cunning city managers are waiting for the Dutch-German-Swiss conglomerate to install a megawatt, mesmerizing blaze of glory to guide crowds to the omniplex.

Believe it or not, on this night of nights, this night he expected a new life to begin, riding off with the Globies, the players exhausted but hungry for another town tomorrow, laughing, telling lies, picking salty slivers of the town they've just sacked out their teeth, on this penultimate night before the dawning of the first day of his new life, Rastus displays patience and self-denial worthy of Harriet's Tom. Accepts the sudden turn of fate delaying his flight from Hinckley. Takes time out to rescue a damsel in distress.

One more job, just one more and I'm through, outta here. Trotting with the Globies or flying on my own two feet, I'm gittin out. Giddy-up. Yeah. Tell folks it was Rastus singing dis sad song, now Rastus up and gone.

Determined to do the right thing, he stoops and raises the girl's cold, heart-shaped face, one large hand under her neck so her head droops backward and her mouth flops open, the other hand flat against her tiny bosom. Figures he'll blow breath into her mouth, then pump her rib cage like you would a bellows till her lungs catch fire again. In other words Rastus is inventing CPR, cardiopulmonary resuscitation, a lifesaving technique that will catch on big in America one day in the bright future when hopefully there will be no rules about who can do it to whom, but that night in

Hinckley, well, you can imagine what happened when a crowd of citizens hopped up and confused by Globie shenanigans at the armory came upon Rastus in the shadows crouched over a bloody, unconscious little white girl, puckering up his big lips to deliver a kiss.

To be fair, not everyone participated in the mayhem you're imagining. Experts say the portion of the crowd returning home to the slum bordering the former colored quarter must shoulder most of the blame. In other words, the poor and fragrant did the dirty work. The ones who live where no self-respecting white person would, an unruly element, soon themselves to be evicted when Consolidated Enterprises clears more parking space for the pleasure center, the same people, experts say, who had constituted by far the largest portion of the mob that had burned and chased all the Negroes out of town, these embarrassing undesirables and unemployables, who would lynch foreign CEOs too if they could get away with it, are responsible, experts will explain, for perpetrating the horror I'm asking you to imagine. And imagine you must, because I refuse to regale you with gory, unedifying details.

Clearly, not everyone's to blame. Certainly not me or you. On the other hand, who wouldn't be upset by an evening of loud, half-naked, large black men fast breaking and fancy dribbling, clowning and stuffing and jamming and preening for white women and kids screaming their silly heads off. Enough to put any grown man's nerves on edge, especially after you had to shell out your hard-earned cash to watch yourself take a beating. Then, to top it all off, once you're home, bone tired, hunkered down on your side of the bed, here comes your old lady grinning from ear to ear, bouncy like she's just survived a naked bungee-dive from the top of the goddamned pleasure center's twin-towers-to-be.

The Studebaker's wipers flop back and forth, bump over scabs of ice. The driver's view isn't improving. We inch along a long, long black tunnel, headlights illuminating slants of snow that converge just a few yards beyond the spot where a hood ornament would sit, if Studebakers, like Mercedes-Benzes, were adorned with bowsprits in 1927. Bright white lines of force, every kamikaziing snowflake in the universe sucked into this vortex, this vanishing point the headlights define, a hole in the dark we chug, chug behind, the ever receding horizon drawing us on, drawing us on, a ship to Zion, the song says.

Our driver's appalled by the raw deal Rastus received. During an interview he asserts, I'd never participate in something so mobbishly brutal. I would not assume appearance is reality. I would never presume truth lodges in the eyes of the more numerous beholders. After all, my people also a minority. We've suffered unjustly too. And will again. I fear it in my bones. Soon after the great depression that will occur just a few years from now, just a few miles down this very road we're traveling in this hot, *fluup*ing car, some clever, evil motherfucker will say, Sew yellow stars on their sleeves. Stars will work like color. We'll be able to tell who's who. Protect our citizens from mongrels, gypsies, globetrotters, migrants, emigrants, the riffraff coming and going. Sneaking in and out of our cities. Peddling dangerous wares. Parasites. Criminals. Terrorists. Devils.

Through the slit in his iron mask the driver observes gallows being erected by the roadside. Imagines flyers nailed and taped all over town. Wonders if it had been wise to warn them we're coming.

So *who* invented the jump shot. Don't despair. All the panelists have taken seats facing the audience. The emcee at the podium taps a microphone and a hush fills the vast hall. We're about to be told.

What We Cannot Speak About We Must Pass Over in Silence

I have a friend with a son in prison. About once a year he visits his son. Since the prison is in Arizona and my friend lives here on the East Coast, visiting isn't easy. He'd told me the planning, the expense, the long day spent flying there and longer day flying back are the least of it. The moment that's not easy, that's impossible, he said, is after three days, six hours each, of visiting are over and he passes through the sliding gate of the steel-fenced outdoor holding pen between the prison visitation compound and the visitors' parking lot and steps onto the asphalt that squirms beneath your feet, oozing hot like it just might burn through your shoe soles before you reach the rental car and fling open its doors and blast the air conditioner so the car's interior won't fry your skin, it's then, he said, taking your first steps away from the prison, first steps back into the world, when you almost come apart, almost lose it completely out there in the desert, emptiness stretching as far as the eye can see, very far usually, ahead to a horizon ironed flat by the weight of blue sky, to the right and left zigzag mountain peaks marking the edges of the earth, nothing moving but hot air wiggling above the highway, the scrub brush and sand, then, for an unending instant, it's very hard to be alive, he says, and thinks he doesn't want to live a minute longer and would not make it to the car, the airport, back to this city if he didn't pause and remind himself it's worse, far worse for the son behind him still trapped inside the prison, so for the son's sake he manages a first step away, then another and another. In these faltering moments he must prepare himself for the turnaround, the jarring transition into a world where he has no access to his son except for rare ten-minute phone calls, a blighted world he must make sense of again, beginning with the first step away and back through the boiling caldron of parking lot, first step of the trip that will return him in a year to the desert prison.

Now he won't have it to worry about anymore. When I learned of the friend's death, I'd just finished fixing a peanut butter sandwich. Living alone means you tend to let yourself run out of things. Milk, dishwasher detergent, napkins, toothpaste—staples you must regularly replace. At least it happens to me. In this late bachelorhood with no live-in partner who shares responsibility for remembering to stock up on needful things. Peanut butter a choice I didn't relish, but probably my only choice that evening, so I'd fixed one, or two, more likely, since they'd be serving as dinner. In the day's mail I'd ignored till I sat down to my sorry-assed meal, a letter from a lawyer announcing the death of the friend with a son in prison, and inside the legal-sized manila envelope a sealed white envelope the friend had addressed to me.

I was surprised on numerous counts. First, to learn the friend was gone. Second, to find he'd considered me significant enough to have me informed of his passing. Third, the personal note. Fourth, and now it's time to stop numbering, no point since you could say every event following the lawyer's letter both a surprise and no surprise, so numbering them as arbitrary as including the sluggish detail of peanut butter sandwiches, "sluggish" because I'd become intrigued by the contents of the manila envelope and stopped masticating the wad in my jaw until I recalled the friend's description of exiting prison, and the sludge became a mouthful of scalding tar.

What's surprising about death anyway, unless you count the details of when and how, the precise violence stopping the heart, the volume of spilled blood, those unedifying, uninformative details the media relentlessly flog as news. Nothing really surprising about death except how doggedly we insist on being surprised by what we know very well's inevitable, and of course, after a while, this insistence itself unsurprising. So I was (a) surprised and (b) not surprised by the death of a friend who wasn't much of a friend, after all, more acquaintance than intimate cut-buddy, a guy I'd met somewhere through someone and weeks later we'd recognized each other in a line at a movie or a bank and nodded and then ran into each other again one morning in a busy coffeeshop and since I'm partial to the coffee there, I did something I never do, asked if it was okay to share his table and he smiled and said sure so we became in this sense friends. I never knew very much about him

and hadn't known him very long. He never visited my apartment nor I his. A couple years of casual bump-ins, tables shared for coffee while we read our newspapers, a meal, a movie or two, a playoff game in a bar once, two middle-aged men who live alone and inhabit a small, self-sufficient corner of a large city and take time-outs here and there from living alone so being alone at this stage in our careers doesn't feel too depressingly like loneliness. The same motivation, same pattern governing my relationships with the occasional woman who consents to share my bed or if she doesn't consent to sleep with me entertains the option long enough, seriously enough, with attitudes interesting enough to keep us distracted by each other for a while.

Reconsidering the evening I received notice of the friend's death, going over my reactions again, putting words to them, I realize I'm underplaying my emotions. Not about the shock or sadness of losing the friend. He's the kind of person you could see occasionally, enjoy his company more or less, and walk away with no further expectations, no plan to meet again. If he'd moved to another city, months might have passed before I'd notice him missing. If we'd lost contact for good, I'm sure I wouldn't have regretted not seeing him. A smidgen of curiosity, perhaps. Perhaps a slight bit of vexation, as when I discover I haven't restocked paper towels or Tabasco sauce. Less, since his absence wouldn't leave a gap I'd be obliged to fill. My usual flat response at this stage in my life to losing things I have no power to hold on to. Most of the world fits into this category now, so what I'm trying to say is that something about the manila envelope and its contents bothered me more than I'm used to allowing things to bother me, though I'm not sure why. Was it the son in prison. The friend had told me no one else visited. The son's mother dead of cancer. Her people, like the friend's, like mine, old, scattered, gone. Another son, whereabouts unknown, who'd disowned his father and half-brother, started a new life somewhere else. I wondered if the lawyer who wrote me had been instructed to inform the son in prison of his father's passing. How were such matters handled. A phone call. A registered letter. Maybe a visit from the prison chaplain. I hoped my friend had arranged things to run smoothly, with as little distress as possible for the son. Any alternatives I imagined seemed cruel. Cruel for different reasons, but equally difficult for the son. Was he even now opening his manila envelope, a second envelope tucked inside with its personal message. I guess I do know why I was upset—the death of the man who'd been my acquaintance for nearly two years moved me not a bit, but

I grieved to the point of tears for a son I'd never seen, never spoken to, who probably wasn't aware my grief or I existed.

Empathy for the son not surprising, even logical, under the circumstances, you might say. Why worry about the father. He's gone. No more tiptoeing across burning coals. Why not sympathize with a young man suddenly severed from his last living contact with the world this side of prison bars. Did he know his father wouldn't be visiting. Had the son phoned. Listened to it ring-ring-ring and ring. How would he find out. How would he bear the news.

Of course I considered the possibility that my reaction or overreaction might be a way of feeling sorry for myself. For the sorry, running-down-to-the-ground arc all lives eventually assume. Sorry for the prison I've chosen to seal myself within. Fewer and fewer visits paid or received. No doubt a bit of self-pity colored my response. On the other hand I'm not a brooder. I quickly become bored when a mood's too intense or lasts too long. Luckily, I have the capacity to step back, step away, escape into a book, a movie, a vigorous walk, and if these distractions don't do the trick, then very soon I discover I'm smiling, perhaps even quietly chuckling at the ridiculous antics of the person who's lost control, who's taking himself and his commonplace dilemmas far too seriously.

Dear Attorney Koppleman,

I was a friend of the late Mr. Donald Williams. You wrote to inform me of Mr. Williams's death. Thank you. I'm trying to reach Mr. Williams's imprisoned son to offer my belated condolences. If you possess the son's mailing address, could you pass it on to me, please. I appreciate in advance your attention to this matter.

In response to your inquiry of 6/24/99: this office did execute Mr. Donald K. Williams's will. The relevant documents have been filed in Probate Court, and as such are part of the public record you may consult at your convenience.

P.S. Wish I could be more helpful but in our very limited dealings with Mr. Williams, he never mentioned a son in or out of prison.

I learned there are many prisons in Arizona. Large and small. Local, state, federal. Jails for short stays, penitentiaries for lifers. Perhaps it's the

hot, dry climate. Perhaps space is cheap. Perhaps a desert state's economy, with limited employment opportunities for its citizens, relies on prisons. Perhaps corporate-friendly deals make prisons lucrative businesses. Whatever the reasons, the prison industry seems to flourish in Arizona. Many people also wind up in Arizona retirement communities. Do the skills accumulated in managing the senior citizens who come to the state to die readily translate to prison administration, or vice versa. I'm dwelling on the number of prisons only because it presented a daunting obstacle as I began to search for the late friend's son.

Fortunately, the state employs people to keep track of prisoners. I'm not referring to uniformed guards charged with hands-on monitoring of inmate flesh and blood. I mean computer people who know how to punch in and retrieve information. Are they one of the resources attracting prisons to Arizona. Vast emptiness plus a vast legion of specialists adept at processing a steady stream of bodies across borders, orchestrating the dance of dead and living so vacancies are filled and fees collected promptly, new residents recruited, old ones disposed of. Was it the dead friend who told me the downtown streets of Phoenix are eerily vacant during heatstroke daylight hours. People who do the counting must be sequestered in air-conditioned towers or busy as bees underground in offices honeycombed beneath the asphalt, their terminals regulating traffic in and out of hospices, prisons, old folks' homes, juvenile detention centers, cemeteries, their screens displaying Arizona's archipelago of incarceral facilities, diagrams of individual gulags where a single speck with its unique identifying tag can be pinpointed at any moment of the day. Thanks to such a highly organized system, after much digging I located the son.

Why did I search. While I searched, I never asked why. Most likely because I expected no answer. Still don't. Won't fake one now except to suggest (a) curiosity and (b) anger. Curiosity since I had no particular agenda beyond maybe sending a card or note. The search pure in this sense, an experiment, driven by the simple urge to know. Curiosity motivating me like it drove the proverbial cat, killing it until satisfaction brought it back. Anger because I learned how perversely the system functions, how slim your chances of winning are if you challenge it.

Anger because the system's insatiable clockwork innards had the information I sought and refused to divulge it. Refused fiercely, mindlessly, as only a mindless machine created to do a single, repetitive, mindless task can mindlessly refuse. The prison system assumes an adversarial stance the instant an inquiry attempts to sidestep the prerecorded labyrinth of logical menus that protect its irrational core. When and if you ever reach a human voice, its hostile tone insinuates you've done something stupid or morally suspect by pursuing it to its lair. As punishment for your trespass, the voice will do its best to mimic the tone and manner of the recorded messages you've been compelled to suffer in order to reach it.

Anger, because I couldn't help taking the hassle personally. Hated equally the bland bureaucratic sympathy or disdain or deafness or defensiveness or raw, aggressive antagonism, the multiplicity of attitudes and accents live and recorded transmitting exactly the same bottom-line message: yes, what you want I have, but I'm not parting with it easily.

I won't bore you or myself by reciting how many times I was put on hold or switched or switched back or the line went dead after hours of Muzak or I weathered various catch-22 routines. I'll just say I didn't let it get the best of me. Swallowed my anger, and with the help of a friend, persevered, till one day—accidentally, I'm sure—the information I'd been trying to pry from the system's grip collapsed like an escaping hostage into my arms.

      I'm writing to express my condolences sympathies upon the death of your father at the death of your father your father's passing though I was barely acquainted only superficially I'm writing to you because I was a friend of your father by now prison officials must have informed you of his death his demise the bad news I assume I don't want to intrude on your grief sorrow privacy if in fact hadn't known your sorrow and the circumstances of our lives known him very long only a few years permitted allowed only limited opportunities to become acquainted and the circumstances of our lives I considered your father a friend I can't claim to know him your father well but our paths crossed often frequently I considered him a good valuable friend fine man I was very sorry to hear learn of his death spoke often of you on many occasions his words Please allow me to express my sympathy for your great loss I don't claim to know to have known him well but I your father fine man good man considered him a valuable friend heartfelt he spoke of you many times always quite much good love affection admiration I feel almost as if I you know you though I'm a complete stranger his moving words heartfelt about son compelled me to write this note if I can be helpful in any fashion manner if I can be of assistance in this matter at this difficult time place don't hesitate to let me know please don't

I was sorry to hear of your father's death. We were friends. Please accept my heartfelt regrets on this sad occasion.

Some man must have fucked my mother. All I knew about him until your note said he's dead. Thanks.

It could have ended there. A case of mistaken identity. Or a lie. Or numerous lies. Or a hallucination. Or fabrication. Had I been duped. By whom. Father, son, both. Did they know each other or not. What did I know for sure about either one. What stake did I have in either man's story. If I connected the dots, would a picture emerge. One man dead, the other good as dead locked up two thousand miles away in an Arizona prison. Was any of it my business. Anybody's business.

I dress lightly, relying on the weather lady's promises.

A woman greets me and introduces herself as Suh Jung, Attorney Koppleman's paralegal. She's a tiny, pleasant Asian woman with jet-black hair brutally cropped above her ears, a helmet, she'll explain later, necessary to protect herself from the cliché of submissiveness, the china-doll stereotype people immediately applied when they saw a thick rope of hair hanging past her waist, hair her father insisted she not cut but wear twisted into a single braid in public, her mother combing, brushing, oiling her hair endlessly till shiny pounds of it were lopped off the day the father died and then, strangely, she'd wanted to save the hair she had hated, wanted to glue it back together strand by strand and drape it over one of those pedestaled heads you see in beauty shops so she and her mother could continue forever the grooming rituals that had been one of the few ways they could relate in a household her father relentlessly, meticulously hammered into an exquisitely lifelike, flawless representation of his will, like those sailing ships in bottles or glass butterflies in the museum, so close to the real thing you stare and stare waiting for them to flutter away, a household the father shattered in a fit of pique or rage or boredom the day she opened the garage door after school and found him barefoot, shitty-pantsed, dangling from a rafter beside the green family Buick.

In the lawyer's office she listened to my story about father and son, took notes carefully, it seemed, though her eyes were cool, a somewhere-else distracted cool while she performed her legal-assistant duties. Black, distant eyes framed in round, metal-rimmed, old-lady spectacles that belied the youthful freshness of her skin. Late at night when she'd talk about her dead father, I'd notice the coolness of the first day, and as I learned more about him—or rather, as I formed my own impression of him, since she volunteered few details, spoke instead about being a quiet, terrified girl trying to swim through shark-infested water without making waves—I guessed she had wanted to imitate the father's impenetrable gaze, practicing, practicing till she believed she'd gotten it right, but she didn't get it right, probably because she never understood the father's coldness, never made her peace with the blankness behind his eyes where she yearned to see her image take shape, where it never did, never would. Gradually I came to pity her, her unsuccessful theft of her father's eyes, her transparent attempt to conceal her timidity behind the father's stare, timidity I despised because it reminded me of mine, my inadequacies and half-measures and compromises, begging and fearing to be seen, my lack of directness, decisiveness, my deficiency of enterprise and imagination, manifested in her case by the theatrical gesture of chopping off her hair when confronted by the grand truth of her father's suicide. Timidity dooming her to cliché—staring off inscrutably into space.

Given her history, the lost-father business in my story must have teased out her curiosity. Otherwise, why would she take notice of me. Going by appearances—her pale, unlined face, my stern, dark, middle-aged mask—I was too old for her. I could suggest (a) she was older than she looked and (b) I'm younger than you might guess at first glance, but then I'd be hedging, suggesting some middle ground we shared almost as peers, and such turned out not to be the case. I wasn't old enough to be her father, but that dreadful plausibility enforced a formal distance between us, distance we maintained in public, distance that at first could be stimulating erotically, for me at least, until the necessity of denying difference, denying the evidence of my eyes, became less a matter of play than a chore, a discipline and duty, even when we were together in private.

Behind a desk almost comically dwarfing her (seeing it, I should have been alerted by its acres of polished blond wood to the limits, the impropriety of any intimacy we'd establish), she listened politely, eventually dissuaded me from what I'd anticipated as the object of my visit—talking to Attorney Koppleman. She affirmed her postscript: no one in the office knew anything about a son in prison. I thanked her, accepted the card she offered to substantiate her willingness to help in any way she could.

Would you like me to call around out in Arizona. At least save you some time, get you started in the right direction.

Thanks. That's very kind of you. But I probably need to do some thinking on this.

And then I realized how stupidly wishy-washy I must sound. It galled me, because I work hard to give just the opposite impression. Appear to be a man sure of himself, not the kind of jerk who bothers people, wasting their valuable time because he doesn't know what he wants. So perhaps that's why I flirted. Not flirted exactly, but asserted myself in the only way I could think of at the moment, by plainly, abruptly letting her see I was interested. In her. The woman part of her. A decisive act, yet suspect from the beginning, since it sprang from no particular spark of attraction. Still, a much more decisive move than I'm usually capable of making—true or false. Hitting on her, so to speak, straight up, hard, asking for the home number she hastily scribbled on the back of her card, hurrying as if she suddenly remembered a lineup of urgent tasks awaiting our interview's termination. Her way of attending to a slightly embarrassing necessity. The way some women I've met, and men too, I suppose, treat sex. Jotting down the number, she was as out of character as I was, but we pulled it off. A silly, halfhearted, doomed exchange in a downtown office, pulling it off in spite of ourselves. Me driven to retrieve dignity I was afraid I'd compromised. Her motive opaque, then as now. Even though the lost-father business leaps out at you, it doesn't account for her lifting her gaze from her cluttered desk, from the file on top of the pile on which she'd laid her card, staring at me, then dashing off her number on the back.

Thanks again. And thank you for this, I said, pressing my luck, nodding at the card I was holding back side up, my arm extended toward her, as if I were nearsighted and needed distance to read what she'd written, but she didn't raise her eyes again to the bait I dangled or she dangled or whatever it was either of us believed we were accomplishing in the lawyer's office that afternoon.

The world is full of remarkable things. Amiri Baraka penned those words when he was still LeRoi Jones writing his way back to Newark and a new name after a lengthy sojourn among artsy, crazy white folks in the Village. One of my favorite lines from one of my favorite writers. Back in the day when I still pretended books worth talking about, people were surprised to discover Baraka a favorite of mine, as quietly integrated and nonconfrontational a specimen as I seemed to be of America's longest, most violently reviled minority. It wasn't so much a matter of the quality of what Jones/Baraka had written as it was the chances he'd taken, chances in his art, in his life. Sacrifices of mind and body he endured so I could vicariously participate, safely holed up in my corner. Same lair where I sat out Vietnam, a college boy while my cousin and most guys from my high school were drafted, shot at, jailed, murdered, became drug addicts in a war raging here and abroad.

Remarkable things. With Suh Jung I smoked my first joint in years. At fifty-seven learned to bathe a woman and, what was harder, learned to relax in a tub while a woman bathed me. Contacting the son in prison not exactly on hold while she and I experienced low-order remarkable things. I knew which Arizona prison held him and had received from the warden's office the information I'd requested about visiting. Completing my business with this woman was a necessary step in the process of preparing myself for whatever I decided to do next. Steaming water, her soapy hands scrubbing my shoulders, cleansed me, fortified me. I shed old skins. When the son in prison set his eyes on me, I wanted to glow. If he saw me at my best, wouldn't he understand everything.

The dead friend my age more or less, so that could mean the son more or less Suh Jung's age. He should be the suitor. The shoulders she lathered, the hand stubbing out the roach in a mayonnaise jar cap, could be his. What would he see, turning to embrace the woman sitting up naked next to me in bed. She's small, boy-hipped, breasts slight pouches under long nipples that attract attention to an absence rather than presence they crown, twin sentry towers on her bony chest, guarding an outpost no aggressor's likely to target. Is she a woman the son would desire. What sort of woman does the son fantasize when he masturbates. What if the son awakened here, his cell transformed to this room, the son imprisoned here with this woman, sweet smoke settling in his lungs, mellowing him out after all the icy years. Me locked in the black Arizona night imagining a woman. Would it be the same woman in both places at once or different limbs, eyes, wetnesses, scents, like those tigers whirling about Sambo, tigers no longer tigers as they chase each other faster and faster, overwhelming poor little Sambo's senses, his Sambo black brain, as he tosses and turns in waking-sleep, a mixed-up colored boy, the coins his mother gave him clutched in a sweaty fist, trying once more to complete a simple errand and reach home in one piece.

Why would I be ashamed if caught with a woman who might be the age of the son rotting in prison. What difference to the son whether or not I have a lover or what her age might be. If I'm celibate till I die, would my abstinence buy him freedom one instant sooner. If my trip or possible trip's stalled while I dally with a woman, so what. I'm going to visit, not bring him home. What's wrong with sorting out my motivations, my ambivalence, calculating consequences. Always plenty to sort out, isn't there: fathers, sons, daughters, deaths, the proper care and feeding of the selfish, greedy animal each of us is, the desirability of short-lived affairs to distract us from the awful humiliations we're born to suffer aging and dying. I'm more alone now, fifty-seven years later, than when I arrived spanking brand-new on the planet. Instead of being delayed, my trip to Arizona is beginning here, being born here in this grappling, this tangle.

Have you written again.

No, just the once. His answer enough to cure me of letter writing forever.

But you say you're ready to visit. Do you have a ticket. Or are you going to stamp your forehead and mail yourself to Arizona.

The city bumps past, cut up through the bus windows. We had headed for the last row of seats in the back, facing the driver. Seats on the rear bench meant fewer passengers stepping over, around, on you during the long ride uptown to the museum. Fewer people leaning over you. Sneezing. Coughing. Eavesdropping. Fewer strangers boxing you in, saying stuff you don't want to hear but you find yourself listening anyway, the way you had watched in spite of yourself the never-turned-off TV set in your mother's living room. Fresh blood pooled on one of the butt-molded blue seats you intended to occupy. A wet, silver-dollar-sized fresh glob. You consider changing buses. Could you transfer without being double-fared. What about the good chance you'd hop from frying pan to fire, catch a bus with a raving maniac on board or a fleet of wheelchairs docking or undocking every other corner. Better to leave well enough alone. Take seats catty-corner from the bloody one. The blood's not going to jump the aisle and bite you. Fortunately, you noticed it before either of you splashed down in it. You check again, eye-balling one more time the blue seats you're poised above, looking for blood, expecting blood, as if blood's a constant danger though you've never seen blood before on a bus bumping from uptown to downtown, downtown to uptown in all the years of riding until this very day.

We almost missed the Giacometti.

Not there yet.

It closes next weekend.

Right on time, then. I'm away next week.

Oh, you're going to Arizona next week.

I've been letting other things get in the way. Unless I set a hard date, the visit won't happen. You know. Like we kept putting off Giacometti.

You booked a flight.

Not yet.

But you're going for sure. Next week.

I think so think so think so think so think so.

I loved the slinky *dog*. He was so . . . so . . . you know . . . dog. An alley-cat dog like the ones always upsetting the garbage cans behind my father's store. Stringy and scrawny like them. Swaybacked. Hunkered down like they're hiding or something's after them even when they're just pit-patting from place to place. Scruffy barbed-wire fur. Those long, floppy, flat dog feet like bedroom slippers.

To tell the truth, too much to see. I missed the dog. I was overwhelmed. By the crowd, the crowd of objects.

Two weeks after the Giacometti exhibit, I could make more sense of it. A fat, luxurious book by a French art critic helped. It cost so much I knew I'd force myself to read it, or at least study the copious illustrations. The afternoon in the MoMA I'd done more reading than looking at art. Two floors, numerous galleries, still it was like fighting for a handhold on a subway pole. Reading captions shut out the crowd. I could stand my ground without feeling the pressure of somebody behind me demanding a peek.

I wondered why Giacometti didn't go insane. Maybe he did. Even without the French critic I could sense Giacometti didn't trust what was in front of his eyes. He felt the strangeness, the menace. He understood art always failed. Art lied to him. People's eyes lied. No one ever sees the world as it is. Giacometti's eyes failed him too. He'd glance away from a model to the image of it he was making, he said, and when he looked back to check the model, it would be different, always different, always changing.

Frustrated by my inability to recall the dead friend's face, I twisted on the light over the mirror above the bathroom sink, thinking I might milk the friend's features from mine. Hadn't we been vaguely similar in age and color. If I studied hard, maybe the absence in my face of some distinctive trait the friend possessed would trigger my memory, or vice versa, a trait I bore would recall its absence in the friend's features, and bingo, his whole face would appear.

There is an odd neurological deficit that prevents some people from recognizing faces. Seeing the stranger in the mirror, I was afraid I might be suffering from the disorder. Who in God's name was this person. Who'd been punished with those cracks, blemishes, the mottled complexion, eyes sunk in deep hollows, frightened eyes crying out for acknowledgment, for help, then receding, surrendering, staring blankly, bewildered and exhausted, asking me the same questions I was asking them.

Rather than attempt to account for the wreckage, I began to repair the face, working backward, a makeup artist removing years from an actor, restoring a young man the mirror denied. How long had I been losing track of myself. Not really looking when I brushed my teeth or combed my hair, letting the image in the mirror soften and blur, become as familiar and invisible as faces on money. Easier to imagine the son than deal with how the father had turned out, the splotched, puffy flesh, lines incised in forehead and cheeks, strings dragging down the corners of the mouth. I switched off the light, let the merciful hood drop over the prisoner's head.

People don't really look, do they. Experiments have demonstrated conclusively how unobservant the average person is and, worse, how complacent, how unfazed by blindness. A man with a full beard gets paid to remove it and then goes about his usual day. The following day a researcher asks those who regularly encounter the man, his coworkers for example, if he had a beard when they saw him the previous day. Most can't remember one way or the other but assume he did. A few say the beard was missing. A few admit they'd never noticed a beard. A few insist vehemently they saw the invisible beard. I seem to recall the dead friend sporting a beard at one time or another during the period we were acquainted. Since I can't swear yes or no, I consign myself, just as Giacometti numbered himself, among the blind.

Are prisoners permitted to cultivate beards. Would a beard, if allowed, cause the son to resemble the father more closely. How would I recognize a resemblance if I can't visualize the father's face, or rather see it all too clearly as the anonymous blur of an aging man, any man, all men. Instead of staring without fear and taking responsibility for the unmistakable, beaten-up person I've apparently become, I prefer to see nothing.

Time at last for the visit. I'd written again and the son had responded again. A slightly longer reply with a visiting form tucked inside the flimsy prison envelope. Of course I couldn't help recalling the letter within a letter I'd received from the lawyer, Koppleman. The son instructed me to check the box for family and write *father* on the line following it. To cut red tape and speed up the process, I assumed, but for a second I hesitated, concerned some official would notice the names didn't match, then realized lots of inmates wouldn't bear (or know) their father's name, and some wouldn't claim it even though it's registered on their birth certificate, so I checked the family box, printed *father* in the space provided.

Aside from a few sentences re the enclosed form, the second letter actually shorter than the first: *Why not. My social calendar not full.* A smiling leopard in a cage. Step closer if you dare.

An official notice from the warden's office authorizing my visit took months to reach me. I began to regret lying on a form that had warned me, under penalty of law, not to perjure myself. Who reads the applications. How carefully did prison officials check facts applicants alleged. What punishments could be levied against a person who falsified information. The form a perfunctory measure, I guessed, so bureaucrats in charge of security could say they'd followed the rules. A form destined to gather dust in a file, properly executed and stamped, retrievable just in case an emergency exploded and some official needed to cover her or his ass. Justify his or her existence. The existence of the state. Of teeming prisons in the middle of the desert.

During the waiting my misgivings soured into mild paranoia. Had I compromised myself, broken a law that might send me too packing off to jail. I finally calmed down after I figured out that short of a DNA test (a) no one could prove I wasn't the prisoner's father and (b) it wasn't a crime to believe I was. If what the son had written in his first letter was true, the prison would possess no record of his father. The late friend past proclaiming his paternity. And even if he rose from the dead to argue his case, why would his claim, sans DNA confirmation, be more valid in the eyes of the law than mine. So what if he had visited. So what if he'd married the prisoner's mother. So what if he sincerely believed his belief of paternity. Mama's baby, Daddy's maybe. Hadn't I heard folks shout that taunt all my life. Didn't my own mother recite the refrain many times. Nasty Kilroys scrawled everywhere on the crumbling walls of my old neighborhood hollered the same funny, mean threat. Careful, Jack. Don't turn your back. Kilroy's lurking. Kilroy's creeping. Keep your door locked, your ole lady pregnant in summer, barefoot in winter, my man. In more cases than people like to admit, paternity nothing but wishful thinking. Kilroy a thief in the night, leaves no fingerprints, no footprints. Mama's sweet baby, Daddy's, maybe.

Psychologists say there's a stage when a child doubts the adults raising it are its real family. How can parents prove otherwise. And why would kids want to trade in the glamorous fairy tales they dream up about their origins for a pair of ordinary, bumbling adults who impose stupid rules, stifling routines. Who needs their hostile world full of horrors and hate.

Some mornings when I awaken I look out my window and pretend to understand. I reside in a building in the bottom of somebody's pocket. Sunlight never touches its bricks. Any drawer or cabinet or closet shut tight for a day will exude a gust of moldy funk when you open it. The building's neither run-down nor cheap. Just dark, dank, and drab. Drab as grown-ups that children are browbeaten into accepting as their masters. The building, my seventh-floor apartment, languish in the shadow of something falling, leaning down, leaning over. Water, when you turn on a faucet first thing in the morning, gags on itself, spits, then gushes like a bloody jailbreak from the pipes. In a certain compartment of my heart where compassion's sup-posed to lodge, but there's never enough space in cramped urban dwellings so I store niggling self-pity there too, I try to find room also for all the mil-lions of poor souls who have less than I have, who would howl for joy if they could occupy as their own one corner of my dreary little flat. I invite these unfortunates for a visit, pack the compartment till it's full far beyond capacity, and weep with them, share with them my scanty bit of prosperity, tell them I care, tell them be patient, tell them I'm on their side, tell them an old acquaintance of mine who happens to be a poet recently hit the lottery big-time, a cool million, and wish them similar luck, wish them clear sailing and swift, painless deaths, tell them it's good to be alive, whatever, tell them how much I appreciate living as long as I've managed and still eating every day, fucking now and then, finding a roof over my head in the morning after finding a bed to lie in at night, grateful to live on even though the pocket's deep and black and a hand may dig in any moment and crush me.

With Suh Jung's aid—why not use her, wasn't it always about finding uses for the people in your life, why would they be in your life if you had no use for them, or vice versa, and if you're using them, doesn't that lend purpose to their lives, you're actually doing them a trickle-down favor, aren't you, allowing them to use you to feel themselves useful and that's some-thing, isn't it, better than nothing anyway, than being useless or used up— I gathered more information about the son in prison. Accumulated a file, biography, character sketch, rap sheet a.k.a. his criminal career.

You're going to wear out the words, she joked as she glanced over at me sitting beside her in the bed that occupied the same room with a Pullman fridge and stove. Her jibe less a joke than a complaint: I'm sick and tired of your obsessive poring over a few dog-eared scraps of paper extracted from Arizona's bottomless pit of records, is what she was saying with a slight curl of one side of her thin mouth, a grimace that could have been constructed as the beginning of a smirk she decided was not worth carrying full-term.

I kept reading. Avoided the swift disappointment another glance at her tidy body would trigger. Its spareness had been exciting at first, but after the slow, slow, up-close-and-personal examination of her every square inch afforded by the bathing rituals she performed on me and I learned to reciprocate once my shyness abated, after we'd subjected each other's skin to washcloth, oil, the glide, pinch, stroke of fingertips and tongue, her body had become in a few months much less intriguing, less compensation for her tart remarks. Now I had no patience for her impatience with me, her taunts. The eroticism between us had dulled rather too quickly, it seemed. An older man's childish unreasonableness partly at fault. Why else would I be disappointed after a few weeks because her hips didn't round nor the negligible mounds beneath her nipples swell. Her boyish look not a stage, it was what I was going to get, period, even if the business between us survived longer than I had any reason to expect. No, things weren't going to get better, and I was wasting precious time. Given my age, how many more chances could I expect.

Here's what the papers said: He's done lots of bad things, the worst kinds of things, and if we could, we'd kill him, but we can't, so we'll never, never let him go.

Are you surprised, she'd asked.

I didn't know what to expect, I had replied.

Heavy-duty stuff. If only half the charges legit, he's a real bad actor.

I'm not traveling out west to forgive him or bust him out or bring him back. Just visit. Just fill in for the dead father. Once. One time enough and it's finished.

No matter how many times you read them, she says, the words won't change. Why read the same ugly facts over and over.

(A) Because my willing, skilled accomplice gathered them for me. (B) Curiosity.

His crimes would make a difference to me, I mean if I were you. This whole visiting business way over the top, you admit it yourself, so I don't pretend I can put myself in your shoes, but still. The awful crimes he's committed would affect anybody's decision to go or not.

Is he guilty. How can you be certain based on a few sheets of paper.

A lot's in the record. A bit too much for a case of mistaken identity. Huh-uh. Plus or minus a few felonies, the man's been busy.

Are you casting the first stone.

A whole building's been dumped on the poor guy. And he's thrown his share of bricks at other folks. I'd hate to bump into him in a dark alley.

Maybe you already have, my friend. Maybe you have and maybe you've enjoyed it.

You're more than a little weird about this, you know. What the hell are you talking about.

Just that people wind up in situations there's no accounting for. Situations when innocence or guilt are extremely beside the point. Situations when nothing's for sure except some of us are on one side of the bars, some on the other side, but nobody knows which side is which.

I know I haven't robbed or kidnapped or murdered anyone. Have you.

Have I. Do you really want to know. Everyone has crimes to answer for, don't they. Even you. Suppose I said my crimes are more terrible than his. Would you believe me. Would my confession start your heart beating a little faster.

(a) No. And (b) you're not scaring me. Put those damned papers away and turn off the light. Please. I have work tomorrow.

You don't want to hear my confession. It might sound better in the dark.

I'm tired. I need sleep, and you're acting stupid because you can't make up your mind to go to Arizona.

My mind's made up. The prison said yes. I'm on my way.

I'll be glad when it's over and done.

And me back in the arms of my love. Will you be faithful while your sweet serial killer's away.

She tries to snatch the papers but misses. I drop them over the side of the pull-out bed. Like the bed, she is small and light. Easy to fold up and subdue even for an older fellow. When I wrap myself around her, my body's so much larger than hers, she almost vanishes. When we fuck, or now, capturing her, punishing her, I see very little of her flesh. I'm aware of my size, my strength towering over her squirming, her thrashing, her gasps for breath. I am her father's stare, the steel gate dropping over the tiger pit in which she's naked, trapped, begging for food and water. Air. Light.

I arrive on Sunday. Two days late, for reasons I can't explain to myself. I flew over mountains, then desert flatness that seemed to go on forever. It must have been Ohio, Illinois, Iowa, Nebraska, not actual desert but the nation's breadbasket, so they say, fruited plains, amber waves of grain, plowed, fertilized fields irrigated by giant machines day after day spreading water in the same pattern to create the circles, squares, rectangles below. Arable soil gradually giving way to sandy grit as the plane drones westward, through clouds, over another rugged seam of mountains, and then as I peer down at the undramatic nothingness beyond the far edge of wrinkled terrain, the surface of the earth flips over like a pancake. What's aboveground buried, what's belowground suddenly exposed. Upside-down mountains are hollow shells, deep, deep gouges in the stony waste, their invisible peaks underground, pointing to hell.

A bit of confusion, bureaucratic stuttering and sputtering when confronted by the unanticipated fact of my tardy arrival, a private calling his sergeant, sergeant phoning officer in charge of visitation, each searching for verification, for duplication, for assurance certified in black and white that she or he is off the hook, not guilty of disrupting the checks and balances of prison routine. I present myself hat in hand, remorseful, apologetic, *Please, please, give me another chance please kind sir*, forgive me for missing day one and two of the scheduled three-day visit, for checking in the morning of day three instead of day one. Am I still eligible or will I be shooed away like starving beggars from the rich man's table.

I overhear two guards discussing a coyote whose scavenging brought it down out of the slightly elevated wilderness of rock and brush beginning a few miles or so from the prison's steel-fenced perimeter. I learn how patiently guards on duty in the tower spied on the coyote's cautious trespass of their turf, a blip at first, up and back along the horizon, then a discernible shape—skinny legs, long, pointed ears, bushy tail—a scraggly critter drawn by easy prey or coyote curiosity closer and closer to the prison until it was within rifle range and the guards took turns profiling it through their sharpshooting sniper scopes, the sad-faced, cartoon coyote they christened whatever guards would christen a creature they probably will kill one day, a spook, a mirage, it seems so quick on its feet, bolder as it's allowed to approach nearer without being challenged, believing perhaps it can't be seen, flitting from shadow to shadow, camouflaged by hovering darkness, by mottled fur, a shadow itself, instantly freezing, sniffing the air, then trotting again back and forth along the skyline, skittish through coverless space, up and back, parry, thrust, and retreat, ears pricked to attention when the rare service vehicle enters or leaves the prison parking lot before dawn. Murky predawn the coyote's time, the darkness divulging it, a drop from a leaky pipe, a phantom prowling nearer and nearer as if the electrified steel fence is one boundary of its cage, an easy shot now the sharpshooters forbear taking, too easy, or perhaps it's more fun to observe their mascot play, watch it pounce on a mouse and pummel it in swift paws bat-bat-bat before its jaws snap the rodent's neck or maybe the name they named it a kind of protection for a while till somebody comes on duty one morning or premorning really when the first shift after the night shift has to haul itself out of bed, out of prefab homes lining the road to the prison entrance, shitty box houses, a few with bright patches of something growing in flower boxes beside the front steps, boxes you can't see at that black hour from your pickup, eyes locked in the tunnel your headlights carve, a bad-head, bad-attitude morning, pissed off, thinking about quitting this stinking job, getting the fuck out before you're caught Kilroying or cuckolded in the town's one swinging joint, cussed out, serving pussy probation till further notice, cancer eating his mama, daddy long gone, kids sick or fighting or crazy on pot or dead or in prison so he draws a bead and *pow*, blood seeps into the sand, the coyote buzzard bait by the time I eavesdrop on two guards badmouthing their assassin colleague, laughing at him, at the coyote's surprise, the dead animal still serving time as a conversation piece, recycled in this desert sparseness, desert of extremes, of keepers and kept, silence and screams, cold and hot, thirst and drunkenness, too much time, no time, where all's lost but nothing's gone.

A spiffy, spit-and-polish platinum blond guard whose name tag I read and promptly forget, Lieutenant, another guard addresses her, Lieutenant, each breast under her white blouse as large as Suh Jung's head, smiles up at me from the counter where she's installed, hands me the document she's stamped, slides me a tray for unloading everything in my pockets, stores it when I'm finished. Now that wasn't so bad, was it, sir. Gives me a receipt and a green ticket with matching numbers. Points me toward a metal detector standing stark and foursquare as a guillotine whose eye I must pass through before I'm allowed to enter the prison.

Beyond the detector one more locked door I must be buzzed through and I'm outside again, in an open-air, tunnel-like enclosure of Cyclone fencing bristling on sides and top with razor wire, a corridor or chute or funnel or maze I must negotiate while someone somewhere at a machine measures and records my every step, false move, hesitation, scream, counts drops of sweat, of blood when my hands tear at the razor wire, someone calibrating the before and after of my heart rate, my lungs.

I pass all the way through the tunnel to a last checkpoint, a small cinder-block hut squatting beside the final sliding gate guarding the visiting yard. Thirty yards away, across the yard, at a gated entranceway facing this one, guards are mustering inmates dressed in orange jumpsuits.

In a slot at the bottom of the hut's window you must surrender your numbered green ticket to receive a red one. Two groups of women and children ahead of me in line require a few minutes each for this procedure. Then I hold up the works. Feel on my back the helplessness and irritation of visits stalled. Five, ten minutes in the wire bullpen beside the hut, long enough to register a miraculous change in temperature. Less than an hour ago, crossing the parking lot from rental car to waiting room, I'd wondered if I'd dressed warmly enough for the visit. Now Arizona sun bakes my neck. I'm wishing for shade, for the sunglasses not permitted inside. My throat's parched. Will I be able to speak if spoken to. Through the hut's thick glass, bulletproof I'm guessing, I watch two officers chattering. One steps away to a wall phone. The other plops down at a shelflike minidesk, shuffles papers, punches buttons on a console. A dumb show since I couldn't hear a thing through the slab of greenish glass.

Did I stand in the cage five minutes or ten or twenty. What I recall is mounting heat, sweat rolling inside my clothes, blinking, losing track of time, not caring about time, shakiness, numbness, mumbling to myself, stiffening rage, morphing combinations of all the above, yet overriding each sensation, the urge to flee, to be elsewhere, anywhere other than stalled at that gate, waiting to be snatched inside or driven away or, worse, pinned there forever. Would I be knocked down to my knees, forced to recite my sins, the son's sins, the sins of the world. If I tried to escape, would my body—*splat*—be splashed and pulped on the razor wire or could I glide magically through the knives glinting like mirrors, not stopping till I reach a spot far, far away where I can bury my throbbing head in the coolness miles deep below the sand, so deep you can hear the subterranean chortle of rivers on the opposite face of the planet.

At last someone arrives from a door I hadn't noticed, addressing me, I think.

Sorry. Your visit's been canceled. Computer says the inmate you want to visit is not in the facility. Call the warden's office after nine a.m. Monday. Maybe they can give you more information. Sorry about the mix-up. Now please stand back. Step away from the gate so the next . . .

Briefs
(2010)

Witness

Sitting here one night six floors up on my little balcony when I heard shots and saw them boys running. My eyes went straight to the lot beside Mason's bar and I saw something black not moving in the weeds and knew a body lying there and knew it was dead. A fifteen-year-old boy the papers said. Whole bunch of sirens and cops and spinning lights the night I'm talking about. I watched till after they rolled him away and then everything got quiet again as it ever gets round here so I'm sure the boy's people not out there that night. Didn't see them till next morning when I'm looking down at those weeds and a couple's coming slow on Frankstown with a girl by the hand, had to be the boy's baby sister. They pass terrible Mason's and stop right at the spot the boy died. Then they commence to swaying, bowing, hugging, waving their arms about. Forgive me, Jesus, but look like they grief dancing, like the sidewalk too cold or too hot they had to jump around not to burn up. How'd his people find the exact spot. Did they hear my old mind working to lead them, guide them along like I would if I could get up out this damn wheelchair and take them by the hand.

To Barry Bonds: Home Run King

When I was a young man, like you, I, too, experimented with anything I could lay my hands on to make me better at what I wanted to be. Like you—maybe—I feared only my color, my tainted blood and tainted, incriminating history, and occasionally late at night fretted over whether I could sustain the strength of will to save myself, but beyond these distractions, I really believed and told myself deep down inside that nothing could stop me. I'd get it done. Be a superstar beyond belief, in spite of or because of any doubts I entertained. And accordingly allowed myself excesses. The right to hurt others. The right to damage myself. Woke up more than one morning in a puddle of piss, blood, and snot and never gave a thought to turning around, going back home. Too much world to win and I was damned good at winning. People loved me for being very good and footed bills I couldn't have imagined once upon a time running up. Bills for things the poor boy I once was had never heard of. Things I didn't recognize till after they passed through my body and my shit stank differently. I became truly so good, so much better than the competition, I forgot anybody ever needed to pay. Least of all me. And let me tell you that standing here now swinging my bat as you must swing yours, at air, at mosquitoes, at slow, dreamy curve balls I whack but can't halt their flight and they splash gooey in my face, like you now, I'm half clown, half star, half martyr and half something else if that makes any sense, you know, or makes as much or little sense, anyway, as being called out if you swing and miss a ball three times.

War Stories

I have a friend, a kind of friend, anyway, I talked with only once and that once we'd seemed simpatico. I let him know I had learned a lot from a story he'd written about things men carried when they fought in Vietnam. Years have passed and I've lost track of him, so to speak. I need to talk with him now because I'm trying to understand the war here in America, the worst war, in spite of mounting casualties in wars abroad, this war filling prisons, filling pockets, emptying schools, minds, hearts, a war keeping people locked down at home, no foreign nations to defeat, just ourselves defeated by fear of each other, a war incarcerating us all in killing fields where the only rule is feed on the bodies of fellow inmates or surely they will feed on yours. What do combatants carry in this war, I want to ask him, in this civil strife waged within stone walls, in glass cages, barbed wire enclosed ghettos of poverty and wealth, behind the lines, between the lines. Can friend be distinguished from foe by what they carry, what they wear. By the way they walk, how they talk. Their words, their silence? This war different, though not entirely unlike others in Afghanistan, Iraq, and soon Iran or wherever else folly incites us to land our young men and women with whatever they will carry into battle this time and carry when they return like the chickens Malcolm warned always come home to roost. Not separate wars, really. No more separate than different colors of skin that provide logic and cover for war. No more separate than the color of my skin from yours, my friend, if we could meet again and talk about carrying the things we carry, about what torments me, an old man ashamed of this country I assume you still live in, too.

Close

The twins born so alike that their doting mother, blessed be her memory, tied a ribbon around one infant's chubby ankle to tell them apart. Red, the ribbon's color, also served as a name, and aside from the red ribbon always visible on one twin's body, they grew up identical into nearly identical lives, until at the age of twelve, Red contracted a terrible disease. A barrage of radiation, medicine, and prayers spared her life but not without leaving behind a sterile womb. Seven years later her twin, Rachel, gave birth to twins and presented one of the boys to her beloved sister to raise as her own son, a gift so generous and unprecedented it was recorded in the *Book of Perfect Intentions* and Red received honorable mention in the same volume for the generous lack of bitterness she displayed with no choice but to be on the receiving end of the gift. Because the thought of separating their separated boys unbearable as the thought of losing the nearly mystical companionship the twin sisters enjoyed, they all resided for many years under the same roof, one unit of three, one of two, a single happy family. The arrangement worked far better than town gossips predicted and might have lasted longer, except one afternoon while her sister was out shopping, Red (many say the ribbon's color doomed her) decided that sharing the penis of her twin's husband would place very little strain on the generosity of a sister able to share one of her babies. But as everybody knows, husbands are not babies, and the family's domestic arrangements rapidly deteriorated. A secret at first, the sexual trespassing never exactly confessed but allowed to leak out in dribbles. One morning Rachel awakens with wet cheeks, another morning wet feet, then she and the others paddle daily in a slough of jealousy, recriminations, despair. No one likes anyone anymore, and during a particularly vicious exchange of the dozens one boy hollers, *Yo mama's a ho*, and his twin curses back, *She your mama, too,* and from that moment on the sons and their sons and their son's sons, even unto the present generation, have waged murderous wars upon one another, perpetuating the slaughter and chaos that give humanity such a bad name.

Automatic

They stole my money, my father says. I know exactly what you mean, man, I could have responded, but don't want to get him started on the frozen poem of frustration and rage he can't help reciting, stanza by stanza, because the thieves won't send him the prizes their letters declare he's won. I've come to take away his car keys. Or rather do what our worried family has decided, Ask for his car keys. We'd tried before. No way, Jose, he let us know. Me and that old girl automatic. Drive this whole city blindfolded. Today it's as if he knew before I knocked, someone would be coming by and there would be less of him left as soon as he opened his door, so he's reminding me, whatever my good intentions, that I'm also just like those others who'd lied, stripped and stolen things from him his entire life and aren't finished yet, vultures circling closer and closer, withholding his prizes, picking his bones clean because an old black man too tired to shoo them off anymore. His quick mind leaving him fast but thank goodness my father no pack rat. Until the end his apartment fairly neat. He keeps only the largest letters in their boldly colored, big print envelopes guaranteeing a Corvette or condo in Acapulco or million in cash mega prize. Beside his bed and on the kitchen table large stacks of these lying motherfuckers that taunt and obsess him, his last chance, a glorious grand finale promised though how and when not precisely spelled out in the fine print. He never quite figures out the voices on the other end of his daily 800 calls are robots. Curses the menus white women's voices chirp. His response to my request he surrender his keys gentler. A slightly puzzled glance, a smile breaking my heart, *No, Daddy, no. Don't do it*, I'm crying out helplessly, silently, as he passes me the keys.

Writing

All the years I never learned to write. Stop. Start. A man on a bicycle passes down Essex Street in the rain. Gray. Green. Don't go back. You won't write it any better. More. You can only write more or less. That's all. A man in a greenish gray slicker pedals down Essex in a slashing downpour. Leaves behind a pale brushstroke of color that pulsates, coming and going as you stare into empty slants of rain. A flash of color left behind. Where is the man. Where gone. What on his mind. The color not there really. Splashed and gone that quick. A bit of wishful thinking. A melancholy painting on air. Do not go back. It doesn't get better. Only more. Less. The years not written do not wait to be written. Wait nowhere. No. An unwritten story is one that never happens. A story is never until after the writing. Before is pipe dream. Something lost you wish you hadn't or wish you had. Gone before it got here. There is no world full of unwritten stories waiting to be written. Not even one. To hang people's hopes on, the hope that their story will be revealed one day, worth something, true, even if no one else can see it or touch it, a beautiful story like in that girl's sad eyes on the subway, her life story real as anyone's, as real as yours, her eyes say to me, a story no one has written, desperate to be written. Never will be. Rain blurs the image of a man steadfastly splashing down Essex Street on his bike through driving rain, rain whose force and weight any second will disintegrate the gray sheet of paper on which the figure's drawn, a man huddled under a gray-green slicker who doesn't know he's about to disappear and take his world with him. Except for a stroke of gray-green hovering in my eyes like it did the day we crossed the dunes and suddenly, for a moment; between steep hills of sand I saw framed in the distance what I thought might be a sliver of the sea we'd come so far to find.

Breath

Sometimes you feel so close it's like we're cheek to cheek sucking the breath of life from the same hole.

In a few hours the early flight to Pittsburgh because my mom's life hanging by a thread. Thunder and lightning you're sleeping through, cracks the bedroom's dark ceiling like an egg. About 4:00 a.m. I need to get up. Drawing a deep breath, careful as always to avoid stress on the vulnerable base of my spine when I shift my weight in bed, I slide my butt toward the far edge, raise the covers, and pivot on one hipbone to a sitting position, letting my legs fold over the bed's side to find the floor, still holding my breath as I get both feet steady under me and slowly stand, hoping I didn't bounce the mattress, waiting to hear the steady pulse of your sleep before I exhale.

In the kitchen a yellowish cloud presses against the window. A cloud oddly lit and colored it seems by a source within itself. A kind of fog or dust or smoke that's opaque, unsettling, until I understand the color must come from security lights glaring below in the courtyard. It's snow. Big flakes not falling in orderly rows, a dervishing mob that swirls, lifts, goes limp, noiselessly spatters the glass. Snow obscuring the usual view greeting me when I'm up at crazy hours to relieve an old man's panicked kidneys or just up, up and wondering why, staring at blank black windows of a hulking building that mirrors the twenty-story bulk of ours, up prowling instead of asleep in the peace I hope you're still enjoying, peace I wish upon the entire world, peace I should know better by now than to look for through a window, the peace I listen for beside you in the whispering of our tangled breaths.

Message

A message in red letters on the back of a jogger's T-shirt passed by too quickly for me to memorize exactly. Something about George Bush going too far in his search for terrorists and WMDs. A punch line sniggering that Bush could have stayed home and found the terrorist he was looking for in the mirror. I liked it. The message clever I thought and jacked the idea for my new line of black-lettered T-shirts: America went way too far looking for slaves. Plenty niggers in the mirror for sale.

Manhole

On South Street where it parallels the East River, only a hundred yards or so from the water, next to a tall Cyclone fence enclosing a parking lot for emergency vehicles, a stubby guy, rubbing his hairy-backed hands together briskly, clambers out of a manhole to join his partner who leans on a huge white slurping tank truck. Both workers in official coveralls so my taxes pay their salaries and I think that means we're on the same page and think in these uptight times a little humor always helps and think it might be funny when I cruise past to smile and point at the open manhole and say, Ah-hah. So that's where you white guys come from, and I do say it but they don't appreciate my joke and I surely don't think it's funny either when I glance back and catch the one beside the truck dragging a pistol out the back pocket of his baggy yellow jumpsuit. Eyes wide, asshole squeezed tight, I accelerate the pace of my jogging. Hear over my shoulder, Run, nigger, run—you better run, you black shine, and then the unmistakable pop which takes me down sprawling on the asphalt, hitting hard as if I'd been pitched from a speeding drive-by, but I'm not dead I'm rolling, rolling fast to my feet, haul-assing like a turkey through the corn for cover round a bend as if a bullet couldn't catch me if it wanted to. No laugh meter in the vicinity so I don't know whose joke funnier, mine or theirs. One man, one vote, but one of me, two of them, and bullets trump ballots anyway just like Malcolm said, but maybe I get the last laugh because the white guy on a bench staring out at the East River, traffic reports buzzing from his tiny radio, still sits there on my return leg and I crackle his eyeglasses into the bridge of his nose with a precise, surprise elbow, all this in not much more than the usual forty-five minutes my jog consumes, a sure sign the weather's warming, the city cleaning up for another long, hot summer of being the biggest, baddest apple in the world.

Martyr

God's wonders never ceasing. A child, a mere girl of five or six begs not for the torture to end, but to be scalded again with the others, her tender flesh peeling, defenseless before the onslaught of boiling water the priests pour over her naked limbs. Yet her soul's untouched, cries out not in agony but joy, asking only to be returned to the bosom of her Christian family, united with them as they cross to the Kingdom that no earthly power can deny. Moved in spite of themselves, Satan's saffron-robed minions restore the tiny, quivering body to her mother's arms. The poor child's flesh, once pale and pure as driven snow, blistered now, the soles of her feet blackened and torn by the terrible mountain, the many, many crude steps carved in rock we ascended to reach this pinnacle of suffering. So high, so far from city crowds the officials would turn against us by shaming us, defaming our faith with the spectacle of apostasy. Hidden here because these shoguns, though they scorn us, fear God's strength inside our frail flesh. Fear His truth will shine forth no matter how ingeniously they torment us. God teaching the multitudes that with faith even the weak and helpless can endure every horror evil men invent. A child's pure soul undefeated by the fires of Hell, though I, king's envoy and chief of the Jesuit band, quake and cringe, hung by my heels above a pit of steaming dung, and renounce my father's name.

Ruins

Pepe, dead ten years now, in his late sixties when he wrote a phrase I admire, a phrase translated from his Spanish as *ruins of her backside*. Perhaps because I'm over sixty now myself, a long-ago student of Pepe and like him a fiction writer, I'm remembering that striking phrase and recite it to my wife.

Stunning, isn't it, I say. How perfectly Pepe's image evokes the sadness of the body.

Did you ever consider how his wife might have felt reading those words in her husband's book. Words that expose and judge and take away her privacy forever. The cruelty of writers is unbelievable. How could he say such an awful thing.

Whoa. Hold on. I didn't write the words. And in the novel they're thought, not spoken. And Pepe's not the one thinking the words. It's a sixtyish man, a character whose name I've forgotten, in bed watching his wife undressing or maybe she's dressing for work in the morning. Either way the point is the man's touched by his wife's nakedness. You know. Flesh as site of eros and death. I hear tenderness in the words. The guy's identifying with his wife. The ruins are everybody's flesh. The flesh that betrays us all. I admire Pepe's unflinching gaze.

But why is the wife's backside displayed for readers to gawk at. Why not Pepe's. C'mon. Be honest. You're just defending Pepe's right to write whatever he damn well pleases. Even if it's waving his poor wife's aging, bare ass around in public.

My wife never met Pepe nor Miranda, his wife and love of his life who had survived Pepe's passing less than a year. Nor read Pepe's novels as far as I know and sometimes I wonder if she really reads mine, since her upset with Pepe is a replay of numerous upsets with me when she confuses my fiction with our lives. What do you think, Dear Reader. Does she have a case.

Cleaning Up

I was jogging on the green shoulder of a country road, enjoying the quiet and solitude of a bygone time, a world lost forever it seems except for rare moments when nature helps us recall the peace and plenty of our original state, then suddenly, directly in my path, a slightly squashed, blue-banded plastic water bottle appeared. I considered my options—around, over, kick it aside. Of course I could have slowed, picked it up, and carried it till I could dispose of it properly. Didn't. A few strides later admitted to myself I should have picked it up, would have if I'd believed someone was watching. And thought how sad it would be to become a hopeless case. To skip good deeds because no one applauds. To sink to the level of people incapable of doing the right thing for its own sake. The incorrigible ones who toss beer cans from car windows.

A few days later, just beyond a heap of horse dung steaming like a judgment on this fallen earth, the bottle is still there. And then I encounter more . . . six . . . eight . . . ten at least in a half-mile stretch, each identical almost to the first, unpleasant likenesses breeding, multiplying. I don't disturb them, but promise myself to return. Return with friends and remove every last one of them. We'll dress in white like angels, wear surgeons' masks and rubber gloves. Bring rakes to comb them from the grass. Large black garbage bags to haul them away in our trucks.

me happy when skies are gray . . . , and hum them softly to myself as I write, the same words by the way that Richard Berry (of "Louie, Louie" fame) translated in his fashion and got much of the song right because his version playing in my head brings my son here right beside me, with me, wherever else he must be.

You Are My Sunshine

E-mail from my French translator, Jean-Pierre Richard, asking for clarification of inconsistencies between text of novel *Hiding Place* and family tree appended as preface to novel—particularly the character Shirley, who in text noted several times as middle child, though on tree she's an oldest child.

Shirley's not either, she's both, I want to respond—not only my sister, not only a character—the world of the novel depends on fact and fiction and I'm just a mediator with no answers or changing answers, always more questions than answers, as curious as you are, Jean-Pierre, a translator like you, who at best attempts to mediate irreconcilable differences. My wife, Catherine who's bilingual, says she hates it when she's stuck between friends who speak only French and friends who speak only English and she's forced into translating for both groups. Exhausting, she says. Frustrating. Like being pulled apart. I can't relax. Nobody's satisfied. And you feel like you're to blame, don't you, I add to commiserate with her and myself in my chosen/appointed role as go-between for people not from different countries, not speaking different languages exactly but people sharing a country who choose often not to understand or like each other, people who use things like prisons to translate an ancient need to remain separate.

As for your other query, those words in italics are a line from "You Are My Sunshine," a favorite of my Culpepper, Virginia, grandfather, John French, who used to sing it to me riding on his shoulders when I was very young. I wish I could translate his singing, Jean-Pierre, but it's as hopeless as translating love into words and sending it in a letter to my son in prison. I can't translate my grandfather's singing, only put words on a page, *You make*

New Work

There are pages there called new work I keep turning to find nothing there are pages called new work there I keep turning to find nothing new there is work there called new I keep finding turning to nothing new there I keep turning to nothing there are pages turning to nothing there I keep turning to find new work there turning to nothing called new work I keep turning pages to find.

Short Story

Slowly, slow, tiny sips from a bottle of water after a jog on a hot July morning. Drinking slowly a habit learned the hard way on the hoop court when I was one of the best young bloods and between games one Saturday afternoon some of us robbed ice-cold cases of lemonade from an untended delivery truck and everybody lollygigged in the little shade at one end of the playground, chugging endless lemonade, loud and sweaty and full of ourselves, our luck, our power, our thirst, winners of the last run grinning and bragging, the losers trash talking about other times, next times. Lemonade trickling down my chin, sticky on my bare chest. Lemonade till my stomach bloats and cramps and I lose a whole half day of good ball. A camel forever afterward. No drink till play's over or tiny, tiny sips slowly. Sixty-five years old now and asking myself if that lesson from the court connects with the drastically pared-down stories I've begun attempting. The parallel's seductive. Teaching myself to cut back on the ambition of long forms. Settling for the satisfaction of well-wrought miniatures.

I still shiver inside, thinking about a game starting up. No plan for handling the speed of the best games. Shuttling through my mind now, they don't pass more swiftly than they did back in the day. Faster than the speed of light. Everything, then nothing, then gone, gone. We were nothing. All the players nothing. Ghosts gliding in from the sidelines. No name. No rep. Everything to prove one more time. Nobody till the games rolling, your legs and heart pumping. Will you get abused or do your thing and hear everybody holler.

Games sweet as cold gallons of stolen lemonade pouring down my throat, and before I notice, the whole bottleful of water is gone. Dizzy when I stand. My legs buckling under me, I nearly fall like my wife's father fell, old, white-haired man, sprawled blinking on the grass. Old enough to know better but jumped up from the table too quick after a good, long meal in our garden.

Swimming

After sixty years of never venturing into water deeper than I'm tall, learning to swim in the sea isn't easy. My colleague Bernard couldn't understand why I had a problem with believing water would hold me up. For him the body's buoyancy a simple fact, demonstrated once, convincingly, never questioned since his first time floating alone in the ocean. I felt obliged to explain I'm a sinker—my body's weight relative to its surface area means I'm more like lead than feathers. I'd hoped to impress Bernard by citing the law of physics my body violated, but he shook his head, returned to whatever problem my problem had momentarily distracted him from solving. Bernard's a math/science pragmatist. No frills. Fluent in formulas, manuals, and maps. Abrupt occasionally to the point of abrasiveness. No patience often, for daydreamers like me, yet his brief, no-nonsense description of his first time afloat in deep water a kind of reassuring mantra this summer of teaching myself to swim. Not his words. I don't remember his words or repeat his words as I nudge myself inch by inch farther from shore, closer to a depth where my feet can't touch bottom unless my head's underwater. It's his silence I chant, not words, to calm and shape my breathing, the silence of a boy floating alone in the ocean the first time, a boy receiving a simple revelation—no metaphysics, no god, no promises, no fear of death—just experiencing how the sea outside unconditionally accommodates the sea inside, on my back, stretched out on a carpet of water, arms extended like oars, feet slowly churning, not bothered by the fact there's nothing solid beneath me, nothing certain except believing nothing's enough.

Answering Service

Now I'll call my dad. But I can't. He's dead. The thought *now I'll call my dad* coming naturally, faster than the speed of light before I could censure it or laugh or cry at the unthinking thought of phoning my father, dead now for six years, the thought coming because I'd just hung up after talking with my mom and the thought mize well call old pops since I'm on the phone anyway and it's been a while since we last talked so I'll call daddy even though it's never easy talking with him, that thought comes naturally you see because I've done my calling in spurts or in a serial fashion, you could say, for many years now, extended sessions of one call after another, maybe kicked off by one call I desire to make or one I must make and since I've got it going, in a groove or stuck, you might say, and the phone sits there, no excuse, ready again if I'm ready, I go on and make a bunch of calls until, forgive the dumb pun, I'm off the hook. I've just hung up after talking to my mom who at the moment is alive but very, very ill. And so am I. Alive. That's the thing about the phone, isn't it. When you call, there's a chance you'll get an answer. Life continues. Yours. Someone else's. Not always. These days even if you do get an answer it's likely to be a machine and very likely a machine's the last thing you want to hear. Machines aren't alive and they can make you wonder if you are. But a phone call's a chance, at least, of talking to someone alive besides yourself. Unless like my father the someone you call's dead. Then there's no chance. Unless you get their machine.

Ghetto

The King's dead. He lifts his wet son from the crib. A quiet, quiet baby, soaked and he protests not. No outcry yesterday when a waterbug prowled the crib, settled on his fat beige cheek. His son's mother the one who hollers when she discovers the huge black insect. Flicks it off. Snatches up her baby and screams in fear, for help, for the father to kill or shoo or rescue, a bloodcurdling cry if ever he'd heard one, him racing naked from bed to the alcove they called the baby's room to find her backed against the wall farthest from the crib, clutching their son to her breast, her face aged a hundred years since he'd switched off the bed lamp that night. How could the baby still be so young, so quiet in the arms of this ancient woman who sobs, *Out of here . . . please . . . we've got to get out of here.* Yesterday. Scared woman with baby clamped to her bosom, bare-ass man gawking at the monster in the crib. A scene from a movie or book, familiar with a kind of déjà vu authority. A frozen moment that waits for him to renew their acquaintance. Yesterday. The day they shot King in Memphis. Just yesterday, at this same early morning hour, he'd run here naked, summoned by a scream yanking him from the usual tired conversation with himself, *C'mon boy. Move your sorry black ass, boy.* Tired before he rolls out of bed, tired of waking up in the same dead-end place where he'd dropped off to sleep.

Still dark outside yesterday when he'd run here and scooped the beetle from the crib in a mitt of Pamper, lucky to grab a wet not shitty one from the waste basket on the changing table. With all his might he'd squeezed the thick wad, hoping to hear a nasty pop. Twice he slammed it down on the dresser top under the hard meat of his hand, then hurled it to the floor, stomping, grinding white plastic and paper flat under his bare heel. Just yesterday. The baby quiet through the whole silly business. Quiet this morning twenty-four hours later. Lifted wet from his crib. What does his son remember about yesterday. What will he tell him.

Review

You don't have to be very smart to write a review of a book of short stories. All you need to say is that some stories in the book are better than others. Everybody agrees that's the way it works with collections of short stories. It's not necessary to read the stories, just scan the table of contents and cite in your review the title of one story you say you like and one you don't like. This specificity will impress the readers of your review, establish your credibility and seriousness. Don't stress yourself selecting which title to admire or pan since almost none of your readers will ever read any of the stories you're reviewing. Readers will be less favorably disposed toward your review if you say all the stories in the collection suck or all the stories are great because your readers, based upon their previous experience of reading or not reading books of stories and reading or not reading reviews of books of stories and based upon their previous experience of life in general which is, after all, what stories are about, will have concluded that some things are better than other things and this being the case, for stories as well, why stir up readers by suggesting you think your experience of reading stories or your experience of life in general is different than your reader's experience and maybe you believe you're smarter than they are, whereas everybody knows you don't need to be born all that smart to write a review of a book of stories or write the stories either.

Party

I go up to Aunt May's wheelchair. She gives me her crinkly hand and I take it. Why are you sprouting warts and whiskers, I want to ask her, looking down to find Aunt May's tiny green eyes twinkling in the folds of her moon face, the same pitted, pale flesh of the hand my pale hand squeezes, not too hard, not testing for bones I'm very curious about. Are they brittle or soupy soft or sea-changed altogether to foam like is stuffed inside cloth animals to hold their shape. Draped by bead necklaces dangling to her waist, her hips snug in a sequined flapper dress hemmed with fringe that starts at her knees and almost touches the silver buckles of her shoes, May smiles at me from a sepia-toned photo. No. That's not true. Same smile but May smiles it here, now, her hand in mine, during this celebration of her eighty-third birthday, although unbeknown to everybody at the party (and everyone at the party in the old photo) the surgeon forgot a metal clip in May's gut last week that's festering and will kill her next Christmas Eve. Not one party and then another and another. It's all one big party. Life ain't nothing but a party, May grins at me after I sugar her cheek, dance her hand, the long strings of fringe swish, swishing, brushing my trouserleg as she swirls out, spins, spools in, jitterbugging, camel walking, fox-trotting, buzzard lope. My, my, Miss May. Oh-blah-dee. Watch out, girl. You have only eighty-three years or eight months or eight seconds to live before the party's over and the flashbulb freezes you forever, portions of the brownish photo the color of batter I used to lick from my finger after swiping it around the mixing bowl when my grandmother, your cousin, your fine running partner, light, bright, and almost white as you, May, finished pouring her cake in a pan, set the pan in the oven to bake, and turned me loose on that bowl. Don't miss none, she'd grin. Get it all, Mr. Doot.

Now You See It

You come to a space on the page and can't read farther because in this space resides everything the writer does not know, pretends to know, cannot know—the face of a god, for instance, the emptiness and fullness of time, perfect silence, voices of the dead returning—all crammed clamoring into this white space between two words or space dividing blocks of print on a page, as if the unnameable, unimaginable can be put on hold in a space the writer may have chosen to leave blank in order to suggest a plan or design or transition or simply provide a rest stop for pilgrims in the story before they pick up their burdens again and continue their journey, but whatever the writer's intent, the space suddenly uncrossable, too much missing, too much erased, you falter, unclear why you've read this far, the space yawns wider and wider and sucks in the whole world, including the writer's dream dreamed up to fashion a story, to fashion a space within the story for you, your dreams, and there's no going forward, no going back, nothing survives the space, no words, no page, no safe passage the writer promised through roaring silence that closes like the sea over heads of creatures who cannot swim, the story gone before the writer's next word.

Fall

She happens to be glancing at him when he lets go the handlebar of his piled-high shopping cart and turns his head fast like somebody's called his name over his shoulder—lets go and turns and takes a quick step in the opposite direction he had been pushing the cart—a step too fast for an old man—where's he think he's going in such a big hurry—then clearly not a step—he's falling—falling and dead before he hits the pavement—not catching hisself—falling chin first—face all twisted up sideways on the pavement—snaggleteeth in the wrong place—and she's surprised by none of this—goes to him—kneels—not surprised by stink almost suffocating her—yes, yes, like once long ago when she sneaked up under her rocking chair great-granny's long black dress—not surprised he's not finished shitting and pissing hisself—though one wide-open eye saying dead, dead, dead—not surprised he shudders and one last twitch lifts a foot clean off the pavement—not surprised blood and nastiness leak down his chin—been here, done this—her turn soon—dying in broad daylight out in the street—that hood over her head of bad, sweet smell—she pats his old, dead shoulder, says, So long, Mister, Sorry Mister—unsurprised till he answers, Hush child. Everything gon be all right.

First Love Suite

On a rainy day with nothing better to do three guys sit around telling stories of first loves. The first two stories of first love never happen. What you mean, *first love*, man. First time I copped some pussy, you mean, the first guy wonders aloud. The second guy smiles, sighs, closes his eyes like he's died and gone to whatever heaven on earth he roamed with his first love, leaving the other two guys far behind, neither one very interested in the second guy's reverie anyway, one guy because he's still scratching his head, trying to figure out what constitutes a first love, and the other guy disinclined to follow very far into the enchanted forest of the second guy's daydream which might be a bit like watching the second stalled storyteller masturbate, not an alluring activity to consume time even on a rainy day, he thinks, unless it's him, himself getting off, which he isn't, doesn't while he contemplates two failed story-telling attempts and the prospect of his own failure since what else could he say or anyone say that wouldn't be, more or less, a repeat of the stories untold so far, the first one being not having a fucking idea what a first love is, and the second being consumed by dropping off an edge and plummeting arms flailing toward a bottom, to which there is no bottom, thus how or why would you attempt to tell another guy or two guys in this case, your story if you're busy falling, your mouth full of hollering or screaming and a sweet, juicy tongue you've been searching for, waiting for, dreaming of for years, root, root, rooty-toot-toot all up in your gums and tickling your sinus passages and tonsils from the wet pink inside.

Ralph Waldo Ellison

The snoring of two brown bodies inside an abandoned car rattles its cracked windshield. Rattling keeps the glass almost free of ice and turns into the shiver of a freight train within the dream of one of the teenaged brothers bundled inside the jalopy in all the clothes he owns, shake, rattle, rolling boxcars the boy running away from Oklahoma will hear the final night of his life rattling on rails beneath the daybed in the living room of a New York City apartment rich with African masks, fabrics, and carvings, the apartment he never leaves his last days, an apartment, a daybed become nightbed he can't escape except on the el rattling blocks away or memories of trains recorded in old jazz or blues licks on records or ancient nightmares, a boy shaken by teeth sunk deep in his tender neck, the boxcar he's hopped split open like a watermelon's pink belly by a booted foot, dozens of roachy black seeds scattering, a claw catching him by the scruff of his skull, a train at night in the distance passing by, the train he's been waiting for, listening for, he blows on his icy hands, hears the shivering car window, rattle of coffee perking, shadowy figures circled round a fire, posse of railroad bulls raiding the camp in the woods at dawn, bust up, burn, he's nabbed, pleads high ambitions and for some goddamn reason he never sorts out, the rednecks release him, maybe with smirks and a *keep this nigger running* pat on the ass he thinks he remembers telling it that way later to his wife he instructed absolutely, precisely how to do it so the coffee snaps him awake but doesn't panic him, so much to do he tells the men armed with state-issue cattle prods and shotguns, so little time, the coffee should remind him but not abandon him, his icy hands glowing in the dark, his brother snoring, the Oklahoma City moon a frozen, pockmarked thing with a dangling, sticky-glue tongue that wags and drools, whips at warp speed along invisible tracks chasing unwary colored boys, gobbling them up.

Genocide

The first time I watched him play he was so good I wanted to cry. He had it all. The body, mind, will. A big black bouncey kid everywhere at once on the hoop court. So good the game came to him. And all the other players knew, whether they liked the fact or not, knew if they wanted the game's shine a moment on the best they could bring when they played the game the way it should be played, they needed him. The best action starting up and swirling round him, choosing him, opening its heart to him each time he set foot on the asphalt court.

First time I saw him playing the court shrunk infinitesimally small then zoomed infinitely large, as small then large as the invisible Buddha head floating above it, the gaze of whose curled, hooded eye fixed on the game turns the play perfect because a Buddha could see it in no other fashion, though everything out there imperfect, yearning to be more, to be less, to be other than it is, all that sadness and incompleteness forgotten in the Buddha's smiling certainty this universe and all the universes containing it are moving along just fine, thank you, nothing out of place, everything present without the pain of birth or death, just give the boy the ball and get out of the way, the Buddha's golden gaze speaking palpable as a cityscape, a sunset or sunrise framing tacky, crooked backboards and poles on Homewood court the July day I first saw him play.

Like seeing myself out there playing perfectly. Or rather seeing for the first time the game played the way I'd always dreamed of playing it and seeing the one playing the game that perfect way didn't need to be me for my dream to come true and make me happy beyond words, so happy I understood instantly it couldn't last, wouldn't last, and tears began welling up behind my eyes, ready to mourn, to concede and despair since nothing this good every stays this good long. I wanted to kill him. Grab that big nigger and put him on ice. Set him free so I wouldn't have to watch the pop or slide of him going down slowly, coming apart. Stash his ass somewhere safe. Somewhere nothing, no one could touch him with a corrupting touch. Me first.

Haiku

Toward the end of his life, a time he resided in France in self-imposed exile from America, the Negro novelist Richard Wright chose the Japanese form haiku, an unrhymed poem of three lines, seventeen syllables, as his principle means for speaking what burned inside him, the truths he needed to express each day till he died. Thousands of haiku and the thought of him working hour after hour, an ailing colored man from Mississippi, fifty-two years old, his international renown lynched by his fellow countryman, a brown man, trying again, one more time, to squeeze himself into or out of a tiny, arbitrary allotment of syllables dictated by a tradition conceived by dead strangers in a faraway land, Richard Wright in Paris hunched over a sheet of paper midwifing or executing himself within the walls of a prison others built without reference to dimensions required by a life that arched gigantically like his from almost slavery in the South to almost men on the moon, the idea of this warrior and hero falling upon his own sword on a battlefield rigged so he's doomed before he begins, the still multiplying and heartbreaking ironies of the man's last, quiet, solitary efforts—counting 1, 2, 3 . . . 5, 6, 7, up and back like a salsa dancer, or however, whatever you do, pacing, measuring your cage in order to do the thing he'd ended up doing, haiku, the thought makes me want to cry, but also sit back, shout in wonder.

Passing On

Why couldn't he choose. Blue suit or brown suit for the funeral. Throughout a long life, he'd endeavored to make sense of life, and now, almost overnight it seemed, the small bit of sense he'd struggled to grasp had turned to nonsense. Even the toys his grandkids played with mocked him, beeping, ringing, squealing, flashing products of a new dispensation he'd never fathom. Only pickly pride remained, pride in how he dressed, how he spoke the language, pride he hoped would allow him a dignified passage through final disappointments and fickleness. Unbending pride a barely disguised admission he's been defeated by that world he no longer pretends to understand and refuses to acknowledge except as brutal intervention, as disorder and intimidation constructed to humiliate him personally, pride wearing so thin he's desperate to recall skills his father might have taught him. Not the meager list of the skills themselves—not shining shoes, not tying a tie—but evidence of intimate exchange. Traces of the manner in which, through which, his father might have said, Here are some things I know, some things I am, and I want to pass them on so you know them, too, and I hope they will serve you well. In other words he was aching to remember any occasion when or if his father had granted him permission to enter the unknown world his father inhabited, a world that intersected only rarely with rooms shared with a wife and children. Who was his father. How was it possible to be the man his father was. A man attached and absolutely unattached. Where did he go when he left home. Did anything his father ever say suggest a son would be welcome in those other spaces that men occupied. Closure what he had learned from his father. The absolute abandonment of shutting down, disappearing. Cover-ups. Erasing all tracks. Eluding pursuit. Were those the skills. Teaching the shame of bearing an inexhaustible bag of useless tricks he knew better than to pass on.

Wolf Whistle

At first I think it's a mad boy let out of the attic or basement for air an hour a day whistling at me from the rear of a long yard, a demented boy unfamiliar with skin darker than his but crazy enough not to be afraid, not to care, and whistles scorn, racial epithets, his shrill keening anger at being surprised, intruded upon by a trespasser black as the devil or *ooh-la-la*, cutie pie, what the fuck do we have here, sweetie, shrieked loud enough for the whole neighborhood to enjoy in the long silence of Le Moustoir at the eastern lip of Arradon on the Gulf of Morbihan in the vicinity of Vannes in Brittany in France in Western Europe in a universe with ample space to incarcerate boys in Turkish-looking, rusty cages crowned with minarets, hung on trees, two of them, two cages umbrellaed by trees at the front of the long yard belonging to a house on the corner of rue Saint Martin and rue de la Touline I passed without seeing on daily walks to the part tavern, part grocery store or morning strolls to the closest sea or jogging five kilometers to Toulindac that opens like a tourist's postcard dream when you turn a corner and coast parallel to the coastline, Isle aux Moines, a gray lump framed in endless blue distance by the long, slow smile of curve embracing double-deck ferries, white sails, striped sails, a sailing school with pennants flapping where kids try to learn to fly like fish and birds, a convincing advertisement for the good life, a trick, achieved with mirrors, even though happy, piping voices reach me there, all the way up there on a road above Toulindac when I glide or pretend to glide invisibly, effortlessly as the wind toward the fence-lined path that cuts steep and straight down to the beach, to acres of naked flesh, rocks and rocks and rocks, large as elephants, tiny as stinging gnats, families packed on weekends into this small, select space with stunning views almost to open sea, sea a bright lawn of water barely rippling as it laps the beach whose gently sloping sandy bottom remains visible underwater, many steps from shore, the footing awkwardly rocky through knee-high puddles of nodding algae, but soon smooth enough except for stones sharp as nails, blue, chilling water shallow for youngsters to wade far, far out, clear and calm, never a black triangle of fin crossing parallel to the horizon, no pain till you step out shivering, blue, slit open, the kids can play while you half watch, half doze, stupid in the sun, no need to ever get your feet wet or cold again, gashed again, your mad boy free a minute or two in the yard to wolf whistle or coo or cackle at Le Moustoir neighbors passing by, at children from the kindergarten across rue Saint Martin who break out early afternoons to car doors slamming then in again, their young mothers waiting naked and dazed as sunbathers or hiding in drab colors of little doughnut cars jammed in the shade of trees adjacent to the house with a long yard on the corner where if I could ever get its attention, if I could ever master its language or the French language it might bilingually understand, I would teach one of the parrots or the other to be a mad boy again, not so mad he's locked in a cage but mad enough to whistle and hoot horribly obscene, scary things at kids and their mothers, warning them about the bright razor sea you can smell from here and all the dead things in it, including pale skin of mothers burned to ash, including children set out to play, set out nonchalantly like they're turned out to play in traffic on busy streets of this universe shaped like a long yard from whose shadowy rear-end a hoarse, mocking, insane voice chops at me, cuts my legs from under me so I never make it to Toulindac one day, just kneel here, bleed here, outside the house's white stucco, chin-high wall, begging forgiveness of a boy born mad and almost mute but he's picked up the gift of assaulting others with a few choice, nasty noises picked up from his universe, on my knees imploring him to forgive me for blaming and cursing him because I saw for the first time two parrots staring, swaying, pecking gently at the bars of their rusted oriental cages, two lynched birds I'd teach to warble *Emmett Till, Emmett Till* if I could, but they just sit there preening, ruffling their ratty feathers, each twin nailed to its perch, neither one making a sound in response to my coaxing, my artless imitations of them, and I give up.

Shadow

He notices a shadow dragged rippling behind him over the grass, one more silent, black presence for which he's responsible.

American Histories
(2018)

JB & FD

I

To need his glasses and be struck by an awareness that they are not at hand, an ordinary-enough circumstance for Frederick Douglass, except sometimes it's accompanied by a flash of extraordinary dread. If not quite panic, certainly an unease disproportionate to a simple recurring situation. Dread that may be immediately extinguished if he locates his horn-rimmed, owlish-eyed spectacles exactly where he anticipated they should be.

He sees them and almost sighs. Nearly feels their slightly uncomfortable weight palpable on his nose. Finding the glasses is enough to reassure him that he remains here among the living in this material world where he depends on glasses to read, glasses to help him negotiate stubbornly solid objects he cannot glide through. Enough to remember that he's able to recall or backtrack, anyway, and understand how the present moment connects to moments preceding it, a trail of hows and whys causing him to wind up where he is now, at this particular moment, stretching out a hand to pick up eyeglasses because he is the same person who placed them on the desk, beside a stack of three books at the desk's upper-left-hand corner so he wouldn't forget, and there, here they would be when he needed glasses.

Sometimes dread does not vanish when he locates his glasses. They turn up where he thinks they should, his fingers curl, prepare to reach out for them. But glasses are not enough. Not convincing enough. They do not belong to him. Not glasses. Not hand. He vaguely recognizes both. Glasses too heavy to lift.

Or hand too heavy. He's observing from an incalculable distance. Sometimes that detachment is a gift, sometimes it dooms him, and he cannot animate or orchestrate what he desires to come next. John Brown spreads his ancient, musty wool cloak—cloak the brown color of his name—over glasses, books, desk, study, house, wife, him, and when John Brown snatches the cloak away, nothing's there. Douglass has fled to the mountains, the woods to join him.

2

Ah, Frederick, my friend. Look at you, Fred Douglass. I knew after a single glance you could be the one. Your manly form and bearing left no room for doubt. And today, these dozen hard years later, you still stand tall, straight, gleaming. I see God's promise of freedom in you. Yours. Mine. Our nation's. A man who could lead his people, all people, out of slavery's bondage. Your beard dark that day we first spoke and now tinged with spools of gray, but you gleam still, my friend. Despite the iron cloud of suffering and oppression slavery casts over this land.

Douglass remembers no beard. Not wearing one himself, nor a beard on Brown's gaunt face. Certainly not the patriarch's thicket of white flowing—no, a torrent—today, halfway down John Brown's chest. He misremembers me.

But if God ignites a man to believe himself a prophet, if visions burst upon him and seize him, as an ordinary man is seized by a roiling gut and must rush behind a bush to squat and relieve himself, if such urgency is the case, I suppose, Douglass instructs himself, a prophet can be forgiven for mistaking petty details. Prophecies forgiven for confusing time and place, for compounding truth and error, wisdom and foolishness, for mixing wishful thinking with logic. John Brown thus forgiven for believing that ignorant, isolated slaves, cowed into submission by a master's whip, will grasp the purpose of a raid on Harpers Ferry and flock instantly to his banner. Enraptured by his vision, Brown foresees colored slaves armed with sticks and stones prevailing against cannon, Sharps carbines, the disciplined troops of a nation dedicated absolutely to upholding the principle that color makes some men less equal than others. I embrace the fiery justness of

John Brown's prophecies, his unflinching willingness to sacrifice himself and his sons, yet I cannot forgive my friend for untempered speech, demagoguery, the impetuosity and rage that grip him. That transform dream to madness.

3

Douglass watches himself step out from behind the curtain and stride to the bunting-draped podium. They will welcome him. He is famous. Broad chest bemedaled, gold baton, field marshal's crimson sash decorating his resplendent uniform, veteran of a terrible war, though he never fired a shot in anger. Fine figure of a man still. After seven decades on earth. After a protracted, blood-drenched conflict settling nothing. Certainly not settling his fate. Nor his color's fate. Nor his nation's.

A drumroll of applause greets him, deepening as he moves step-by-step across the stage, a thunder of hands accompanying him. In the front rows his new white wife's white women friends. When a journalist asked Douglass to speak about his marriage, seeking details to spice the story he intended to write about newlyweds whose union scandalously ignored great disparities of age and race, Douglass replied, "My first wife the color of my mother, second the color of my father."

Tonight in this hall where he'd spoken once before, where once he'd been property, a fugitive hosted by abolitionists, a piece of animated chattel curiously endowed with speech, tonight in this hall he would address "The Woman Question." Proclaim every woman's God-granted entitlement, like his, to all the Rights of Man.

A born orator. Born with that gift and many glorious others, his mother assured him in stories told at night, whispering while she lay next to him in the darkness, their only time together, half hours she stole from her master, slipping away to walk an hour each way, plantation to plantation, to earn their half hour.

Second rumble of applause when he concludes his remarks. Head bowed, he waves away the noise and stirs it, conducts it, loves it even as his gesturing arm seems dismissive, seems modest, a humble man, a veteran tempering, allaying the crowd's enthusiasm just as he strokes and soothes and quiets and fine-tunes his new young wife's pale hair and pale skin, her passion that makes him tender, wistful, as often as aroused. These happy newlyweds. Her ferocious coven of female friends among the loudest of clappers.

The evening will be a success, and he will return home to drop dead. Douglass dead as suddenly as Lincoln felled by an assassin's bullet. Except the president lingered. Douglass won't. Dead. He sees this as surely as he sees his old face in the vanity mirror in their freshly papered bedroom. As surely as old man Brown saw blood. Only pools, rivers, an ocean of blood, John Brown swore, would cleanse the sin of man-stealing. No. Not cleanse. Not expunge or redeem or expiate. No. Blood must be shed. No promises. No better, cleaner South or North. Only a simple certainty that blood must be shed. Douglass read that dire text in Brown's distracted gaze, his stare. Same fire in himself as a boy who struck back, no fear of consequences, at bullying slave driver Covey. Same fire fanned by waves of hands striking hands that primes him, guides, draws him as he crosses to a podium. Fire in the young woman he's taken after forty years with his colored first wife, this second wife who will discover him lying comfortably on the floor as he would have been lying comfortably across their canopied bed awaiting her had his heart not stopped and dropped him like an ax drops an ox, Douglass lying there on the Turkish carpet he sees so clearly now and never will again. Won't see it when he falls, when the abyss blackens suddenly and his head slams down into the rug's elaborately woven prayers.

4

Through a smallish window in a small motel I watched snow falling, a heavy snow, probably more than enough coming down to transform in a couple of hours the unprepossessing landscape framed within the motel window.

Big white flakes dropping effortlessly from the sky as I'd hoped all morning words would materialize on the page while I sat here in this unprepossessing room attempting to imagine a boy alone on a wilderness trail who drives his father's cattle along a shore of Lake Erie. How many miles there and back to supply a military encampment during the War of 1812, the boy on a horse or a mule, I assume, although it's possible he may have been on foot, armed with a long stick or a cudgel to protect himself and prod the stream of cattle along whichever edge of Lake Erie he advances—north, south, east, west— from Hudson, a small, new town in Ohio's Western Reserve, where the boy's family resides, to a base on the Detroit front occupied by a General Hull and his troops.

I had never been a white teenager with a strict, pious Calvinist father named Owen Brown whom I had accompanied often on cattle drives, never punched cows alone, never a slave like the boy his age John Brown immediately would befriend and never forget, the colored boy encountered in an isolated cabin located somewhere along his route. Very likely John Brown himself couldn't say exactly where, disoriented by an unexpected snowstorm that erased the usual familiar terrain and forced him for caution's sake to seek shelter for his animals and himself before nightfall, before he found himself lost completely, not sure how far he may have drifted from the trail, not even clear in which direction the trail might lie after hours of thick, swirling snow, certain of nothing but snow, wind, chilling cold, and the necessity to keep track of the cattle, perhaps round them up, count them, maybe drive them into a tight circle for warmth, cows huddled, hunkered down in a ring, and maybe him or him and his horse or mule bedded down close enough to share the heat of three, five, seven large beasts in a heap, a dark snowdrift in the middle of nowhere. Or perhaps drawn by the sight of a cabin ahead, you keep the animals moving as best you can and ride toward it, then dismount, or you've been plodding on foot and you reach a door and knock, embolden yourself, a shy, stranded twelve- or thirteen-year-old, to share the unhappy story of your plight, the errand your father entrusted to you, his livestock, his livelihood, delivering beef for General Hull's soldiers to eat so the Brown family can eat, so there's food on the table back in Hudson. Not army beef—cornmeal mush his mother measures, spoons out to John Brown and his siblings Ruth, Salmon, Oliver, and Levi Blakeslee, an orphan who, thanks to Owen Brown's charitable heart, was adopted and traveled as part of the Brown family to Hudson from New York State. Taut, hungry, lean faces at home, and now John Brown's duty to feed them.

Night deepening. Storm trapping him, a boy who's desperately seeking assistance, refuge, only or at least till daylight and he can relocate trail or landmarks and be on his way. I compare his predicament to mine, and I'm ashamed. My problem simply finding words, simply pretending to be in another time and place, another consciousness while settled in the comforts of a motel room along the interstate, fumbling around in storms of my own making, staring out a window at an increasingly postcard-perfect snowscape.

John Brown's storm does not subside but intensifies, lasting through the next afternoon perhaps, so he stays a night and half the following day in a cabin with a settler and his family, stranded here in a stranger's cabin for far too long, too far away from accomplishing his task. Owen Brown's cows outside maybe wandering off, lost in blinding snow. How many of them. Count them, band them together, search for strays, coax up the slovenly ones who otherwise would be content to die where they kneel, sunken into the snow.

These people are pioneers of sorts, like his, hovering at the edge of raw wilderness. Dark inside the cabin. Fireplace logs shiver, smolder, smoke. Spit loud as mountain streams thawing in spring. A question arising daily, as predictable as the sun: will they survive for another twenty-four hours on this not-quite-civilized frontier. Prayers each time they awaken, each time they break bread. Bread coarse, dark, hard, a little milk on occasion or water to soften it, a rare dab of honey to sweeten, or it's cornmeal porridge or cornmeal fried in grease to make a square of hot mush like John Brown receives that night in a cabin familiar to him from home, the wooden plates and heavy mush no strangers, nor the wife who smiles twice—John Brown notices, counts—during the hours of his stay.

She reminds him of his mother—busy without a pause, quiet as a shadow, a kindly shadow, she lets you know without saying a word, nor could you say how you know that deep kindness and deep fear hide inside her busyness. Her mouth like his mother's a tight line, lips nearly invisible even when she unseals them to address briskly, not often above a tight whisper, her three tiny girls or the man who is her husband, who's quite impressed by any youngish boy a father would trust to drive cattle along miles and miles of wilderness trail, a man who offers encouragement to John Brown to linger longer, though the boy and perhaps the host know he must refuse and he will, politely, this well-spoken boy. A boy who understands his mission. Determined, as long as he can draw breath into his body, to reach his destination and discharge his responsibilities. Then walk, ride, or crawl back to Hudson, money collected in hand. Hurry, hurry, not a moment to spare, so many crucial hours consumed, lost, wasted already.

Not a problem for me to identify with his anxious state of mind, his despondency and disappointment with himself, with John Brown's sense he could, should have been better prepared for any emergency that might sap precious time. His sister Ruth would not understand why her bowl is empty. Her big eyes, severe even when a very young child, hold back tears she knows better than to shed, not because she fears being disciplined for weeping at the dinner table—her parents love her, teach her, pray over her and with her every day. Tears would vex her mother, worry her father, tears might cause them to think she is blaming them for no food or, worse, blaming the Good Lord she knows is always watching over her, His grace abounding, more precious than thousands of earthly platters heaped with food.

John Brown imagines Ruth inside him and peeks out at himself with her deep, famished eyes, the way the slave boy looks at him, speaking with eyes, gestures, a silent conversation, a wordless friendship struck up with the first glances they exchange in the cabin, fellow outsiders, alien presences, raw boys of similar size, age.

John Brown winces but holds his tongue, his tears, when the dark boy cowers under a sudden flurry of blows, many thuds, cracks across his back, shoulders, arms, not ducking or fleeing, hands not thrust up to protect himself from blows delivered by a stout stick that must have been leaning against the head of the rough log table, stationed there at the man's hand, John Brown immediately perceives, for exactly this purpose. Rapid, loud blows that are—is it fair to suggest—as painful in John Brown's mind as they are on the slave boy's body, fair to say the sting of this not-uncommon beating cools soon and is forgotten by a black boy's tough flesh, but a white boy's shock endures. Surprise, surprise for John Brown the evil in the heart of this grown-up man nothing but kind to him, offering succor from a storm to one of his kind, a stranger, a mere feckless boy who let down his father, his family. I've lost my way, good sir. A father like his father but unlike, too, as John Brown feels himself like and unlike the black slave boy his age who serves them, who eats and sleeps under the same roof with this family, with him that night, but in a corner. Eats over there, sleeping there under rags, rags his bedding, clothes, roof, walls, floor all nothing but rags, a dark mound of rags the wind has blown into the house perhaps when the door opened to let John Brown enter or leave or when the man who's father of the house passes in and out to piss or the slave boy's endless chores drive him into the storm to do whatever he's ordered to do until he's swept by a final gust of wind one last time back into the cabin, a piece of night, ash, cinder trying to stay warm in a corner where it lands.

5

Spring rains swelled the rivers the year my sons John and Jason set off to join their brothers in Kansas and be counted among antislavery settlers when the territory voted to decide its future as a free or slave state. They left Ohio with their families, traveling by boat on the Ohio, then Mississippi River to St. Louis, Missouri, where they bought passage on a steamer, the *New Lucy*, to reach the camp at Osawatomie that the family had taken to calling Brown's Station.

A long, cold, wet journey to Kansas, Douglass, and on the final leg God saw fit to take back the soul of my grandson, four-year-old Austin, Jason's elder son, stricken during an outbreak of cholera on board the steamer. When the boat docked at Waverly, Missouri, the grieving families of Jason and John, despite a drenching thunderstorm, disembarked to bury young Austin. The boat's captain, a proslavery man surrounded by his Southern cronies, the same ruffians who had brandished pistols and Bowie knives, swearing oaths, shouting obscenities, swaggering, and announcing their bloody intent to make Kansas a slave state, the same brigands who had terrorized their fellow passengers night and day, singling out my sons, whose accent and manner betrayed them as Northerners. All those devils must have laughed with the captain at the cruel joke he bragged he was playing on the bereaved families, dumping their meager baggage to soak and rot on the dock, steaming away from Waverly before the distraught mourners returned from their errand, abandoning them during a downpour in a slave state though they had paid fares to Kansas.

No simple business to slaughter men with broadswords. To hack and slice human flesh with less ceremony than we butcher sheep and pigs. Dark that late night, early morning in Kansas when we descended upon homesteads of the worst proslavery vigilantes and fell to killing along Pottawatomie Creek. I was in command. Ordered the guilty to come out from their homes. Ordered executions in the woods. I knew the men I condemned had assaulted and murdered peaceful settlers, and among their victims were members of my family. Still, I stood aside at first, appalled by the fury, blood, screams, the mayhem perpetrated by weapons wielded by my sons Owen and Salmon and our companions. Though I entertained not the slightest of doubts, Frederick—the awful acts committed that day were justified, even if they moved the clock only one minute closer to the day our nation must free itself from the sin of slavery—yet I stayed my hand until the quiet of dawn had returned. Then, in silence broken only by pitiful moans, I delivered a pistol shot to the brain of a dying James Doyle.

6

Here is a letter (some historians call it fiction) written by Mahala Doyle in the winter of 1859 and delivered to John Brown awaiting execution in his prison cell in Virginia:

> *I do feel gratified to hear that you were stopped in your fiendish career at Harpers Ferry, with the loss of your two sons, you can now appreciate my distress in Kansas, when you . . . entered my house at midnight and arrested my Husband and two boys, and took them out of the yard and shot them in cold blood, shot them dead in my hearing, you can't say you done it to free slaves, we had none and never expected to own one, but has only made me a poor disconsolate widow with helpless children. . . . Oh how it pained my heart to hear the dying groans of my Husband & children.*

7

On the road between Cleveland and Kansas, gazing up at the stars, John Brown's son Frederick said, "If God, then this. If no God, then this."

John Brown remembers the wonder in Frederick's voice, how softly, reverently his son spoke, so many stars overhead in the black sky, remembers the wagon wheels' jolt, yield, bounce had spun a seemingly unending length of rough fabric from the road's coarse thread, then a seamless, silky ride for John Brown lasting until Frederick's words returned him to an invisible chaos of slippery mud, rocks, craters that snatch them, tumble them, rattle their bones. Any moment a sudden, unavoidable accident might pitch both men overboard or smash the wagon to splinters as it traverses this broken section of road between Cleveland and Kansas, and there is no other road except the one spun for a few minutes during John Brown's forgiving sleep, his forgetful sleep.

How many minutes, hours, how much unbroken silence of sleep before he awakened abruptly to hear his son Frederick's voice asking how many miles covered, how many more miles to go to Kansas, Father. His poor, half-mad, feeble-brained son, the one of all his children, people agree, who resembles him most in face and figure, Fred, loyal and uncomplaining as a shoe. Tall, sturdy Frederick, who will die in a few weeks in Kansas. Dead once before as an infant, then reborn, rebaptized Frederick in remembrance of his lost little brother. Frederick's second chance to live cut short by ruffians in a border war, my second perished Frederick. Then a third chance, a dark son or dark father or mysteriously both, bearing the same Christian name my sons bore, Frederick. And John Brown trembles after his sleeping eyes pop open when he hears his son's declaration, Frederick's soft blasphemy revealing his wonder at a thought he had brewed all by himself while he drove the wagon transporting father and son to the killing fields of Missouri and Kansas, driving through this great holy world, this conundrum, John Brown thinks, far too perplexing, too fearful for a father to grasp or explicate.

In his cell in Virginia, John Brown will remember riding in a wagon at night with his dead son Frederick on the way to rejoin family in the camp in Kansas. His arm stiffens, his fist grips the hilt of an imaginary broadsword, and he mimics blows he witnessed in predawn darkness, blows his sons Salmon and Owen inflicted on outlaws they attacked on Pottawatomie Creek. This stroke for a dead grandson, Austin. This one for dead baby Frederick. This for Frederick who shared his lost brother's name and died too soon, twenty-six years old, in those Kansas Territory wars. And more blows struck for other, darker Fredericks, all of them his children, God's children, Brown almost shouts aloud as he presses again a revolver's actual barrel against the skull of whimpering, murdering night-rider Doyle. An act of mercy or vengeance, he will ask God in his cell, to end the suffering of a nearly dead evil wretch when he pulls the trigger.

8

(1856)

Mrs. Thomas Russell wrote: *Our house was chosen as a refuge because no one would have dreamed of looking for Brown therein . . .*

> *John Brown stayed a week with us, keeping to his room almost always, except at meal time, and never coming down unless one of us went up to fetch him. He proved a most amiable guest, and when he left, I missed him greatly . . .*
>
> *First time that I went up to call John Brown, I thought he would never open his door. Nothing ensued but an interminable sound of the dragging of furniture.*
>
> *"I have been finding the best way to barricade," he remarked, when he appeared at last. "I shall never be taken alive, you know. And I should hate to spoil your carpet."*
>
> *"You may burn down the house, if you want to," I exclaimed.*
>
> *"No, my dear, I shall not do that."*

Mrs. Russell goes on to record: *John Brown had the keenest possible sense of humor, and never missed the point of a joke or of a situation. Negroes' long words, exaggerations, and grandiloquence afforded him endless amusement, as did pretentiousness of any sort . . .*

> *He was acute in observing the quality of spoken English, and would often show himself highly diverted by the blunders of unedu-cated tongues. He himself spoke somewhat rustically, but his phrases were well formed, his words well chosen, and his constructions always forcible and direct. When he laughed he made not the slightest sound, not even a whisper or an intake of breath; but he shook all over and laughed violently. It was the most curious thing imaginable to see him, in utter silence, rock and quake with mirth. . . .*

(1858)

John Brown thinks of it as molting. His feathers shed. A change of color. Him shriven. Cleansed. Pale feathers giving way to darker. Darker giving way to pale. Not seasonal, not a yearly exchange of plumage as God sees fit to arrange for birds or for trees whose leaves alter their hue before they drop each fall. His molting occurs in an instant. He stands naked. A tree suddenly stripped of leaves. Empty branches full again in the blink of an eye.

I see such alterations in myself, Douglass, in my dreams and often in God's plain daylight, and wonder if others notice my skin falling away, turning a different color, but I do not ask, not even my wife or children, for fear I will be thought mad. One more instance of insanity my enemies could add to discredit me. Old Brown thinks he changes colors like a bird or a leaf.

Free slaves, mad Brown shouts. Free the coloreds, as if color simply a removable outer shell, as if color doesn't permanently bind men into different kinds of men. As if feathers, leaves, fur, skin, fleece, all one substance, and all colors a single color. Yet I believe they are the same in God's eye.

I thank you again for the kindness and generosity you and your wife have extended towards me. I arrived here weary, despondent, exhausted by the Kansas wars, and you offered shelter. A respite from enemies who pursue me as if there's a price on my head here in the North as well as in the South. Your welcoming hand and spirit have revived me. I have been able to think. Write my Constitution.

When not occupied by my pen, I have benefited from your willing ear, your thoughtful responses to my poor attempt to draft a document that protects every American instead of a privileged few. I am eternally indebted to you for the sanctuary you provided, for your unceasing hospitality these last three weeks, and to demonstrate my gratitude, I'm ashamed to admit, I ask for even more from you. Not for myself this time, but for the grand cause we both are destined to serve. You must join us in Virginia, Frederick Douglass.

Why are you certain that my enslaved brethren will "hive" to you, as you put it. Why certain that a general insurrection will follow the Harpers raid and topple the South's slaveholding empire, free my people from bondage. I agree with much of your reasoning and share your sense of urgency, but do not share your certainty. Envy it, yes, but do not share it. You cite Toussaint's successful revolt in Haiti and Maroons free in the hills of Jamaica. Yet Virginia is not Jamaica, not Haiti. I believe there must be better ways than bloody rebellion to end the abomination of slavery. Why are you so certain God looks with favor on your plan. What if, despite your fervor and good intentions, you are wrong.

Wrong, you say. Wrong. In this nation where a man's color is reason enough to put him in chains. Where cutthroats in Kansas murder settlers whose only offense is hatred of slavery. Where a senator is caned in the halls of Congress for condemning manstealers. In a nation where every citizen is compelled by law to aid and abet slave masters who seek to recover escaped "property," why is it difficult to separate right from wrong.

I tremble as I utter this chilling thought, Frederick Douglass, but what if no God exists except in the minds of believers. Would it not behoove us more, not less, to bear witness to what is right. To testify. To manifest, in our acts, the truth of our God's commandments.

I make no claim to be God's chosen warrior. I have studied an assault on the Virginia arsenal for a very long while. Devised a strategy I believe will exploit a powerful enemy's weaknesses. Recruited and trained good men to fight alongside me and my sons. Weighed both moral and practical consequences. Asked myself a thousand times what right do I have to commence such an undertaking. Still, I would be a fool to think I'm closer to knowing God's plan. We serve Him in the light or darkness of our understanding.

(1859)

Stand with us. You would be a beacon, Frederick. Let Southerners and Northerners, freemen and the enslaved, see the righteous power, the fierce, unquenchable spirit I recognized in you the first time we met. Let the world know that you are aroused, aggrieved. That you will not rest until your brethren are free. Teach your fellow countrymen there can be no peace, no forgiveness as long as slavery abides. Accompany us to Virginia. Strike a blow with us.

I must die one day, John Brown, sure enough. But I feel no need to hurry it. I don't reckon that ending my life in Virginia will make me a better man than one who chooses to survive and dedicates himself to serving God and his people. I shall continue my work here in the North. Offer my life, not my death, to my people.

I respect your well-known courage and principles. Nevertheless, I must speak bluntly, and say that I believe you quibble. You speak as if a man's time on earth is merely a matter of hours, days, years.

In this business we cannot afford to bargain. To quibble about more time, less time, a better time. We are not accountants, Fred. Duty requires more than crying out against slavery, more than attempting to maintain a decent life while the indecencies of slavery are rife about us. To rid the nation of a curse, blows must be struck. Blood shed. I am prepared to shed blood. Mine. My sons'.

And my blood. And the blood of young Green here, fresh from chains, who, after listening to us debate, not quibble, chooses to accompany you to Virginia.

Some days, I assure you, my feet, my mind rage. Yet a voice intercedes: do not give up hope for this intolerable world. Change must come. Like you, I believe the Good Lord in Heaven has grown impatient with this Sodom. Soon He may perform a cleansing with His glorious, stiff-bristled broom. I will rejoice if He calls me to that work.

I have made up my mind as you have made up yours, John Brown. And this man, Green, his mind. Godspeed to you both.

9

My name is John Brown and I want my son to hear the story of my name so I will talk the story to this good white lady promises she write down every word and send them in a letter to my son in Detroit on Pierce Road last I heard of him and his wife and three children, a boy, two girls, don't know much else about them, must be old by now, maybe those three children got kids and grandkids of they own and I never seen none them with my own two eyes, these old eyes bad now don't see much of anything no more, wouldn't hardly see them grands nor great-grands today if they standing here right beside this bed so guess I never will see them in this life and that fact makes me very sorry, son, and old-man sorry the worse kind of sorry, I believe, and let

me tell you, my son, don't you dare put off to tomorrow because tomorrow
not promised, tomorrow too late, too late, but don't need to tell you all that,
do I, son, you ain't no spring chicken, you got to be old your ownself cause I
comes into the world in eighteen and fifty-eight just before the war old John
Brown started and seem like wasn't hardly no time before here you come behind me, me still a boy myself, but I want to tell you the story of my name not
my age and how you supposed to know that story less I tell it and this nice
lady write the words and maybe you read them one day to my grands and
great-grands, son, then they know why John Brown my name and why John
Brown a damn fine name, but listen, son, don't you ever put off to tomorrow trying to be a good man, a honest man, hardworking, loving man, don't
put it off cause that gets a man in trouble, deep-down trouble, cause time is
trouble, time full of trouble, and time on your hands when your hands ain't
doing right fills up your time with trouble, then it's too late, your time to do
right gone, you in the middle of doing evil or trying not to or trying to undo
evil you done and time gone, too late, like me in a cage a dozen and some
years locked up behind bars for killing a fella didn't even know his name till I
hears it in the courtroom and lucky he black everybody say or you wouldn'a
made it to no damn courtroom, no jail, crackers string your black ass up, the
other prisoners say, you lucky nigger, they say, and cackle, grin, and shake
they heads and moan and some nights make you want to cry like a baby all
them long, long years when if I ain't slaving in the fields under a hellfire sun
I'm sitting in a cell staring at a man's blood on a juke-joint floor, never get my
time back once I yanks a Bowie knife out my belt and he waving his knife and
mine quicker finds his heart, the very same bowie knife my father Jim Daniels give to me and John Brown give to him, said, Use this hard, cold steel, Mr.
Jim Daniels, on any man try to rob your freedom, same knife old John Brown
stole from the crackers like he stole my daddy, mama, my sister and brother,
and a passel of other Negroes from crackers down in Kansas and Missouri,
it's too late, too late, knife in my hand, I watched a man bleed to death inside
those stone walls every day year after year, hard time, son, you wait too long
to do right it's too late and you can't do nothing, can't change time, and that's
that, like the fact I never seen my grands, never seen you but once, one time
up there on the Canada side in that cold and snow and wind, your mama carried you all them miles, had you wrapped up like you some little Eskimo or
little papoose. It was only once only that one time I ever seen you, there you

was with your mother, she come cross with you on the ferry, and me and her talked or mize well tell it like it was, she talked and I kinda halfway listened but I didn't want to hear nothing I wasn't ready to hear, nodded my head, smiled, chucked you under your chubby double chins, patted her shoulder, smooched her beautiful brown Indin-color colored cheek a couple times, always liked your mama, but the problem was I didn't know then what I know now, son, or excuse me, yes I did, I knowed it just as clear as day, course I did, just didn't want to hear it cause I had other plans, knucklehead, young-blood plans, what I'ma do with a wife and baby, it was rough up there, barely feed myself, keep a roof over my head, if you could call a tent a roof, so how am I supposed to look out for youall, anyway, it was only that once I seen you, then same day she's back on the ferry, she's gone, you gone, nothing, no word for lots and lots of years cept a little tad or tidbit the way news come and go in prison or hear this or that happened from people passing through up there in Canada, me asking or somebody telling tales they don't even know my name who I am or know you or know who your mama and who you is to me or who my peoples is, but I'd overhear this or that in somebody's story and so in a manner of speaking I kept up, knew you still alive, then your mama dead and you married living on Pierce Road in Detroit, three grandkids I ain't never laid eyes on, never will now . . . Excuse me, Miss, you got that all down so far or maybe I should slow up or maybe just go ahead and shut up now, stop now cause how you think this letter find him anyway even if I say it right and you catch every word I say on paper it still don't sound right to me hearing myself talk this story, it just makes me sad, and it's a damned shame, a mess anyway, too late to tell my son my daddy, his granddaddy, Jim Daniels, give me John Brown's name because John Brown carried us out from slavery in the fall of 1858, my brother and sister, mama, and Jim Daniels, my father cross seven states, eleven hundred miles, eighty-two days in wagons, railroad trains, on foot, boats, along with six other Negroes John Brown stole from slavery in Kansas and Missouri and Daddy say one them other six, a woman slave, ask John Brown, "How many miles, how many days, Captain Brown, we got to go before freedom?" and John Brown answer her and the lady slave say back, "That's a mighty far piece you say, Captain, sir. Ole Massa pitch him a terrible conniption fit we ain't back to fix his dinner," and then me born on one them last couple days before they cross the river to freedom, so my daddy Jim Daniels named me John Brown, he told me, and if I'da been more than half a man when you and your mama come up there I woulda took care of youall and passed my name on to you and you be another John Brown whatever else my sweet Ella called you you'd be John Brown, too, and if you knew the story of the name, son, maybe you would have passed the name on, too, John Brown, and maybe not, Miss, what do you think, Miss, is it too late, too much time gone by, Miss, what do you think.

10

Along an edge of the Gulf of Morbihan I walk through woods, on gravelly, rocky beaches, in sand, on a narrow walkway atop a mile-long stone seawall, then climb a bluff overlooking the wall where I can peer way, way out to dark clumps of island in the gulf's glittering water, toward open sea invisible beyond the islands. I imagine an actor assigned to deliver the colored John Brown monologue in a film version of "JB & FD." The actor asks me why I choose to make the nice lady in the script white, not colored. Asks why I invented a colored John Brown.

Powerful sea winds have shaped trees I stand next to on the bluff, winds that would shape me, too, no doubt, if I stood here very long. Trees with thick, ancient-looking gray trunks, bark deeply furrowed as old John Brown's skin, multiple trunks entwined, branches big as trunks, twisted, tortured, though a few trees shoot more or less straight up to vast crowns that form a layered green canopy of feathery needles high overhead. A row of maybe seven, eight survivors of probably hundreds of years of battering wind, and spaced among them another four or five cut down to stumps a couple yards across you could sit on and stare out at endless water beyond the edge of land, beyond the seawall and Roman ruins below.

Next to trees, still standing and fallen, I forget who I am, who I'm supposed to be, and it is perfection. Doesn't matter who I am or believed I was or all the shitty jobs performed to get to France—I listen for the voices of Frederick Douglass and John Brown sealed within the silence of those huge trees. Trees I don't know a name for, thinking maybe pine or fir or conifer, and I never will need to look up the name because for a small instant I'm inside them, and it lasts forever.

and my next brother, Otis. Other siblings arrived after the empty four years. New lives, two years separating each birth from the next, regular as rain, until five of us, four boys, one girl in the middle. With her hands full, heart full of caring for the ones alive, why would my mother allow herself to sink back into that abyss of watching two infants, so perfectly formed, so freshly dropped from inside her, leave the world and disappear as if her womb harbored death as naturally as life.

My brother was named Otis for our mother's brother and Eugene for our father's brother. Uncle Otis was very much alive, but Uncle Eugene dead already or soon to die on Guam, when my brother born. Uncle Eugene dying needlessly, or, you could say, ironically, since war with Japan officially declared over, a truce in force the sniper who shot Eugene didn't know about or perhaps refused to honor because too much killing, too many comrades dead. Why not shoot one more American soldier beachcombing for souvenirs where he had no right to trespass, no palpable reason to continue to live in the mind of an enemy whose duty was to repel invaders, to follow in his rifle's scope their movements. Not exactly easy targets, but almost a sure thing for a practiced marksman, even a sniper very weary, beat-up from no sleep, constant harassment of enemy planes, tanks, flamethrowers, a shooter trained to take his time, forget hunger, thirst, his dead, his home islands far too close to this doomed Guam as he gauges, tracks his prey, picks out a brown man who will surely, fatally fall before the others scatter for cover, before he, himself, is observed or snipered on this day he's not aware the war's over or is aware and doesn't care as he chooses someone to kill, freezes the rifle's swing, stops breathing, squeezes the trigger.

Uncle Otis, like our father and our father's brother, Eugene, served in World War II. Uncle Otis returned home to become a part of family life, always around until I was grown up with kids and my youngest sibling a teenager. We all still remember him fondly, Big Ote to distinguish him from Little Ote, my brother, who also carried the name of the uncle none of us in my generation had ever seen. Except I claimed to recall my uncle Eugene, even though my mother insistently objected, no-no-no you were way too young, just a baby when he

My Dead

Edgar Lawson Wideman: sept 2, 1918–dec 14, 2001

Bette Alfreda French Wideman: may 15, 1921–feb 7, 2008

Otis Eugene Wideman: march 6, 1945–jan 11, 2009

David Lawson Wideman: may 7, 1949–oct 19, 2014

Monique Renee Walters: nov 21, 1966–feb 6, 2015

I list my dead. Father. Mother. Brother. Brother. Sister's daughter. For some reason their funeral programs share a manila folder. During a bad ten months I had lost a brother, a niece, and they joined the rest of my dead. The dead remembered, forgotten, adrift. The dead in a folder. There and not here. Dead whose names never change. The dead who return secretly, anonymously, hidden within other names until they vanish, appear again.

March 6, the date I noted in my journal after I had compiled a list and returned the programs to their folder, happens to be my brother Otis Eugene's birthday, a date like others in the list I tend to forget, as he is often forgotten when I revisit family memories. My younger brother Otis who survived our unforgettable mother barely a year. My quiet, forgettable brother, his birth separated from mine by four years, by twins, a boy and girl, neither living longer than a week.

Their deaths, of course, a terrible blow for our mother. She never spoke of those lost babies, and late in her life denied to my sister that the births had occurred. No dead twins in the four-year interval between me, her eldest,

left for the war. I persisted in my claim, wrote my first published story to bear witness to his living presence within me, my closeness with a long-dead man more intimate, continuous, and attested, I'm almost ashamed to admit, than recollections I have of his namesake, my brother. A brother who, for reasons never shared with me, preferred to be called Gene once he became an adult.

Gene, the name everybody I met in Atlanta called him when I traveled there for his funeral. Over the years I had taught myself to say *Gene* when I addressed my brother in groups not family or introduced him to strangers or on those rare occasions when just the two of us were conversing and I wanted to show him I treated his wish to be called Gene seriously, how once, anyway, in this specific case I would make an effort to forget I was his elder, oldest of the siblings, and follow his lead. Act as if his right to name himself might really matter to me, and for once he could set the rules. My little brother Gene in charge, and me behaving as if he has escaped the box, the traps I spent so much evil time elaborately, indefatigably laying for him during our childhood. Not much use for a younger brother when we were growing up. Except when he served as temporary or potential victim and I was, yes, yes, like some goddamned sniper drawing a bead on an enemy soldier totally unaware his life dangled at the end of a thread in my fingers.

Gene. In Atlanta the name didn't sound like the affectation I had once considered it, my brother's rather late in the day, thus partly funny, partly irrelevant and futile striking out for independence. An attempt perhaps to wipe the slate clean by rebaptizing himself and answering only to a name he had chosen. A not-too-subtle effort to cancel prerogatives and status other members of the family had earned over the long haul of growing up inter-twined, separate and unequal. Like the privilege I had granted myself, no blame or guilt attached, to seldom phone him. To not recall or acknowledge him whatsoever for long stretches of time if I chose. My forgettable brother.

Now I concede it was less a matter of qualities he possessed or didn't possess that caused him to be forgettable, but my presumptions, my bottomless un-ease. Wasn't I the most worthy, important brother in the family, the world. The one who, therefore, must occupy all space available, even if no space left

for anyone else. Forgetting a brother a convenient tactic to ensure I never found him in my way. An annoyance. A barrier. A ghost.

I went to Atlanta to bury a brother and found Gene. Not Otis or Little Ote. Not Otis Eugene. Once my brother chose Gene as his new name, I stopped associating that name with the uncle who had died in the Pacific war. Eugene whose big sneakers I believed I remembered seeing on live feet. People in Atlanta who knew my brother had probably never heard of Eugene, our dead uncle. When they talked about a Gene, the name transformed me into a stranger, an intruder. I recalled names I had made up to keep my brother in his place, tease him to tears in ugly games while we were kids stuck in the same small house. Names I'd forgotten after we both left home. Then for years and years almost no name necessary for him. Few occasions arose to speak of a brother or speak to him or summon him into my thoughts.

I could have let him be Gene in Atlanta. Isn't that what he asked. Wasn't that one reason for his long, self-imposed exile. No trips back home unless someone very sick, dying, dead. Another city, another state, another start with another name he had picked. A new family, not necessarily to replace the old but to fill emptiness where maybe he'd always felt homeless or smothered or locked down in spaces like the ones I allowed him. Spaces with room for him only if he stayed in them alone.

I could have let myself be satisfied with seeing Gene, convinced myself I was saying goodbye to a stranger in Atlanta, but it was him, his neat, pencil-thin mustache, elegant features, my brother's unbegrudging silence in the open casket.

probably all of them white which made everything worse she didn't need to say because I heard it in her voice by the fifth or sixth word, her voice that didn't belong in the chair's office, a story not for a chairperson's ears, but he was Southern gentleman enough as well as enough of a world-renowned Chaucer scholar to hand me the phone and excuse himself and shut the office door behind him so I could listen in peace to my mother crying softly and trying to make sense of a dead man and my father in jail for killing him, his cut-buddy I can say to myself now and almost smile at misunderstandings, bad jokes, ill will, superiority, inferiority stirred up when I switch between two languages, languages almost but never quite mutually intelligible, one kind I talked at home when nearly always only colored folks listening, another kind spoken and written by white folks talking to no one or to one another or at us if they wanted something from us, two related-by-blood languages that throttled or erased or laughed at or disrespected each other more often than engaging in useful exchange, but I didn't slip once in my conversation with the chair, didn't say my gotdamn daddy cut his gotdamn cut-buddy, no colored talk or nigger jokes from either of us in the office when a phone call from my mom busted in and blew away my cover that second or third day of my first or second week of my first college teaching job.

My aunt C got my father a lawyer. Aunt C lived five doors away on our street, Copeland, when I was growing up. My family of Mom, Dad, five kids had moved into an upstairs three-room apartment in a row house at the end of a block where a few colored families permitted because the housing stock badly deteriorated and nobody white who could afford not to wanted to live on the busted block, after coloreds had been sneaked into a few of Copeland's row houses or modest two-story dwellings squeezed in between, like the one Aunt C and her husband could afford to buy and fix up because he was a numbers banker, but most of us coloreds, including my mother and father, had to scrimp and scuffle just to occupy month by month, poaching till the rent man put us out in the street again, but residents long enough for their kids to benefit for a while from better schools of a neighborhood all white except for a handful of us scattered here and there down at the bottom of a couple streets like Copeland.

    Aunt C a rarity, a pioneer you might say because she worked in the

Maps and Ledgers

My first year teaching at the university my father killed a man. I'm ashamed to say I don't remember the man's name, though I recall the man a good buddy of my father and they worked for the city of Pittsburgh on a garbage truck and the man's family knew ours and we knew some of them, my sister said. Knew them in that way black people who lived in the same neighborhood knew each other and everybody else black in a city that divided itself by keeping all people of color in the same place back then no matter where in the city you lived.

I did not slip up, say or do the wrong thing when the call that came into the English Department, through the secretary's phone to the chairman's phone, finally reached me, after the secretary had knocked and escorted me down the hall to the chair's office, where I heard my mother crying because my father in jail for killing a man and she didn't know what to do except she had to let me know. She knew I needed to know and knew no matter how much a call would upset me, I would be more upset if she didn't call, even though calling meant, since I didn't have a home phone yet nor a direct line in my office and no cell phones, she would have to use the only number I'd given her and said to use only for emergencies and wasn't this an emergency, hers, mine, we had to deal with, she and I, her trying not to weep into the phone she was holding in Pittsburgh while she spoke to strangers in Philadelphia, white people strangers to make it worse, a woman's voice then a man's before she reached me with the news I needed to know and none of it anybody's business, terrible business breaking her heart to say to me even though I needed to know and would want to know despite where I was and who I was attempting to be, far away from home, surrounded by strangers planning office of the city, a good job she finessed, she explained to me once, by routing her application through the Veterans Administration since she'd served as a WAC officer during WW II and guessed that by the time the city paper pushers noticed her color disqualified her, the military service record that made her eligible for a position and elevated her to the top of the list would have already gotten her hired, only woman, only colored, decades before anybody colored not a janitor or cleaning woman got hired by the city to work in downtown office buildings. Aunt C who I could always count on to find some trifling job around her house for me to earn a couple quarters when I needed pocket change or bigger jobs car washing, neatening up and cutting the grass in her tiny backyard when I needed new sneakers or a new shirt my parents couldn't buy, and then counted on her again years later because she was the one who knew everybody and everybody's dirt downtown, and got my father—her elder brother—an attorney, a colored one who also knew everybody and everybody's dirt downtown, the man as much or more of a rarity, an exception in his way as my aunt since he not only practiced law but served in the state legislature as majority speaker, an honor, achievement, irony, and incongruity I haven't been able to account for to this day, but he wound up representing my father and saving him from prison, thanks to Aunt C. That same colored lawyer one day would say to me, shaking his head and reaching out and placing his hand on my shoulder, *Family of poor old Aeschylus got nothing on yours, son,* as if to inform me, though he understood both of us already knew, that once my mother's phone call had caught up with me, Aunt C doing her best or no Aunt C— things would only get worse.

No, my father didn't serve time for murder. Lawyer plea-bargained self-defense and victim colored like my father anyway so they chose to let my father go. But things did get worse. My father's son, my youngest brother, convicted of felony murder. And years later my son received a life sentence at sixteen. My brother, my son still doing time. And my father's imprisoned son's son a murder victim. And a son of my brother's dead son just released from prison a week ago. And I'm more than half ashamed I don't know if the son, whose name I can't recall, of my brother's dead son has fathered a son or a daughter. My guess is the rumor of a child true since if my grandnephew was old enough for adult prison, he would be way past the age many young colored men father babies back home.

Gets confusing doesn't it. Precedents from Greek mythology or not. Knowing or not knowing what variety of worse will probably come next if you are a member of my colored family hunkering down at the end of Copeland or on whatever divided street you think of as home or whatever you may think a home is. Gets damned confusing. I lose track of names. Generations. No end in sight. Or maybe I already know the end and just don't want to think about it out loud. Whose gotdamn business is it anyway. Knucklehead, fucking hardhead youngbloods and brothers. Got-damned Daddy. Gotdamned cut-buddy. Words I didn't slip and say out loud that day attempting to explicate an emergency to my chairman in the departmental office.

Get away, I kept telling myself, and none of this happens.

I always had been impressed by my grandmother Martha's beautiful hand. Not her flesh-and-blood hand. Her letters. Her writing. Perfect letter after letter in church ledgers and notebooks year after year in my grandmother Martha's beautiful hand. You almost felt a firm, strong hand enfolding, guiding yours if your turn to read Sunday school attendance or minutes of the Junior Deacons' board, each letter flowing into the next into the next word then next sentence so you didn't stumble or mumble repeating aloud what you found waiting for you so peacefully, patiently, perfectly shaped between faint blue lines on each page. Not that her hands weren't hands a person might notice and think something nice about. Maybe a bit mannishly large but my grandmother Martha wasn't a small woman, her wide-boned hips not swaying side to side when she walked, more of a tall person's rocking-chair lean and tipping-forward-then-back momentum that propelled her strides, striding down the sidewalk purposefully though never in a hurry, walking like you'd probably imagine she probably writes when she records church business, her hand's fingers slim, smooth-jointed, tapering to big teardrop nails she often painted plum to complement light brown skin.

Letter after letter perfect as eggs. Perfect as print. But better. Her hand cursive. Letters flow like alive things that grow. One growing live into or from the other whether connections visible or not. As the Bible grows if you are taught to read it in the fashion I was. Each verse, each psalm, parable, book, sermon connected. Truths alive and growing in the pages after you learn in church how to read Bible words. Cursive you learn in school. *Cursive* one of many strange words telling you a different language spoken in school and you will always be a stranger in that strange land. Not everybody good at cursive, not every boy or girl in class remembers new words, nor gives a flying fuck if they do or don't, but my grandmother's cursive flows seamlessly page after page when you leaf through one of the old Homewood AME Zion notebooks and ledgers with thick, ornate covers she filled and you are not aware until you discover one more time as you always do how shabby the world will be, how much it hurts when her hand drops yours and perfect writing stops.

My grandmother picked her husbands as carefully, perfectly as she performed her church secretary cursive. Except every now and then she decided it was time to change scripts. After she abandoned then divorced her first husband—a dark-skinned workingman, shy emigrant from rural Promised Land, South Carolina, father of my father and my aunt C, the man I grew up calling Grandpa—my grandmother Martha chose to marry preachers. A series of three or four preachers whose names I often could not remember when they were alive, names mostly lost now they are dead, like the name of the man my father killed. Uncle this or Uncle that is what I called my grandmother's husbands and one I called "Reverend" because he addressed me as "Professor," a darkie joke we shared, minstrels puffing each other up with entitles, *Yo, Mr. Bones . . . Wuss up, Mr. Sambo.*

Same grandmother who wrote beautiful cursive played deaf (almost but not quite her version of darkie joke) when people were saying things she preferred not to hear. A highly selective deficit she displayed only when she chose. For instance, sitting on her pink couch she protected with a transparent plastic slip-cover, chattering away with a roomful of other family members, if someone mentioned the name of one of ours in trouble or prison, my grandmother Martha would shut her eyes, duck her head shyly, totally absent herself as if she'd suddenly nodded off like very old folks do. If you didn't know better, you'd think she was missing the conversation. Elsewhere. Immune. But if the unpleasant topic not dropped quickly enough to suit her, she would shush the person speaking by tapping an index finger against her pursed lips. *Not nice . . . Shhhh.* Some mean somebody might be listening and spread nasty news about a son or grandson or nephew shot dead in the street three years ago or locked up in the pokey twenty years, or a slave two hundred years ago. *Shhhh.* Whisper, she orders as she leans over, pouts, and mimics whispering. Best whisper in a family member's ear so cruel strangers can't overhear, can't mock names of our dead, our wounded, our missing ones.

I regard my empire. Map it. Set down its history in ledgers. Envy my grandmother's beautiful hand. Her cold-bloodedness. I've done what I needed to do to get by, and when I look back, the only way to make sense of my actions is to tell myself that at the time it must have seemed I had no other choice.

As far back as I can remember, I was aware the empire I was building lived within an empire ruled by and run for the benefit of a group to which I did not belong. *Mm'fukkahs, the man, honkies, whitey, boss, peckerwoods, mam, fools, mister, sir, niggas* some of the names we used for this group not us, and the list of names I learned goes on and on, as many names probably as *they* learned to call us by. Growing up, if I found myself talking to people, small gathering or large, almost always it would be composed exclusively of members of my group or, except for me, members of the other. On the other hand nothing unusual about contact between the two groups. Ordinary, daily mixing the rule not exception. In public spaces we politely ignored each other or smiled or evaded or bumped, jostled, violently collided, or clashed. Passed through each other as easy as stepping through a ghost. Despised, killed each other just as easily, though since the others held the power, many, many more fatal casualties in our group resulting from those encounters than in theirs.

Majority rules, we learned. Fair enough. Except, since we spent most of our time among our own kind talking, interacting only with each other, slippage occurred naturally. Reinforced by the presence of friends and family, we considered ourselves among ourselves the equal of others. Or considered ourselves better. Considered our status as minority, as inferior not to be facts. Or at best relative facts, irrelevant to us unless we assumed the point of view of the group not our group. On good days members of our group would make fun of such an assumption. Bad-mouth the other group with all the nasty names we dreamt up for them. Names and laughter like talismans—string of garlic, sign of the cross—European people in the old days would brandish to fend off a vampire. A survival strategy we practiced while the other group survived by arming themselves, by erecting walls, prisons, churches, laws. By chanting, screaming, repeating, believing their words for us.

Ain't nothing but a party, old Aunt May always said. How long, how long, sighed Reverend Felder, in Homewood AME Zion's pulpit, Dr. King in Atlanta's Ebenezer Baptist.

Aunt May's skin a lighter color than my grandmother Martha's light brown, and the difference, slight though it was, cowed my grandmother enough to look the other way or pretend to be deaf when May got loud, raunchy, or ignorant at family gatherings. May, tumbler of whiskey held down with one hand on the armrest pad of her wheelchair while the hand at the end of her other arm points, wiggles, summons all at once, a gesture synced with a holler, growl, and mm-mm, boy, you better get yourself over here and gimme some sugar, boy, get over here and dance with your aunt May, boy, you think you grown now, don't you, you sweetie pie, past dancing wit some old, crippled-up lady in a wheelchair, ain't that what you thinking, boy. Well, this old girl ain't done yet. Huh-uh. You all, hear me, don't, you. Ain't nothin but a party. Woo-wee. Get your narrow hips over here, you fine young man, and dance wit May.

They left something behind in Aunt May's gut they shouldn't have when they sewed her up after surgery. Staple, piece of tape, maybe a whole damn scalpel, my sister rolled her eyes telling me. You know how they do us, my sister said, specially old people can't help themselves, won't speak up—poor May in terrible pain, belly blew up and almost dead a week after they sent her home. So weak and full of drugs poor thing lying there in her bed could barely open her eyes. But you know Aunt May. Ain't going nowhere till she ready to go. Hospital didn't want her back, but we fussed till they sent an ambulance. Opened her up again and took out whatever festering. May got better. Didn't leave from here till she was good and ready to leave. You know

May. Hospital assholes never even said they were sorry. Threw May away like a dirty old rag after they saw they hadn't quite killed her, and then got busy covering their tracks. May dead two years before anybody admitted any wrongdoing. Too late to hold the hospital accountable. Simple-minded as all those pale folks on May's side the family always been, couldn't get their act together and sue the doctors or hospital or some cotton-picking somebody while May still alive.

May's nephew, Clarence, you remember him. Browner than I am, I reminded my sister as if she didn't already know. I ran into him five, six years ago, when I was in town for something. Clarence a cook now. Guess at some point May and her pale sisters decided some color might be a good idea. Two, maybe three married brothers from the same brown-skinned family, didn't they, and broke the color line so Clarence and a bunch of our other second cousins or half cousins or whatever after a couple more generations of marrying and mixing got different colors and names and I've lost track, but Clarence I knew because he was my age and a Golden Gloves boxer and everybody knew him and knew his older brother, Arthur, in jail for bank robbing, put away big-time in a federal penitentiary, so when Clarencie walked into Mrs. Schaefer's eleventh-grade class, which was a couple grades further than Clarencie ever got, he wasn't supposed to be in that eleventh-grade classroom or any other, he just happened to be hanging out, strolling the high school halls and saw me and came in and hollered, Hey, cuz, how you doing, man . . . and me, I kind of hiss-whispered back, Hey, what you doing here, him acting like nobody else in the classroom when he strutted in, walked straight to my seat in the back, loud-talking the whole way till I popped up, Hey, cuz, and hugged him, shocking the shit out of Mrs. Schaefer because I was her nice boy, good student and good citizen and example for all the other hoodlums. You could tell how terrified the poor white lady was most the time, coming every day into a school not all colored yet but getting there and getting worse and she needed me as much as I needed her we both understood so who in hell was this other tall colored boy acting like he owned her classroom with nobody he had to answer to but himself and that was my cousin Clarencie, he couldn't care less what anybody else thought, Cousin Clarence, and you could tell just looking at him once, stranger to you or not, that you better go on about your own business and hope this particular reddish-brown-skinned negro with straight, dago-black hair and crazy eyes got no business with you, you heard the stories didn't you, sis. You most likely told some of them to me—bouncer at a club downtown, mob enforcer maybe, got paid for doing time for the crime of some mafia thug don and afterward Cousin Clarence a kind of honorary made-man people say, but most of the worst of that bad stuff long after we hugged and grinned and took over Mrs. Schaefer's class a minute because he didn't care and I forgot for once to care whom it belonged to.

Aunt C, my father's sister, got him a fine lawyer. But things continued to get worse. Worse is what you begin to expect if worse is what you get time after time. Worse, worser, worst. Don't let the ugly take you down, my mother said. Don't let it make you bitter and ugly, she said. She had led me by the hand to a few decent places inside me where she believed and tried to convince me that little sputtering lights would always exist to guide how I should behave once I left home and started a grown-up life. Her hand not as powerful and elegant as my grandmother Martha's, but my mother wrote good letters, clear, to the point, often funny, her cursive retaining features of the young girl she'd been when she learned to write. Neat, precise, demonstrating obviously she'd been an attentive student, yearned to get right the lessons she was taught.

Earnest another way of putting it, it being my mom's character when she was a schoolgirl and then when she fell in love with my father, I bet, and that sort of mother, too, I absolutely know, serious, conscientious without being boring, never boring because whatever she undertook she performed in the spirit partly of girls in grade school nearly junior high age, always a little scared but bold, too, both idly mischievous and full of hidden purpose, full of giggles and iron courage adults could never comprehend, often dismiss, yet stand in awe also, charmed, protective of the spark, that desire of young colored girls to grow and thrive, their hunger to connect with an unknown world no matter how perilous that new-to-them world might turn out to be for girls determined to discover exciting uses for limbs, minds, hearts still forming, still as stunning for them to possess as those girl hearts, minds, limbs were stunning for adults to behold. In the case of my mother, from girlhood to womanhood, an infectious curiosity, a sense of not starting over but starting fresh, let's go here, let's do this, not because she had mastered a situation or a moment previously but because uncertainty attracted, motivated, formed her.

Look at this writing, I can almost hear her say, look at these letters, words, sentences, ideas, feelings that flow and connect when we attempt something in this particular, careful fashion, with this cursive we studied and repeated in a classroom, but mine now, see, see it going word by word, carefully, and I follow her words, her writing like that of a bright child's who is occasionally distracted while she busily inscribes line after almost perfect line from manual to copybook. Going the way it's supposed to go. And where it's going, nobody knows exactly where but it looks the way it should and worth the trouble, the practice, because it's mine now and yours, too, she tells me, if you wish, and work hard at it. Whatever. Take my hand. Hold it as I hold yours, precious boy, and let's see, let's see what we shall see.

That's the message I read in her hand, in letters my mother sent when I went away to college. Letters I receive today from home beyond these pages. Home we share with all our dead.

I thought at the time, the time when I'd just begun university teaching, that the worst consequence of my father stabbing another man to death would be my first meeting with the chair in his office after I returned from Pittsburgh. After I'd said to my mother, Don't worry, I'll be home soon, and hung up the phone and tried to explain an ugly, complicated situation in as few words as possible and the chair had generously excused me from my teaching duties and granted me unconditional license to attend to family affairs, *A terrible business. Sorry it hit before you could get yourself settled in here.* The worst would be wisdom, commiseration, condolences I'd have to endure one more time animating his face, in his office, in his position as departmental chair after I completed my dirty work at home and stood in his office again, forgiven again by his unrufflable righteousness.

A good man, my mother would call him. Ole peckerwood, May would say. I heard both voices, responded to neither. Too busy worrying about myself. Too confused, enraged, selfish. Not prepared yet to deal with matters far worse afflicting my father, his victim, the victim's family, all my people back home, our group that another more powerful group has treated like shit for centuries to intimidate and oppress, to prove to themselves that a country occupied by many groups belongs forever, solely, unconditionally to one group.

My sister needs a minute or so to summon up the name, but then she's certain, "James . . . and I think his first name Riley . . . uh-huh . . . Riley James . . ." she says is the name of the man our father killed. Neither of us speaks. Silence we both maintain for a while is proof probably she's correct. Silence of a search party standing at the edge of a vast lake after the guide who's led them to it points and says the missing one is out there somewhere. Silence because we've already plunged, already groping in the chill murkiness, holding our breath, dreading what we'll recover or not from the gray water.

Thought I'd recognize the name if I heard it. That jolt, you know, when you're reminded of something you will never forget. But James sounds right, anyway. And Riley James had kids, didn't he. Yes, my sister says. Three. One a girl about my age I'm pretty sure. Used to run into her before it happened.

Coming up, did you ever think we might need to have this conversation one day. Daddy killing someone else's daddy.

Oh, we knew. Children understand. Don't need adults to tell them certain things. Kids supposed to listen to grown-ups, better listen if you don't want a sore behind, but we watch them, too. Kids always watching, wondering why big people do what they do. Understand a whole lotta mess out there adults not talking about. Scary mess kids can't handle. Or maybe nobody kid or adult can handle it, so you better keep your eyes wide open. Don't even know what you looking for except it's bad. Gonna get you if you not careful. But no. Thank goodness, no. Huh-uh, I'm not standing here today saying that when I was a little girl I could see my father would kill another man. But we knew, we saw with our own eyes awful stuff happening day after day and worse just around the corner waiting to happen. Grownups didn't need to tell us all that mess happening to them. We watched while it happened.

Wish I could disagree, Tish. Wish I could say no, but no, I think we probably did know. You're remembering right again, my sweet lil sis.

Whoa. Don't remember everything, but some things I sure don't forget, so lighten up some on the sweet sister bullshit. As if you always treated me like I was your sweet lil sister. Like youall's favorite game back then wasn't

teasing and beating on me to see me cry. My little brothers torturing me as
soon as they were big enough. And you, too, eldest brother. They learned it
from you. You . . . you not me always the sweet one. Oldest, sweetest one. At
least that's what you had all the adults in the family calling you and believing
about you. Him so nice. All those good grades in school and talks so nice to
grown-up people, so smart and a good boy takes care of his little brothers
and sister to help out his mother. What a sweet, nice boy. Wasn't hardly bout
no sweet lil sis, you devil. My sweet eldest brother the king. Making me pay
in spades if I dared to sass you or look at you cross-eyed or stick out my
tongue or beg please, Mom, could I please have that last little wing, the wing
you had your eye on since you sat down at the table and counted the pieces
of chicken on the plate and figured an extra one left after everybody got their
share and that extra wing meant for you.

Okay. Warm and safe and nice as we felt home was, maybe not always
but lots of the time, really, still there was the worry about worse coming.
Could hear it when Daddy slammed the door behind himself going out.
Or I peeped at Mom's red eyes. Or checked out the thumb she chewed on.
Or Daddy's clean, ironed white shirts he pitched in the laundry basket and
wouldn't wear till they came back starched in cellophane wrappers from
the cleaners. Or Mom forgets she's scrubbed a pot clean and stands at the
kitchen sink humming gospel and scrubs and scrubs and scrubs.

Thinking now about Mom's poor thumb, didn't I suck on mine when I
was a little girl. Yes indeed I did. Seems to me I recall you sneaking off when
nobody paying attention and you sucking yours, too.

Yes, all that's so. Still, whether or not we knew things would get worse,
our fear doesn't answer the question, why. You must wonder now like I do.
Why. Why did things get worse.

Wish I knew the answer to that one, older brother.

Will it always be like this, then. Too late. Damage done. Another
victim. Trial. Funeral. Inquest. Story in the newspaper, on TV. More tears.
Hand-wringing.

Stop now. Stop. Don't need to go there this morning, do we. Been there.
Done it far, far too many times. Wish you were here, brother dear, to gimme
a hug. Some sugar, May used to say.

Is it worse now. Doesn't seem possible, but it just might be. Not only for
our family. Shit no. Not just us. Everybody. Everybody jammed up here wit

us in this stinking mess. Everybody just too scared or too dumb to know it, is what our brother said with his eyes when I came to town to visit and we let go of each other and time for me to leave the prison and he has to stay where he is and nothing to do but look at each other one more time, one more sad, helpless stinking time. Clang, bang, gate shuts behind me and they still got the key.

We had talked about power during that visit. Talked in the cage. Power how long, too long stolen by the ruling group to diminish and control the ruled. Power of this political system that has operated from its start as if vast gaps dividing us from the ruling group either don't exist or don't matter. Same ole shit. Ask the brothers in here, our brother says. Ask the outlaws. Ask them about law supposed to protect everybody—rulers and ruled—from each other equally. Law calling itself the will of the people. Law that got all us in here blackened up like minstrels. Color, His-Honor-Mr.-Law says, No problem. While out the other side of his mouth he's saying color gives law power to abuse color. Look at the color around us in here. Some days I look and cry. Laugh some days. Our colors, our group. Power serves itself. Period. Exclamation point. Truth and only truth, our locked-up brother says. And he's not wrong, our brother's not wrong, so how can I be right. My empire. They slam the gate shut. Blam. Time to leave my brother's cage, go back in mine. My maps. Ledgers. Theirs.

Remember when I called you couple weeks ago, sis, and asked the man's name Daddy killed. Conversation got long, much longer than usual, nice in a way because usually conversations shortish because we skip over awful things and don't want to jinx good things by talking too much about them but I remember I think we both got deep into the begats, both trying to recall Daddy's grandmother's name and neither could and Owens popped into my mind and I said Owens to you and you said, Sybil Owens—wasn't she the slave from down south who came up here to found Homewood, and you were right of course and I laughed because I was the one who wrote down the Sybela Owens story and you knew the story from my books or from family conversations. Same family conversations from which I'd learned, mostly from May, about May's grandmother or great-grandmother Sybela, who had fled slavery with a white man who stole Sybela from his

slave-plantation-owner father and settled in or near what's now called
Homewood where one day when May was a little girl she saw, according
to her, an old, old woman on a porch in a rocking chair smoking a pipe,
woman in a long black dress, dark stockings, and head rag who smiled at her
and she'd hear people say later the old woman was her grandmother, maybe
great-grand, and May never forgot and passed on the memory or tale or
whatever to us, a story about Mom's side of the family, not Daddy's, and I
wrote or talked my version of it and you probably heard May herself tell it
like I did but years and years ago and the best we usually do as we try to sort
out the family tree and put names to branches, to people, is most likely to
mix up things the way I did with *Owens* before you corrected my memory
and I reminded myself and you how family stories were partly what one of
us had heard live from the mouth of the one who had lived the story or heard
it second- or thirdhand and passed it on but partly also stuff I had made
up, written down, and it got passed around the family same as accounts of
actual witnesses telling stories the way May told hers about Sybela so that
day on the phone we were begatting this one from that one and so on, you
said, Hold on a minute and went up to the attic where you keep those boxes
and boxes of Mom's things, the papers and letters she saved from the old
people in the family, because you believed there was an obituary in rough
draft in Mom's hand on tablet paper that might tell us Daddy's grandmother's name, the name I could hear my father and Aunt C saying plain as day
but could not raise beyond a whispering in my ear too faint to grasp or repeat aloud to myself. And sure enough you quickly retrieved information
Mom had written down long ago for a church funeral program, maybe for
the colored newspaper, too, a couple sheets of blue-lined school-table paper, lines and handwriting faded, creases in the paper also cuts, the obituary
notice we both had remembered but neither could repeat the exact contents
of. You had the folded sheets in your hand in a minute once you got up those
steep-assed attic steps I worry about my little sis climbing because she's not
little sis anymore but sweet, still sweet.

   Yes, you hear me talking to you, girl. This is eldest brother speaking, and
you're my sweet sister and don't you dare sass me, girl. Two of our brothers
gone, just us two left and our brother in the slam and when you read me
Mom's notes for her father's obituary they included Daddy's name but do
not mention our father's mother's mother so of course they solved nothing

just deepened the puzzle of how and why and where and who we come from and here we are again, and whatever we discover about long ago, it never tells us enough, does it. Not what we are nor what comes next after all that mess we don't even know maybe or not happened before . . . well, we try . . . and after I listened to you reading bits of information the note compiled, I thought about the meaning of long ago, and how absolutely long ago separates past and present, about the immeasurable sadness, immeasurable distance that well up in me often when I hear the words *long ago*, and on another day, in another conversation, I will attempt to explain how certain words or phrases reveal more than I might choose to know, an unsettling awareness like seeing an ugly tail on an animal I know damn well has no tail or a tail negligible as the one people carry around and can't see, and I will ask you, Tish, what if I'm trying to imagine *long ago* and a shitty, terrible-looking tail appears, a tail like the one I'm sure doesn't belong on a familiar animal but grows longer, larger, and hides the animal. Wraps round and round and takes over. Will there be nothing left then, I will ask you. Nothing. Not even wishful thinking. The life, the long ago, once upon a time I am trying to imagine—gone like the animal not supposed to own a tail and the tail I inflicted upon it.

Williamsburg Bridge

Quick trip yesterday so today I'm certain and determined to jump, though not in any hurry. Why should I be. All the time in the world at my disposal. All of it. Every invisible iota. No beginning. No end. Whole load. Whole wad. All mine the moment I let go. Serene, copious, seamless time.

How much of it do you believe you possess. Enough of it to spare a stranger the chump change of a moment or two while he sits on the Williamsburg Bridge, beyond fences that patrol the pedestrian walkway, on a forbidden edge where a long steel rail or pipe runs parallel to walkways, bikeways, highways, and train tracks supported by this enormous towering steel structure that supports us, too, sky above, East River below, this edge where the bridge starts and terminates in empty air.

To be absolutely certain, I rode the F train yesterday from my relatively quiet Lower East Side neighborhood to Thirty-fourth Street and set myself adrift in crowds always flailing around Penn Station and Herald Square. To be certain of what. Certain I had no desire to repeat the experience. Certain that experience consists of repetition and that what repeats is the certainty of nothing new. Short subway ride uptown in dark tunnels beneath New York's sidewalks, twenty-five, thirty minutes of daylight aboveground, among countless bodies shrieking, shuddering, hurtling ahead like trains underground, each one on its single, blind track, and I was certain once more of the sad, frightening thoroughness of damage people inflict upon themselves and others, of a fallen city embracing us, showcasing the results of a future beyond repair. Certain I was prepared to sit here a short while and then let go.

I believe I heard Sonny Rollins playing his sax on the Williamsburg Bridge one afternoon so many years ago I can't recall the walkway's color back then. Old color was definitely not what it is now: pale reds and mottled pinks of my tongue as I wag it at myself each morning in the mirror. Iron fences with flaking paint that's cotton-candy pink frame the entrance to the bridge at the intersection of Delancey and Clinton streets where I stepped onto it today for the very last time, passing through monumental stone portals, then under a framework of steel girders that span the bridge's 118-foot width and display steel letters announcing its name.

Just beyond shoulder-high, rust-acned rails, a much taller crimson barrier of heavy-gauge steel chicken wire bolted to sturdy steel posts guards the fences. Steel crossbeams, spaced four yards or so apart, form a kind of serial roof over the walkway, too high by about a foot for me to jump up and touch, even on my best days playing hoop. Faded red crossties overhead could be rungs of a giant ladder that once upon a time had slanted up into the sky but now lies flat, rungs separated by gaps of sky that seem to open wider as I walk beneath them, though if I lower my eyes and gaze ahead into the distance where the bridge's far end should be, the walkway's a tunnel, solid walls and ceiling converge, no gaps, no exit, a mauvish gray cul-de-sac.

Tenor sax wail is the color I remember from the afternoon decades ago I heard Sonny Rollins the first and only time live. Color deeper than midnight blue. Dark, scathing, grudging color of a colored soldier's wound coloring dirty white bandages wrapped around his dark chest. An almost total eclipse of color while dark blood slowly drip drop drip drops from mummy wrap into the snow. A soldier bleeding, an unknown someone testifying on a sax and the chance either one will survive the battlefield highly unlikely.

I don't want to weigh down my recollection with too much gloomy symbolism so let's just say it was a clear afternoon a sax turned blacker than night. Color of all time. Vanished time. No time. Dark smudge like I mix from ovals of pure, perfect color in the paint box I found under the Christmas tree one morning when I was a kid. Unexpected color with a will of its own brewed by a horn's laments, amens, witness. That's what I remember, anyway. Color of disappointment, of ancient injuries and bruises and staying alive and dying and being born again all at once after I had completed about half the first lap of a back-and-forth hump over the Williamsburg Bridge.

Walking the bridge is an old habit now. One I share with numerous other walkers whose eyes avoid mine as I avoid theirs, our minds perhaps on people down below, people alive and dead on tennis courts, ball fields, running tracks, swings, slides, benches, chairs, blankets, grass plots, gray paths alongside the East River. Not exactly breaking news, is it, that from up here human beings seem tiny as ants. Too early this morning for most people or ants, but from this height, this perch beyond walkway fences, this railing or pipe along an out-of-bounds edge of the Williamsburg Bridge, I see a few large ants or little people sprinkled here and there. Me way up here, ants and people way down there all the same size. Same weight. Same fate. Same crawl. Inching along inside the armor of our solitary-nesses. Hi-ho. Hi-Ho. Off to work we go.

So here I am, determined to jump, telling myself, telling you that I'm certain. Then what's the fool waiting for, it's fair for you to ask. My answer: *certain* an old-fashioned word in a world where, at best, I'm able only to approximate the color of a bridge I've walked across thousands of times, a world where the smartest people acknowledge an uncertainty principle and run things accordingly and own just about everything and make fools of the vast majority of the rest of us not as smart, not willing to endure lives without certain certainties. In this world where desire for certainty is a cage most people lock themselves in and throw away the key, I don't wish to be a victim, a complete dupe, so I hedge my bets. I understand certainty is always relative, and not a very kind, generous, loving relative I can trust, especially since the uncertainty principle enfolds everybody equally, smart or dumb, no matter. Which is to say, or rather to admit, that although I'm sure I'm up here and sure this edge is where I wish to be and sure of what I intend to do next, I can't be truly certain, only as close to certain as you or I will ever get, before the instant I let go.

Many years passed before I figured out it had to be Sonny Rollins I had heard. Do you know who I mean. Theodore Walter Rollins, born September 7, 1930, New York City—emerges early fifties, "most brash innovative creative young tenor player"—flees to Chicago to escape perils of NYC jazz scene—reemerges 1955 in NYC with Clifford Brown, Max Roach group—nicknamed Newk for resemblance to Don Newcombe, star Brooklyn Dodgers pitcher—produces string of great albums before he withdraws from public again—practices on the Williamsburg Bridge "to get self together after too much fame, too soon"—returns with new album, *The Bridge*—another sabbatical, Japan, India, "to get himself together" . . . thinks, "it's a good thing for anybody to do" . . . etc. etc.—all this information available at Sonny Rollins website—although cocaine addiction, a year he did at Rikers for armed robbery are not in his website bio.

Once I'd become sure I had heard Sonny Rollins playing live, my interest, my passion for his music escalated. As did my intimacy with the Williamsburg Bridge. Recently, trying to discover where it ranks among New York bridges in terms of its attractiveness to jumpers, I came across AlexReisner .com/NYC2 and a story about a suicide in progress on the Williamsburg Bridge that Mr. Reisner claimed to witness. Numerous black-and-white photos illustrate his piece. In some pictures a young colored man wears neatly cropped dreads, pale skin, pale undershorts, a bemused expression, light mustache, shadow of beard, his hands curled around a pipe/rail running along the outermost edge of the bridge where he sits. Water ripples behind, below to frame him. His gaze downcast, engaged elsewhere, a place no one else on the planet can see. No people there, no time there where his eyes have drifted, settled. His features regular, handsome in a stiff, plain, old-fashioned way. Some mother's mixed son, mixed-up son.

If I could twist around, shift my weight without losing balance, rotate my head pretty drastically for a chronically stiff neck and glance over my left shoulder, I'd see what the pale young man probably saw, the superimposed silhouettes of the Manhattan and the Brooklyn Bridges downriver, grand cascades of steel cables draped from their towers, and over there if I stay steady and focused, I could pick out the tip of the Statue of Liberty jutting just above the Brooklyn Bridge, Miss Liberty posed like the sprinters Tommie Smith and John Carlos on the winners' stand at the 1968 Mexico City Olympics, her torch a black-gloved fist rammed into the sky: Up yours. We're number one. Stadium in an uproar, Go boys go. I see a fuming Hitler grab his cockaded, tricornered hat and split like he did in '36. In the haze where sky meets sea and both dissolve, a forest of tall cranes and derricks, arms canted at the exact angle of the statue's arm, return her victory salute.

Dawns on me that I'll miss the next Olympics, next March Madness, next Super Bowl. Dawns on me that I won't regret missing them. A blessing. Free at last. Dawns on me I won't miss missing them any more than all the sports I won't be watching on TV will miss me.

If I still have your attention, I suppose I should say more about why I'm here, prepared to jump. It's not because I won or didn't win a gold medal. Not up here to sell shoes or politics. Nor because my mom's French. Not here because of my color or lack of color. My coloring pale like the young colored man in website photos who sat, I believe, precisely on the spot where I'm sitting. Color not the reason I'm here nor the reason you are here, whatever you call your color. Mine, it appears, gives an impression of palish sepia or beige. The sprinters' black fists, taut arms holler forget about it. Forget the yes or no, misfortune or fortune, lack or surplus of pigment your skin displays. Ain't about color. Speed what it's about. Color just a gleam in the beholder's eye. Now you see it, now you don't.

On the other hand, no doubt, color matters. My brownish tinge, gift of the colored man my mother married, confers added protection against sunburn in tropical climates and a higher degree of social acceptance generally in some nations or regions or communities within nations or regions where people more or less my color are the dominant majority. My color also produces in many people of other colors an adverse reaction as hardwired as a worker ant's love for the nest's queen. Thus color keeps me on my toes. Danger and treachery never far removed from any person's life regardless of color, but in my case, danger and treachery are palpable, everyday presences.

No surprise at all. Unpleasantness life inflicts, no matter how terrible, also glimmers with confirmation. Told you so, Color smiles.

Gender not the reason I'm here either. A crying shame in this advanced day and age that plenty of people would tag my posture as effeminate. See a little girlish girl on a couch squeezing her thighs together because she's too shy in company to get up and go pee. A suspicious posture for a male, especially a guy with pale cheeks and chin noticeably shadowed by stubble. Truth is with my upper body tilted slightly backward, weight poised on my rear end, arms thrust out to either side for balance, hands like the young man's in the photo gripping a fat pipe or rail, I must press my thighs together to maintain stability. Keep my feet spread apart so they serve as bobbing anchors.

Try it sometime. Someplace high and dangerous, ideally. You'll get the point. Point being of course any position you assume up here unsafe. Like choice of a language, gender, color, etc. People forced to choose, forced to suffer the consequences. No default settings. Like choosing which clothes to wear on the Williamsburg Bridge or not wear. I've chosen to keep my undershorts on. I want to be remembered as a swimmer not some naked nut. Swimmer who has decided to swim away, dignity intact. Homely but perfectly respectable boxers serving as proxies for swimming trunks. Just about naked also because I don't wish to be mistaken for a terrorist. No intent to harm a living soul. Or dead souls. No traffic accidents, boat accidents caused by my falling body, heavier and heavier, they say, as it descends. No concealed weapons, no dynamite strapped around my bare belly. No excuse for cops to waste me unless they're scared of what's inside my shorts, and I sympathize with their suspicions. Understand cops are pledged to protect us, guarantee our security. We live in troubled times. Who doubts it. Who can tell what's in the mind of a person sitting next to you on a subway or standing at the adjacent public urinal. Anyway, either way, gunned down or not, I've taken pains to situate myself on the bridge's outermost edge to maximize the chance I hit nothing but water, no collateral damage.

And contrary to what you might be thinking, loneliness has not driven me to the edge. I'm far from lonely. With all the starving, homeless people on the planet, don't waste any pity on me, please. In addition to my undershorts

I have pain, grief, plenty of regrets, dismal expectations of the future to keep me company, and when not entertained sufficiently by those companions I look down below. Whole shitty world's at my feet.

My chilly toes wiggle like antennae, my chilly thighs squeeze together not because of loneliness. They move with purpose like my mother's hands forming a steeple. You might think she's about to pray, but then she chants: *Here's the church / See the steeple*, words that start a game Mom taught me in ancient days. Hand jive. I can't stop a grin spreading across my face even here, today, when she begins rhyming and steeples her pale, elegant fingers. I'm a sucker every time. *Here's the church / See the steeple.* I close my eyes— cathedrals, towers, castles, cities materialize in thin air—la-di-da . . . la-di-da. I drift entranced till she cries: *Open the doors / Out come the people.* Then her fingertips hordes of tiny wiggly people who poke, tickle, grab, nibble, pinch. I giggle, and she laughs out loud. I double over to protect my softest, most ticklish spots. Her nails dig into my ribs, fingers chase me up under my clothes. My small body squirms, thrashes every which way on her lap. No escape. Stoppit. Stoppit. Please, Mom. Stop or I'll fall. Please don't stop.

Yes, Mom. One could say I drink a lot, Mom, and drink perhaps part of the problem, but not why I'm up here. Do I drink too much—yes/no—lots of wine—it's usually wine—often good French wine and even so, yes, too much disturbs my customary way of coolly processing things and making sense of what I observe. Drink a bad habit, I admit. Like hiring a blind person to point out what my eyes miss. But I'm grateful to the potbellied wine god. Drink simpatico, an old, old cut-buddy. I gape at his antics, the damage he causes, stunned by the ordinary when it shows itself through his eyes. The ordinary. Only that, Mom. Nothing evil, nothing extreme, nothing more or less than the ordinary showing itself as gift, a wolf in sheep's clothing. Then naked. The ordinary exposed when I'm drinking. You must know what I mean. I'm the hunter who wants to shoot it. Wants to be eaten.

French my dead mother's mother tongue and occasionally I think in French. Mother tongue swabs my gums, wraps around my English, swallows it. Gears of the time machine whir in sync with French—ooh-la-la. I nearly swoon. Mother's tongue, French words in my mouth. Thinking in French. French the only language in the universe.

If another person appeared next to me sitting on the steel rail where I sit and the person asked—What do you mean by "mother tongue"—what do you mean, "think in French"—I would have to answer: "I don't know." Carefully speak the words aloud in English, those exact words repeated twice to keep track of language, of where I am, to keep track of myself.

Truth is, "I don't know." I falter, no more truth follows. Too late. Time machine whirs on, leaves nothing behind, nothing ahead, no words I'm able to say to steady myself after I scramble to make room for another on the rail. Desperate to explain before we tumble off the edge. Desperate to translate a language one and only one person in the universe speaks, has ever spoken. I struggle to open a parenthesis and hold it open, keep a space uncluttered, serene, safe. Me inside it able to gather my thoughts, my words before they disintegrate, before the machine whirs on, before its spinning gears crush, consume, before the temple walls collapse, rubble around my feet, rats darting through the ruins from corpse to bloated corpse for the sweetest bits, blood squishing between my toes. Words silenced, rushing away, tongue dead meat in my mouth.

What words will I be saying to myself the instant I slip or pitch backward into the abyss. Will French words or Chinese or Yoruba make a difference. Will I return from the East River with a new language in my head, start up the universe again with new words, or do I leave it all behind, everything behind forever, the way thoughts leave me behind. Thoughts which smash like eggs on the unforgiving labyrinth's walls. Can I scrape off dripping goo. Twist it into a string to lead me out of whitespace.

East River behind me, below me, is not whitespace. River showing off today. Chilly ripples scintillate under cold, intermittent sunshine. If someone snapped pictures of me, like the ones Reisner snapped of a young colored man, several photos would show water darkly framing my pale flesh, in others my skin darker than water. Water colors differently depending on point of view, light, wind, cosmic dissonance. Water shows all colors, no color, any color from impenetrable oily sludge to purest glimmer. Water a medium like whitespace yet drastically unlike whitespace. From water springs mother, father, posterity, progress, all vitality, even so-called insensible matter. Whitespace empty. Above, below, before, after, always. Whitespace thin, thin ice. Blank pages words skate across before they vanish. Whitespace disguises itself as spray, as froth, as bubbles, as a big white splash when I let go and land in the East River. My ass-backwards swan dive, swan song greeted by white applause, a bouquet of white flames while deep down below, whitespace swallows, burps, closes blacker than night.

But no. Not yet. I'm in no hurry this morning. Not afraid either. Fear not the reason I'm up here, ready to jump. I may be clutching white-knuckled on to the very edge of a very high bridge, but I don't fear death, don't feel close to death. I've felt more fear of death, much closer to death on numerous occasions. Closest one summer evening under streetlights in the park in the ghetto where I used to hoop. Raggedy outdoor court, a run available every evening except on summer weekends when the high-flyers owned it. A daily pickup game for older gypsies like me wandering in from various sections of the city, for youngblood wannabes from the neighborhood, local has-beens and never-wases, a run perfect for my mediocre, diminishing skills, high-octane fantasies, an aging body that enjoyed pretending to be in superb condition, at least for the first five or six humps up and down the Cyclone-fenced court, getting off with the other players as if it's the NBA finals, our chance at last to show we're contenders. Ferocious play war, harmless fun unless you get too enthusiastic, one too many flashbacks to glory days which never existed and put a move on somebody that puts you out of action a couple weeks, couple months, for good if you aren't careful. Anyway, one evening a hopped-up gangster and his crew cruise up to the court in a black, glistening Lincoln SUV. Bogart winners and our five well on the way to delivering the righteous ass-kicking the chumps deserved for stealing a game from decent folks waiting in line for a turn. Mr. Bigtime, bigmouth, big butt dribbles the ball off his foot, out of bounds. Calls foul. Then boots the pill to the fence. Waddle-waddling after it, he catches up and plants a foot atop it. Tired of this punk-ass, jive-ass run, he announces. Motherfucker over, motherfuckers. Then he unzips the kangaroo pouch of a blimpy sweat top he probably never sheds no matter how hot on the court because it hides a tub of jelly-belly ba-dup, ba-dupping beneath it, and from the satiny pullover extracts a very large pistol. Steps back, nudges the ball forward with his toe and—Pow—kills the poor thing as it tries to roll away. Pow—Pow—Pow—starts to shooting up the court. Everybody running, ducking to get out the goddamned fool's way. Gwan home, niggers. Ain't no more gotdamn game today. Pow. King of the court, ruler of the hood, master of the universe. Pow. Busy as he is during his rampage brother finds time to wave his rod in my direction. What you looking at, you yellow-ass albino motherfucker. Gun steady an instant, pointed directly between my eyes long enough I'm certain he's going to blow me away and I just about wet myself. If truth be told, with that cannon in my mug, maybe I did leak a little. In the poor light of the playground who could tell. Who cares is what I was thinking if I was thinking anything at that moment besides dead. Who knows. Who cares. Certainly not me, not posterity, not the worker ants wearing rubber aprons and rubber gloves who dump my body on a slab at the morgue, drag off my sneakers, snip off my hoop shorts and undershorts with huge shears before they hose me down. Sweat or piss or shit or blood in my drawers. Who knows. Who cares.

A near-death experience I survived to write a story about, a story my mother read and wrote a note about in one of the pamphlets from church she saved in neat stacks on top and under the night table beside her bed, pamphlets containing Bible verses and commentary to put herself to sleep.

I saw the note only after Mom died. A message evidently intended for my benefit she never got around to showing me. She had underlined words from Habakkuk that the pamphlet deemed appropriate for the first Sunday after Pentecost—"destruction and violence are before me; strife and contention arise. So the law becomes slack and justice never prevails—their own might is their god"—and in the pamphlet's margin she had printed a response to my story.

Of course I had proudly presented a copy of the anthology containing my story to my mother, one of two complimentary copies, by the way, all I ever received from the publisher as payment. Mom thanked me profusely, close to tears, I believe I recall, the day I placed the book in her hands, but afterward she never once mentioned my story. I found her note by chance years later when I was sorting through boxes full of her stuff, most of it long overdue to be tossed. Pamphlet in my hand and suddenly Mom appears. Immediately after reading her note, I rushed off to read all of Habakkuk in the beat-up, rubber-band-bound Bible she had passed on to me, the Bible once belonging to my father's family, only thing of his she kept when he walked out of our lives, she said and said he probably forgot it, left it behind in his rush to leave. I searched old journals of mine for entries recorded around the date of the pamphlet, date of my story's publication. After this flurry of activity, I just about wept. My mother a busy scribbler herself, surprise, surprise, I had discovered, but a no-show as far as ever talking about her writing or mine. Then a message after she's gone, ghost message Mom doesn't show me till she's a ghost, too: This reminds me of your story about playing ball.

Why hadn't she spoken to me. Did she understand, after all, my great fear and loneliness. How close I've always felt to death. Death up in my face on the playground in the park. Nobody, nothing, no time between me and the end. Probably as near to death that moment as any living person gets. Closest I've ever felt to dying, that's for damn sure. Still is. So absolutely close and not even close at all, it turns out, cause here I sit.

Yo. All youall down below. Don't waste your breath feeling sorry for me. Your behinds may hit the water before mine.

With my fancy new phone I once googled the number of suicides each day in America. I'm a latecomer to the Internet, cell phones, iPads, all the incredible devices invented to connect people. Remain astounded by what must be for most younger folk commonplace transactions. By speaking a few words into my phone I learned 475 suicides per year, 1.3 daily in New York City. With a few more words or clicks one could learn yearly rates of suicide in most countries of the civilized world. Data more difficult obviously to access from prehistory, the bad old days before a reliable someone started counting everything, keeping score of everything, but even ancient numbers available, I discover, if you ask a phone the correct questions in the proper order. Answers supplied by sophisticated algorithms that estimate within a hairbreath, no doubt, unknown numbers from the past. Lots of statistics re suicide, but I could not locate the date of the very first suicide nor find a chat room or blog offering lively debate on the who, when, why, where of the original suicide. You'd think someone would care about such a transformative achievement or at least an expert would claim credit for unearthing the first suicide's name and address, posting it for posterity.

Suicide of course a morbid subject. Who would want to know too much about it. Let's drop it. I'm much more curious about immortality and rapture, aren't you. Houston airport my prime candidate for a site where immortality might be practiced. First time I wandered round and round, part of a vast crowd shuffling through the maze of Houston airport's endless corridors and gates, my unoriginal reaction was: I did not know death had undone so many. But since I'm not morbid, I revised my thinking—perhaps these countless souls, these faces morphing into every face I've ever seen or remembered or forgotten, folks I had yet to meet or never would, faces from dreams, very specific avatars of flesh-and-blood faces (John Wayne's for instance) from books, magazines, TV, films, faces from the Rolodex of my imaginary lives, perhaps all these travelers not the dead. Maybe they are an ever-changing panorama of all people ever born and still to be born roaming through Houston airport. Immortality one colossal, permanent game of musical chairs. If one chair pulled out from under you, keep on trucking. Another empty chair to plop down on soon as that stranger or old buddy moves his or her fat ass. Just be patient, keep shuffling along, we're all old friends here, the whole gang's here. No planes arrive, no planes leave anybody's got to catch. Just keep strolling, smiling. Plenty of refreshments, souvenirs to buy. TV monitors and restrooms handy everywhere. The possibility of romance or peace and quiet or maybe even rapture, who knows what you'll find. Immortality a single life, a single airport waiting area we all share materializing as ourselves and others, moving round and round, swimming in an ocean, a drop of ourselves, same water, same airport no one leaves no one enters but everybody winds up there. Like you wind up a clock to tell time, to see time. Hear it and pretend time exists because the clock tick-tocks and whirs on—ba-dup, ba-dup.

If a person intent on suicide also seeking rapture, why not choose the Williamsburg Bridge. Like the young man in the website photos who probably believed his fall, his rapture would commence immersed within the colors of Sonny Rollins's tenor sax. Sonny's music first and last thing heard as water splashes open and seals itself—ba-dup. Rapture rising, a pinpoint spark of immortal dazzle ascending the heavens, wake spreading behind it, an invisible band of light that expands slowly, surely as milky-white wakes of water taxis passing beneath the bridge expand and shiver to the ends of the universe.

Sometimes it feels like I've been sitting up here forever. An old, weary ear worn out by nagging voices nattering inside and outside it. Other times I feel brand new, as if I've just arrived or not quite here yet, never will be. Lots to read here, plenty of threats, promises, advice, prophecies in various colors, multiple scripts scrawled, scrolled, stenciled, sprayed on the walkway's blackboard of pavement—*We will be Ephemeral*—*Mene Mene Tekel*—*Ends Coming Soon*. I've read elsewhere that boys in Asia Minor duel with kites of iridescent rainbow colors, a razor fixed to each kite's string to decide who's king, decide how long.

Clearly my kite's been noticed. Don't you see them. Bridge crawling with creepy, crawly cops in jumpsuits, a few orange, most the color of roaches. Swarms of them sneaky fast and brutal as always. They clamber over barriers, scuttle across girders, shimmy up cables, skulk behind buttresses, swing on ropes like Spider-Man. A chopper circles—Whomp-Whomp-Whomp-Whomp. One cop hoots through a bullhorn or karaoke mic. Will they shoot me off the bridge like they blasted poor, lovesick King Kong off the Empire State Building. Cop vehicles, barricades, flashing lights clog arteries that serve the bridge and its network of expressways, thruways, serviceways, overpasses, and underpasses, which should be pumping traffic noise and carbon monoxide to keep me company up here.

With a cell phone, if I could manage to dial it without dumping my ass in the frigid East River, I could call 911, leave a number for SWAT teams in the field to reach me up here, an opportunity for opposing parties to conduct a civilized conversation this morning instead of screaming back and forth like fishwives. My throat hoarse already, eyes tearing in the wicked wind. I will threaten to let go and plunge into the water if they encroach one inch farther into my territory, my show this morning. On my way elsewhere and nobody's business if I do, chirps my friend, Ladyday.

Small clusters of ant people, people ants peer up at me now. What do they think they see tottering on the edge of the Williamsburg Bridge. They appear to stare intently, concerned, curious, amused, though I've read numerous species of ant and certain specialists within numerous ant species are nearly blind. Nature not wasting eyes on lives spent entirely in the dark. But nature generous, too, provides ants with antennae as proxies for vision and we get cell phones to cope with the blues.

Shared cell phone blues once with a girlfriend I had high hopes for once who told me about a lover once, her Michelangelo, gorgeous she said, a rod on him hard as God's wrath is how she put it, a pimp who couldn't understand why she got so upset when he conducted business by cell phone while lying naked next to naked her, a goddamn parade of women coming and going in my bedroom and Michelangelo chattering away as if I don't exist, him without a clue he was driving me crazy jealous she said and her with no clue how crazy jealous it was driving me, the lethal combination of my unhealthy curiosity and her innocent willingness to regale me with details of her former intimacies, her chattering away on her end and me listening on mine, connected and unconnected, cell phone blues until listening just about killed me and I had to let her go and lost her like she lost her sweet Michelangelo.

Not expecting a call up here. Nobody on the line to giggle with me as I describe a cartoon in my head of people wearing phones like snails wear shells. Sidewalks mobbed by see-through booths, each occupied by a person chattering away. Booths elbow for position like guys on the playground fight for a rebound or booths waddle-waddle-waddle by like young men of color, pants below their ass cracks waddle like toddlers with loads in their diapers. A few rare ones walk booths with old-school cool—sexy, macho, etc., but booths very difficult to maneuver, shaped a bit too much like upright coffins. Then Emmett Till's glass casket joins the mix and nothing's funny. Booths collide. Booths crush bodies contorted inside them. Booths burning. Apoplectic faces of trapped occupants, fists pounding glass walls. Riders dumped, mangled, heads busted, bleeding on the curb.

If I could explain whitespace, perhaps I could convince everyone down there to take a turn up here. Not that it's comfortable here, no reasonable person would wish to be in my shoes, I'm not even wearing shoes, tossed overboard with socks, sweatshirt, jeans, jacket, beret. Stripped down to skivvies and intermittent sunshine the forecast promised not doing the trick. Each time a cloud slides between me and the sun, wind chills my bare skin, my bones shiver. On the other hand the very last thing any human being should desire is comfort. World's too dangerous. Pulse of the universe ba-dup, ba-dup beats faster than the speed of light. Nothing stops, nothing stays, a blur of white noise. People, cities, whole civilizations wiped out in an instant, steeped in blood, obliterated. If we could see it, not a pretty picture. Ba-dup. Comfort never signifies less peril, less deceit, it only means your guard's down, your vigilance faltering.

On the bridge one dark day, thick clouds rolling in fast, sky almost black at two in the afternoon, I caught a glimpse of a man reflected in a silvery band of light that popped up solid as a mirror for an instant parallel to the walkway fence, a momentary but too, too crystal-clear image of a beat-up hunched-over colored guy in a beret, baggy gray sweats, big ugly sneakers scurrying across the Williamsburg Bridge, an old gray person beside me nobody loves and he loves nobody. He might as well be dead. Who would know or care if he dies or doesn't, and this man scurrying stupid as an ant in a box, back and forth, back and forth between walls it can't scale, is me, a lonely, aging person trapped in a gray city, a vicious country, me scurrying back and forth as if scurrying might change my fate, and I think what a pitiful creature, what a miserable existence, it doesn't get any worse than this shit, and then it does get worse. Icy pellets of rain start pelting me, but between stinging drops a bright idea—universe bigger than NYC, bigger than America. Get out of here, get away, take a trip, visit Paris again, and even before the part about where the fuck's the money coming from, I'm remembering I detest tourism, tourists worse than thieves in my opinion, evil and dangerous because tourists steal entire lands and cultures, strip them little by little, stick in their pockets everything they can cart back home and exchange for other commodities until other lands and cultures emptied and vanish, tourists worse than thieves, worse like false-hearted lovers worse than thieves in the old song, you know how it goes, a thief will just rob you . . . ba-dup, ba-dup . . . and take what you have . . . but a false-hearted lover leads you to the grave. Tourists worse than thieves, like false-hearted lovers worse than thieves, but a false-hearted lover far worse than any worst thing you can imagine. So where to go, where to hide, what to do after seeing that ghost.

Once I had hopes love might help. Shared rapture once with a false-hearted lover. I'll start with your toes, my gorgeous lover whispered, start with your cute crooked toes she says, your funny crooked toes with undersides same color as mine, skin on top a darker color than mine she grins and when I'm finished with your toes she promises my false-hearted lover promises I'll do the rest.

Hours and hours later she's still doing toes, she's in no hurry and neither am I. Enraptured. Toes tingle, aglow. How many toes do I own. However many, I wished for more and one toe also more than enough. Toe she's working on makes me forget its ancestors, siblings, posterity, forget everything. Bliss will never end. I read *War and Peace*, *Dhalgren*, *Don Quixote* and think I'll start Proust next after I finish *Cane* or has it been Sonny Rollins's mellow sax, not written words, accompanying work she's busy doing down there.

Whole body into it, every tentacle, orifice, treacly inner wetness, hers, mine. I'm growing new toes or does one original toe expand, proliferate, bud, bloom, breed. Could be one toe or many, who knows who cares, she's still at it and who's counting.

I floated miles above her, us, them, it, far removed from this "inextricable place," as a favorite writer of mine named the world. Time stopped—yes/ no—then here it comes. I hear it whirring, starting up again. No. Nobody turned off the time machine. I just missed a beat. Missed one tick or tock and fell asleep before the next tick or tock. Time only seemed to stop, as during a yawn, blink, death, rapture, as in those apparently permanent silences between two consecutive musical notes Sonny Rollins or Thelonious Monk brew, or between heartbeats, hers, mine, ours. A hiccuping pause, hitch, an extenuating circumstance like being tickled by my mom while I'm attempting to act grown-up, dignified, serious.

Falling . . . slipped out of love. It's afterward and also seamlessly before she starts on my toes and she's still in no hurry. No hurry in her voice the day that very same false-hearted lover tells me she's falling . . . slipped out of love.

Shame on me, but I couldn't help myself, shouted her words back in her face—*falling . . . slipped out of love.* Who wouldn't need to scream, to grab her, shake her, search for a reflection in the abyss of her eyes, in the dark mirror of whitespace. I plunged, kicked, flailed, swallowed water, wind, freezing rain.

Sad but true some people born unlucky in love, and if you're jinxed that way, it seems never to get any better. No greeting this morning from my neighbor ghost, not even a goodbye wave. Can't say what difference it might have made if she had appeared in her window. I simply register my regret and state the fact she was a no-show again this morning.

I believe it's her I speak to politely in the elevator. Her I nod at or smile or wave at on streets surrounding this vast apartment complex or when we cross paths in the drab lobby shared by the buildings we inhabit. When I moved into my fifteenth-floor, one bedroom, kitchenette, and bath, the Twin Towers still lurked at the island's tip, biggest bullies on the block after blocks of skyscrapers, high-rises, the spectacle still novel to my eyes, so much city out the window, its size and sprawl and chaos would snag my gaze, stop me in my tracks, especially the endless sea of glittering lights at night, and for the millisecond or so it took to disentangle a stare, my body would expand, fly apart, each particle seeking out its twin among infinite particles of city, and during one such pause, from the corner of one eye as I returned to restore the building, the room, my flesh-and-blood self, I glimpsed what might have been the blur of a white nightgown or blur of a pale, naked torso fill the entire bright window across the courtyard from my kitchenette window, a woman shape I was sure, so large, vital, near, my neighbor must have been pressing her skin against the cool glass, a phantom disappearing faster than I could focus, then gone when a Venetian blind's abrupt descent cut off my view, all but a half-hand-high/thirty-inch-wide band of emptiness at the window's bottom edge, increasingly familiar and intimate as years passed.

What if she had known that today was her last chance. For a showing as in Pentecost. Jewish ghost to Gentile apostles, their eyes all a-goggle, flabbergasted, humbled, scared. Nobody's fault it didn't occur. No different this morning, though it's my last. Her final chance, too. Sad she didn't know. Sad she may have moved out years ago. Too bad I won't be around tomorrow to tell her I'm up here today so we can be unhappy about it together, laugh about it together. Her name, if I knew it, on the note I won't write and leave behind for posterity.

Posterity. Pentecost. With a phone I could review both etymologies. Considered bringing a phone. Not really. Phone would tempt me to linger, call someone. One last call. To whom. No phone. Nowhere to put it if I had one. Maybe tucked in the waistband of my shorts. Little tuck of belly already stretching the elastic. Vanity versus necessity. So what if I bulge. But how to manage a call if I had a phone and someone to call. Freeing my hands would mean letting go of the thick pipe/railing, an unadvisable maneuver. Accidental fall funny. Not so funny, not acceptable, not my intent. Would spoil my show. A flawless Pentecost this morning, please.

Posterity, Pentecost, old-fashioned words hoisting themselves up on crutches, rattling, sighing their way through alleys and corridors of steel girders, struts, trusses, concrete piers. Noisy chaos of words graffitied on the pedestrian walkway: *Dheadt Refuse—Eat Me—Jew York—Poop Dick Dat*

Bitch—Honduras. Ominous silence of highway free of traffic as it never is except rarely after hours and even during the deepest predawn quiet a lone wolf car will blast across or weave drunkenly from lane to lane as if wincing from blows of wind howling, sweeping over the Williamsburg Bridge.

Why the most outmoded, most vexing word. Staggering across the Williamsburg Bridge one morning, buffeted by winds from every direction, headwind stiff enough to support my weight, leaning into it at a forty-five-degree angle, blinded by the tempest, flailing, fearing the undertow, the comic strip head-over-heels liftoff and blown away—goodbye, goody-bye, everybody—and I asked myself why the fuck are you up here, jackass, walking the bridge in this godforsaken weather, and that question—*why*—drum-drum-drumming in my eardrums, the only evidence of my sanity I was able to produce.

Why not let go. Escape whitespace. Fly away from this place where I teeter and totter, shiver, hold on to a cold iron rail, thighs pressed together like sissy girls afraid of the dark, clinging, hugging each other for warmth and company, fingers numb from gripping, toes frozen stiff, no air in my lungs or feathers. If I possess feathers. If I possess wings.

Always someone's turn at the edge, isn't it. Aren't you grateful it's me not you today. I'm your proxy. During the Civil War a man drafted into the Union Army could pay another man to enlist in his place. This quite legal practice of hiring a proxy to avoid a dangerous obligation of citizenship enraged those who could not afford the luxury, and to protest draft laws which in effect exempted the rich while the poor were compelled to serve as cannon fodder in Mr. Lincoln's bloody, unpopular war, mobs rioted in several Northern cities, most famously here in New York, where murderous violence lasted several days, ending only after federal troops were dispatched to halt the killing, beatings, looting, burning.

Poor people of color by far the majority of the so-called draft riots' victims. A not unnatural consequence given the fact mobs could not get their hands on wealthy men who had hired proxies and stayed behind locked doors of their substantial mansions in substantial neighborhoods protected by armed guards during the civil unrest. Poor colored people on the other hand easy targets. Most resided in hovels alongside hovels of poor whites, thus readily accessible, more or less simple to identify, and none of them possessed rights a white man required by law or custom to respect. Toll of colored lives heavy. I googled it.

So much killing, dying, when after all, a proxy's death can't save a person's life. Wall Street brokers who purchased exemption from death in the killing fields of Virginia didn't buy immortality. Whether Christ dies for our sins or not, each of us obligated to die. On the other hand the moment you learn your proxy killed in action at Gettysburg, wouldn't it feel a little like stealing a taste of immortality. Illicit rapture.

If suicide a crime, shouldn't martyrdom be illegal, too. Felony or misdemeanor. How many years for attempted martyrdom. Neither a life sentence nor capital punishment would have deterred Jesus. Terrorists not deterred either. Was Jesus serving time on Rikers Island when Sonny Rollins showed up. Did they jam together.

Sitting here today folded wings heavy as stone I can still imagine how it might feel to fly. I can imagine whitespace parting as wings, strokes, words enter it and form stories with beginnings, middles, ends. I can imagine such stories being written and printed, imagine myself and others inhabiting them, reading them, imagine how memories of what's been said or written seem real, but I cannot imagine where whitespace begins or ends. White pages whir past and dissolve. Myself printed, my invisible colored ink pushed across blank space. Blind leading the blind.

When you reach the edge you must decide to go further or not, to be free or not. If you hesitate, you get stuck like the unnamed, fair-skinned, young colored man in Reisner's photos. Better to let go quickly and maybe you will rise higher and higher because that's what happens sometimes when you let go—rapture. Why do fathers build wings if they don't want sons to fly; why do mothers bear sons if they don't want sons to die.

On TV I watched the arm of a starfish float away from its body. The diseased fish captive in a huge tank in a lab so its death could be observed and filmed by scientists. Arm separates, glides away, leaves a hole behind where it had detached itself, a dark wound leaking vital fluids and fluttery shreds of starfish. Loose arm long and straight, slightly tapered at one end, a hard, spiky-looking outer shell, interior soft, saturated with suckers. Off it floats, slowly, serenely, as if motivated by a will of its own. I could have easily believed the arm a new fish foraging in the tank's floodlit, murky water. Except an absolutely unimpeachable voice-over informed me the starfish is unable to regenerate lost limbs and a severed starfish limb unable to grow into a new starfish.

When I let go and topple backward, will I cause a splash, leave a mark. After the hole closes, how will the cops locate me. I regret not having answers, not completing my essay on whitespace. The plunge backward off my perch perhaps the last indispensable piece of research. As Zora Neale Hurston said, You got to go there to know there.

At the last minute for comfort's sake, for the poetry of departing this world as naked as I arrived, maybe I will remove these boxers. Why worry about other people's reactions. Trying to please other people a waste of time. At my age, I understand good and well my only captive audience is me. Myself. I. Any person paying too much attention to an incidental detail like shorts is dealing with her or his own problems, aren't they, and their problems by definition not mine. Allowing other people's hang-ups to influence my decisions gets things ass-backwards as the elders used to say. Perhaps people down below are my proxies—halt, lame, blind, broken-in-spirit, lost, abandoned, terrified, starving proxies saving me to live another day, ba-dup, ba-dup, buying time for me with their flesh-and-blood lives while I shiver and sway up here. Their sacrifices in vain, no doubt. I'm too close to the edge, too much whitespace to fall or fly or crawl across. I have no words to soothe other people's pain, to quiet their cries drum, drumming in my ears.

Can't seem to get underwear off my brain this last morning. Not mine, we're finished with mine, I hope. Though a woman's underwear in Paris, my undershorts today on the Williamsburg Bridge surprisingly similar, both made of the same no-frills white cotton cloth as little girls' drawers used to be. I'm seeing a lady's underwear and recalling another unlucky-in-love story. Last one I'll tell, I promise. A civil war precipitated by underwear. Not a murderous war like ours between the states. A small, bittersweet conflict. Tug-of-war when I begin pulling down a lady's underwear and she resists.

I was young, testing unclear rules, slippery rules because of slippery eel me. Civil war waged inside me by my slippery parts. I wished/wish to think of myself as a decent person, an equal partner, not tyrant or exploiter in my exchanges with others, especially women. Which meant that whatever transpired in Paris between a lady and me should have been her show, governed by her rules, but I was renting her time, thus proxy owner of her saffron skin, slim hips, breasts deep for a young woman. Why not play. Wrap a long, black, lustrous braid around my fist, pull her head gently back on her shoulders until her neck arches gracefully and she moans or whimpers deep in her throat.

I had asked her name and when she didn't respond immediately, repeated my French phrase—*comment t'appelles-tu*—more attention to pronunciation since she was obviously of Asian descent, a recent immigrant or illegal, maybe, and perhaps French not her native language. *Ana*, I thought she replied after I had asked a second, slower time. Then I shared my name, and said I'm American, a black American—*noir*—I said in case my pale color confused her. I asked her country of origin—*de quel pays*—another slight hesitation on her side before she said—*Chine*—or she could have said Ana again or the first Ana-like sound could have been *China*, I realized later. Her name a country. Country's name spoken in English, then French, an answer to both my inquiries.

Anyway her eagerness to please teased me with the prospect that perhaps no rules need inhibit my pleasure. I assumed all doors open if a tip generous enough added to the fee already collected by a fortyish woman on a sofa at the massage parlor's entrance on rue Duranton. Only unresolved issue the exact amount of *pourboire*. I didn't wish to spoil our encounter with market-stall haggling, so like any good translator, I settled for approximate equivalences and we performed a short, silent charade of nods, looks, winks, blinks, fingers to express sums and simulate acts, both of us smiling as we worked, hi-ho, hi-ho.

I trusted our bargain had reduced her rules to only one rule I need respect: pay and you can play. Her bright, black eyes seemed to agree. Resistance, they said, just part of the game, monsieur. Just be patient, *s'il vous plaît*. Play along. I may pretend to plead—no no no no—when your fingers touch my underwear, but please persist, test me.

Easy as pie for a while. Underwear slid down her hips to reveal an edge of dark pubic crest. Then not so easy after she flops down on the floor next to the mat, curls up knees to chest, and emits a small, stifled cry. Then it's inch by inch until underwear finally dangled from one bobbing ankle, snapped off finally, and tossed aside. A minute more and not a bit of shyness. Time machine purrs, rolls on, da-bup, da-bup.

Wish I could say I knew better. Knew when to stop, whether I paid or not for the privilege of going further. Wish I believed now that we were on the same page then. But no. Huh-uh. Like most of us I behaved inexcusably. Believed what I wanted to believe. Copped what I could because I could. No thought of limits, boundaries. Hers or mine. No fear of AIDS back then. Undeterred by the threat of hordes of Chinese soldiers blowing bugles, firing burp guns, ba-do-do-do-do-do as they descend across the Yalu River to attack stunned U.S. troops, allies of the South in a civil war, Americans who had advanced a bridge too far north and found themselves stranded, trapped, mauled, shivering, bleeding, dying in snowdrifts beside the frozen Chosin Reservoir.

No regrets, no remorse until years later, back home again ba-dup, ba-dup, and one afternoon Sonny Rollins practicing changes on the Williamsburg Bridge halts me dead in my tracks. Big colors, radiant bucketfuls splash my face. I spin, swim in colors. Enraptured. Abducted by angels who lift me by my droopy wings up, up, and away. Then they let go and I fall, plunge deeper and deeper into swirling darkness.

Am I remembering it right, getting the story, the timing right, the times, the fifties, sixties, everything runs together, happens at once, explodes, scatters.

I will have to check my journals. Google. Too young for Korea, too old for Iraq, student deferments during Vietnam. Emmett Till's exact age in 1955, not old enough to enlist nor be on my own in New York City, slogging daily like it's a job back and forth across the Williamsburg Bridge those years of Sonny's first sabbatical. When I hurried back to rue Duranton next morning to apologize or leave a larger tip, it was raining—*il pleut dans la ville*. No Ana works here I believe the half-sleep women on the sofa said.

I wish these dumb undershorts had pockets. Many deep, oversize pockets like camouflage pants young people wear. I could have loaded them with stones.

Before I go, let me confide a final regret: I'm sorry I'll miss my agent's birthday party. To be more exact it's my agent's house in Montauk I regret missing. Love my agent's house. Hundreds of rooms, marvelous ocean views, miles and miles of wooded grounds. One edge of the property borders a freshwater pond where wild animals come to drink, including timid, quivering deer. Stayed once for a week alone, way back when, before my agent had kids. Quick love affair with Montauk, a couple of whose inhabitants had sighted the *Amistad* with its cargo of starving, thirsty slaves in transit between two of Spain's New World colonies, slaves who had revolted and killed most of the ship's crew, the *Amistad* stranded off Montauk Point with a few surviving sailors at the helm, alive only because they promised to steer the ship to Africa, though the terrified Spaniards doing their best to keep the *Amistad* as far away from the dark continent as Christopher Columbus had strayed from the East Indies when he landed by mistake on a Caribbean island.

I know more than enough, more than I want to know about the *Amistad* revolt. Admire Melville's remake of the incident in *Benito Cereno*, but not tempted to write about it myself. One major disincentive, the irony of African captives who after years of tribulations and trials in New England courts were granted freedom, repatriated to Africa, and became slave merchants. Princely, eloquent Cinquez, mastermind of the shipboard rebellion, one of the bad guys. Cinquez, nom de guerre of Patty Hearst's kidnapper and lover. Not a pretty ending to the *Amistad* story. Is that why I avoided writing it. Is the Williamsburg Bridge a pretty ending. Yes or no, it's another story I won't write.

Under other circumstances, revisiting my agent's fabulous house, the ocean, memories of an idyll on Montauk might be worth renting a car, inching along in bumper-to-bumper weekend traffic through the gilded Hamptons. My agent's birthday after all. More friend than agent for years now. We came up in the publishing industry together. *Muy* simpatico. Rich white kid, poor black kid, a contrasting pair of foundlings, misfits, mavericks, babies together at the beginning of careers. *Muy* simpatico. Nearly the same age, fans of Joyce, Beckett, Dostoevsky, Hart Crane (if this were a time and place for footnotes, I'd quote Crane's most celebrated poem, *The Bridge*—"Out of some subway scuttle, cell or loft / A bedlamite speeds to thy parapets / Tilting there momently"—and add the fact Crane disappeared after he said "goodbye-goodbye-goodbye, everybody"—and jumped off a boat into the Gulf of Mexico). We also shared a fondness for Stoli martinis in which three olives replaced dry vermouth and both of us loved silly binges of over-the-top self-importance, daydreaming, pretending to be high rollers, blowing money neither had earned on meals in fancy restaurants, until I began to suspect the agency's charge card either bottomless or fictitious, maybe both.

Muy simpatico even after his star has steadily risen, highest roller among his peers, while my star dimmed precipitously, surviving on welfare, barely aglow. How long since my agent had sold a major piece of my writing, how long since I submitted a major new piece to sell. In spite of all the above, still buddies. Regret missing his party, Montauk, the house. House partly mine, after all. My labor responsible for earning a minuscule percentage of the down payment, *n'est-ce pas*. For nine months of the year no one inhabits the Montauk mansion. In France vacant dwellings are whitespace poor people occupy and claim, my mother had once informed me. Won't my agent's family be surprised next June to find my ghost curled up in his portion of the castle.

Last time in Montauk was when. Harder and harder to match memories with dates. One event or incident seems to follow another, but often I misremember. Dates out of sync, whitespace conflates and erases everything.

Except rapture. Rapture unforgettable, consumes whitespace. Sonny Rollins's sax squats on the Williamsburg Bridge, changes the sky's color, claims ownership of a bright day. Was I in fact walking the bridge those years Sonny Rollins woodshedding up here. I'll have to check my journals. But the oldest journals temporarily unavailable, part of the sample loaned to my agent to shop around.

I'm sure I can find a university happy to pay to archive your papers, he said.

Being archived a kind of morbid thought, but go right ahead, my friend. Fuckers don't want to pay for my writing while I'm alive, maybe if I'm dead they'll pay.

Stoppit. Nobody's asking you to jump off a bridge. Nothing morbid about selling your papers. Same principle involved as selling backlist.

So do it, okay. Still sounds like desperation to me, like a last resort.

Just the opposite. I tempt publishers with posterity, remind them the best writing, best music never ages. Don't think in terms of buying, I lecture the pricks. Think investment. Your great-great-grandkids will dine sumptuously off the profits.

Whoa. Truth is I've got nothing to sell except whitespace. What about that. How much can you get for whitespace.

What in hell are you talking about.

Come on. You know what I mean: whitespace. Where print lives. What eats print. White space. That Pakistani guy. Ana . . . Ana . . . la-di-la-di-da-da . . . something or other who wrote the bestseller about black holes. Prize client of yours, isn't he. Don't try and tell me you or all the people buying the book understand black holes. Black holes. White space. White holes. Black space. What's the difference.

Whitespace could be a bigger blockbuster than black holes. No words . . . just whitespace. Keep my identity a secret. No photos, no interviews, no distracting particulars of color, gender, age, class, national origin. Anonymity will create mystery, complicity—whitespace everybody's space, everybody welcome, everybody will want a copy. Whitespace an old friend, someone you bump into in the Houston airport lounge. Wow—look who's here. Great to see you again. Big hug, big kiss. Till death do us part.

The *Amistad* packed with corpses and ghosts drifts offshore behind me. Ahoy—ahoy, I holler and wave at two figures way up the beach. No clue where we've landed. I'm thinking water, food, rescue, maybe we won't starve or die of thirst after all. The thought dizzying like too much to drink too fast after debilitating days of drought. Water, death roil around in the same empty pit inside me. Faraway figures like two tiny scarecrows silhouetted against a gray horizon. They must be on the crest of a rise and I'm in a black hole staring up. Like me they've halted. I stop breathing, no water sloshing inside me, no waves slap my bare ankles, roar of ocean subsided to a dull flat silence. My companions stop fussing, stop clambering out of the flimsy rowboat behind me. Everybody, everything in the universe frozen. Some fragile yet deeply abiding protocol of ironclad rules, obscure and compelling, oblige me to wait, not to speak nor stir until those alien others, whose land this must be, wave or run away or beckon or draw swords, fire muskets.

The pair of men steps in our direction, then more steps across the grayish whitespace. They are in booths making calls. Counting, calculating with each approaching step, each wobble, what it might be worth, how much bounty in shiny pieces of silver and gold they could collect in exchange for bodies, a rowboat, a sailing ship that spilled us hostage on this shore.

My Friends, calls out the taller one in a frock coat, gold watch on a chain. His first words same words Horatio Seymour, governor of New York, addressed in 1863 to a mob of hungover, mostly Irish immigrants, their hands still red from three or four days of wasting colored children, women, and men in draft riots.

I'm going to go now. What took you so long, I bet you're thinking and maybe wonderingly why—*why* this moment, and since you've stuck with me this long, I owe you more than, *why not*—so I'll end with what I said to my false-hearted lover in one of our last civil conversations when she asked, What's your worst nightmare.

Worst nightmare. Good question.
So answer me already.
Never seeing you again.

Come on. Seriously.
Seeing you again.
Stoppit. Stop playing and be serious.
Okay. Serious. Very super serious. My worst nightmare is being cured.
Cured of what.
What I am. Of myself.
Cured of yourself.

Right. Cured of who I am. Cured of what doesn't fit, of what's inappropriate and maybe dangerous inside me. Cured absolutely of me, myself, I. You know. Cured like people they put away—way, way far away behind bars, stone walls, people they chain, beat on, shock with electric prods, drug, exile to desert-island camps in Madagascar or camps in snowiest Siberia or shoot, starve, hang, gas, burn, or stuff with everything everybody believes desirable and then display in store windows, billboard ads, on TV, in movies, perfectly stuffed, lifelike, animated cartoon animals.

Lying naked in bed next to naked her I said that my worst nightmare is not the terrible cures nor fear I fit in society's category of people needing cures. Worst nightmare is not damage I might perpetrate upon others or myself. Worst nightmare, my Love, the thought I might live a moment too long. Wake up one morning cured and not know I'm cured.

P.S.—the other day, my friends, believe it or not, I saw a woman scaling the bridge's outermost restraining screen. Good taste or not I ran toward her shouting my intention to write a story about a person jumping off the Williamsburg Bridge, imploring her as I got closer for a quote. "Fuck off, buddy," she said over her naked shoulder. Then she said—*Splash.*

Nat Turner Confesses

N at Turner no stranger to me. The grad-school education I'd been privileged to receive in the early 1960s included an American Studies course which mentioned slave revolts and named a few slaves responsible for bloody, short-lived, essentially futile outbreaks of violence that occurred before Lincoln's Emancipation Proclamation and the Civil War ended legal slavery in America. My curiosity led me to discover a handful of radical, left-wing scholars who specialized in uncovering and preserving evidence of slave resistance to bondage. Thanks to the research of those scholars I learned more about Gabriel Prosser, Denmark Vesey, Nat Turner, etc., and rebellions they had perpetrated. More information, of course, piqued my curiosity for more. But not the kind of curiosity that killed the cat. My good liberal education was also instilling moderation. Instructing me how to divide and conquer. Conquer and divide myself first. A very large, unforgiving, ruthless world out there and no one—especially some lucky someone like me who had been granted a special pass to enter places reserved for people not my color—could afford to squander time and resources on projects leading nowhere. Except to the dead ends of history, to dead people buried in the rubble who had wasted their lives in hopeless quests.

Nat Turner addresses the spectators with silence. A goodly number had turned out to see him hanged and he is pleased. The more of them shivering under a slight drizzle this dismal morning, the easier it is for him to say nothing. Easier to wish he'd begun the work of killing them sooner, these strangers and the few he might recognize if he cast his eyes about the throng, dark faces here and there among white faces he's sure, the ones ordered by masters to attend this edifying spectacle, or dark faces peeking curious, wide-eyed, pretending to be invisible at the edges of the crowd, and though he blinds himself to it, he hears and smells the mob fragrant as the pig yard where someone not him, thank goodness, must be shoveling mud and shit already at this hour. A rabble boiling around the hasty scaffold, this cross erected in a farmer's field just beyond Jerusalem. So many white faces it's easier to forgive himself and his band for not completing the work of eliminating them all, every single one, as he'd conceived in his plan and exhorted the others, returning in one instance to a ransacked dwelling, strewn with corpses of a family they had just murdered, to bash in the skull of an infant girl he remembered they'd missed in an upstairs nursery. One by one, every single guilty one of them, man, woman, child slaughtered until he and his recruits had emptied Southampton, Virginia, the entire world, or until they, themselves, cut down.

Not a word Nat Turner desires to speak to anyone today, not a person he wishes to see, only the dead, his loyal troops who did not survive, scores of innocent folk, men, women, children rounded up on plantations, from village streets, swamps, woods, and rumored to have paid with their lives for his sins, the Emmetts and Trayvons murdered as if guilty of riding with Nat Turner that August night of killing, and yes, oh yes, speak a last word to his poor wife beaten unmercifully until she produced, they say, "odd papers written in blood" then stripped and whipped again, as if a flesh-and-blood woman whose husband long a ghost to her could reveal his whereabouts, as if her naked flesh privy to his secrets. Sorry, sorry, he might whisper to his lost bride, to those victims he served.

Then Thomas Gray intrudes. Not his face picked out from the crowd. Thomas Gray's gray face not seen from the scaffold this last morning. He's invisible as the other spectators, invisible as I had been while he read my so-called confession to the court at my trial. Confession Gray had written himself and claimed that I, the accused, had dictated to him. Gray's lying voice heard again here in this moment of truth, the moment people say no one dares violate with an untruth because death imminent, and we fear God's all-knowing stare.

I would relish an opportunity to watch the eyes of Thomas Gray—my inquisitor, lawyer, judge, jury, priest, executioner as he variously styled himself—watch his eyes consume letter by letter, word by word, not the counterfeit confession he authored. Watch him pelted by the witness I bear, the truth of this unfolding tale I compose to occupy myself during these final minutes while I stand beneath a gallows fitted with three hooks and ropes, standing above a mob that now mutters and seethes as it grows more restless, impatient because I say nothing, my lips stones, though I believe, in the instant Gray meets his creator, he must listen to every word I brew now, words scourging him, words streaming, stinging up from my belly to my heart to my silent mouth this morning.

May Thomas Gray hear my confession, not his. My words. Not the words he's written and intends to publish for great profit, a businessman like others in the crowd who wait for my body to be cut down so they can strip patches of my skin, chunks of my flesh and peddle them as Christians once peddled splinters of the true cross.

As a boy I learned to read. Taught myself names of letters, sounds of letters that are also their names. Learned the alphabet: A–Z.

A = an apple. Apple bitten ends darkness. Animals wake up to light which is another dark. Animals see what they have never seen before. See themselves and see one another and it's the beginning of the end. A–Z. Alone. Not alone. A–Z begins with first taste of A for apple. First open eye. First glimpse of what a world is. What a person is not. World holds others like you and unlike you. Creatures with nothing to do with you. Separate. Like rivers, trees, mountains, sky, snow, a bird, shadows. And everything not you burns, roars loudly or silently. Creatures hungry, hunt, haunt a world beginning and ending with the alphabet that begins with letter A. Ends with letter Z.

B = Book = Bible. Be. Bee bee busy bumble bee. Buzzy, fuzzy, striped B for bug with wings, stings, hives, honey. To be in pain. b. To begin to read the Bible letter by letter because each letter a sound, the world an empire of sounds buzzing in your ears, noises people make, world makes. Bee crawls, slow, striped black and yellow, and you catch it in your fist, listen, crush, squash it. No buzz. Before it was a bug, a bee, but nothing now, even when you open your fist, open your eyes, only darkness. Read dark, darker, darkest. Bible opens to letter A, to letter B, alpha to beta, A–Z, I read somewhere and learn to sound out names for god, suckle at the alpha-beta tit, listen to

blood-red, white milk squeezed up sweet inside, singing inside warm pillow of skin, sometimes it puts me to sleep, wakes me up in the deep, down
darkness, deep quiet again—being alone with only God again—still as a
squashed bug, squashed b—it's not Him, not me, not it—broken—but,
because many, many Bs—busy, busy b's—b b b—you could spell a world
with nothing but b. Beginning begotten baby born black butt big boy bigger
better best blest bought beaten beast behave beg blind until he learns C,
the next letter, and learns next, and next creature, because black boy learns
(A–Z) to read God's Book.

    C: See with eye. C sounds like see. Eye sounds like I. Eyes C. I see
sounds like *icy*. Icy makes you slip and fall. Feet up over head. Head down
under feet. Happy little white girls and boys bundled in bright, happy colors
skate on ice in Lil Miss book. What is ice. Ice cold, dummy. White, smooth,
slippery ice. You slip and fall and fall, if you not careful. Boom down you
go. C, I told you so, dummy. Crack your noggin. Hard head nigger noggin. I
told u so. U better b careful. Or when you C eyes first time you fall. What is
ice. Not nice. White, white eyes everywhere, cold, colder, coldest after dark,
after sun goes down. No ice here, see, c, it's there in picture book, God's
snow and tall mountains and his children in bright colors fast as deer, his
cold ice and hot sand of his deserts you will never see, you sleep, fall asleep
and darkness wakes u, u C, eyes see pictures in books with pages u cannot
turn, pages turning too fast, too slow, pictures with no pages your eyes see.
Icy. You slip and fall. See nothing. Eyes cold white as God's ice everywhere.

    D for Dread. Dream. Did. Dirty. Deed. I did it. I admit I did. Fucked her,
yes. Did it, but swear I'm not happy or proud I did it. Swear she said okay.
Not all slave masters enjoyed screwing their slaves. Whipping slaves. Slavery, yes, a terrible, terrible institution, I admit it, and we all agree, but still
not all masters the same. There were good guys and bad guys. Bad apples but
some decent, too. Not everybody roots for the same team. Always winners
and losers. Heroes and goats. Why shouldn't I be a winner for a change. Me,
Nate Parker, and my underdog, underground railroad team. We did it. Made
a Nat Turner movie and everyone promises it's a hit. On top for once. Let
me tell you it hasn't been easy. Making a movie not a cakewalk. Not one easy
step along the way. And not easy now. Even now after a winning score in the
book declares me a winner. On top at last. Free at last. Film in the can. Hand
in the till. Here, let me sprinkle some this honey money on your tongues,

my brothers. No fun all these years being exploited. Called bad or evil or flatout ignored. But if you are willing to forget and forgive, I am. We can go from here. New start. New season. Put the bad times behind us. What's over is over. And done. Let's put that bad stuff out our minds. I'm willing if you are. New day. New game. What makes America great, the game great, is it not, my sisters and brothers of all colors. Thank you for this opportunity. This chance to perform. Said I was sorry, didn't I. Didn't Mr. Gray read my confession. Can't you hear my sobs of remorse. Let bygones be bygones. Let's all us be free at last. Why lynch me now. Won't bring back the dead. We got our whole history in front of us. Let's do it, Maceo. Give the drummer some. Let the good times roll. Promise youall I'll be a good boy. Hardest worker in showbiz.

E: With about forty Es lined up in a row, a long chain gang of Es maybe different sizes, shapes, colors, letters strung out one after another, would the sound of all those Es make the sound of a mule you might hear dawn or dusk mad cause it's tired, hurt, broke, pissed, weary, tired of being whipped, winded, trembling at the knees, long mule neck aching so bad, not one more mule step left in skinny mule legs, emaciated mule muscles, nothing left to do except squeal eeeeeeeeeeeeeeeeee till the final mule breath exits its mule-assed body, mule-assed soul. Eeeeeeeeeeeeeeeee.

F: Father. Fast, flee, freedom, friend. Fount of wisdom. Foundation. Founder. Fire, fear, flee, feast, famine. Father forgive. Flay me. Fly me. Far, far away.

G: Only one sound, one letter, and I am unworthy. They say I am forbidden to utter, to spell it—only G. No other letters. Only an empty space after G—— for my god's name.

If you believe you already know my story, perhaps you should stop here. The story you know suffices. You will discover nothing useful in what I have to relate. Nothing that will raise doubts or supplant truths or untruths inside you that you have transported until your life's journey progressed to this point where you find me offering my alphabet, my tale, my confession as if it begins here, gushing new like pure water from a pristine mountain stream, when both of us, though we speak separate languages, understand the fact my life, like yours, has been unraveling a long, long time and we are both past the point of going back or starting over, strangers in this moment we might prefer to be a moment of truth, strangers to each other and ourselves as we pass by, as we exchange words weightless as strangers passing by.

Sad day yesterday.

Heavy day, sure enough.

Lil Miss coffin didn't weigh much. Mize well be feathers in there.

Not carrying a coffin what I'm talking bout. Talking about tears. All that crying. Ole Missus and them so sad. And fixing to rain all morning before we dig that hole put the box in the ground.

See. You just didn't want get wetted up. Fraid your black ass gon melt it get wet.

Know what you can do for my black ass, nigger.

Turrible day. Turrible sad, what I'm saying.

Not your mama in the box. Nor your daughter they sold away last planting season.

I decided to kill white people when the voice I hear sometimes in my head reasoning with me said you don't need them. Need no one to tell me I am not one of them and never would be. Don't need masters. Do not need the heaven and hell in their churches. Nor the hell on earth they make of this Virginia. Don't need fellow slaves. Nor slave rags and slave rations and slave quarters. Don't need nasty sheep to tell me I am a nasty goat and don't belong in the sheep pen.

I found it strange then, since I had been persuaded, agreed whole-heartedly, I thought, with the voice of reason, strange that once I had commenced the killing, strange that at first, each time my turn to strike a fatal blow, fear or panic or pity or something else I have yet to fathom, caused me to hesitate. Standing over the bed of sleeping Joseph Travis—appropriately our first victim since he was owner of the plantation on which I, leader of the plot, resided—I struck him several times with a hatchet, but Will's assistance necessary to dispatch him. When I attacked Miss Newsome with my sword, Will's implacable ax was required again to deliver the fatal blow. In the side yard of her family's dwelling, Mrs. Margaret Whitehead grabbed my hand and pleaded, but I struck her numerous times with my sword, causing her to collapse to the ground, though she didn't die until I snatched up a loose fence railing and crushed her skull. Were these mishaps the result of small, inadequate weapons, or my novice's ineptitude at killing. Or did I hesitate, temper blows in each instance, because I still believed if I eradicated them, I might miss the presence of white people.

I am called Nat Turner, a name made up for the convenience of sellers and purchasers of me. A made-up name like I invented a name for the voice inside me, calling it God's voice when I endeavored to describe the source of words no one besides me able to hear. Though that source, I must admit, far beyond my poor wits to fathom and remains impossible for me to explicate, I tried with all my powers to share the words of the source with my brethren in chains. Attempted to convince them that if they listened carefully to words that seemed to issue from my lips, they would hear more than Nat Turner speaking. Prophecies and mysteries would descend upon all of us when we gathered in secret places in the woods.

WHITE PEOPLE DO NOT CHANGE. WILL NOT CHANGE. SO THEY HAVE CHANGED YOU. WROUGHT YOU—BENT, TWISTED, EMPTIED YOU—TO BE WHO YOU ARE. ARE YOU SOMEONE YOU WISH TO BE. OR SOMEONE WHITE PEOPLE WISH YOU TO BE. YOU ARE INSIDE THEIR PLAN, NAT TURNER. BUT NOT INSIDE THEM, NAT TURNER. THEY ARE INSIDE YOU. REMOVE THEM. REMOVE YOURSELF FROM THEIR PLAN.

I began life with a mother and father. Like everyone does. Like you, like Mr. Thomas Ruffin Gray, I started with an Eve, an Adam. Though Eve and Adam not my parents' names, just conveniences I'm making up, like the name slavers fabricated for me. My mother's and father's names lost and forgotten long ago. The names they happened to bear when I was born had been passed out like tools passed out to field hands to serve their masters. Name to distinguish one piece of livestock from another, a name obliging you to come when it's called and face dire punishment if you don't respond quickly enough, names to shame or make fun of our condition, names stamping us as belonging to somebody, somebody's property branded with a name not connecting us to our mothers, fathers, sisters, brothers, ancient blood families preceding us in time, names erasing kin we are supposed to, taught to forget, names like mine, Nat Turner, who as far as I know never possessed another. Nor a family in whose bosom I was secure, protected as it was said white people we slaved for guarded their offspring.

Nevertheless, I was an extremely fortunate child. Still inside my mother's belly when she was ordered to the big house to serve Mrs. Travis and wet-nurse the infant Mrs. Travis expected. Extremely fortunate that after a baby everybody called Lil Miss born to the Travises, I was born, too, and accompanied my mother daily to the big house where she waited upon Mrs. Travis— suddenly Big Miss or Ole Miss or Ole Missus behind her back—and nursed the new daughter with whom you might as well say I shared a birthday.

My mother, less fortunate than me, told me, You two babies long wit everything else I had to do just bout killed me, boy. Said she carried us two, one on either hip, one at either titty, she said youall alike as two peas in a pod, except one pea white, other pea black, and my mother smiled when she said it, and said, Young and strong as I was you two wore me out said too much work to do around the house, always more, chore after chore, kitchen, nursery, them two older chillens needing me, scrub, tidy this room then that and you babies hanging on to me mize well be twins, twin trouble, double whining and double hollering and double wet and stinky and sick and mischief, and running off and hiding or fighting or into something you ain't got no business being in soon as the two of you large enough to get up on two legs or four legs you could say, my, my, the two of you had my poor head spinning round trying to keep up, lay you down at night, my son, then dropped down myself like a dead person on that mat in the little closet kinda room behind Ole Miss Travis room lots of nights but seem like quick as a person could say Jack Robinson one or the other of you screaming in one or the other room, then both fussing and it's starting up again weary as I am it's starting again and I'ma tell you the God's truth you two little devils just bout killed me and Ole Miss all laid up in bed all whiskey-headed and mumble bout this or that nothing or laid up under her soft sheets and wool blankets snoring never lift a finger to help.

They say Lil Miss made funny down there.
   Say no babies
   Say husband say he gon send her back to her daddy's house
   Say Ole Miss say you got her, keep her
   Say the husband beat her like a dog, hurt her bad like he beat his people
   Say his people say he turrible mean
   Say listen at you, fool, they all mean
   Say Lil Miss not mean
   Say uh-huh and Lil Miss dead

When you fall asleep in another person's dream, what happens if you awaken. Where are you. Who will you be. Have you become the dream's dreamer. The Dream. Perhaps you awaken and see yourself sprawled like one of her rag dolls Lil Miss props up to imitate the way she sits when she pretends to read, or perhaps she copies a doll sprawling in a corner, crumpled, soft, head drooping, wide-apart legs and butt resting flat on the floor, or knees steepled, seamed white cotton crotch exposed, back leaned against the wall, sitting so she appears alive reading or dead or asleep, you watching, waiting for her to scold and chase you away or coodle-coo and say come play.

We were children. Two of us growing up alone, many, many hours, most of most days and some nights spent together. Curious children. We looked at, touched, tasted each other. Playmates. Curious children. Play-named each other. My mother's duty to care for both of us daily. Blackee. Missee. My mother occupied by other duties, left us to fend for ourselves at an early age. No, no, no, Mrs. Travis hollered at my mother, her peer in age and both about to give birth. No daughter of mine raised in the nigger pen full of little dirty niggers. No. You bring yours here to keep her company.

Many hours. Many days alone. Children together. Curious. Learning. Uncovering secrets. Inventing games, names. One mother busy, busy. One mother absent. One burdened with way too many duties. One burdened with no duties. We were children left alone. Explored secret patches of yard outdoors, secret patches of rooms indoors. We learned every inch, inside and out. Every hidden hiding place. Laughed, tickled, scratched, whispered. Shared secrets. And when tired or bored or outraged we fought like beasts. Screamed. Sulked. Sullen. Made up riddles so the other one couldn't know the answer. Teased. Hurt each other. Licked. Pinched. Sniffed each other. Children growing inside each other. Away from each other. Girl. Boy. One of us could be both, or be the other one or chase away the other until the other missed too much by both, until the other returned and we could be one again.

As a convenience—like the convenience of naming slaves—in order to shape the telling of my story and to deliver my confession in the most convincing fashion, I could name that period of my life before the great and total separation demanded then and now, the separation of children into different kinds and different worlds, I could call my first four or five years on earth "Eden," except to borrow that name for any time or place in Virginia would mock both Bible story and mine.

Blackee. Missee. Children. I watched her squat and pee. Nap. Weep. Ash on your black legs, she said. Nasty, ashy white. Go away. Or said, "Sulphur." Never heard that word, I bet, dummy boy. Devil smell. Preacher Wilson said it's Devil smell. Sulphur. You stink like the Devil, natty. Go way, you dum-dum dummy boy. Stinkee, Sulphur boy. No. Come over here, nattykins. Let me lick your round black pot of belly. Tummy boy. Boy tummy with a little sprouty root down there. Weedy sprout. Not like nigger sprouts, nigger bare bottoms in the fields. Bare black asses under long shirts. Bend over show their bottoms. Bend over chopping weeds, grass. Show their business. Show long, rooty nigger legs. Long knives chop, swing back and forth, back and forth. Chop grass, weeds, cotton. Blades swing, swinging like Nanny used to tie us a swing on a low branch and swing us back and forth. Low branch above low roots running along the ground, roots popping out the ground like old, twisted gray old Devil fingers. No hair, no weeds around your tiny rooty little hair down there. Not like grown hairy niggers. Not like my mama. My father I seen him, too. See. Come here, scaredy cat. Mama dead drunk look like she sleeping she dead as a dead frog. Look, Blackee. Don't be scaredy cat. See me touch her, see, Mama's black black bush. See I touch it. Dare you. I see your big white eyes looking. Go on and touch it. Look at all that black nigger hair dead as a dead frog, natty, touch it, dare you touch it. Someday mine growing black like her. Promise I let you touch mine. Let you sleep in it, let you live in my dark patch, natty boy.

Somewhere before the age of five or six, as they used to do things and will continue doing forever would be my guess, the great separation prevented me from accompanying my mother to the big house and I was assigned endless, mindless chores each day, chores to keep me busy, keep me with all the other little niggers in the little nigger yard or pigpen or garden, barn, outhouse, chicken coop, manure pile, garbage pit, etc. Anywhere except the big house. No errand, no question or urgent need for my mother served as an excuse to go anywhere near the Travis dwelling. A few scoldings and beatings clarified the dangers, the price of breaking the rule. Soon I was a boy large enough to go chop down forests, drain swamps, dig out stumps and boulders to clear fields that became new land where we would sow, cultivate, reap, and harvest white people's crops, a perpetual round of labors which profited others and kept niggers possessionless, hungry, poor, dependent, evil, exhausted. One day someone told Mr. Travis, Nat Turner can read, and I confessed to him and he tested me, discovered not only was I literate but could write and cipher. You are a peculiar one, Nat Turner, he said, finally, and a peculiarly smart one and steady, too, a hard worker, the overseers tell me, and I'd be a foolish businessman not to take advantage of your skills, to waste you on nigger work, wouldn't I, Nat Turner.

Little by little, step by closely watched step, I found myself assigned new tasks that required me to be decently dressed and reasonably clean of field muck and stench, tasks performed in the big house under the scrutiny of Travis, who gradually put more and more trust in me until I was more or less his jack-of-all-trades assistant (not immune, however, from occasional episodes of nigger work) summoned daily to receive a long list of chores, though very different chores than those my mother had complained almost killed her, but chores that kept me constantly occupied, like her, sunup to sundown and many hours more. By then, during my apprenticeship as clerk, overseer, buyer, seller, manager, etc., learning to fulfill impeccably the expectations of Travis and on my good days even anticipate them, Lil Miss was long gone, naturally, from the big house I frequented.

With a burnt black end of stick I had practiced writing letters of the alphabet on my palm. If caught, one hard swipe, rub against my shirttail or trouser leg and no evidence. Just a dirty nigger hand like nigger hand supposed to be dirty. Dark ash shows well on pink palm of hand. Easy to trace letters there. My hand not a large hand, not small, a middling size for a middling-sized fellow like me. Middling-size hands, feet, and the rest. Good enough, I think. No hand big enough to fit the whole alphabet. Even drawing letters with a point not clumsy as the nub of stick. How many letters fit if I practice smaller and smaller, I wondered. If letters small enough, how many words might fit on my palm. If hand bigger, letters smaller, could my palm hold a book. How many words in a book. Did I know enough words to fill a book. How many words could I spell. A book is many words spelled correctly with letters of the alphabet to make sentences, make sense, make a book. If I could spell many words correctly and write them with smaller and smaller letters, how many books might fit on my palm. Books so small, how would anybody read them. But if I wrote the letters, words, books, tracing them on my skin, wouldn't they be there whether anybody else able to see them or not.

Look, Nat, Mr. Joseph Travis said. My eyes obey and fasten on a brightly painted wooden ball, recently purchased, hollow inside as a dried gourd. I can detect the seam gluing together two halves of this globe, as Travis calls it, gripped by an iron claw that allows it to rotate atop a black iron pedestal in this room he calls a study. This ball a map of the entire world, he confides. This globe you're looking at, Nat, holds every place on earth—England, Italy, China, France, Rome, America. Brings every place on earth here for us to see in this room in Southampton, Virginia, where we stand. A round map of the known world. North Pole. Africa. No place missing. Almost magical, isn't it, Nat.

Both my hands, as if tied together at the wrists, are behind me, invisible to Travis. The globe too large. Too much of it for a runaway's feet to flee. Too much world to fly across to freedom. Fingers of one hand tighten, crush all the countries. All the white people inhabiting them, all the people wearing black, yellow, red skins, gaudy colors like the painted globe wears. Squeeze, crush until the map, the miles, people, the globe shrink small as a kernel of corn in my fist. I can throw it away or put it in my mouth and chew it, swallow or spit it out. This small, round world large enough to hold a master's study, this room in which Travis speaks and I listen, both taller than the globe Travis spins now atop its black iron pedestal. Travis taller than me as he rotates the globe and talks, talking as if he owns it, understands every place on it, this room with two men in it, his dwelling with its cellars, porches, shutters, columns, portico, stairways, attics, kitchens on a slave plantation, the map large enough to hold me, hold every alphabet letter, every word, and small enough to fit on one of my palms.

I refuse to believe the globe. No magic. No map. The North Star—God's cold, bright eye—only map a runaway should trust. Distant as it seems, that faraway light also inside, leading, guiding, all the map required to escape earthly bondage.

Show me my footprints on this globe you purchased. Where do the quarters fit. The chains. How could every shifting grain of grit or sand or puddle of pig shit under my bare toes be repeated here, preserved, doubled exactly, once and for all, but then again and again as it spins, here like mountains, rivers, clouds, animals, leaves, leaf by leaf and all leaves growing, dying over and over on a globe holding this room, this land holding us and being embraced in turn, Virginia a convenient name for a place holding this house, the silence, order, and tranquillity of this moment I can hear Travis yearning to hold, embrace, celebrate, to sing a little praise song inside himself about this place, about this precise present moment, as if he could, as if he were a singing type of man, though he isn't, though in the silence I can imagine hearing him sing, as if he could, and I imagine Lil Miss propped up in a corner of wall, legs spraddled, mouth moving, pretending to read a book before she could read, before we helped each other learn. Travis praising the globe he rotates, his fingertips giving more a glancing caress than hitting the empty shell's wooden skin to keep it turning, Travis silent now so he can listen as if there's a song in this room coming from his lips.

I lean a ladder against a chimney behind the house and will climb it, step through a window into the bedroom where Travis sleeps. The day is August 21, 1831. I've known how to read since I was a boy. Taught myself at an early age clock time, calendars, how to write the name Nat Turner, the name Joseph Travis of the man who claims to own me, whom I intended to kill the past spring but I took ill, so will kill him today, August 21, 1831. Him first, then every other plantation owner, their women and children, relatives, white minions from here to Jerusalem. Perhaps when our work completed, I will write their names in a ledger. A thick black ledger to save names of whites murdered tonight, and runaways, and those who die trembling with fear of us and disappear into thin air. We must cleanse the countryside of them because we no longer require white people to tell us what to do, tell us our names, the hour, day of the week, month, year, color of our flesh.

Until we rid ourselves of them, until they are gone, we will not truly cleanse ourselves of the belief that we are nothing without them.

With each step up a ladder leaned against the back chimney's stones, rung by rung, I feel my feet rising higher, closer to freedom. Still, surrounded by night's darkness and silence, afloat, suspended as always between one instant and the next, when I enter the window open against August's sweltering heat, when my feet are planted on a solid wooden floor, will the first blow of my hatchet prove fatal. Or will I hesitate, temper the blow because I'm still afraid I might need white people. Nowhere, no one without them.

What's Egyptland, natty boy. Niggers sing Egyptland when they sad, sometimes sing it happy. My blanket my Egyptland, little nat. Wraps it round me at night. Rub my nose with a corner when I suck my thumb. Smell my sweet blankey, nat-nat. Egyptland in it. Me, you in it.

No, you say. No-no. Stinky, you say. How dare you. Get your black ass over here this instant. Get over here and bend over. Take your beating, bad, bad boy. Say yes. Say sweet. Say Egyptland.

Ole Miss sent for me and here I am standing at the foot of her bed. Does she remember me. Does she know she will die asleep in this same room adjacent to her husband's while we dispatch him. Who is this large boy, I hear her eyes asking herself. No. I'm grown now. Man-size. No. Not man. Boy. Because if boy her girl still lives. This black something, standing here eyes lowered, mute as a mule, thick as a mule. Stink of him filling the room or is it already full she's asking, her dank flesh, hot breath reeking, room crowded with stench of death, sick vapors rising off wet, rumpled bedclothes. She is not afraid of dying, except if she dies, how will her poor baby find her, her poor lost girl wandering, haunting dark corners of the room: I'm back. I'm here, Mama. Where are you.

Who sent you here, you black imp. To mock me with your "condolences," your white word in nigger lips. You know better than to enter my bedroom. Someone put you up to this. A meddler. A fool.

You say I sent for you. "Summoned," you say, minstrel man. You grinning pillar of salt. You Devil mask. Why would I ever "summon" you. Your presence an abomination. Here where I grieve. Reminding me God took her and let you live. Breath in your body belongs to her. Stolen from her. As you stole her time. Why does God let your heart beat while hers has stopped. If I could snatch your bloody beast heart from your chest and plant it in her, I would. I detest you, Nat Turner. Your hateful presence reminding me she's not here . . .

Oh, Nat. Pitiful Nat. And pitiful me. If only I could take you like a baby in my arms. Hug you close to me. As if it would bring her back. Please. Please, go away. Let me die. Leave me my empty peace. My oblivion. My mother's grief. Make my child alive again, Nat Turner. My baby. Oh, let me touch you. Let me hug.

I could have begun this confession by speaking first of my father. With my time for telling stories almost over now, with a bloodthirsty mob milling around me, I regret I have not talked more about him, with him. I must admit—chagrined, ashamed—that I know very little about him aside from my mother's stories, mentions of him by my brethren in recollections they exchange to entertain one another. I'm able to put a face on gray Thomas Gray, but no face for my father. Except perhaps a shadowed version of my colored face. Yet at a crucial juncture when I needed to gain my brethren's trust in order to go forward with my plan to liberate us all, I called upon my father, used my father to allay their suspicions and doubts.

I confess today I again need his name. To steal his name. Be him. As if his name bestows his determination, clarity of purpose, ruthlessness, refusal to turn back and accept failure. My story could not exist without his. No promise of freedom, no uprising, no bloodshed, no record of violence released or violence suppressing violence, no numbing sense of futility, no guilt without him. Without the denial, the silencing of him.

A father, of course, part of a story you know already about me. No person on earth begins life without a father's seed. I could have started my story there—with his undeniable presence, but a presence slavery's evil constantly denied so that when I attempt memories of my father, I can only recall times he was absent. Father separated. Father withheld. Father embodied in words, thoughts, not a flesh-and-blood father. Father a runaway, a fugitive before I reached my fourth year. Runagate who escaped and never returned, never seen again.

My father must have been strong-minded and probably accumulated much wisdom and many practical skills he began perhaps to pass on to me before he ran away. I will never know what kind of man I might have turned out to be with him beside me daily. I am certain I inherited his strong back. They say a brother of my father was whipped to a whimpering pulp by an overseer's slave lackey and lay bleeding in a cotton field miles from the big house. Overseer said, Leave the nigger, but my father begged, Please, please, let me carry him, and overseer didn't stop my father from kneeling and slinging his brother over his shoulder and trudging all those miles back. But like Lil Miss returning to her father's house after what everybody said was a miscarriage, my daddy's brother dead when he arrived.

At the point it was necessary to enlist them, I began to share with my brethren my plan to seize freedom for us all. At first Will, Hark, Henry, Nelson did not trust me. Nor my plan, nor the spirit voice I claimed instructed me, nor secret meetings in the forest, nor my sudden enthusiasm for freedom. My initial four recruits—court would call them "co-plotters"—proved loyal, brave to the end. Despite their initial misgivings and mine. They had long been accustomed to regarding Nat Turner as odd—a solitary, private one who maintained a distance from his fellow sufferers, one who unless conveying orders from the big house seldom spoke, waited for others to start conversations. I worshipped differently, was rumored to speak to voices no one else could hear. My privileges and small property were resented. My seeming intimacy with Travis compromised any prospect of intimacy with them. Perhaps most disquieting and inexplicable was the fact I had been a successful runaway, then returned voluntarily to servitude. How could they trust a man who had spurned his own precious freedom.

Obviously, my plan required soldiers, so I was desperate to regain my brethren's confidence. Used my father. Most knew he was a runaway, a true runagate who had fled, disappeared, never seen again. I told them my mother had shared stories of my father with me. His promise to return at night and steal away with wife and son he dearly loved, she said. As a young man I had waited, anxiously anticipating the great day, the dark of night when he would arrive and carry us north to freedom. Gradually, I grew impatient—I explained to Will, Hark, and the rest—and became a runaway like my father.

Had no notion, I told them, of where I was headed, of what might lie in store for me, but whatever transpired, I assured them, I knew I was seeking my father. Wherever he abided, no matter how far away, no matter under what conditions, no matter what had prevented him from returning for us—captivity, dangers, even death—I believed I could run, run, run and one day I would join him.

Didn't find him, I told them. My father had vanished into a howling wilderness, so to speak. I was a fugitive, heart full of despair, loneliness, disappointment, and my sorrow, my yearning drove me back here. Here to reunite with my mother and wait for him again.

Thus, my brothers, in my fashion, I'm still seeking him here where my father has walked the land, cleared forests. Only here could I listen to my mother's stories, to stories in which other people recalled him or others like him. Here where he'd sowed and reaped, tended beasts, drank the water, smelled the air, wept for missing family, friends, sang the old songs you and I still sing together, I said to them. I stayed on this so-called plantation waiting, waiting, though part of me remained a runaway, runagate like my father, at liberty, no one's property, waiting until a voice announced, Now's the time, a new burning day of both darkness and light.

The voice speaks to us now. A fire burns, now, this very moment. Wait no longer, the voice exhorts, you must rise up, body and spirit. You, all your brethren. Reason together, rally together, the voice demands, now, today. All of us—men, women, runagates—we must seek out our fathers, mothers, daughters, sons, enslavers, murderers, strangers, ones loved, ones hated, invisibles, accused, accusers, prisoners, jailers, ourselves, the forgotten, forgiven and unforgiven, the forsaken and, Oh what a morning, Oh, what a meeting it will be, the old song promises, song we still sing, singing as we seek.

My confession ending now as it started. Alphabet letters (A–Z) spelling my story, telling it (A–Z). Ending. Beginning (A–Z).

Collage

In this collage I want Romare Bearden to save the life of Jean-Michel Basquiat. It never happened. Or happened and no witness of the conversation between Bearden and Basquiat while they spray-paint graffiti in a vast graveyard of subway cars:

Do you believe writing changes a wall.

You mean make a wall fall down. Make a new wall. That what you mean.

Yeah. Different after we scratch on it. Different wall.

Gotta be.

How you know that. Who told you that.

We're different each time we write. You. Me. Wall gotta be.

Scratch on a wall, it belongs to us, right.

No. Huh-uh. Write on it, nobody owns it. Anybody walk right through it.

No wall, where's the writing.

Still there. Inside the other side.

You full of shit now. Talking shit now. Say any damned thing.

You're the one asking questions.

Not asking questions. Just want to know, is all.

Just write.

Sometimes I think you think you some kind of wall.

Keep scratching. Maybe you make me go away.

Sometimes I think you think you write on me.

Maybe scratch on your scratching, maybe. Not on you. Why you think I wanna make my main man go away.

I ain't nobody's damn wall.

That's what I'm talking about, main man.

You bout done, man.

Ready to split if you ready, main man.

Let's get the fuck gone. Scratching make me hungry.

One last lick. *Phziff.* Can empty. Done. Finished. And there. See it. A hungry mouth like yours. We outta here, main.

Main can sound like *man. Man* can sound like *main.* Trains overhead can sound like trains underground, Basquiat says to himself. Though trains can't fly. Though they sound like they up there in the sky. Like thunder. Can't see thunder either. Can't see trains underground either. They shake, rattle, roll. Invisible though you know they underfoot shake, rattle, rolling you and you think you see them, dark and invisible as it is under there. Like you see rumbles inside the stomach when you hungry. Like you know it's trouble coming. No money. No home. No food. How you spozed to eat if you don't go on and do wrong. How you spozed to write.

August Wilson, who grew up in Pittsburgh, Pennsylvania, wrote:

> *In Bearden I found my artistic mentor and sought, and still try to make my plays the equal of his canvases . . . I never had the privilege of meeting Romare Bearden. Once outside 357 Canal Street in silent homage, daring myself to knock on his door . . . sorry I didn't . . . often thought of what I would have said to him that day if I had knocked on his door and he had answered. I probably would have just looked at him. I would have looked and if I were wearing a hat, I would have taken it off in tribute.*

Romare Bearden born September 2, 1911, in Charlotte, North Carolina. Jean-Michel Basquiat born December 22, 1960, in Brooklyn. Both men died in New York City on the twelfth day of different months in 1988. Bearden in March. Basquiat the following August. Basquiat resided at 57 Great Jones Street until a drug overdose killed him. Bearden's last address, 357 Canal Street, a short walk on the Lower East Side from Great Jones.

Romare Bearden, world-famous collagist, attended Peabody High, same public school in Pittsburgh my sister, my two dead brothers, my brother in prison for life, and I attended. Very same Bearden who heard from a friend that some artists at the beginning of the Italian Renaissance resisted demands of their patrons for paintings that conformed to fashionable rules of perspective mandated by the new science and math of rendering perspective. Artists feared deep cuts opening like doors into a canvas. Tintoretto, for example, screwed up on purpose. Believed illusory holes in a painting might become real holes into which the gaze, maybe the gazer's body and soul, might plunge and be lost forever. Who knows, Bearden says to Basquiat. Point is resist. Painters might tumble in, too.

Bearden's collages remind Basquiat of how his mother used to talk. Still talks on her good days. Her stories flatten perspective. Cram in everything, everyone, from everywhere she's been. Spanish, her native language, and her English flow seamlessly, intimately when she's telling tales. Like the mix of materials Bearden combines to construct collage. Her words may be foreign, her accent unfamiliar, but listeners able to follow. Anecdotes she relates fill space to the brim without exhausting it. Moments she has experienced become large enough, thank goodness, to include everybody. Nobody feels left out.

Bearden's collage and Mom's narratives truly democratic—each detail counts equally, every part matters as much as any grand design. Size and placement don't highlight forever some items at the expense of others. Meaning depends upon point of view. Stop, Basquiat tells himself. I sound like a museum audiocassette guide when all I really want to say is *dance*. Mom talking story or Bearden at the turntable mixing cutouts with paint with fabrics with photos with empty spaces invite people to dance.

Basquiat loved to make music. Played in bands with his homies from scratching, hanging out. Jammed in clubs, recorded hours of tapes, their sound a mix of all the kinds of music they heard around them and noises in the streets, drug noises inside their heads. Basquiat disappointed when the band cooking and everybody in the audience too stoned to dance.

No one's fault, Romare Bearden supposes, if a gift he fashions doesn't quite fit in the box it was meant to fill with love. He tilts the collage board. Lets fragments he'd chosen slide back down to the worktable. Discovers they no longer fit there either. Collage board empty. Table overflowing. He must start again. Decide again what to include or discard. He believes his life depends on each choice. His feet shuffle beneath the worktable like Monk's feet under a piano. Working collage is too hard, impossible really, unless he hears something resembling music whose rhythms guide his eyes, hands.

Not surprising, given the scope of his ambitions, that Bearden misremembers occasionally the dimensions of a board he's preparing for collage or forgets how large a medley of ingredients he has assembled. Anyone observing him labor could have told him he's undertaking a doomed task. Too much on the table, limited room, after all, within a frame. Bearden's extremely smart so he knows better, too, but gets seduced by the privilege of paying absolute attention, piece by piece, to every item he selects. If pushed, he'd probably insist that losing track of the bigger picture a mercy, even a momentary state of grace, Bearden might add, especially when you are an older man. Why not linger over a swatch of antique Alabama patchwork quilt alive under his gaze as he rotates and rubs it, discovering new, mellow harmonies among its once brightly colored threads. Sweet funk of it, he brings it closer to his nose.

Collage should prepare brand-new space, Bearden says to Basquiat. I do not wish to abandon things I gather for collage into a space previous occupants own. I think collage envisions new pasts as well as new futures. Wonder if *thinking* is the proper word to express how I decide, separate, test.

Bearden recalls Alberto Giacometti lamenting a fatal skewering of attention as he sculpted the face of his brother Diego Giacometti. No matter how swiftly his eyes travel from flesh-and-blood brother to clay and back, Alberto wrote, he confronts the enigma of a Diego whose face changes. Never the face seen an instant before. Often the face of a stranger. Mysteriously troublingly to Giacometti, as my brother's face can appear to me after six months, nine, a year between visits to the prison.

Space framed within collage at least as elusive as any human face. Each time Bearden studies an element he considers adding to a collage—a color, a photo, a triangle of denim—the total composition vanishes. To see it whole again, his eyes must relinquish their grip on the element. Same way I lose my brother when I exit prison walls. The way I must exit the world outside prison bars to visit my brother.

Well, Basquiat asks, how does an artist resolve this dilemma, Maestro. This perpetual losing battle, this shifting back and forth, this absence, gap, this oblivion between a reality the senses seize and a reality the imagination seizes.

You guess. You believe, Bearden would respond to Basquiat or anyone else curious and serious enough to ask. A kind of wishful thinking, he might admit to himself. Each step of building collage precarious. Unleashes energy. Revelation. Loss. Grasping something concrete in your hand, you leave this *inextricable place*, as a fellow artist, Samuel Beckett, called it, and revisit a remembered place. You understand the fragment you grasp is as fragile, fallible as memory. Understand no former place remains fixed, unchanged. But you guess, believe a reunion will occur. Not in a space waiting patiently as a prison cell. A generously welcoming place, you hope.

Bearden worries about things that may have slipped off the worktable to the floor. He's unable to explain to Basquiat why removal of objects from an array sometimes makes the array more plentiful, not smaller. Nor can he explain how a board upon which he's arranging things becomes more spacious as he packs it. He learns to live with the necessity of letting go. Enjoys the idea of himself being as surprised as the stranger who opens one of these gift boxes he prepares.

Our eyes observe waves rippling the sea. But where exactly is a wave, Bearden winks and asks Basquiat. We can't see water molecules bobbing up and down. We think we see waves rippling. If my collages work, the stuff composing them gets agitated, makes waves.

Or you might say each collage starts with the bare bones of a story. For instance, me and two other colored boys beat up on Eugene, a crippled white boy. My grandmother intervenes, rescues the boy, and he becomes my best friend. Grandma discovers he lives in a brothel with his prostitute mother and rescues him again. He comes with his birds to stay in our house a short year then dies. A collage I built is layer upon layer of questions about that simple story.

Takes lots and lots of Angels and Devils hopping around to make a world anybody can see, Basquiat agrees. But where you spozed to put stuff that doesn't belong in the picture, he would ask Bearden. How you get a genie back in the bottle once the genie's out. What disease crippled poor Eugene. What names he give his birds. How much did Eugene's mom charge for a piece of pussy. What's her name. Did she earn more or less in a lifetime of selling herself than the price one of your collages or my paintings commands today. Rumor in the street says nobody survives. Who tries. Who asks.

There are about thirty words around you all the time, like *thread* and *exit*, Basquiat claimed.

I met a man who looked after Bearden in Bearden's old age when he was cancer-ridden, too weak to drive himself to his studio in Long Island City or climb stairs to the second floor of his apartment or handle heavy collage boards. Man told me Romare Bearden loved collards. Loved even more the pot liquor in which collard greens cooked. *Collards*, if you say it like the man said it, sounds like *coloreds* and *coloreds* sounds like *collards*. Bearden a gentle, easy person to care-take, the man told me, and being with the old, dying artist probably best time of the man's life, he confides, smiling as he recalled their long conversations he taped, how scared he was carrying Bearden piggyback up and down steps. But you best not forget that bowl of pot liquor to start Romare's day. Evil all day when no cup of steaming collard juice first thing.

More than once found myself up at 4:00, 5:00 a.m., the man said, cooking collards so the liquor could simmer down a couple hours to where it would taste just right by the time Mr. and Mrs. B up and I had him washed, shaved, dressed, and ready at his little table kind of desk in the workroom downstairs. Most days I made sure some leftover liquor in the pot to save and heat up next morning, but to tell the God's truth, I was getting old, too. Worried I'd stumble with him on my back and kill us both on those damned steps. Getting older every day along with Mr. Bearden. Starting to forget things with so much to do to keep his days running smooth and regular the way he liked it. Every day he could manage the trip, I'd drive him out to Long Island City. Be in the studio by noon working with Teabo, his assistant.

Sometimes I'd wake up in my bed, *Oh, shit*, and remember the greens pot empty on the stove. *Damn.* Too poor to ever own a watch when I was growing up. Taught myself to keep time in my head. Could tell you the minute and hour, just as good as if a watch on my wrist. Must have been born with the gift of a clock in my head or maybe I figured out I'd have one if I made a habit of paying attention. Won a whole lot of bets in college with that trick. Could tell you the time today. And still wake up at exactly the time I tell myself before I go to sleep. Wide awake, no alarm, no watch. Part of the gift, I guess. Me and time always been on good speaking terms, you might say, so when I remembered an empty pot on his stove, I'd know the hour and, *Oh, shit, man.* Get your big behind out the bed, man. Go fix Romare's greens so they be simmered down perfect—greasy, salty, tiny bits of grit in the juice, too strong for most people, but just how he liked it.

Basquiat owned an illustrated encyclopedia of signs and symbols that included signs hobos chalked and scratched on small town walls to warn other hobos. Basquiat often drew on his paintings the hobo sign meaning "nothing to be gained here" or the sign meaning "a beating awaits you here."

Once upon a time, Basquiat says to Bearden, I painted the Devil on a door to scare myself away. *Go away, fool.* Never come back here again and stand here staring at this damned drug-den door. And fuck sure never again knock. And if you hear steel bolts unbolted, don't you dare push it open and walk through to where you know the Devil's crouched down inside, nasty, hairy, bare black ass all up in your face first thing you see in there. Devil bent down munching on garbage inside dead people's stomachs.

Basquiat thinks he scratched not painted the goddamn door. Samo again. Scratching again. Never will be a painter. Always Samo. *Samo* sounds like *Sam O*. Means S-O-S: Same Ole Shit. Same ole Samo. Never not Samo. Means help me. Means help Samo. Samo. Samo. Stuck like a record. Samo over and over. Or Samo maybe sounds like *Sa Mo*, and means some more. Like Devil, please give Samo some more. *Gimme s' mo.* Samo wants s' mo.

Samo scratching Devil on a door. Ugly door. Ugly Devil. Paints words in the Devil's ugly mouth. Words in his red, empty eyehole tunnels. Go away, fool. Go away, Samo. Go away, Devil. Go away. No more. Never again, Samo. For Samo's sake do not enter. Do not forsake. Don't just go away, Samo. Run, nigger, run. Far away. Way. Way. But rumor in the street says you are Samo. Always. Scratcher not painter. You cannot change. Why in hell would you want to change anyway, even if the fool you are could change. *Samo* sounds like *S' mo*. Gotta git me some more.

Confess. You the same Samo. Confess to the few who would listen. As if any fool would listen to Samo. Samo who can't paint. Samo scratching. *Scratch* one of Devil's names. *Scratch* means graffiti. *Scratch* means money. Means itch. Means fuck wit a record. Kill it. Same ole itch. Scratch it. Scratch buys a bag. Ten bags a day. Hundred. Here's s' mo, Samo. More scratch than you can count. Devil on the door. Behind the door. Sees you. Loves to see you coming. Everybody loves you, Samo. You the man.

Wuzzup, Dude. Wuzzup, Money. Wuzzup, Main Man. They can see you through the door. See through you. Watch you ache to paint the door shut. Shut. Shut. Shoot. Shooted. Shut away. Shoot away. Paint away the Devil. No. Not paint. Scratch. Roll of bills in your fist like a chunk of bloody bandages.

Devil means money means bags and bags of dope. As many bags as dead bodies stashed inside the door. They watch you. Dead eyes looking through the wooden door at you. Staring. Waiting. Scratching. They love you. Funny, you think. Run, you think. You want to paint it shut forever. Paint Devil on it, inside it forever.

Devil on door grins back at you. Thinks it's funny, too, Samo. Same ole Samo. Funny Samo. Funny Devil. Dead eyes see you push through. Not a door. It's a window, a mirror. Glass breaking. You fall through. Glass everywhere. Nails falling down like rain. Knives. You are falling. Down you go flat on your black skinny ass. Funny. You crack up. No. You step through. Glass slippery under bare toes. Step on a crack break your mama's back. You hip-hop, whistle, snap your fingers, wiggle, squirm through untouched. To the other side. Samo.

Giddy-up, Jean-Michel Basquiat hollers. Rides a good horse he owns. Own all this, too, he thinks. This Paradise on this island where he bounces in the saddle, astride a thoroughbred Arabian, nigger-colored horse. Giddy-up. Giddy-up, cowboy. As far as the eye can see owns waves of green of sea of clouds of blue sky above and below him owns the hooves of the animal squeezed between his knees, his thighs be-dumping, be-dumpety-dumping in a place called Hawaii he believes where sits this island he owns, rides and nobody can see him, bother him. He owns it, all of it, all of this place stretching to a horizon that shimmers, bobs out there, as far as he's able to see. Finish line floats out there somewhere, finished like a painting stretched wet to dry on its frame of spears, a horizon opening as a dream stretches open. You clomp, clomp closer and closer to it, through it, and beyond each time you reach it forever.

There are about thirty words around you all the time . . . all of them DEVIL.

Perhaps it's 1986 when Basquiat watches a fine young French thing pedal past, bare-legged on her bicycle. She's K, a lady I will meet fifteen years or so later, marry eventually, long after that momentary encounter between notorious Jean-Michel Basquiat's eyes and hers.

His eyes on her nice, tanned legs, big, cute frizzy hair, sweet hips, and lips that speak French, mother tongue of Jean-Michel's father. A sure-enough fox, petite like he prefers, graced by that perfection nature reserves for smallish, compact women's bodies like hers. She's wearing short shorts that day. Then he sees her everywhere, Tribeca, Lower East Side—Mudd Club, Studio 54, Area—and she sees him and sees he's very aware of seeing her she's sure. They are very aware of each other she's sure, and he sure is, too. They speak briefly sometimes in passing. Greetings, smiles exchanged usually always except when he's doing sullen or lost in space or mounted on his gray Dürer death horse or plain sleepy from no sleep for days or plain high or testing maybe if it's true he's truly, truly famous, beyond fame, everybody who's somebody or not recognizes him and counts coup whether or not he notices them or nods or looks back or not or mocks like a blackface minstrel with a wiggly tongue their stares.

He notices her and she notices cute, brown him everywhere around LES until one night in Area when he waves her over she goes as far as to stand smiling beside the table where he sits with an older man, and though the painter doesn't know her name he halfway introduces, halfway pimps her in a teasing, funny way she thinks to the dapper man who turns out to be his Haitian father.

Quick, hot surge of jealousy, envy of the Devil flashing in Basquiat's eye as I listen, but just as instantly I'm pleased, profoundly grateful beyond words for brightness in K's eyes while she reminisces about her encounters with a famous artist. My wife who has been suffering brutal insomnia, her gaze, her affect dulled by the wages of sleeplessness, despair, and anxiety over a string of deaths, of sudden serious illnesses striking family and closest friends, her own increasingly frequent attacks of tachycardia and other ominous, unresolvable threats to her health, so of course I worry with her, about her. No, not worry. I quake inside with fear I may be losing her. Thus losing everything. Though I must believe, must trust, trust, trust her mind's deepdown toughness, her small body strong as a horse.

On the worst days I launch endless searches for reassuring signs of our former, familiar selves. Walk for hours alone to empty my head of anything except the effort, the noise of my footsteps through this dreary time capsule of a latter-day Lower East Side, this remnant of a boundless universe we once roamed together. Boy wonder, colored painter, victim, heir, wife, husband, kids, scratchers, thieves, flirtatious Haitian fathers, all of us, the fallen and survivors, coloreds and not, then and now, too many to count or keep track of, or touch or talk with. Bridges and high-rises, ghettos, music, fashion, meatpacking districts, financial districts, hi-line, traffic, parks, news, ethnic and religiously cleansed slums, and racialized enclaves battered, bruised, cowering. Foreign nations collapsing here, bleeding, museums, sprawl of new construction, prisons, galleries, cell phones, war, murder, terrorists.

Who dat. Who she. Pedaling down Spring Street. Crazy little French mama come *Knock/Knockin* at my front door. *Bon jour. Bonjour.* Not the Devil, are you, you French sweetie pie. Open up and let me in, Samo almost scratches on the door, the window, the mirror within which he sees her welcoming eyes, sees his. Sees the grinning Devil's face.

The door a forgery, experts almost unanimously agree. Wannabe. Imposter. Fraud. If the original Jean-Michel Basquiat ever painted a Devil on the door of a dope den or even just scratched one, this ain't it. Clearly the work of another, obviously inferior artist, opines one expert, and not only am I certain, he adds for spite and to needle his colleagues, I happen to know the person's name whose work it is. Guy even admitted it to me, risked forfeiting the million or so door was worth if he claimed it as his. Says he's an admirer of the great Basquiat. Knew him back in the day, on the street, the scratching scene. Frequented same dealers, dope joints, etc. Sorry Samo dead, he said. Miss him. Bad luck to diss him, said my informant. But he winked, and added that the rumor on the street is boy never painted anything anyway. Samo a scratcher. Keeps on scratching. Once a scratcher, always a scratcher. Ask Samo. If you can stand the look on his face. Looks like the Devil when he grins. Bad grill. Gaps. Bad speckled, bumpy, pimply skin. Bad color. Bad boy smile when he looks at you says, Hi. I'm spooky Samo. No way you'd believe he had it all once, looking at him today. Half dead. Or dead. Depending on which expert you believe.

Ask the Authentication Committee organized, authenticated by his colored West Indian daddy. They/he determine who, when, what comes and goes through gallery doors and how much it goes for. And what goes *phizzz* in the night because nobody loves it. Committee makes paintings real. Not scratch. Not not worth squat. They decide what's art. They make Samo real. Same ole Samo. Stamped with Samo Copyright Stamp.

To this collage of conversations, which perhaps never took place, let me add one more. Behind bars of a ten-by-ten-inch, four-inch-deep stainless steel rack anchored low on our bathroom wall—packed, squeezed so tightly not one more could fit—K, my wife of twelve years, saves, for reasons known only to her, old copies of French home decorating magazines. On two covers—*Elle Décoration* (nov 2014) and *Marie Claire Maison* (fev-mars 2012)—are phrases that struck and stayed with me as I browsed through K's collection while I sat on the toilet. In my mind many times since, I've cut out and pasted up the phrases. Formed them into an exchange that very likely could have occurred between two extremely smart, curious, intense young people. Two immigrants, wayfaring strangers in the teeming metropolis of NYC circa 1986:

N'ayez Plus Peur de Noir
Petits Espaces/Grande Idées

In the spirit of English editions of Tolstoy's novel *War and Peace* that supply translations of the French Tolstoy liberally mixes with his Russian, I offer translations of the French words above that captured my attention:

Fear Black No More
Great Ideas for Small Spaces

Since I'm unsure who thought which thought, I won't attach speakers' names to the phrases. Anyway, in their original arrangement of bright colors and a variety of fonts on glossy magazine covers that first caught my eye, the French words express ideas no one in particular owns. Thus I float or rather scratch those words here, a collage in this collage, above the heads of K and Basquiat, not as evidence the thoughts were ever spoken aloud by either of them, but as thoughts that belong to them—embedded, released in conversations their eyes struck up.

One luxury of growing old, Bearden says to Basquiat, says it a bit shyly, self-consciously, since he knows Basquiat will not get very old, is more time to ask questions about simple stories. Stories that make us up as we make them up. Will I be born again. Alive again once this particular allotment of years runs out. Is a city called Pittsburgh still reachable by catching a train north from Mecklenburg, North Carolina, or a train south from Harlem that passes through Philadelphia then climbs over and tunnels through many mountains, rounds a gigantic horseshoe curve. If Pittsburgh continues to exist—a golden triangle cordoned by bridges and three rivers, clinging to steep hills like Rome—and if I reach Pittsburgh and walk its streets, am I a boy there or old like I am here and now, still asking a boy's questions. Is teasing my nearly bald head with such idle speculations a less forgivable luxury now than when I was a kid. Am I stuck forever, man or boy, with a bad habit, perhaps, of wasting precious time daydreaming. As if living and questioning never ends, as if a simple question might stump time, buy time, stop time long enough for a boy, a man, to slip past the conductor and ride back and forth to Pittsburgh on a beam of light without paying the price of a ticket.

Anyway, Romare Bearden confides, my first drawings, like your Devil on a door, not very nice. I learned from my friend Eugene how to draw nasty stuff we spied through rotting floorboards of the attic he shared with his mother over a whorehouse that sat down Spring Street and around the corner from my grandmother's boardinghouse. One Saturday afternoon Grandma saw us extremely busy, busy, drawing on big, greasy, blood-speckled sheets of paper chickens came wrapped in from the butcher shop, and she marched over: What you boys up to. Why you so quiet over here. When she saw what we were up to, her eyes got wide. She hollered. Snatched our drawings. Ripped them up and rained the tiny pieces into the kitchen garbage pail.

I expected a good whack or two. My grandmother one of those pillow-bosomed women who love children dearly, especially me, but when you made her mad, watch out. Pow. Trouble was Grandma so nice and easy most the time you don't notice her getting mad. First sign of mad. Pow. Then it's too late to move out her way cause with Grandma getting mad also a matter of getting even. Fact is I didn't exactly understand why she might be hitting mad when I saw her coming over to where we were busy at the kitchen table, though I sort of knew the pictures Eugene and I were drawing had something very secret, very private about them I surely didn't want Grandma of all people to see.

What I had peeked at between the raggedy floorboards had scared me, main man. People hurting one another my first thought. Noisy, ugly thrashing about. Mean grabbing, mean pushing and squeezing, spilled whiskey, dirty sheets, cigarettes. Bare skin of grown-up body parts I'd never seen so naked before. More scary because it was colored bodies and white bodies down there mixed up closer than I had ever seen colored and white mixing on Spring Street and in the little checkerboard patches of neighborhood around Spring around the rolling mill where a few lucky colored folks had regular jobs. All kinds of people living in the neighborhoods. Poor the only requirement. Mixing on one hand but on the other hand definitely not mixing. No trespassing the Golden Rule. Only colored men rented my grandmother's rooms, and different houses, different blocks, different barbers, different churches for white and colored because people believed in sticking to their own kind. Even kids believed it, so the first time I met up with Eugene, it was me, Mumps, and Bo, the three of us teasing then beating on him unmercifully because what the hell a white boy think he's doing standing there staring at us, him ugly as a fresh knot on somebody's head got conked by a rock. Probably him being crippled as much as being the wrong color (though my skin wore almost the same color, by the way) made us jump him, smack him down so he'd go away and never bring his pitiful self back to our alley behind Spring where Mumps, Bo, and me played.

My grandmother busted in that time, too. Set down her shopping bags on the cobblestones, yelled, Stoppit. Stop that, you bad boys, and whacked whoever she could lay her hands on, running us away from that skinny white kid. Whacking Mumps and Bo like she whacked me because that's how it worked back then around Spring Street. You were everybody your color's child and if you got caught doing wrong by any colored adult friendly with your people, they had the right to whip your behind and send you home for another good beating because you should know better and not shame yourself, not shame your family by doing wrong in public as if you hadn't been raised to know better.

Anyway, going back to the other, later time after she tore up those butcher paper drawings and shredded them or maybe burned them to ashes in the kitchen sink, Grandma calmed down and asked me and Eugene what in

Jesus name did we think we were doing and where did we get the idea of those terrible pictures. We told her about the room under the attic room Eugene lived in with his mother, about a spy hole in one corner of the floor covered over by just a ratty piece of linoleum we lifted to check out the action below. Told Grandma in which particular house Eugene resided around the corner from Grandma's, the house I went to almost every day after school and many evenings, too, if Grandma said okay.

My, oh, my. Good Lord have mercy, Grandma groaned and snatched Eugene by the hand after she let go the ear she was pinching, and he gimped off beside her, though I know Eugene didn't hardly want to go home but he knew he better go with her and did, dragging his bad leg to slow things down as much as he dared without letting on he was scared or stubborn or just plain didn't want to go. But off he went with Grandma and when she came back to our house, I was surprised to see she still had Eugene by the hand and he got a little plaid cardboard suitcase and Grandma carrying his birdcages and Eugene stayed with us till he got sick and passed.

Nineteen twenty-seven the year Eugene buried, Bearden says, and in 1978 I tried to pack all that Eugene story and Homewood, East Liberty, Pittsburgh story, the whole damned known world and probably the unknown, too, Bearden smiles, into a 16¼-inch by 20½-inch collage pasted on board I titled *Farewell Eugene*. All those worlds as they appeared to me fifty years afterward in my memories of how crowded a time, a city, a boy's universe can be at any moment once you teach yourself to look closely and practice patiently for a lifetime the skills of cutting and pasting, gluing down textures, colors, fabrics, layer after layer to picture what the past may have been and how it rises again, solid and present as the bright orange disc of sun I put at the top-right corner of *Farewell Eugene*.

Same sun shining almost red over Eugene's funeral fifty years before with everybody on earth in attendance or at least nobody missing who should be there. Eugene's friends, his people, mine, his pigeons, Grandma, me, we're all there in the crowd back then and this time, too, if I got the collage close to right. All of us remembered, revived beneath an orange sun coloring the city, coloring flowers Eugene's pale mother holds that day. Same old sun, same old Pittsburgh, same old simple questions asking to be asked. The crowd of us then and now, living and dead saying our goodbyes, our hellos to Eugene. As many of us you might say as boarded Noah's Ark or as many as in the number religious thinkers in the Middle Ages used to bicker over if asked how many angels fit on the head of a pin.

17   John Edgar Wideman, *God's Gym*, New York: Mariner, 2005, 41.

18   John Edgar Wideman, "In Praise of Silence," *Callaloo*, 24, no. 2 (Spring 2001), 549.

19   Wideman, *The Stories of John Edgar Wideman*, 152.

20   John Edgar Wideman, "Playing Dennis Rodman," *The New Yorker*, April 29, 1996.

21   John Edgar Wideman, *Hoop Roots*, Boston: Houghton Mifflin, 2001, 12–13.

22   Alberto Giacometti, the Swiss sculptor, has also had a significant influence on Wideman's theories of form, time, vision, and aesthetic process.

23   Wideman, *American Histories*, 201.

24   Ibid., 204.

25   Ibid., 205

26   John Edgar Wideman, *Fanon*, New York: Mariner Books, 2008, 21. In *Fanon*, the novel's protagonist, Thomas (who is likely a stand-in for Wideman), explains that his mother's stories "flatten and fatten perspective" and crammed "everything, everyone, everywhere in the present, into words that flow, intimate and immediate as the images of a Bearden painting." Thomas also halts his riff, realizing that all he really must say is "dance."

27   John Edgar Wideman, "The Architectonics of Fiction," *Callaloo*, 13 no.1, (Winter 1990), 45.

28   Wideman, *Briefs*, 110.

29   Ibid., 2.

30   Wideman, "Surfiction," *The Stories of John Edgar Wideman*, 190.

31   Ibid., 192.

32   Wideman, *Briefs*, 155.

33   Wideman, "The Architectonics of Fiction."

34   Wideman, *American Histories*, 26.

Notes

1   Ralph Waldo Ellison, *Invisible Man*, New York: Vintage, 1952, 1980, 269.

2   John Edgar Wideman, *American Histories*, Scribner: New York, 2018, 85.

3   John Edgar Wideman, *Briefs*, Lulu.com, 2010, 61.

4   Tracie Church Guzzio, *All Stories Are True: History, Myth, and Trauma in the Work of John Edgar Wideman*, Jackson: University Press of Mississippi, 2011, 99.

5   Lisa Baker, "Storytelling and Democracy (in the Radical Sense): A Conversation with John Edgar Wideman," *African American Review*, 34, no. 2 (2000), 267.

6   Wideman, *American Histories*, 120.

7   Ibid., 93.

8   John Edgar Wideman, "To Robby," *The Stories of John Edgar Wideman*, 1st ed., New York: Pantheon, 1992, 269.

9   Ibid., 3.

10 Ibid., 111.

11 Wideman, *American Histories*, 60–61.

12 Ibid., 61.

13 Wideman. *The Stories of John Edgar Wideman*, 378.

14 John Edgar Wideman, *The Cattle Killing*, New York: Mariner Books, 1996, 212.

15 Ralph Waldo Ellison, *Shadow and Act*, New York: Vintage 1964, 78.

16 John Edgar Wideman, "Stomping the Blues: Ritual in Black Music and Speech." *The American Poetry Review*, 7 no. 4 (July/August 1978), 42. Also see "Luzana Cholly and the Citizens of Gasoline Point, Ala.," *New York Times Book Review*, May 12, 1974.

JOHN EDGAR WIDEMAN'S books include *American Histories, Writing to Save a Life, Philadelphia Fire, Brothers and Keepers, Fatheralong, Hoop Dreams,* and *Sent for You Yesterday.* He is a MacArthur Fellow, has won the PEN/Faulkner Award twice, won the 2019 PEN/Malamud Award for the Short Story, has been a finalist for the National Book Award, and has twice been a finalist for the National Book Critics Circle Award. He divides his time between New York and France.

YOU MADE ME LOVE YOU

Selected Stories, 1981–2018

JOHN EDGAR WIDEMAN

Jefferson Madison
Regional Library
Charlottesville, Virginia

SCRIBNER
New York   London   Toronto   Sydney   New Delhi

Scribner
An Imprint of Simon & Schuster, Inc.
1230 Avenue of the Americas
New York, NY 10020

To all those coming up after: stay in the struggle.

Contents